Name	
Registration Number	

TOEIC

Test of English for International Communication

TEST 1

三民書局

請掃描左方 QR code 或輸入下方網址進入音檔網站。
https://elearning.sanmin.com.tw/Voice/
1. 於搜尋欄輸入「實戰新多益：全真模擬題本 3 回」或點擊「英文」→「學習叢書」→「Let's TOEIC 系列」尋找音檔。請依提示下載音檔。
2. 若無法順利下載音檔，可至「常見問題」查看相關問題。
3. 若有相關問題，請點擊「聯絡我們」，將盡快為你處理。

三民・東大音檔網

LISTENING TEST

In the Listening test, you will be asked to demonstrate how well you understand spoken English. The entire Listening test will last approximately 45 minutes. There are four parts, and directions are given for each part. You must mark your answers on the separate answer sheet.

Do not write your answers in your test book.

PART 1

Directions: For each question in this part, you will hear four statements about a picture in your test book. When you hear the statements, you must select the one statement that best describes what you see in the picture. Then find the number of the question on your answer sheet and mark your answer. The statements will not be printed in your test book and will be spoken only one time.

Statement (D), "They are taking photographs," is the best description of the picture, so you should select answer (D) and mark it on your answer sheet.

1.

2.

GO ON TO THE NEXT PAGE →

3.

4.

5.

6.

PART 2

Directions: You will hear a question or statement and three responses spoken in English. They will not be printed in your test book and will be spoken only one time. Select the best response to the question or statement and mark the letter (A), (B), or (C) on your answer sheet.

7. Mark your answer on your answer sheet.

8. Mark your answer on your answer sheet.

9. Mark your answer on your answer sheet.

10. Mark your answer on your answer sheet.

11. Mark your answer on your answer sheet.

12. Mark your answer on your answer sheet.

13. Mark your answer on your answer sheet.

14. Mark your answer on your answer sheet.

15. Mark your answer on your answer sheet.

16. Mark your answer on your answer sheet.

17. Mark your answer on your answer sheet.

18. Mark your answer on your answer sheet.

19. Mark your answer on your answer sheet.

20. Mark your answer on your answer sheet.

21. Mark your answer on your answer sheet.

22. Mark your answer on your answer sheet.

23. Mark your answer on your answer sheet.

24. Mark your answer on your answer sheet.

25. Mark your answer on your answer sheet.

26. Mark your answer on your answer sheet.

27. Mark your answer on your answer sheet.

28. Mark your answer on your answer sheet.

29. Mark your answer on your answer sheet.

30. Mark your answer on your answer sheet.

31. Mark your answer on your answer sheet.

PART 3

Directions: You will hear some conversations between two or more people. You will be asked to answer three questions about what the speakers say in each conversation. Select the best response to each question and mark the letter (A), (B), (C) or (D) on your answer sheet. The conversations will not be printed in your test book and will be spoken only one time.

32. What product are the speakers discussing?
(A) A digital camera
(B) A flat-screen television
(C) A tablet computer
(D) A mobile phone

33. Why is the woman disappointed with the product?
(A) The screen is not bright enough.
(B) The menus are too complicated.
(C) The battery life is too short.
(D) The monthly fee is too high.

34. What does the man say will happen on Saturday?
(A) A product will be launched.
(B) A new store will open.
(C) A review will be published.
(D) A sale will begin.

35. What is the man interested in learning about?
(A) Foreign languages
(B) Healthy eating
(C) Hair styling
(D) Massage therapy

36. What does the woman say is provided after the training course?
(A) A job placement
(B) A cash bonus
(C) A certificate
(D) A membership card

37. What information does the woman ask for?
(A) A phone number
(B) A mailing address
(C) Credit card details
(D) Directions to a business

38. Why did the man arrive late?
(A) He missed his bus.
(B) His car broke down.
(C) He went to the wrong location.
(D) He had another appointment.

39. Why will the coffee shop close temporarily?
(A) A training session will be held.
(B) Some furniture will be replaced.
(C) A safety inspection will take place.
(D) Some lighting will be installed.

40. What does the man say he will do next?
(A) Contact the staff
(B) Post a work schedule
(C) Make a payment
(D) Review some documents

41. What kind of business does the man work for?
(A) A packaging company
(B) A catering firm
(C) A food manufacturer
(D) A security agency

42. What does the woman mean when she says, "we're struggling to keep up"?
(A) There is a lot of competition in her field.
(B) Her monthly profits are decreasing.
(C) Her business cannot cope with the demand.
(D) Several employees have been absent.

43. What does the man offer to do?
(A) Reschedule a delivery
(B) Send a catalog
(C) Visit the woman's business
(D) Prepare an estimate

44. What type of product does the man want to exchange?
(A) A laptop computer
(B) A mobile phone
(C) A set of speakers
(D) A pair of headphones

45. What was the problem with the item?
(A) The battery life
(B) The performance
(C) The size
(D) The color

46. What does the woman offer to do?
(A) Issue a partial refund
(B) Provide store credit
(C) Have a product modified
(D) Present alternative items

47. Who is the man?
(A) A journalist
(B) An author
(C) A talk show host
(D) A college professor

48. What does the man remember during the interview?
(A) His prior meeting with the woman
(B) A vacation he went on with his family
(C) His time spent studying at a local college
(D) A previous employment experience

49. What does the man recommend the listeners do?
(A) Read many books
(B) Create a portfolio
(C) Attend job fairs
(D) Enroll in a class

50. Why is the man calling?
(A) To point out an invoice error
(B) To report a product defect
(C) To add an item to an order
(D) To inquire about a delivery

51. What information does the woman ask the man for?
(A) His phone number
(B) His home address
(C) His credit card number
(D) His e-mail address

52. What will the man do tomorrow?
(A) Move into a new house
(B) Leave for a vacation
(C) Attend a business meeting
(D) Visit the woman's workplace

53. What did the woman do this morning?
(A) She interviewed job candidates.
(B) She purchased materials.
(C) She compared prices.
(D) She revised a document.

54. What does the man suggest the woman do?
(A) Conduct a survey
(B) Visit a business premises
(C) Reschedule an appointment
(D) Request estimates

55. What does the woman want to do first?
(A) Speak with a colleague
(B) Make a payment
(C) Send invitations
(D) Visit some Web sites

56. Why is the man at the hotel?
(A) To discuss a merger
(B) To deliver supplies
(C) To arrange an event
(D) To have an interview

57. What will take place at the hotel in April?
(A) A live performance
(B) A renovation project
(C) A business convention
(D) A training session

58. What does Joanna want to see?
(A) A work schedule
(B) Some blueprints
(C) A budget proposal
(D) Some references

---

59. Where do the speakers work?
(A) At a restaurant
(B) At a gym
(C) At a university
(D) At a factory

60. Why is the man unable to help?
(A) He is going on vacation.
(B) He misplaced an ID card.
(C) He is not experienced.
(D) He has a schedule conflict.

61. Why does the man say, "I did that during my first week"?
(A) To explain why he is qualified
(B) To confirm that a deadline was met
(C) To disagree with a viewpoint
(D) To volunteer for a role

The 7th Technology Trade Show Main Hall—Vendors

Display Zone A—Digitech

Display Zone B—Photon

Display Zone C—Trident

Display Zone D—Quasar

---

62. According to the speakers, what is different about this year's technology trade show?
(A) The start time
(B) The venue
(C) The registration fee
(D) The duration

63. Look at the graphic. Which display zone will the speakers probably visit?
(A) Display Zone A
(B) Display Zone B
(C) Display Zone C
(D) Display Zone D

64. What does the man remind the woman to do?
(A) Arrange accommodations
(B) Confirm a spending allowance
(C) Purchase event tickets
(D) Speak to a supervisor

Step 1. Connect to our Wi-Fi **Step 2.** Enter your credit card details **Step 3.** Select data amount and rate **Step 4.** Click "Confirm"	

Date	Hotel Service	Fee
July 12	Dry Cleaning	$35.00
July 13	Pay-Per-View Movie	$11.50
July 14	Room Service	$27.98
July 15	Late Check Out	$40.00

65. Where is the conversation most likely taking place?
(A) In an airport
(B) In an office
(C) In a hotel
(D) In an electronics store

66. Look at the graphic. Which step does the man need to do next?
(A) Step 1
(B) Step 2
(C) Step 3
(D) Step 4

67. What will the woman probably do next?
(A) Contact a coworker
(B) Replace an item
(C) Provide a password
(D) Give a demonstration

68. What information is the man asked to provide?
(A) A room number
(B) His surname
(C) His credit card details
(D) An invoice number

69. Look at the graphic. Which amount does the man say should be removed?
(A) $35.00
(B) $11.50
(C) $27.98
(D) $40.00

70. What does the woman advise the man to do?
(A) Complete a form
(B) Call a number
(C) Send an e-mail
(D) Change a reservation

Directions: You will hear some talks given by a single speaker. You will be asked to answer three questions about what the speaker says in each talk. Select the best response to each question and mark the letter (A), (B), (C), or (D) on your answer sheet. The talks will not be printed in your test book and will be spoken only one time.

71. What is the radio show mainly about?
(A) Finance
(B) Careers
(C) Health
(D) Parenting

72. According to the speaker, why does Ms. Morrison travel?
(A) To train employees
(B) To raise money
(C) To speak at events
(D) To create new businesses

73. What will be launched this spring?
(A) A documentary
(B) A class
(C) A new Web site
(D) A book

74. Who most likely is the speaker?
(A) A landscaper
(B) A chef
(C) A mayor
(D) An event promoter

75. What event is the speaker preparing for?
(A) A concert
(B) A food fair
(C) A convention
(D) A grand opening

76. Why does the speaker tell the listener to call him?
(A) To request additional supplies
(B) To confirm his arrival at a location
(C) To arrange a site inspection
(D) To receive further instructions

77. Who is Ray Wilson?
(A) A painter
(B) A tour guide
(C) A sculptor
(D) An art critic

78. Why does the speaker say, "Admission is half-price until the end of the month"?
(A) To apologize for an earlier inconvenience
(B) To inform the listeners of a pricing error
(C) To announce the closure of the art gallery
(D) To encourage the listeners to visit a museum

79. What will happen in July?
(A) An outdoor festival will take place.
(B) A talk will be given.
(C) An art class will begin.
(D) A business will be relocated.

80. Who is the speaker?
(A) A business owner
(B) A tour guide
(C) An award winner
(D) A city official

81. What did Mr. Bennett do three years ago?
(A) He quit his job.
(B) He opened a store.
(C) He moved to a new country.
(D) He founded an organization.

82. According to the speaker, what is Mr. Bennett knowledgeable about?
(A) Money management
(B) Property prices
(C) Community needs
(D) Consumer trends

83. What kind of activity is the speaker leading?
    (A) A product demonstration
    (B) A job interview
    (C) A press conference
    (D) A staff orientation

84. What does the speaker imply when he says, "my office is on the third floor"?
    (A) He would prefer to work on a different floor.
    (B) He is unable to attend an event.
    (C) He is available to offer assistance.
    (D) He will distribute materials to the listeners.

85. What does the speaker say he will do in December?
    (A) Move to a different branch
    (B) Recruit additional employees
    (C) Revise a company handbook
    (D) Post a seasonal work schedule

86. Where is the speaker?
    (A) At a grand opening event
    (B) At a software convention
    (C) At a training workshop
    (D) At a shareholders meeting

87. What feature does the speaker mention about a product?
    (A) It can be purchased online.
    (B) It comes with a warranty.
    (C) It updates automatically.
    (D) It won an industry award.

88. What should the listeners do to get a discount?
    (A) Take a product catalog
    (B) Apply for a membership
    (C) Make an advance order
    (D) Use a gift certificate

89. According to the speaker, how should the listeners leave a message?
    (A) By visiting a Web site
    (B) By calling a different number
    (C) By sending an e-mail
    (D) By staying on the line

90. What is Pro Form Gym most likely known for?
    (A) Offering the lowest prices
    (B) Providing the newest exercise machines
    (C) Employing the best instructors
    (D) Having the most locations

91. What is Pro Form Gym offering until the end of this month?
    (A) Free exercise classes
    (B) Complimentary gifts
    (C) Discounted equipment
    (D) Reduced membership fees

92. What kind of event is taking place?
    (A) An awards show
    (B) An orientation session
    (C) A retirement meal
    (D) A press conference

93. Who is Joshua Park?
    (A) An actor
    (B) A director
    (C) A camera operator
    (D) A talent agent

94. Why does the speaker say, "It's still on Channel 7 today"?
    (A) To indicate that a show remains popular
    (B) To propose a new work project
    (C) To suggest changing a programming schedule
    (D) To congratulate the listeners on their success

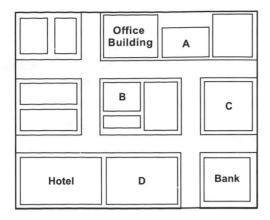

West Air	$275
Easy Wings	$295
DC Airlines	$300
Smart Jet	$315

95. What kind of business is the speaker planning to open?
(A) A clothing store
(B) A real estate agency
(C) An art gallery
(D) A bakery

96. Look at the graphic. Which location is the speaker interested in?
(A) Location A
(B) Location B
(C) Location C
(D) Location D

97. What does the speaker want to find out about?
(A) The parking availability
(B) The building size
(C) The cost of rent
(D) The local transportation

98. Who is the message intended for?
(A) A client
(B) A supervisor
(C) An airline employee
(D) An accountant

99. Look at the graphic. How much will the speaker's ticket cost?
(A) $275
(B) $295
(C) $300
(D) $315

100. What does the speaker ask the listener to send?
(A) A travel itinerary
(B) A client's contact details
(C) An authorization form
(D) A payment receipt

This is the end of the Listening test. Turn to Part 5 in your text book.

GO ON TO THE NEXT PAGE

READING TEST

In the Reading test, you will read a variety of texts and answer several different types of reading comprehension questions. The entire Reading test will last 75 minutes. There are three parts, and directions are given for each part. You are encouraged to answer as many questions as possible within the time allowed. You must mark your answers on the separate answer sheet. Do not write your answers in your test book.

PART 5

Directions: A word or phrase is missing in each of the sentences below. Four answer choices are given below each sentence. Select the best answer to complete the sentence. Then mark the letter (A), (B), (C), or (D) on your answer sheet.

101. Chef Harrington likes the food ------- cooks for hotel guests, but would prefer to create more complex dishes.
(A) he
(B) him
(C) his
(D) himself

102. Luxo Cosmetics is seeking female consumers between the ages of 18 ------- 35 for its market research study.
(A) or
(B) for
(C) and
(D) but

103. The bank manager is so busy that clients typically wait at least one week for an ------- with her.
(A) appoint
(B) appointment
(C) appointed
(D) appoints

104. Situated in the heart of the tourist district, York History Museum displays the ------- collection of tapestries in the UK.
(A) lightest
(B) partial
(C) creative
(D) oldest

105. The white earphones are the only ------- in stock at our High Street branch at the moment.
(A) shipping
(B) several
(C) there
(D) ones

106. Mr. Burns was presented with a gold wristwatch in ------- of his 30 years of service to the company.
(A) recognition
(B) authorization
(C) decision
(D) proposition

107. Once ------- probationary period ends, the new employees will attend a performance review at head office.
(A) them
(B) their
(C) theirs
(D) themselves

108. Astrid Financial Services is hoping to expand its business ------- opening new branches throughout Europe.
(A) as
(B) of
(C) at
(D) by

109. Many record stores have gone out of business because of the ------- demand for CDs and other physical formats of music.
(A) limitation
(B) limits
(C) limited
(D) limit

110. Printing on both sides of each sheet of paper will result in fewer sheets being required, ------- reducing waste.
(A) consequently
(B) formerly
(C) once
(D) more

111. Before he relocated to the New Zealand office, Mr. Marlowe spent several weeks training his -------.
(A) replacement
(B) replace
(C) replacing
(D) replaced

112. DCA Web Design provides price ------- to business owners who wish to strengthen their online presence.
(A) addresses
(B) estimates
(C) industry
(D) markets

113. There were ------- 75 dishes on the restaurant menu when the owner added a new range of vegetarian options.
(A) every
(B) already
(C) so that
(D) just as

114. To attract more visitors, Mount Jefferson National Park developed numerous hiking trails ------- for a wide range of fitness levels.
(A) successful
(B) historical
(C) appropriate
(D) probable

115. Alford Dental Clinic allows patients to arrive up to 15 minutes late, after which the appointment -------.
(A) rescheduled
(B) is rescheduled
(C) had been rescheduled
(D) be rescheduled

116. The employee break room will be inaccessible to staff ------- the walls are being painted.
(A) even
(B) yet
(C) although
(D) while

117. Ms. Gupta recommended sending information packets to convention participants ------- after their registration is confirmed.
(A) immediate
(B) more immediate
(C) immediately
(D) most immediately

118. Arnold Schneider will be ------- employee absences over the Christmas period and reporting them to the HR Director.
(A) developing
(B) recruiting
(C) providing
(D) monitoring

119. ------- tenants must hand in their door entry keycards to the security office at the main entrance.
(A) Depart
(B) Departed
(C) Departing
(D) Departure

120. ------- Mr. Dawson graduated from university, he began working as an architect with Raleigh & Associates.
(A) Either
(B) As soon as
(C) Because of
(D) In order to

121. The first sales representative ------- the monthly target will be awarded with three extra paid vacation days.
(A) reach
(B) for reaching
(C) to reach
(D) is reached

122. After a customer has purchased a laptop from Digital Direct, the business will perform repairs free of charge at any time ------- a six-month period.
(A) except
(B) around
(C) during
(D) close

123. The interviewer felt that Ms. Howden's experience working in Asia was ------- to the job duties and responsibilities of the position.
(A) apply
(B) applicable
(C) application
(D) applicator

124. Lowden Corporation ------- its social media ban on all departments in its head office.
(A) appraises
(B) obeys
(C) instructs
(D) enforces

125. Now that the company has employed several part-time office assistants, our workload is ------- lighter.
(A) consider
(B) consideration
(C) considering
(D) considerably

126. Hotels in the city's Old Town district have experienced a boom in popularity lately thanks to an ------- of tourists.
(A) influx
(B) intrigue
(C) intention
(D) induction

127. After ------- Internet providers, Mr. Moss noticed regular disruptions to his wireless connection.
(A) switching
(B) switch
(C) to switch
(D) has switched

128. Most snack food manufacturers ------- design their advertisements to appeal to young children.
(A) formerly
(B) abruptly
(C) severely
(D) purposely

129. Interior King furniture is popular among consumers for its simple design and ------- of assembly.
(A) ease
(B) easy
(C) easier
(D) eased

130. Ironman Nutritional Supplies will ------- its shipping fee for anyone who spends at least $300 on an order.
(A) prevent
(B) concede
(C) waive
(D) exceed

Directions: Read the texts that follow. A word, phrase, or sentence is missing in parts of each text.
Four answer choices for each question are given below the text. Select the best answer to complete the text. Then mark the letter (A), (B), (C) or (D) on your answer sheet.

Questions 131–134 refer to the following e-mail.

To: Feltman Corporation Employees

From: Lee Durst

Subject: Cafeteria trash

Date: June 19

To All Staff,

The board of directors has decided to implement a new policy ----- the serving of food and
131.
disposal of trash in the staff cafeteria. Starting from next Monday, all meals served in the cafeteria will come on new stainless steel trays, instead of the typical disposable plastic trays. These should be returned to the kitchen after use, where they will be cleaned and sanitized for reuse. This policy will ----- the amount of trash created. -----, all drinking
132.   133.
cups will be replaced with metal ones that can be reused for many years. This will help our company to be more eco-friendly. -----. Should you have any questions or suggestions, feel
134.
free to contact me.

Best wishes,

Lee Durst
General Operations Manager

131. (A) regards
(B) regardless
(C) regarding
(D) regarded

132. (A) promote
(B) cease
(C) minimize
(D) estimate

133. (A) As a result
(B) Instead
(C) In addition
(D) However

134. (A) Please let us know what you think of the new menu items.
(B) During this renovation work, some foods will be unavailable.
(C) This project has been successful thanks to your hard work.
(D) We would appreciate your cooperation with this effort.

Questions 135–138 refer to the following letter.

Dear Valued Customer,

Do you think there is an error in your monthly electricity bill? If so, _____ it to Northern
135.
Electric's customer service department as soon as possible, either by mail or by e-mail. We
encourage our customers to alert us of any billing errors within 3 days of receiving their bill
so that we can address the matter immediately. _____. Our representatives will evaluate and
136.
make a decision on all _____. If we determine that you have been mistakenly overcharged
137.
on your monthly bill, the appropriate _____ will be deducted from the next monthly bill you will
138.
receive.

135. (A) sends
(B) sent
(C) send
(D) sending

136. (A) Northern Electric has recently
launched a new payment plan.
(B) Northern Electric hopes to fill several
positions in the department.
(C) The electricity supply will be
temporarily disrupted this week.
(D) Please also clearly state the nature
of the problem.

137. (A) claims
(B) properties
(C) installations
(D) applications

138. (A) currency
(B) amount
(C) replacement
(D) solution

Questions 139–142 refer to the following memo.

To: Horizon Hotel Front Desk Staff

From: Mike Rowan

Subject: Conference Halls

Date: August 4

I am delighted to announce that construction of our new conference halls will be finished by the end of next week. The two halls will be _____ from the hotel lobby.
139.

The new halls can each accommodate up to 600 people, and are intended for company training sessions and business presentations. _____. Ms. Tennant will be temporarily
140.
responsible for taking event bookings between now and the end of September. _____, she
141.
will resume her typical duties as Guest Services Coordinator. We plan to create a brand new position for an Events Coordinator, and this will be advertised internally by the end of this month. This successful applicant will be responsible for _____ reservations for the
142.
conference halls.

139. (A) accessible
(B) acceptable
(C) attainable
(D) approved

140. (A) Many of the events have boosted the hotel's reputation.
(B) Rita Tennant has given several business presentations.
(C) Both rooms must be booked in advance.
(D) Interviews will be carried out in early September.

141. (A) Likewise
(B) Nevertheless
(C) After that
(D) In short

142. (A) oversee
(B) oversees
(C) overseen
(D) overseeing

Questions 143–146 refer to the following e-mail.

To: pkilroy@amerimail.net
From: mwagstaff@marksmotors.com
Subject: Bronco Meridian
Date: December 14

Hi Peter,

Thank you for asking about the Bronco Meridian sedan we advertised in the local newspaper. I'm sorry to tell you that I just spoke with my head salesperson, and ____, this 143. car was sold this morning.

If you could give me some specific details about what type of car you would like to purchase, I ____ you in finding something suitable for you. When it's convenient for you, get 144. back to me by e-mail with your spending budget, the brand and type of car you'd like, and any specific features you are looking for. ____. 145.

You also have the option to receive regular ____. By signing up for these, you will receive 146. text messages informing you of new additions to our list of vehicles. Please let me know if you're interested.

Best regards,

Mark Wagstaff
Mark's Motors Used Car Lot

143. (A) apparently
(B) mainly
(C) briefly
(D) frequently

144. (A) am assisting
(B) can assist
(C) have been assisting
(D) assist

145. (A) Of course, you will need to fulfill the job requirements.
(B) I will be receiving these new vehicles at the lot on Monday.
(C) It is a recent trend in the automotive industry.
(D) Then, I will search for vehicles that match your preferences.

146. (A) notifications
(B) repairs
(C) appointments
(D) upgrades

PART 7

Directions: In this part you will read a selection of texts, such as magazine and newspaper articles, e-mails, and instant messages. Each text or set of texts is followed by several questions. Select the best answer for each question and mark the letter (A), (B), (C), or (D) on your answer sheet.

Questions 147–148 refer to the following information.

It's Never Been Easier to Book With Air Transnat!

Looking for a convenient way to book flights, but don't have quick access to a computer? Simply install our new application on your cell phone, and you can do everything in a matter of minutes! All prices for flights are updated every thirty seconds on the application, so the information you see is always accurate.

That's not all! We offer the same perks to application users that we do to Web site users. When making your booking, you can select your seat, choose what you would like to eat on the plane, and even request additional items such as pillows, blankets, and headphones.

Once your booking is complete, you will receive a special reservation code that you can use to make changes to your seat and meal preferences up to one week prior to your departure date.

147. What is true according to the information?
(A) A meal can be selected via an application.
(B) Reservations are confirmed by e-mail.
(C) Flight information is updated hourly.
(D) A Web site was recently redesigned.

148. What is the purpose of the special code?
(A) To speed up a check-in procedure
(B) To receive a discount on flights
(C) To sign up for an Internet service
(D) To allow modification of a booking

Questions 149–150 refer to the following product description.

Enhance Your Health Today!

With a capacity of 0.65L, this blender can accommodate more ingredients than most similar models on the market can. Designed by electrical engineer Manuel Vega, this device is perfect for use both in the home and in a professional setting. The 1000-Watt motor provides impressive power and efficiency, so you can mix ingredients quicker than ever before. And the detachable stainless steel blades cut both horizontally and vertically! Available in white, silver, and black, this product comes with a recipe book and two different sizes of juice cups!

149. What type of product is being described?
(A) A software package
(B) A construction tool
(C) A kitchen appliance
(D) A piece of furniture

150. What is mentioned about the product?
(A) It is powerful.
(B) It is lightweight.
(C) It is affordably priced.
(D) It is easy to use.

Questions 151–152 refer to the following e-mail.

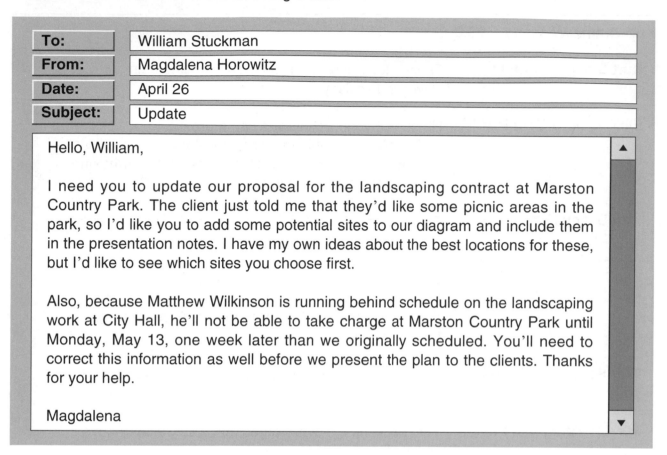

To:	William Stuckman
From:	Magdalena Horowitz
Date:	April 26
Subject:	Update

Hello, William,

I need you to update our proposal for the landscaping contract at Marston Country Park. The client just told me that they'd like some picnic areas in the park, so I'd like you to add some potential sites to our diagram and include them in the presentation notes. I have my own ideas about the best locations for these, but I'd like to see which sites you choose first.

Also, because Matthew Wilkinson is running behind schedule on the landscaping work at City Hall, he'll not be able to take charge at Marston Country Park until Monday, May 13, one week later than we originally scheduled. You'll need to correct this information as well before we present the plan to the clients. Thanks for your help.

Magdalena

151. Why did Ms. Horowitz send the e-mail?
  (A) To accept an employment offer
  (B) To revise a project plan
  (C) To suggest organizing an event
  (D) To request a copy of presentation notes

152. What is Mr. Stuckman asked to do?
  (A) Go to City Hall
  (B) Reschedule a client meeting
  (C) Contact Mr. Wilkinson
  (D) Change a start date

GO ON TO THE NEXT PAGE

Questions 153–154 refer to the following online chat discussion.

🔘 **Online Messenger V3.0**	▲
Kurt Staley [2:11 P.M.]	Thanks for using Spark Software's online help service. How can I assist you?
Iris Cavalera [2:13 P.M.]	Hi, one of your technicians came around to our offices at Ritz Magazine this morning to install a photo editing package on some of our computers. But, I'm having trouble opening the program.
Kurt Staley [2:14 P.M.]	That sounds strange. Do you see any kind of message when you try to start it up?
Iris Cavalera [2:15 P.M.]	Well, it's asking me to input a product activation code. I'm typing AB469, just like the technician wrote down. I didn't have any problems with the previous versions we bought from you.
Kurt Staley [2:17 P.M.]	Oh, I've got it! I'm pretty sure the "B" is actually an "8". There should only be one letter in the code.
Iris Cavalera [2:19 P.M.]	That explains it. I was worried that we'd need to have it installed again. Thanks a lot. ▼

153. What is indicated about Ritz Magazine?
(A) It has returned some faulty products to Spark Software.
(B) It has purchased Spark Software products before.
(C) It requested that a technician repair some equipment.
(D) It will publish an article about graphic design software.

154. At 2:19 P.M., what does Ms. Cavalera most likely mean when she writes, "That explains it"?
(A) She misunderstood Mr. Staley's earlier instructions.
(B) She learned how to order a product from Spark Software.
(C) She found out why she could not use a program.
(D) She would like to discuss her problem with a technician.

```
┌──────────────────────────────────────────────────────────────┐
│                        E-mail Message                         │
├──────────────────────────────────────────────────────────────┤
```

To: All sales executives
From: Terence Materazzo, CEO
Subject: Company cars
Date: Wednesday, July 10

Good morning,

At yesterday's board meeting, it was decided that all of us at Arandell Manufacturing must place greater emphasis on lessening our impact on the environment. One measure that will be taken is the purchase of new company cars that run on electricity and emit no harmful fumes. These cars will be made available to all sales executives and should be used whenever you travel around visiting our clients. We understand that some of you have already made the switch to a gas-free model. If that is the case, please continue to use your own car, and starting from Monday, the company will now cover the costs of all your electricity top-ups.

These new cars will be delivered to our head office on Monday, and I would like all of you to meet in the basement parking lot at 1 P.M. Larger, more advanced vehicles will be offered to our senior executives, while junior executives will receive standard sedans. All vehicles are manufactured by Azari Motors, and one of its representatives will be on hand to show you how to operate the cars and recharge their batteries. At the end of the day, you're free to take your vehicle home with you.

Regards,

Terence Materazzo
CEO
Arandell Manufacturing

---

155. Why is the business offering company cars?
(A) It is celebrating a successful year of business.
(B) It wants staff to travel greater distances to seek clients.
(C) It is trying to be more environmentally-friendly.
(D) It is rewarding its most successful sales executives.

156. What is suggested about some sales executives at the business?
(A) They do not need to travel for their job.
(B) They already own electric vehicles.
(C) They currently receive a monthly travel allowance.
(D) They complained about the cars they drive.

157. What is NOT suggested about the company cars?
(A) They should remain in the company's parking lot.
(B) They will be demonstrated by a motor company employee.
(C) They will be assigned based on seniority.
(D) They will arrive at the headquarters next week.

Questions 158–160 refer to the following advertisement.

Gerber Baked Goods

Gerber Baked Goods has built a reputation as a supplier of high quality cakes and pastries. The company was established 37 years ago by a skilled baker named Paul Gerber, who moved to Gravenhurst to start his own business venture after serving as an apprentice baker in Toronto.

At first, Mr. Gerber handled all of the daily operations himself, not only baking his goods early each morning, but also preparing the store for business and serving customers. Eventually, the bakery became so popular that he had no choice but to ask for the help of his wife, his nephew, and his brother. All of them continue to help out at the main store, although Mr. Gerber has handed over senior management duties to his younger brother, Mark. The business has particularly thrived in the last five years, expanding its range of offerings and opening smaller stores in nearby towns such as Huntsville and Bracebridge.

If you are craving exquisite sweet treats, stop by Gerber Baked Goods to try our products. Our main store is located at 347 Lakeside Road, Gravenhurst, just next to Lloyd's Pharmacy. You can also check out our offerings online at www. gerberbakedgoods.ca.

158. Where would the advertisement most likely be seen?
 (A) In a business journal
 (B) At a culinary school
 (C) In a local publication
 (D) At a career fair

159. What is indicated about Gerber Baked Goods?
 (A) Its founder has won awards.
 (B) Its main branch is in Huntsville.
 (C) It is seeking apprentice bakers.
 (D) It is a family-run business.

160. What is NOT mentioned as a change that the business has implemented?
 (A) The addition of new products
 (B) A change in management
 (C) The launch of new locations
 (D) A decrease in its prices

Need to Read!

Attention, all writers! Alderdale Public Library is organizing a fundraising activity for its Need to Read initiative, which raises money to purchase books and comics for children at the local orphanage. We are seeking writers of all levels and age groups to lend a hand!

Visit the library any time in April during regular business hours (10 A.M. to 7 P.M., Monday through Saturday). We will assign you one historical figure to write about. There is an extensive variety of interesting people to choose from.

Do your own research on the person and then write about their life and achievements. Don't forget to sign your name at the end.

Submit it at the circulation desk by April 30, at the latest, along with your photo. (see below)

These "Life Stories" will be displayed on a wall in the library throughout the month of May. For each story received, the library will donate $10 to our fundraising initiative. Photographs of contributing writers will be posted on the wall next to the main reading area.

For further details, call the Alderdale Public Library directly at 555-2878 or visit www.alderdalelibrary.co.uk/lifestories.

161. What will be the readers of the notice encouraged to do?
(A) Volunteer to help at an event
(B) Participate in a fundraiser
(C) Lead a tour of a local library
(D) Donate money to a charity

162. What is Need to Read's fundraising goal?
(A) To fund the creation of new library facilities
(B) To recycle old books and create new ones
(C) To provide reading materials for children
(D) To host a local book convention

163. What is NOT indicated about the "Life Stories"?
(A) They must be signed by the writers.
(B) They will be displayed in May.
(C) They are about different people.
(D) They will be entered into a competition.

164. Where will library visitors be likely to see photographs of the writers?
(A) At the circulation desk
(B) Near a reading area
(C) On the Web site
(D) At the main entrance

Questions 165–167 refer to the following e-mail.

E-mail Message

To: All staff of Woodgrain Furniture Store
From: Philip Downie, Store Proprietor
Date: June 11
Subject: Summer excursion

Dear staff,

It's almost time for our annual company vacation, and this year I'd like to ask for your opinions on where we should go. Furthermore, we will run a contest to find the best suggestion for our ideal holiday destination! Employees have until the end of this month to come up with ideas for our three-day break in late July. You should each submit your top three choices to Ms. Ogilvie in the administration office by June 30. The individual who submits the winning suggestion, chosen by me, will receive two tickets for a movie at the theater around the corner from us, Galaxy Movie Theater.

Submissions should be made using entry forms that you can pick up from the office. When judging your suggestions, I will consider the following factors: their appeal to our diverse range of employees, as well as the number of activities on offer (the more, the better!) and the affordability of transportation and accommodation.

Best of luck to you all!

---

165. What is the purpose of the e-mail?
(A) To announce a competition
(B) To invite employees to a party
(C) To describe a training opportunity
(D) To give details about a business plan

166. What is indicated about Galaxy Movie Theater?
(A) It has merged with another company.
(B) It will reward its employees.
(C) It will host a special event.
(D) It is near the furniture store.

167. What is NOT mentioned as an aspect of a good destination?
(A) Being inexpensive to travel to
(B) Having spacious hotel rooms
(C) Being enjoyable to all staff members
(D) Having a wide range of available activities

Questions 168–171 refer to the following online chat session.

Lucas Sears [11:25 A.M.]
Good morning, everyone. I'd like you all to make time in your schedules for a meeting after lunch tomorrow. Our new lines aren't selling particularly well. We should consider shifting our focus.

Emma Harding [11:26 A.M.]
What do you have in mind?

Lucas Sears [11:29 A.M.]
Since the target market for High Wave fashion accessories largely consists of teenagers, targeting consumers online rather than through print media seems like a better fit for us.

Murray Henney [11:31 A.M.]
Right. Social media and other Web sites seem to influence buying decisions more and more these days.

Rico Augustus [11:33 A.M.]
I'm totally on board with that idea. Perhaps we can start contacting some social media companies to get some quotes.

Emma Harding [11:35 A.M.]
Good idea. And we could even try to find out which sites receive the most traffic.

Lucas Sears [11:37 A.M.]
Great. It sounds like we're all on the same page. When we meet tomorrow, I'd like to see some data. Look into the different online platforms and find out how much it costs to run ads on each one. Then, I'll compile the findings and pass them on to the board for review.

Rico Augustus [11:38 A.M.]
I'll get right on it.

Lucas Sears [11:39 A.M.]
Thanks, and just let me know if you have any questions. I'll be in my office all afternoon.

---

168. What type of product does High Wave currently sell?
(A) Electronic devices
(B) Fashion accessories
(C) Sports equipment
(D) Cleaning products

169. At 11:25 A.M., what does Mr. Sears mean when he writes, "We should consider shifting our focus"?
(A) The company should discontinue some of its products.
(B) The meeting should be held in a different location.
(C) The company should adopt a new advertising strategy.
(D) The meeting should include a wide variety of topics.

170. What will Mr. Augustus most likely do next?
(A) Revise a marketing budget
(B) Request some price estimates
(C) Send some documents to Mr. Sears
(D) Update the company's Web site

171. What will Mr. Sears submit to the board members?
(A) Suggestions for new product lines
(B) A proposal for increasing Web traffic
(C) Designs for an advertisement
(D) Information about social media

GO ON TO THE NEXT PAGE

Questions 172–175 refer to the following article.

Café Spectacular Coffee Shop Set to Open

(LONDON, February 12)—French coffee house chain Café Spectacular intends to launch its third coffee shop in Bedfordshire, England, next month. It plans to open the shop on Eastlee Avenue in Dunstable. –[1]–.

"Because there aren't many high-end coffee houses in Dunstable, the town is a perfect spot for us to open up our newest store," stated Jerome Lemieux, the owner of the coffee chain. "We are very excited to add another location in Bedfordshire, and we are looking forward to serving our gourmet coffee varieties to the residents of Dunstable." –[2]–.

The Marseilles-based coffee chain also recently opened a coffee shop in the city of Belfast in Northern Ireland. According to Mr. Lemieux, the next step will be to move further north and over the border into Scotland later this year. –[3]–. At this point, the most likely locations are Glasgow and Dundee. –[4]–.

172. What advantage of the new location does Mr. Lemieux mention?
(A) The affordable property prices
(B) The size of the building
(C) The lack of competitors
(D) The large number of residents

173. Where is Café Spectacular's main branch?
(A) In Dunstable
(B) In Belfast
(C) In Glasgow
(D) In Marseilles

174. According to the article, what does the company plan to do in the future?
(A) Expand into Scotland
(B) Announce a new coffee variety
(C) Purchase a local coffee company
(D) Launch a marketing campaign in Bedfordshire

175. In which of the positions marked [1], [2], [3], and [4] does the following sentence best belong?
"Luton and Kempston are the other towns that already have an outlet."
(A) [1]
(B) [2]
(C) [3]
(D) [4]

http://www.woolcroftbusinessinstitute.com

| Home | Building Amenities | Full-time Courses | Upcoming Seminars |

Confidence in Business Speaking Seminar Series
With Catering Provided by Anatolia Restaurant

Woolcroft Business Institute (WBI) is delighted to announce its October seminar series, which is designed to give confidence to those who are often required to speak publicly in the business world. All the seminars will be led by instructors who possess a wealth of experience in a wide range of business fields. Spaces for each seminar will be in high demand, and we can only accept a maximum of 250 people per session. Interested individuals may sign up online or by calling us directly at 555-0127. Participants in each session will be able to enjoy a delicious buffet and drinks after the session, provided by local Turkish restaurant, Anatolia.

Date	Time	Topic	Instructor	Venue
October 7	12:30 P.M.–2:00 P.M.	Introduction to Speechmaking	Kenneth Lee	WBI Main Auditorium
October 14	3:00 P.M.–4:30 P.M.	Understanding Your Target Audience	Vlatko Andonov	WBI Main Auditorium
October 21	4:30 P.M.–6:00 P.M.	Making an Effective Presentation	Sheri Renner	WBI Main Auditorium
October 28	6:00 P.M.–7:30 P.M.	Succeeding in Any Interview Scenario	Karisma Kapoor	WBI Main Auditorium

To:	smeadows@estracorp.com
From:	registration@wbi.com
Date:	October 3
Subject:	Seminar registration
Attachment:	Stanmeadows.docx

Dear Mr. Meadows,

We are contacting you to confirm your registration for one of the sessions in our October seminar series. I have no doubt that the strategies and skills you will pick up at the session will help you to avoid any problematic job interviews in the future.

Please find a document attached that provides detailed information about our institute, including a map of the building, a description of amenities, and details about parking. If you are interested in finding out more about our full-time courses, you can find a full course list on our Web site. Once you arrive at the institute on the day of the seminar, please go directly to the information kiosk to obtain an identification tag.

Woolcroft Business Institute is a proud leader in professional advancement courses. We look forward to helping you to advance your skill set.

Regards,

Registration Department
Woolcroft Business Institute

176. According to the Web page, what is being offered?
- (A) Chances to improve public speaking skills
- (B) Information about employment opportunities
- (C) A financial consultation for business owners
- (D) A networking event for marketing companies

177. What is NOT indicated about the seminars?
- (A) They can be registered for by phone.
- (B) They will be followed by food and beverages.
- (C) They are held in several event venues.
- (D) They are hosted by Woolcroft Business Institute.

178. Who will instruct the session Mr. Meadows is planning to attend?
- (A) Mr. Lee
- (B) Mr. Andonov
- (C) Ms. Renner
- (D) Ms. Kapoor

179. In the e-mail, the phrase "pick up" in paragraph 1, line 2, is closest in meaning to
- (A) carry
- (B) choose
- (C) acquire
- (D) assign

180. What document is attached to the e-mail?
- (A) A list of available courses
- (B) A guide to an institute
- (C) A registration receipt
- (D) An identification tag

GO ON TO THE NEXT PAGE

Questions 181–185 refer to the following advertisement and e-mail.

Cosmo Computer Tune-ups–Special New Year Rate

Tel: 0898-555-0126
E-mail: sales@cosmotuneups.com

To celebrate the start of the new year, we are offering a special rate on all computer tune-ups performed during January and February. This offer is only available to business clients who have used our services in the past. Cosmo technicians use our innovative diagnostic and repair tools to maximize the performance of your computers by removing malicious software, optimizing operating systems, and installing recommended updates. Our standard rate and our limited-time special rate are as follows:

Number of Computers	Standard Rate (per computer)	Special Rate (per computer)
1–9	$20	$17
10–19	$18	$15
20–29	$16	$13
30 or more	$14	$11

Bonus Offer: When contacting us to book our services, if you write the specific advertisement code "MAT123" in the subject line of your e-mail, we'll provide up to 10 Cosmo mouse mats when we visit your workplace to perform the tune-ups.

To:	Bianca Lancaster <blancaster@romacorp.com>
From:	Adam Crenna <adamc@cosmotuneups.com>
Date:	February 2
Subject:	Re: MAT123

Dear Ms. Lancaster,

Thank you for your e-mail in which you requested tune-ups of the computers at Roma Corporation. Based on the information you provided, I've scheduled our service for February 9 at 9 A.M. As you noted in your e-mail, your company qualifies for our special New Year rates. Our technicians will arrive punctually on the scheduled day and tune up the twenty computers in your offices. The work should take no more than three hours.

If you have any questions about our service, please do not hesitate to contact me again. We look forward to once again doing business with you and your company.

Regards,

Adam Crenna
Customer Service Manager
Cosmo Computer Tune-ups

181. What is indicated about the special rate?
(A) It only applies to certain brands of computers.
(B) It will be offered for three months.
(C) It can only be requested through a Web site.
(D) It is available only to existing clients.

182. In the advertisement, the word "performed" in paragraph 1, line 2, is closest in meaning to
(A) conducted
(B) exhibited
(C) improved
(D) strived

183. What is the main purpose of the e-mail?
(A) To request information
(B) To confirm a service
(C) To reschedule an appointment
(D) To promote a special offer

184. How much will Roma Corporation pay per computer tune-up?
(A) $11
(B) $13
(C) $15
(D) $20

185. What is suggested about Ms. Lancaster?
(A) Her computer will be repaired by the manufacturer.
(B) Her company recently purchased new computers.
(C) She is a former employee of Cosmo Computer Tune-ups.
(D) She will receive complimentary mouse mats.

GO ON TO THE NEXT PAGE

Questions 186–190 refer to the following brochure and e-mails.

Brightspark Solar Panel Wholesaler

Brightspark is Europe's leading supplier of solar panels for commercial and residential buildings. We stack a wide range of panels from the world's best solar panel manufacturers. Below, you can learn more about a few of our best-selling panels.

Synergy Solar: Reliable and cost-effective monocrystalline panels that are suitable for all types of roofs, regardless of angle. Each panel is comprised of 72 cells.
Sol Turbo: Similar to Synergy Solar, but 60 cells in each of these panels are polycrystalline, making the panels even more cost-effective.
Solar King: Constructed with heavy anodized aluminum frames, these 60-cell monocrystalline panels are built to withstand high winds and heavy snow.
Sun Catcher: Monocrystalline panels, each containing 72 cells, specifically designed to be placed on the vertical walls of buildings rather than on their roofs.

If you have any questions regarding any of the panels we supply, please contact us by e-mail at: inquiries@brightspark.co.uk.

When purchasing solar panels, it is crucial to take accurate measurements of the surface on which you intend to install the panels. After doing so, and choosing your panel type, our online calculation tool will tell you precisely how many panels you will need to buy in order to cover a given area. Try it out for yourself at www.brightspark.co.uk/calculator.

To:	inquiries@brightspark.co.uk
From:	crundgren@smarthomes.com
Date:	March 17
Subject:	Recent order

Dear Brightspark,

I am the owner of a home renovation firm, and one of your regular customers. On March 15, I placed an order for 25 of your 72-cell monocrystalline solar panels for the home of one of my customers. I'm contacting you because my customer is having doubts about the panels. She is worried that the panels will look unattractive once they have been installed on the roof of her lakeside cottage. I tried to assure her that they are relatively small and discreet. Would you be able to send me any pictures of homes that have these panels installed on their roof? That would put my customer's mind at ease.

And, one more thing. The last time I ordered solar panels from your business, I was able to print out the warranty information online and give it to my customer. However, this time, I can't seem to find it on your site. I'd appreciate it if you could direct me to the information so that my customer will be fully satisfied.

Thanks,

Colin Rundgren

To: crundgren@smarthomes.com
From: anna321@brightspark.co.uk
Date: March 17
Subject: Re: Recent order

Dear Mr. Rundgren,

Thank you for your recent inquiry. The panels that we are preparing to ship to you are our most popular type, and your customer has nothing to worry about. I have attached some images of other satisfied customers' homes so that she can take a look for herself. If she is not satisfied and wishes to select a different type, please inform me by 5 P.M. this afternoon so that I can change the order.

Regarding the other information you inquired about, I'm afraid you'll need to contact the supplier directly if you wish to receive the full, detailed document.

Best Regards,

Anna Thorn

186. According to the brochure, what can customers do on a Web site?
(A) Compare prices of suppliers
(B) Request a consultation
(C) Check panel requirements
(D) Read customer testimonials

187. What aspect of the panels is Mr. Rundgren's customer concerned about?
(A) Their appearance
(B) Their installation cost
(C) Their energy output
(D) Their durability

188. What type of solar panels did Mr. Rundgren most likely order for his client?
(A) Synergy Solar
(B) Sol Turbo
(C) Solar King
(D) Sun Catcher

189. According to Ms. Thorn, why would Mr. Rundgren need to contact her again on March 17?
(A) To receive some documents
(B) To choose different panels
(C) To make a final payment
(D) To reschedule an installation

190. What can be inferred about the product warranty information?
(A) It has recently been revised.
(B) It is included in the product packaging.
(C) It will be mailed out to Mr. Rundgren's customer.
(D) It is no longer available on Brightspark's Web site.

Questions 191–195 refer to the following advertisement, form, and e-mail.

Enroll Your Employees at The Gilford Institute!

By providing your employees with supplementary training, you can create a workforce that is adaptable, efficient, and cohesive. At The Gilford Institute, we offer four highly-regarded professional advancement courses:

Effective Leadership–It is important that companies offer leadership training to all employees, and not only supervisors and managers. By developing your employees' leadership skills at an early stage, you can equip them with the knowledge they need to take on leadership roles in the future.
Maximum class size: 40. Course runs on Mondays and Tuesdays.

Diversity Training–These days, workplaces are more diverse than ever. It is important to make sure that all workers understand diversity issues. Our diversity training course will enhance your employees' knowledge and enable them to embrace diversity in the workplace.
Maximum class size: 70. Course runs on Tuesdays and Thursdays.

Time Management–Time is a valuable but limited resource at all businesses. However, many employees lack the knowledge and training required to manage their time effectively. This often leads to missed deadlines and poor work quality. Our course will help your employees stay organized, focused, and be more productive every day.
Maximum class size: 60. Course runs on Mondays and Wednesdays.

Enhanced Communication–Poor communication can result in decreased productivity and unnecessary disputes. Whether communicating face-to-face or by e-mail, every employee should have an understanding of the basics of communication. Our course will help your staff to develop the essential skills they need to communicate both verbally and in writing.
Maximum class size: 50. Course runs on Tuesdays and Wednesdays.

Please contact us at inquiries@gilfordinstitute.com for more information on course content, course schedules, and registration. All courses are offered at our main campus building in downtown Rutherford.

The Gilford Institute – Advanced Business Training Courses

Course Registration Form

Company Representative: James Buckner
Company: Markley Corporation
Number of Employees Attending: 33
Course: Enhanced Communication

Date of Registration: April 19

To:	The Gilford Institute <inquiries@gilfordinstitute.com>
From:	James Buckner <jbuckner@markley.com>
Date:	April 27
Subject:	Recent Course Registration

Dear Sir/Madam,

I recently registered the employees of Markley Corporation's marketing department for a course at your institute. We are all very eager to begin the course and benefit from the expertise of the instructor. I am contacting you regarding the availability of parking at or near your institute. Because we will be coming from out of town, we will be hiring a bus for our staff members. The vehicle will be quite large—a standard 52-seat bus—so we will need to find an adequate space in which to park. Can you please provide some suggestions, including a map and directions? It would be very helpful to us.

Yours sincerely,

James Buckner
Head of Marketing
Markley Corporation

191. Who is the advertisement most likely intended for?
(A) Recent graduates
(B) Job fair attendees
(C) Course instructors
(D) Business owners

192. Which course can accommodate the most participants?
(A) Effective Leadership
(B) Diversity Training
(C) Time Management
(D) Enhanced Communication

193. When will the employees of Markley Corporation attend a course at The Gilford Institute?
(A) On Mondays and Tuesdays
(B) On Mondays and Wednesdays
(C) On Tuesdays and Wednesdays
(D) On Tuesdays and Thursdays

194. In the e-mail, the word "eager" in paragraph 1, line 2, is closest in meaning to
(A) patient
(B) desirable
(C) apparent
(D) enthusiastic

195. What does Mr. Buckner indicate about Markley Corporation?
(A) It is based outside Rutherford.
(B) It wishes to change some registration details.
(C) It has worked with The Gilford Institute in the past.
(D) It expects The Gilford Institute to provide transportation.

Questions 196–200 refer to the following e-mails and quote.

E-mail Message

To: Joe Turner <joeturner@lla.com>
From: Roberta Fleck <rfleck@fleckevents.com>
Subject: Estimates
Date: December 12
Attachment: Hotel_lists.docx

Dear Mr. Turner,

I received your recent e-mail about your upcoming Lovett Literary Association awards show, which you would like to hold here in Manchester. Please find a list of hotels that have suitable function rooms for holding such an event.

Just like you asked, I have made sure to add a hotel situated in Belmont to the list. Although I have not personally been involved with any events at that hotel, my colleague has assured me that it is well equipped for large functions.

Once you have made a decision, you should put down a 10 percent deposit by December 15 to ensure that the space is reserved. This can be a particularly busy time of the year for securing venues. I look forward to helping make your event a great success.

Sincerely,

Roberta Fleck

Event Space Rental Estimates

Rented by: *Lovett Literary Association*
Approximate number of attendees: *400*

Duration of Event: *4 hours*
Event date: *February 5*

Hotel	Neighborhood	Additional Information	Cost per hour	Total cost
Arlington Hotel	Five Hills	Equipped for live music performances	£250	£1,000
Thames Hotel	Longford	Rooftop event space and bar	£300	£1,200
Yarrow Hotel	Hampton	Easy access and ramps for those with disabilities	£225	£1,100
Musgrove Hotel	Dayton	Newly renovated function room and stage	£275	£1,300
Ascot Hotel	Belmont	Choice of buffet or set menu provided	£325	£1,400

E-mail Message

To: Roberta Fleck <rfleck@fleckevents.com>
From: Joe Turner <joeturner@lla.com>
Subject: Re: Estimates
Date: December 15
Attachment: Hotel_lists.docx

Dear Ms. Fleck,

Thank you very much for the list of locations you compiled for our awards ceremony. You've really worked hard to help us prepare everything. As you advised, I have paid a 10 percent deposit to secure the hotel's event space in advance. Although the rooftop event space at Thames Hotel sounded nice, I felt that it was more important to choose a venue that has recently undergone modifications, as we would like to hold our event in a sophisticated, attractive setting. Furthermore, I'd rather not book a rooftop area, just in case it rains.

The next thing I need to consider is food and drink. Can you recommend a good caterer to provide food at the event? The manager at the hotel recommended hiring a firm that specializes in catering large functions like ours. I'll take a look at some different options, but I'll hold off on making a final decision until I hear back from you.

Best wishes,
Joe Turner

196. What is indicated about Ms. Fleck?
(A) She works at a hotel in Manchester.
(B) She has been nominated for an award.
(C) She is planning a special ceremony.
(D) She lives in the Belmont neighborhood.

197. What hotel did Ms. Fleck include in response to Mr. Turner's request?
(A) Arlington Hotel
(B) Thames Hotel
(C) Musgrove Hotel
(D) Ascot Hotel

198. What is suggested about Yarrow Hotel?
(A) It offers wheelchair access.
(B) Its event space is relatively small.
(C) It can provide live music.
(D) Its guests can enjoy a buffet.

199. How much will Mr. Turner pay for the event space in total?
(A) £1,000
(B) £1,200
(C) £1,300
(D) £1,400

200. According to the second e-mail, what will Mr. Turner do next?
(A) Contact a hotel manager
(B) Consider some live entertainment options
(C) Schedule a meeting with Ms. Fleck
(D) Compare catering companies

Stop! This is the end of the test. If you finish before time is called, you may go back to Parts 5, 6, and 7 and check your work.

NO TEST MATERIAL ON THIS PAGE

ANSWER SHEET

LISTENING COMPREHENSION (PART 1~4)

NO	ANSWER A B C D	NO	ANSWER A B C D	NO	ANSWER A B C D	NO	ANSWER A B C D	NO	ANSWER A B C D
1	ⓐⓑⓒⓓ	21	ⓐⓑⓒ	41	ⓐⓑⓒⓓ	61	ⓐⓑⓒⓓ	81	ⓐⓑⓒⓓ
2	ⓐⓑⓒⓓ	22	ⓐⓑⓒ	42	ⓐⓑⓒⓓ	62	ⓐⓑⓒⓓ	82	ⓐⓑⓒⓓ
3	ⓐⓑⓒⓓ	23	ⓐⓑⓒ	43	ⓐⓑⓒⓓ	63	ⓐⓑⓒⓓ	83	ⓐⓑⓒⓓ
4	ⓐⓑⓒⓓ	24	ⓐⓑⓒ	44	ⓐⓑⓒⓓ	64	ⓐⓑⓒⓓ	84	ⓐⓑⓒⓓ
5	ⓐⓑⓒⓓ	25	ⓐⓑⓒ	45	ⓐⓑⓒⓓ	65	ⓐⓑⓒⓓ	85	ⓐⓑⓒⓓ
6	ⓐⓑⓒⓓ	26	ⓐⓑⓒ	46	ⓐⓑⓒⓓ	66	ⓐⓑⓒⓓ	86	ⓐⓑⓒⓓ
7	ⓐⓑⓒⓓ	27	ⓐⓑⓒ	47	ⓐⓑⓒⓓ	67	ⓐⓑⓒⓓ	87	ⓐⓑⓒⓓ
8	ⓐⓑⓒⓓ	28	ⓐⓑⓒ	48	ⓐⓑⓒⓓ	68	ⓐⓑⓒⓓ	88	ⓐⓑⓒⓓ
9	ⓐⓑⓒⓓ	29	ⓐⓑⓒ	49	ⓐⓑⓒⓓ	69	ⓐⓑⓒⓓ	89	ⓐⓑⓒⓓ
10	ⓐⓑⓒⓓ	30	ⓐⓑⓒ	50	ⓐⓑⓒⓓ	70	ⓐⓑⓒⓓ	90	ⓐⓑⓒⓓ
11	ⓐⓑⓒⓓ	31	ⓐⓑⓒ	51	ⓐⓑⓒⓓ	71	ⓐⓑⓒⓓ	91	ⓐⓑⓒⓓ
12	ⓐⓑⓒⓓ	32	ⓐⓑⓒ	52	ⓐⓑⓒⓓ	72	ⓐⓑⓒⓓ	92	ⓐⓑⓒⓓ
13	ⓐⓑⓒⓓ	33	ⓐⓑⓒ	53	ⓐⓑⓒⓓ	73	ⓐⓑⓒⓓ	93	ⓐⓑⓒⓓ
14	ⓐⓑⓒⓓ	34	ⓐⓑⓒ	54	ⓐⓑⓒⓓ	74	ⓐⓑⓒⓓ	94	ⓐⓑⓒⓓ
15	ⓐⓑⓒⓓ	35	ⓐⓑⓒ	55	ⓐⓑⓒⓓ	75	ⓐⓑⓒⓓ	95	ⓐⓑⓒⓓ
16	ⓐⓑⓒⓓ	36	ⓐⓑⓒ	56	ⓐⓑⓒⓓ	76	ⓐⓑⓒⓓ	96	ⓐⓑⓒⓓ
17	ⓐⓑⓒⓓ	37	ⓐⓑⓒ	57	ⓐⓑⓒⓓ	77	ⓐⓑⓒⓓ	97	ⓐⓑⓒⓓ
18	ⓐⓑⓒⓓ	38	ⓐⓑⓒ	58	ⓐⓑⓒⓓ	78	ⓐⓑⓒⓓ	98	ⓐⓑⓒⓓ
19	ⓐⓑⓒⓓ	39	ⓐⓑⓒ	59	ⓐⓑⓒⓓ	79	ⓐⓑⓒⓓ	99	ⓐⓑⓒⓓ
20	ⓐⓑⓒⓓ	40	ⓐⓑⓒ	60	ⓐⓑⓒⓓ	80	ⓐⓑⓒⓓ	100	ⓐⓑⓒⓓ

READING COMPREHENSION (PART 5~7)

NO	ANSWER A B C D	NO	ANSWER A B C D	NO	ANSWER A B C D	NO	ANSWER A B C D	NO	ANSWER A B C D
101	ⓐⓑⓒⓓ	121	ⓐⓑⓒⓓ	141	ⓐⓑⓒⓓ	161	ⓐⓑⓒⓓ	181	ⓐⓑⓒⓓ
102	ⓐⓑⓒⓓ	122	ⓐⓑⓒⓓ	142	ⓐⓑⓒⓓ	162	ⓐⓑⓒⓓ	182	ⓐⓑⓒⓓ
103	ⓐⓑⓒⓓ	123	ⓐⓑⓒⓓ	143	ⓐⓑⓒⓓ	163	ⓐⓑⓒⓓ	183	ⓐⓑⓒⓓ
104	ⓐⓑⓒⓓ	124	ⓐⓑⓒⓓ	144	ⓐⓑⓒⓓ	164	ⓐⓑⓒⓓ	184	ⓐⓑⓒⓓ
105	ⓐⓑⓒⓓ	125	ⓐⓑⓒⓓ	145	ⓐⓑⓒⓓ	165	ⓐⓑⓒⓓ	185	ⓐⓑⓒⓓ
106	ⓐⓑⓒⓓ	126	ⓐⓑⓒⓓ	146	ⓐⓑⓒⓓ	166	ⓐⓑⓒⓓ	186	ⓐⓑⓒⓓ
107	ⓐⓑⓒⓓ	127	ⓐⓑⓒⓓ	147	ⓐⓑⓒⓓ	167	ⓐⓑⓒⓓ	187	ⓐⓑⓒⓓ
108	ⓐⓑⓒⓓ	128	ⓐⓑⓒⓓ	148	ⓐⓑⓒⓓ	168	ⓐⓑⓒⓓ	188	ⓐⓑⓒⓓ
109	ⓐⓑⓒⓓ	129	ⓐⓑⓒⓓ	149	ⓐⓑⓒⓓ	169	ⓐⓑⓒⓓ	189	ⓐⓑⓒⓓ
110	ⓐⓑⓒⓓ	130	ⓐⓑⓒⓓ	150	ⓐⓑⓒⓓ	170	ⓐⓑⓒⓓ	190	ⓐⓑⓒⓓ
111	ⓐⓑⓒⓓ	131	ⓐⓑⓒⓓ	151	ⓐⓑⓒⓓ	171	ⓐⓑⓒⓓ	191	ⓐⓑⓒⓓ
112	ⓐⓑⓒⓓ	132	ⓐⓑⓒⓓ	152	ⓐⓑⓒⓓ	172	ⓐⓑⓒⓓ	192	ⓐⓑⓒⓓ
113	ⓐⓑⓒⓓ	133	ⓐⓑⓒⓓ	153	ⓐⓑⓒⓓ	173	ⓐⓑⓒⓓ	193	ⓐⓑⓒⓓ
114	ⓐⓑⓒⓓ	134	ⓐⓑⓒⓓ	154	ⓐⓑⓒⓓ	174	ⓐⓑⓒⓓ	194	ⓐⓑⓒⓓ
115	ⓐⓑⓒⓓ	135	ⓐⓑⓒⓓ	155	ⓐⓑⓒⓓ	175	ⓐⓑⓒⓓ	195	ⓐⓑⓒⓓ
116	ⓐⓑⓒⓓ	136	ⓐⓑⓒⓓ	156	ⓐⓑⓒⓓ	176	ⓐⓑⓒⓓ	196	ⓐⓑⓒⓓ
117	ⓐⓑⓒⓓ	137	ⓐⓑⓒⓓ	157	ⓐⓑⓒⓓ	177	ⓐⓑⓒⓓ	197	ⓐⓑⓒⓓ
118	ⓐⓑⓒⓓ	138	ⓐⓑⓒⓓ	158	ⓐⓑⓒⓓ	178	ⓐⓑⓒⓓ	198	ⓐⓑⓒⓓ
119	ⓐⓑⓒⓓ	139	ⓐⓑⓒⓓ	159	ⓐⓑⓒⓓ	179	ⓐⓑⓒⓓ	199	ⓐⓑⓒⓓ
120	ⓐⓑⓒⓓ	140	ⓐⓑⓒⓓ	160	ⓐⓑⓒⓓ	180	ⓐⓑⓒⓓ	200	ⓐⓑⓒⓓ

聽力測驗 Part1 & Part 2

冊次	TEST 1 ☑ TEST 2 ◯ TEST 3 ◯
題號	1
頁數	45
	(A) The man is hanging up a poster. (B) The woman is taking a picture. (C) The man is pointing at something. (D) They are looking at each other.

錯誤原因
圖中的兩個人正看著某個東西，不能因為聽到「在看」就確定答案！ 一定要確定受詞！ Something 也有可能是答案！

重要字彙	hang up　掛 point at　指向 look at each other　看著對方

1. 將答錯及用猜的題目寫下來！
2. 用螢光筆將不知道意思或讀音的單字畫起來！
3. 彙整用螢光筆標示起來的單字及文句！
4. 錯誤原因：(1) 將表「動作」（be being p.p）誤解成表「狀態」。
　　　　　　 (2) 不知道 schedule 的英式發音 [ˈʃɛdjul] 與美式發音 [ˈskɛdʒʊ] 唸法不同。

誤答筆記　聽力測驗 Part1 & Part 2

冊次	TEST 1 ◯　TEST 2 ◯　TEST 3 ◯
題號	
頁數	
錯誤原因	

冊次	TEST 1 ◯　TEST 2 ◯　TEST 3 ◯
題號	
頁數	
錯誤原因	

重要字彙	

誤答筆記　聽力測驗 Part1 & Part 2

＊請將本頁表格剪下，複印後使用。

誤答筆記

找出 Part 5 & Part 6 錯誤的原因

冊次	TEST 1 ○　TEST 2 ☑　TEST 3 ○	
題號	101	
頁數	67	錯誤原因

<table>
<tr>
<td>

~ there has been much _____
in agriculture, with ~.
(A) develop
(B) developed
(C) developing
(D) development

★找出我的弱點！
問題類型　(文法) 句子的結構
　　　　　　　詞彙

</td>
<td>

不知道 [there is/are+ 名詞]
看到 has been 就急忙認定是 P.P
需要看完文句的整體結構！

答案 D
正確原因
there is 句型 → 空格才是主語！
範例中，只有身為名詞的 development
能擔任主語，雖然 there 這個副詞在
主語的位置上，但並不是真正的主語。
實際上真正的主語是接在 be 動詞後的
名詞！

</td>
</tr>
</table>

重要字彙	there is N　有~ develop　發展 agriculture　農業

1. 不用把所有的題目都抄起來！只需要寫下會影響正解的部分，其他以連接號「~」代替！
2. 不要將正解寫在問題裡，需要另外標示！
3. 掌握為什麼答錯才是最重要的！
4. 簡要解釋不懂的部分！
5. 快速掌握題型的話，解題的速度也會提升！確認錯誤的題目屬於什麼類型！
6. 一定要整理題目裡不懂的單字！

誤答筆記　找出 Part 5 & Part 6 錯誤的原因

冊次	TEST 1 ◯　TEST 2 ◯　TEST 3 ◯	
題號		我選擇的答案
頁數		錯誤原因
		答案
		正確原因
★找出我的弱點！		
問題類型	文法	
	詞彙	

冊次	TEST 1 ◯　TEST 2 ◯　TEST 3 ◯	
題號		我選擇的答案
頁數		錯誤原因
		答案
		正確原因
★找出我的弱點！		
問題類型	文法	
	詞彙	

重要字彙	

＊請將本頁表格剪下，複印後使用。

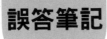
Part 3 & Part 4 & Part 7

Paraphrasing 整理

more detailed report 更詳細的報告	→	a revised document 修訂的文件
drop off your report 留下你的報告	→	turn in an assignment 提交作品
later today 今天稍晚	→	this afternoon 今天下午
	→	
	→	

請整理對話或短文中的線索，再次確認其線索是如何變成正確答案的！

整理對話、短文中的線索是如何變成正確答案的，盡可能精簡。如果將冗長的文句都寫下來，很容易感到厭倦。準備多益最重要的是「跑完全程」。

→	→
→	→
→	→
→	→
→	→
→	→
→	→
→	→
→	→
→	→

＊請將本頁表格剪下，複印後使用。

屬於我的多益單字表

學習時遇到不會的單字，記得整理起來（特別是句子填空題中出現在選項的單字）。

另外，如果在文句中出現跟該單字搭配使用的搭配詞／慣用語，最好也一起寫下來。

也別忘了記下 Part 3、4、7 的文句及選項中影響判斷的單字！

	Sample
sign up 報名；註冊；簽約 sign up for the seminar 報名研討會 = register for	
rarely 很少；不常見 = not often highly 非常 = very	

＊請將本頁表格剪下，複印後使用。

揮別厚重，迎向高分！
最接近真實多益測驗的模擬題本

特色 1 單回成冊

揮別市面多數多益題本的厚重感，單回裝訂仿照真實測驗，提前適應答題手感。

特色 2 錯題解析

解析本提供深度講解，針對正確答案與誘答選項進行解題，全面掌握答題關鍵。

特色 3 誤答筆記

提供筆記模板，協助深入了解誤答原因，歸納出專屬於自己的學習筆記。

TOEIC

Test of English for International Communication

答案與解析

三民書局

TEST 1

TEST 1

PART 1

1. (C) 2. (A) 3. (B) 4. (D) 5. (A) 6. (D)

PART 2

7. (C) 8. (B) 9. (C) 10. (A) 11. (C) 12. (A) 13. (A) 14. (A) 15. (B) 16. (B) 17. (B) 18. (C) 19. (A)
20. (B) 21. (B) 22. (B) 23. (C) 24. (C) 25. (A) 26. (C) 27. (C) 28. (A) 29. (B) 30. (A) 31. (A)

PART 3

32. (C) 33. (C) 34. (D) 35. (D) 36. (C) 37. (B) 38. (B) 39. (D) 40. (A) 41. (A) 42. (C) 43. (B) 44. (D)
45. (C) 46. (D) 47. (B) 48. (D) 49. (A) 50. (D) 51. (B) 52. (B) 53. (C) 54. (D) 55. (A) 56. (D) 57. (B)
58. (D) 59. (B) 60. (D) 61. (C) 62. (B) 63. (B) 64. (D) 65. (C) 66. (C) 67. (A) 68. (D) 69. (C) 70. (B)

PART 4

71. (C) 72. (C) 73. (D) 74. (A) 75. (B) 76. (D) 77. (C) 78. (D) 79. (C) 80. (D) 81. (D) 82. (C) 83. (D)
84. (C) 85. (A) 86. (B) 87. (C) 88. (C) 89. (D) 90. (C) 91. (D) 92. (C) 93. (B) 94. (A) 95. (D) 96. (B)
97. (C) 98. (B) 99. (C) 100. (C)

PART 5

101. (A) 102. (C) 103. (B) 104. (D) 105. (D) 106. (A) 107. (B) 108. (D) 109. (C) 110. (A) 111. (A)
112. (B) 113. (B) 114. (C) 115. (B) 116. (D) 117. (C) 118. (D) 119. (C) 120. (B) 121. (C) 122. (C)
123. (B) 124. (D) 125. (D) 126. (A) 127. (A) 128. (D) 129. (A) 130. (C)

PART 6

131. (C) 132. (C) 133. (C) 134. (D) 135. (C) 136. (D) 137. (A) 138. (B) 139. (A) 140. (C) 141. (C)
142. (D) 143. (A) 144. (B) 145. (D) 146. (A)

PART 7

147. (A) 148. (D) 149. (C) 150. (A) 151. (B) 152. (D) 153. (B) 154. (C) 155. (C) 156. (B) 157. (A)
158. (C) 159. (D) 160. (D) 161. (B) 162. (C) 163. (D) 164. (B) 165. (A) 166. (D) 167. (B) 168. (B)
169. (C) 170. (B) 171. (D) 172. (C) 173. (D) 174. (A) 175. (A) 176. (A) 177. (C) 178. (D) 179. (C)
180. (B) 181. (D) 182. (A) 183. (B) 184. (B) 185. (D) 186. (C) 187. (A) 188. (A) 189. (B) 190. (D)
191. (D) 192. (B) 193. (C) 194. (D) 195. (A) 196. (C) 197. (D) 198. (A) 199. (C) 200. (D)

Part 1

1.

(A) He's taking off his shoes.
(B) He's checking his briefcase.
(C) He's walking down some steps.
(D) He's using his phone.
(A) 他正在脫鞋。
(B) 他正在檢查他的公事包。
(C) 他正在下樓梯。
(D) 他正在使用電話。

解析 照片內僅有一人時，須留意該人物的動作、姿勢及與其有關連性的事物。
(A) 他並未脫鞋，故非正解。
(B) 他並未檢查公事包，故非正解。
(C) 他正在下樓梯，故為正解。
(D) 他並未使用電話，故非正解。

2.

(A) She's wearing a safety helmet.
(B) She's working in the office.
(C) She's painting the wall.
(D) She's inspecting some machines.
(A) 她戴著安全帽。
(B) 她在辦公室辦公。
(C) 她在油漆牆壁。
(D) 她在檢查某些機器。

解析 照片內僅有一人時，須留意該人物的動作、姿勢及與其有關連性的事物。
(A) 她頭上戴著安全帽，故為正解。
(B) 她工作的地方並非辦公室，故非正解。
(C) 她並未進行油漆作業，故非正解。
(D) 她並未檢查機器，故非正解。

3.

(A) They're resting on a wooden bench.
(B) They're looking at a map.
(C) They're climbing a mountain.
(D) They're taking something out of the backpack.
(A) 他們坐在木製長椅上休息。
(B) 他們正在看地圖。
(C) 他們正在爬山。
(D) 他們正從背包拿出東西。

解析 照片內出現兩人時，須留意兩位人物共同的動作、姿勢及人物們周邊的事物。

(A) 照片內沒有長椅，故非正解。
(B) 從兩人的姿勢和視線，能看出他們正在看地圖，故為正解。
(C) 兩人站在原地並未移動，故非正解。
(D) 照片內無人從背包拿出東西，故非正解。

4.

(A) The man is looking at a menu.
(B) A woman is tasting food.
(C) Some plates have been washed in the sink.
(D) A container is being filled with food.
(A) 男子正在看菜單。
(B) 女子正在品嘗食物。
(C) 有些盤子已經在洗碗槽洗過了。
(D) 容器內被裝入了食物。

解析 照片內出現男女二人，須留意兩位人物共同的動作、姿勢及人物們周邊的事物。
(A) 男子看的並非菜單，故非正解。
(B) 女子並未品嘗任何食物，故非正解。
(C) 照片內沒有洗碗槽，也沒有洗好的盤子，故非正解。
(D) 照片內的二人正一起把食物裝進容器中，故為正解。

5.

(A) Boxes are stacked on a warehouse floor.
(B) A ladder is leaning against the wall.
(C) Some packages are being wrapped.
(D) Items are being moved by a forklift.
(A) 箱子堆在倉庫的地板上。
(B) 梯子靠在牆壁上。
(C) 部分包裹正在進行包裝。
(D) 物品正被堆高機搬動。

解析 照片內僅有物品時，必須留意物品的名稱和所在位置。
(A) 倉庫地板上堆了許多箱子，故為正解。
(B) 照片內並無梯子，故非正解。
(C) 照片內並未進行包裝作業，故非正解。
(D) 照片內並未搬動物品，故非正解。

6.

(A) Some people are boarding a boat.
(B) There are lampposts along the walkway.

(C) People are swimming in the ocean.
(D) Some boats are docked at a pier.
(A) 有些人正在登船。
(B) 整條人行道都有路燈。
(C) 人們正在海中游泳。
(D) 有幾艘船停在碼頭邊。

解析 照片內出現多個人物時，須留意人物們的動作、姿勢及周邊事物。
(A) 照片內沒有人在登船，故非正解。
(B) 照片內沒有沿著人行道加設的路燈，故非正解。
(C) 照片內沒有人在游泳，故非正解。
(D) 照片內有幾艘船停在碼頭邊，故為正解。

Part 2

7. Why are you paying by check?
(A) At the bank on Main Street.
(B) Around $500.
(C) Because the company prefers that.
為什麼要用支票支付？
(A) 在主街的銀行。
(B) 大約 500 美元。
(C) 因為那間公司偏好這麼做。

解析 本題為詢問為什麼要用支票支付的 Why 疑問句。
(A) 此為針對 Where 疑問句，告知位置的回答，故非正解。
(B) 此為針對 How much 疑問句，告知金額的回答，故非正解。
(C) 用 that 代指用支票支付，說明這是那間公司欲使用的方式，故為正解。

8. When should we install this software?
(A) It's an anti-virus program.
(B) As soon as we get to work.
(C) Some new laptops.
我們什麼時候必須安裝這個軟體？
(A) 這是一個防毒程式。
(B) 我們開始工作時。
(C) 一些新的筆記型電腦。

解析 本題為詢問何時要安裝某個特定軟體的 When 疑問句。
(A) 只說明軟體的功能，故非正解。
(B) 用表時間點的 As soon as 對應 When 疑問句，說明大概的時間，故為正解。
(C) 用聽到 software 容易聯想到的 laptops 混淆考生，故非正解。

9. Is the customer helpline down?
(A) No. That department is upstairs.
(B) That's very helpful.
(C) Yes. We can't receive any calls.
客服專線故障了嗎？
(A) 不是。那個部門在樓上。
(B) 那很有用。
(C) 對。我們無法接任何電話。

解析 本題為確認客服專線是否故障的疑問句。
(A) 用 No 表否定後，回答了與客服專線無關的答案，故非正解。
(B) 用和 helpline 部分發音相同的 helpful 混淆

考生，故非正解。
(C) 用 Yes 表肯定後，說明客服專線故障帶來的影響，故為正解。

10. What refreshments did you arrange?
(A) Just some drinks and sandwiches.
(B) They've extended their range.
(C) Thanks, I feel better now.
你準備了什麼茶點？
(A) 只是一些飲料和三明治。
(B) 他們擴大了範圍。
(C) 謝謝，我現在感覺好多了。

解析 本題為詢問茶點為何的 What 疑問句。
(A) 明確寫出茶點類型，故為正解。
(B) 用和 arrange 部分發音相同的 range 混淆考生，故非正解。
(C) 表示謝意，但未回覆 What 疑問句，故非正解。

11. I can watch a live performance at this restaurant, can't I?
(A) I'm not much of a music fan.
(B) No, there's no entry fee.
(C) Yes, it starts in 15 minutes.
我可以在這間餐廳看現場表演，對吧？
(A) 我不是狂熱樂迷。
(B) 不，不用付入場費。
(C) 對，15 分鐘後會開始。

解析 本題為確認是否能在某間餐廳看到現場表演的附加問句。
(A) 回答僅表明自己的喜好，與表演無關，故非正解。
(B) 用 No 表否定後提及的內容與是否能看得到表演無關，故非正解。
(C) 用 Yes 表肯定後，用 it 代指 a live performance 告知表演時間，故為正解。

12. Doesn't this hotel have a conference room?
(A) No, I'm afraid not.
(B) A business event.
(C) On May 30.
這間飯店不是有會議廳嗎？
(A) 不，我想沒有。
(B) 一場商業活動。
(C) 在 5 月 30 日。

解析 本題為確認飯店是否有會議廳的否定疑問句。
(A) 用 No 表否定後說明飯店內似乎沒有會議廳，故為正解。
(B) 回答了與問題無關的活動類型，故非正解。
(C) 此為針對 When 疑問句，告知日期的回答，故非正解。

13. Is this travel budget enough, or do you need a little more?
(A) I could use an extra $50.
(B) Just two suitcases.
(C) Here's your itinerary.
這樣的旅遊預算夠嗎？還是需要再多一些呢？
(A) 我可能會多花費 50 美元。
(B) 只有兩個行李箱。
(C) 你的行程表在這。

解析 本題為詢問出差預算是否充足，還是需要更多的選擇疑問句。
(A) 用自己會多花多少錢表達還需要增加一些預算，故為正解。
(B) 用聽到 travel 容易聯想到的 suitcases 混淆考生，故非正解。
(C) 用聽到 travel 容易聯想到的 itinerary 混淆考生，故非正解。

14. Who's writing the article about the stadium renovation project?
(A) I have no idea.
(B) A sports competition.
(C) Just a few improvements.
負責寫體育館翻新工程報導的人是誰？
(A) 我不曉得。
(B) 體育比賽。
(C) 只有幾個改善事項。
解析 本題為詢問誰負責寫體育館翻新工程報導的 Who 疑問句。
(A) 針對問題回答自己不曉得，故為正解。
(B) 用聽到 stadium 容易聯想到的 sports 混淆考生，故非正解。
(C) 用聽到 renovation 容易聯想到的 improvements 混淆考生，故非正解。

15. Where do you want me to leave the printer paper?
(A) At least fifty copies of the report.
(B) In the storage room would be best.
(C) He left at around 3 P.M.
你想要我把影印紙放哪？
(A) 那份報告至少要影印 50 份。
(B) 放在儲藏室裡會比較好。
(C) 他離開的時間大概是下午 3 點。
解析 本題為詢問影印紙該放哪裡的 Where 疑問句。
(A) 此為針對 How many 疑問句，告知所需數量的回答，故非正解。
(B) 此為針對 Where 疑問句，指出特定位置的回答，故為正解。
(C) 回答內容包含無法得知所指對象是何人的 He，故非正解。

16. Does this library have a comic book section?
(A) You'll need to pay the late fee.
(B) Let's ask a librarian.
(C) Here's my library card.
這間圖書館有漫畫區嗎？
(A) 你必須支付滯納金。
(B) 我們去問圖書館館員。
(C) 我的借書證在這。
解析 本題為詢問圖書館是否有漫畫區的疑問句。
(A) 用聽到 library 容易聯想到的 late fee 混淆考生，故非正解。
(B) 提出能夠確認圖書館內有無漫畫區的方法，故為正解。
(C) 此為出示借書證時說的話，與問題無關，故非正解。

17. Could you repair my broken digital camera?
(A) We stock several models.

(B) Only if it's still under warranty.
(C) Unfortunately, it's sold out.
你能修理我故障的數位相機嗎？
(A) 我們備有好幾種型號。
(B) 只要還在保固期間就可以。
(C) 很遺憾，已經賣光了。
解析 本題為詢問是否能修理故障的數位相機，向對方請求允許的疑問句。
(A) 回答自己備有多種型號與修理相機無關，故非正解。
(B) 提及能夠修理商品的條件，故為正解。
(C) 此為購買商品的情境下會有的回答，與修理商品無關，故非正解。

18. Who will be training the new temporary workers?
(A) Just for a couple of days.
(B) Yes. They picked it up quickly.
(C) Gloria would be the best choice.
誰負責訓練新來的臨時工？
(A) 只有幾天。
(B) 對。他們學得很快。
(C) Gloria 會是最佳人選。
解析 本題為詢問負責訓練新臨時工的人是誰的 Who 疑問句。
(A) 此為針對 How long 疑問句，告知時間長短的回答，故非正解。
(B) 此為針對 Yes/No 疑問句的回答，不適用於回覆疑問詞問句，故非正解。
(C) 用特定人物的姓名回答 Who 疑問句，故為正解。

19. Where should we take the clients for some entertainment?
(A) There's no time for that.
(B) Did you have a good time?
(C) Sure, I'd love to join you.
我們要招待客戶們去哪玩好呢？
(A) 我們沒時間那麼做。
(B) 你玩得開心嗎？
(C) 當然，我很樂意加入。
解析 本題為詢問該帶客戶去哪玩的 Where 疑問句。
(A) 用 that 代指招待客戶，接著回答沒有時間那麼做，所以不用想要去哪，故為正解。
(B) 此為針對過去 (Did) 提出的疑問，故非正解。
(C) 此為接受對方提議時使用的句子，故非正解。

20. Edward's designing the concert posters, right?
(A) A live performance.
(B) Yes, he's starting now.
(C) I prefer movies.
Edward 在設計演唱會的海報對吧？
(A) 一場現場表演。
(B) 對，他現在開始做了。
(C) 我比較喜歡電影。
解析 本題為確認 Edward 是否在設計演唱會海報的附加問句。
(A) 用聽到 concert 容易聯想到的 live

performance 混淆考生，故非正解。
(B) 用 Yes 表肯定後，再用 he 代指 Edward，表示他正在設計，故為正解。
(C) 表明自己的喜好，卻未回答 Edward 是否在設計海報，故非正解。

21. Am I working on the main assembly line tonight?
(A) The manufacturing plant.
(B) Didn't you check the new work schedule?
(C) There was a line right around the block.
我今晚是在主要組裝產線工作嗎？
(A) 那個製造工廠。
(B) 你沒看新的工作日程嗎？
(C) 那個街區原本排了一列隊伍。
解析 本題為詢問自己今晚是否在主要組裝產線工作的疑問句。
(A) 此為針對 Where 疑問句，告知地點的回答，故非正解。
(B) 用疑問句告訴對方如何確認他是否在主要組裝產線工作，故為正解。
(C) 回答與問題無關，並用同字異義的隊伍混淆考生，故非正解。

22. When did the Casual Friday policy start?
(A) To make employees happy.
(B) A few months ago.
(C) That's a great idea.
「便服週五」的政策從什麼時候開始實施的？
(A) 為了讓職員們開心。
(B) 幾個月前。
(C) 這個想法很不錯。
解析 本題為詢問「便服週五」的政策何時開始實施的 When 疑問句。
(A) 此不定詞片語是針對 Why 疑問句，表達某目的的回答，故非正解。
(B) 針對 When 疑問句回答了一個大略的過去時間點，故為正解。
(C) 此為表同意或肯定時常用的句型，不適合用來回答疑問詞問句，故非正解。

23. Which vending machine needs to be repaired?
(A) Just some snacks and beverages.
(B) Yes, I'll fix it for you.
(C) The one on the third floor.
需要修理的是哪一臺自動販賣機？
(A) 就是一些零食和飲料。
(B) 對，我會幫你修理。
(C) 3 樓的那一臺。
解析 本題為詢問哪一臺自動販賣機需要修理的 Which 疑問句。
(A) 沒有回答是哪一臺自動販賣機，只說了販售種類，故非正解。
(B) 疑問詞問句的回答不會是 Yes，故非正解。
(C) 用 The one 代指 vending machine，回答特定位置的自動販賣機，故為正解。

24. How many business trips will you be taking this month?

(A) A seminar in Tokyo.
(B) Sure, you can take your time.
(C) I'd guess two or three.
你這個月預計要出差幾次？
(A) 在東京舉辦的研討會。
(B) 當然，你可以慢慢來。
(C) 好像是兩三次。
解析 本題為詢問這個月要出差幾次的 How many 疑問句。
(A) 回答了與 How many 無關的活動和舉辦地點，故非正解。
(B) 疑問詞問句的回答不會是 Sure，故非正解。
(C) 用次數回答 How many 疑問句，故為正解。

25. Would you consider working on this report during the weekend?
(A) I have plans with my family.
(B) It's a 5-minute walk from here.
(C) Typically from 9 to 5.
你可以考慮一下利用週末做這份報告嗎？
(A) 我和家人已經有規劃了。
(B) 距離這裡 5 分鐘的路程。
(C) 通常從 9 點到 5 點。
解析 本題為詢問對方是否有意願在週末做報告的疑問句。
(A) 用和家人已經有規劃來拒絕提議，故為正解。
(B) 此為針對 How long 或 Where 疑問句，告知移動距離的回答，故非正解。
(C) 回答的上班時間與問題無關，故非正解。

26. You're in charge of our most successful sales team, right?
(A) No, thanks. I can't afford it.
(B) I was charged $100.
(C) Yes, I'm the team leader.
你負責帶領我們公司最成功的業務小組對吧？
(A) 不了，謝謝。我買不起。
(B) 我被收了 100 美元。
(C) 對，我是那組的組長。
解析 本題為確認對方是否負責帶領公司裡最成功的業務小組的附加問句。
(A) 此為拒絕提議的句型，故非正解。
(B) 用同字異義的收費混淆考生，故非正解。
(C) 用 Yes 表肯定後，表明自己是該小組的組長，故為正解。

27. Haven't you seen the announcement on the bulletin board?
(A) At the company dinner.
(B) He's the chairman of the board.
(C) I've been off since Monday.
你還沒看布告欄上的公告嗎？
(A) 在公司晚餐聚會上。
(B) 他是董事會的主席。
(C) 我打從週一就休假了。
解析 本題為詢問對方是否沒看布告欄上公告的否定疑問句。
(A) 回答與公告無關的地點資訊，故非正解。
(B) 描述無法知道代指誰的 He 的身分，故非正解。

(C) 用週一開始就休假表達自己沒能看公告，
　　 故為正解。

28. I really want the sofa that's on page 10 of
your catalog.
　　 (A) Let me check if we have one in our
　　 warehouse.
　　 (B) I sent a copy to all mailing list members.
　　 (C) No, I bought it from a Web site.
　　 我真的很想要你們型錄第十頁的那張沙發。
　　 (A) 我去看一下倉庫還有沒有貨。
　　 (B) 我各寄了一份給所有在郵寄名單上的人。
　　 (C) 不，我是在某個網站上買的。
解析 這是個表達自己想要型錄第十頁上那張沙發的
　　 敘述句。
　　 (A) 用 one 代指 sofa，回答對方要去確認是否
　　　 還有存貨，故為正解。
　　 (B) 用聽到 catalog 容易聯想到的 sent a copy
　　　 混淆考生，故非正解。
　　 (C) 本句為購買者會説的句子，等同於購買者
　　　 在回覆購買者，故非正解。

29. Who's responsible for reimbursing travel
expenses?
　　 (A) At the end of the month.
　　 (B) That's the accounting manager.
　　 (C) Oh, I didn't realize that.
　　 誰負責處理出差費用的報銷？
　　 (A) 月底。
　　 (B) 會計部經理。
　　 (C) 喔，我不知道。
解析 本題為詢問誰負責出差費報銷的 Who 疑問句。
　　 (A) 此為針對 When 疑問句，告知時間點的回
　　　 答，故非正解。
　　 (B) 用特定部門的職稱告訴對方誰是負責人，
　　　 故為正解。
　　 (C) 此為不知道某件事或情報時使用的句子，
　　　 無法用來回覆 Who 疑問句，故非正解。

30. Why don't we drive to Los Angeles instead
of taking a flight?
　　 (A) That would certainly be cheaper.
　　 (B) It departs at 4 P.M.
　　 (C) The annual technology convention.
　　 比起搭飛機，我們何不自己開車去洛杉磯呢？
　　 (A) 那麼做的確會比較便宜。
　　 (B) 下午 4 點出發。
　　 (C) 年度科技大會。
解析 本題為詢問對方是否願意不搭飛機，自行開車
　　 前往的疑問句。
　　 (A) 用 That 代指自駕前往目的地這件事，再敘
　　　 述這麼做的優點，故為正解。
　　 (B) 此為針對 When 疑問句，告知某時間點的
　　　 回答，故非正解。
　　 (C) 回答的活動類型與問題無關，故非正解。

31. I'll speak with the elevator engineer when
he arrives this morning.
　　 (A) He's coming tomorrow.
　　 (B) Some urgent maintenance.
　　 (C) Yes, the work didn't take long.

電梯技師今早抵達時，我會跟他談。
　　 (A) 他明天才會來。
　　 (B) 一些緊急維修作業。
　　 (C) 是，那不會花很多時間。
解析 這是描述説話者會在今早電梯技師抵達後跟他
　　 談談的敘述句。
　　 (A) 用 He 代指 elevator engineer，並説明技
　　　 師明天才會來，故為正解。
　　 (B) 回答某維修作業的目的和種類，與問題無
　　　 關，故非正解。
　　 (C) 説話者的未來時態 (I'll) 和本選項的過去時
　　　 態 (didn't) 不符，故非正解。

Part 3

Questions 32–34 refer to the following
conversation.

M: Rhonda, 32 did I see you using the
new tablet computer that Horizon just
launched? I'm considering buying one.
Would you recommend it?
W: Well, I got mine about a week ago. I love
the screen, but 33 the battery runs out
far too quickly. I need to charge it every
couple of hours.
M: I don't like the sound of that. Perhaps I'll
shop around first. In fact, 34 this Saturday
is the first day of Laser Electronics' summer
sale. I'll head along and try to find a good
deal.

男：Rhonda，我是不是看過你用 Horizon 公司剛
　　 出的新平板電腦？我正打算要買一臺。你推薦
　　 這臺嗎？
女：嗯，我大概一週前拿到我的。我很喜歡它的螢
　　 幕，但電池實在消耗得太快了。我幾個小時就
　　 要充電一次。
男：這聽起來不太妙。或許我會先去到處逛逛。事
　　 實上，這週六剛好是 Laser 電子夏季特賣會的
　　 第一天。我會去看看有沒有什麼不錯的商品。

32. 説話者們在討論什麼商品？
　　 (A) 數位相機
　　 (B) 平面電視
　　 (C) 平板電腦
　　 (D) 手機
解析 男子在對話開頭説自己看到女子使用新的平
　　 板電腦 (did I see you using the new tablet
　　 computer)，並表明自己也想要購買該類型的
　　 商品，故本題正解為選項 (C)。

33. 為什麼女子對該產品感到失望？
　　 (A) 螢幕不夠亮。
　　 (B) 功能選單太複雜。
　　 (C) 電池壽命太短。
　　 (D) 月租費太貴。
解析 女子在對話中段説完該產品的優點後，也提及
　　 電池消耗很快的缺點 (the battery runs out far
　　 too quickly)，故本題正解為選項 (C)。

34. 男子說週六會有什麼事？
(A) 商品將上市。
(B) 新店將開幕。
(C) 評論將被刊登。
(D) 特賣會將開始。

解析 男子在提及週六這個時間點後，說明那天為 Laser 電子的夏季特賣會第一天 (this Saturday is the first day of Laser Electronics' summer sale)，故本題正解為選項 (D)。

Questions 35–37 refer to the following conversation.

W: Thank you for calling Acorn Hills Spa. What can I do for you?

M: Hi. 35 I'm interested in signing up for your training course, but I have no formal experience as a massage therapist. Is that a problem?

W: No problem at all. Our course is specifically designed for massage beginners. We'll teach you all of the basics in the first couple of weeks, and move on to advanced techniques later. At the end, 36 you'll get a certificate to show that you passed the course.

M: So, at the end of the course, I'll be a qualified massage therapist? Sounds great! What are the fees and class times?

W: 37 I'll mail you a brochure that contains more information. Can you tell me where to send it to?

女：謝謝你致電 Acorn Hills SPA。有什麼我可以幫你的嗎？

男：嗨。我有興趣申請你們的訓練課程，但我沒有作為按摩治療師的正式經歷。這會是一個問題嗎？

女：完全沒問題。我們的課程特別設計給按摩初學者。前面幾週我們會教你所有基礎，接著再開始學習進階技巧。最後，你將會得到一張證書來證明你已通過所有課程。

男：所以，課程結束後，我就是個合格的按摩治療師了嗎？聽起來很棒！那麼費用和課程時間呢？

女：我會寄一份包含更多資訊的手冊給你。你可以告訴我要寄到哪嗎？

35. 男子想要學什麼？
(A) 外文
(B) 健康飲食
(C) 髮型設計
(D) 按摩療法

解析 男子在對話開頭說明自己想申請訓練課程，不過沒有正式的按摩治療經歷 (I'm interested in signing up for your training course, but I have no formal experience as a massage therapist.)。由此可知男子想學的是按摩療法，故本題正解為選項 (D)。

36. 女子說訓練課程之後會提供什麼？
(A) 工作安排
(B) 現金分紅
(C) 證書
(D) 會員卡

解析 女子在對話中提到，課程結束後男子將會收到一份證書，表明他已經通過了訓練課程 (you'll get a certificate to show that you passed the course)，故本題正解為選項 (C)。

37. 女子要了什麼資訊？
(A) 電話號碼
(B) 郵寄地址
(C) 信用卡資訊
(D) 到某間公司的路

解析 女子在對話最後說要寄送手冊，並問對方要寄到哪裡 (I'll mail you a brochure that contains more information. Can you tell me where to send it to?)，故本題正解為向對方要郵寄地址的選項 (B)。

Questions 38–40 refer to the following conversation with three speakers.

M: Hi, Joanna. I'm sorry I didn't get here on time. I was driving along Tenth Avenue when 38 my car's engine just died. I had to take it to the auto shop and grab a taxi.

W1: No problem. We just got started. Mary and I were just discussing the new lighting we picked out for our store.

W2: Right. We realized that 39 we'll probably need to close the coffee shop for a day to remove our old lights and install the new ones. It's a pretty big job.

W1: And, Tuesday is typically our slowest day, so how about scheduling the work for Tuesday next week?

M: That should work out fine. 40 I'll call our employees now and let them all know in advance.

男：你好，Joanna。抱歉我沒有準時趕到這裡。我沿著第十大道開車時，車子的引擎壞了。我必須先將車子送到車廠，再搭計程車過來。

女1：沒關係。我們才剛開始談而已。Mary 和我剛剛在討論我們為店裡挑選的新照明設備。

女2：對。我們發現我們的咖啡廳可能會需要休業一天，拆除舊有的燈，再安裝新的。這會是個大工程。

女1：另外，週二通常都是我們最不忙的日子，所以把工程安排在下週二怎麼樣？

男：那應該沒問題。我立刻打給我們的職員並提前讓他們知道這件事。

38. 男子為什麼遲到了？
(A) 他錯過公車。
(B) 他的車子故障了。
(C) 他去錯地方。
(D) 他有其他約。

解析 男子在對話開頭針對自己遲到這件事道歉，並說明遲到原因是因為車子的引擎壞掉 (my car's engine just died)，故本題正解為選項 (B)。

39. 為什麼咖啡廳要暫時休業？
(A) 將要舉辦教育訓練。
(B) 某些家具將要被汰換。
(C) 將要進行安檢。
(D) 將要裝明照設備。
解析 其中一名女子在對話中段提到為了把舊的照明設備換成新的，咖啡廳必須要休業一天 (we'll probably need to close the coffee shop for a day to remove our old lights and install the new ones)，故本題正解為選項 (D)。

40. 男子說他接下來要做什麼？
(A) 連絡職員
(B) 公布工作日程
(C) 支付費用
(D) 審查某些文件
解析 男子在對話最後說自己要打給職員，提前告訴他們這件事 (I'll call our employees now and let them all know in advance.)，故本題正解為選項 (A)。

Questions 41–43 refer to the following conversation.

M: Hello, this is Albert Cheng from Lockright Containers. `41` I just listened to your message about needing packaging for your food items.
W: Hi, Albert. Yes, our restaurant recently started a home delivery and takeout service. We've just been using some cheap boxes so far.
M: I see. And, what exactly can I do to help you?
W: Well, `42` the service is more popular than expected, and we're struggling to keep up. We usually run out of boxes a few hours before the restaurant closes.
M: That's not good! Well, we can definitely help you so that you never run out. `43` Why don't I mail a product catalog over to you so you can choose which containers you'd prefer to use?

男：你好，我是 Lockright 容器的 Albert Cheng。我剛剛聽了你關於需要包裝你的食品的需求訊息。
女：嗨，Albert。對，我們餐廳最近開始做外送和外帶的服務。我們目前使用的是一些便宜的盒子。
男：了解。那麼，準確地來說我可以怎麼協助你呢？
女：嗯，這些服務比我想像中的還要受歡迎，我們的速度很難跟上。我們常常在餐廳休息前幾小時就用完包裝盒。
男：這不太妙！那麼，我們能幫助你有用不完的盒子。要不我寄一份產品型錄給你，讓你挑選自

己想要的容器好嗎？

---

41. 男子在什麼樣的公司工作？
(A) 包裝公司
(B) 外燴業者
(C) 食品製造公司
(D) 保全公司
解析 對話開頭提到自己接收到對方有食品包材需求的資訊 (I just listened to your message about needing packaging for your food items.)。由此可知男子在包裝公司工作，故本題正解為選項 (A)。

42. 女子說「我們的速度很難跟上」是想表達什麼？
(A) 她所在的產業競爭很激烈。
(B) 她的月收益持續減少。
(C) 她的店有供不應求的情況。
(D) 有幾位職員缺勤。
解析 女子在對話中段提到外送和外帶服務比想像中受歡迎 (the service is more popular than expected)，速度很難跟得上訂單。這個情形也就代表店內商品太受歡迎，供不應求，故本題正解為選項 (C)。

43. 男子說要做什麼？
(A) 更改配送日程
(B) 寄送產品型錄
(C) 拜訪女子的店面
(D) 準備估價單
解析 男子在對話最後說要寄產品型錄給對方 (Why don't I mail a product catalog over to you)，故本題正解為選項 (B)。

Questions 44–46 refer to the following conversation.

W: Hello. Welcome to Gamma Electronics. Can I help you with anything today?
M: Yes, please. `44` I'm here to exchange this pair of headphones.
W: I see. Do you mind telling me why you want to exchange them?
M: Well, I like the sound quality, but `45` they're too small for my head. They're really uncomfortable.
W: No problem. Well, `46` we have a wide variety of other products that might suit you better. I can show you a few.
M: That would be great. Thanks.

女：你好。歡迎蒞臨 Gamma 電子。今天有什麼我可以為你服務的嗎？
男：是，麻煩你。我來這是想更換這副頭戴式耳機。
女：我明白了。可以告訴我你為什麼想更換嗎？
男：嗯，我很喜歡它的音質，但它對我的頭來說太小了。戴起來很不舒服。
女：沒問題。那麼，我們這裡有不少可能會比較適合你的商品，我拿幾個給你看。
男：那樣就太好了。謝謝。

44. 男子想更換什麼商品？
(A) 一臺筆記型電腦
(B) 一支手機
(C) 一副喇叭
(D) 一副頭戴式耳機

解析 男子在對話前半部說他要更換耳機 (I'm here to exchange this pair of headphones.)，故本題正解為選項 (D)。

45. 商品有什麼問題？
(A) 電池壽命
(B) 性能
(C) 大小
(D) 顏色

解析 男子在對話中段提到這副耳機對他的頭來說太小了 (they're too small for my head)。由此可知商品的問題為大小，故本題正解為選項 (C)。

46. 女子要為男子做什麼？
(A) 退還部分款項
(B) 提供商店紅利
(C) 修正商品功能
(D) 展示可替代的商品

解析 女子在對話後半部說店內有不少比較適合男子的商品，並表示要拿出來給他看 (we have a wide variety of other products that might suit you better. I can show you a few)。由此可知女子要給男子看可更換的替代商品，故本題正解為選項 (D)。

Questions 47–49 refer to the following conversation.

W: We're lucky to have **47** a special guest in the radio studio today! Joseph Fantano, writer of the recently released novel *The Midnight Song*, has joined us for a chat. Joseph, it's great to have you here.
M: Thanks, Tina. I'm happy to be here for this interview. Actually, **48** coming here reminds me of my first ever job, working as a radio show host for a small station in Denver. I really enjoyed my time there.
W: Well, luckily for fans of your books, you changed your career path. On that note... Do you have any advice for listeners who want to pursue a career in writing?
M: **49** I'd say the best way to start is to read a lot of novels. That way, you'll improve your vocabulary and get ideas for how to construct stories.

女：我們今天很幸運地邀請到一位特別來賓來廣播錄音棚！Joseph Fantano，最近剛發行小說 *The Midnight Song* 的作者，要來和我們聊聊。Joseph，很開心你能來這裡。
男：謝謝你，Tina。我很開心能來這裡接受採訪。事實上，來這個地方讓我想起了我第一份工作，我曾在丹佛的一間小電臺裡當過廣播節目主持人。我非常享受那段時光。

女：那麼，你的書迷們還真是幸運，你改變職涯成為了作家。說到這裡…你對想成為作家的聽眾有任何建議嗎？
男：我覺得開始最好的方法就是閱讀大量的小說。這樣一來，能讓你的詞藻更優美並從中得到創作故事的靈感。

47. 男子是誰？
(A) 記者
(B) 作家
(C) 脫口秀主持人
(D) 大學教授

解析 女子在對話開頭說到今天的特別來賓是最近發行的小說的作者 Joseph Fantano (a special guest in the radio studio today! Joseph Fantano, writer of the recently released novel)，故本題正解為選項 (B)。

48. 男子在採訪中想起了什麼？
(A) 之前跟女子見面的事
(B) 和家人一起度過的假期
(C) 在當地大學念書的時期
(D) 先前的工作經驗

解析 男子在對話中段提到自己曾經是丹佛的一間小電臺裡的廣播節目主持人 (coming here reminds me of my first ever job, working as a radio show host for a small station in Denver)。由此可知他想起的是過去的工作經驗，故本題正解為選項 (D)。

49. 男子建議聽眾怎麼做？
(A) 閱讀大量書籍
(B) 製作作品集
(C) 參加徵才博覽會
(D) 登記某項課程

解析 女子在對話中段請男子給聽眾們一些建議，男子回答最好的方式就是多讀一些小說 (I'd say the best way to start is to read a lot of novels.)，故本題正解為選項 (A)。

Questions 50–52 refer to the following conversation.

W: Good morning, and thanks for calling Riley Furniture. How can I help?
M: Good morning. I purchased an office chair through your Web store and paid for express shipping. **50** I expected the delivery to be made to my home on Monday, but it's already Wednesday.
W: Oh, let me check that for you. **51** If you let me know your shipping address, I'll try to find out when your item will arrive.
M: Okay. It's 25 Stratton Street.
W: Thanks. Well, it seems as though the driver is on his way to your location right now. Will you be at home for the next thirty minutes or so?
M: Yes. I'm glad to hear that, as **52** I'll be flying to Cuba on vacation first thing tomorrow.

女：早安，感謝你致電 Riley 家具。有什麼我可以幫你的嗎？

男：早安。我在你們的網路商店買了一張辦公椅，並付了快速到貨的費用。我預期東西會在週一送到我家，但現在已經週三了。

女：喔，我幫你查一下。如果你讓我知道你的郵寄地址，我會試著查詢你的商品何時會抵達。

男：好的。Stratton 街 25 號。

女：謝謝。嗯，看起來配送的司機正在前往你所在的地方。你接下來 30 分鐘左右都會在家裡嗎？

男：是的。我很高興聽到，因為我明天一早就要飛去古巴渡假了。

---

50. 男子為什麼打電話？
(A) 點出帳單上的錯誤
(B) 告知商品的瑕疵
(C) 在訂單上增加商品
(D) 詢問配送相關事項

解析 男子在對話開頭說到預期商品會在週一送到家，但今天已經週三了 (I expected the delivery to be made to my home on Monday, but it's already Wednesday.)。由此可知男子是打電話來詢問配送相關事項，故本題正解為選項 (D)。

51. 女子跟男子要了什麼資訊？
(A) 他的電話號碼
(B) 他家的住址
(C) 他的信用卡號碼
(D) 他的電子郵件地址

解析 女子聽完男子提出的問題後，在對話中段向男子要了配送地址 (If you let me know your shipping address)，故本題正解為選項 (B)。

52. 男子明天要做什麼？
(A) 搬到新家
(B) 去渡假
(C) 參加商務會議
(D) 拜訪女子工作的地方

解析 明天這個時間點出現在對話末段，男子說自己隔天一早就要前往古巴渡假 (I'll be flying to Cuba on vacation first thing tomorrow.)，故本題正解為選項 (B)。

Questions 53–55 refer to the following conversation.

W: Mr. Butler, you mentioned that we should hire an event planner to organize our company's year-end banquet. Well, 53 this morning, I compared some prices quoted by various event-planning agencies. Would you like to take a look at the information now?

M: I'm afraid I have to rush out for a dentist appointment. In the meantime, 54 could you ask some of the companies for some cost estimates? We can talk about it more later.

W: Sure. But, 55 first, I want to speak with Lisa in Accounting to find out what our budget is for this year's banquet.

M: Great idea. I'll stop by your office for a meeting at around 3 P.M.

女：Butler 先生，你提到我們應該要僱用活動企劃來替我們規劃公司的年末晚會。那麼，今天早上，我比較了一下各活動企劃公司的報價。你想要先看一下內容嗎？

男：恐怕我必須趕著去看牙醫。與此同時，你可以跟某些公司要報價單嗎？我們晚點可以細談。

女：當然。但我想先跟會計部門的 Lisa 談談今年晚會的預算。

男：好主意。我大概下午 3 點會去你的辦公室開會。

53. 女子今天早上做了什麼？
(A) 她面試求職者。
(B) 她購買材料。
(C) 她比較價格。
(D) 她修正文件。

解析 今天早上這個時間點出現在對話開頭，女子說自己比較了幾個價格 (this morning, I compared some prices)，故本題正解為選項 (C)。

54. 男子建議女子做什麼？
(A) 調查問卷
(B) 拜訪業者
(C) 調整預約日程
(D) 要報價單

解析 男子在對話中段要女子跟業者要報價單 (could you ask some of the companies for some cost estimates?)，故本題正解為選項 (D)。

55. 女子想要先做什麼？
(A) 跟同事談話
(B) 付款
(C) 寄邀請函
(D) 上某些網站

解析 女子在對話後半部提到為了要知道晚會的預算，必須要先跟會計部門的 Lisa 談談 (first, I want to speak with Lisa in Accounting to find out what our budget is for this year's banquet)。由此可知女子想先跟同事談話，故本題正解為選項 (A)。

Questions 56–58 refer to the following conversation with three speakers.

W1: Welcome to Blue Mountain Hotel. Do you need some help with anything?

M: Hi, 56 I'm here for an interview with Joanna Jackson, the general manager. My name is Nick Santos.

W1: Oh, you must be here about the project manager job for 57 the hotel renovations in April, right? 58 Joanna is on her way now. Oh, here she is.

W2: It's nice to meet you, Nick. Our renovation plans are quite extensive, so we're looking for a very experienced project manager.

M: Well, hopefully you'll decide I'm the best

person for the job. I've managed similar projects at a few large hotels over the years.

W2: Yes, I saw that on your résumé. Now, let's move to my office to have a proper discussion. And, 58 I'd like to take a look at your references before we get started.

女1：歡迎蒞臨 Blue Mountain 飯店。有什麼我可以幫你的嗎？

男：你好，我來這裡是要跟總經理 Joanna Jackson 面試。我的名字是 Nick Santos。

女1：喔，你來應徵 4 月飯店翻新案的專案經理一職，對吧？Joanna 已經在路上了。喔，她到了。

女2：很高興見到你，Nick。我們飯店的翻新規模很廣，所以我們需要一位經驗老道的專案經理。

男：那麼，希望你會覺得我是最適合這個職位的人選。這些年來，我已經做了不少大型飯店的類似案子了。

女2：對，我有在你的履歷上看到這點。我們先移動去我的辦公室，這樣才能好好談談。在這之前，我想先看一下你的推薦信。

56. 男子來飯店做什麼？
(A) 為了討論合併案
(B) 為了配送物品
(C) 為了籌備活動
(D) 為了面試
解析 男子在對話開頭說自己來飯店是要跟總經理 Joanna Jackson 面試 (I'm here for an interview with Joanna Jackson, the general manager.)，說明自己來飯店的理由，故本題正解為選項 (D)。

57. 飯店在 4 月會有什麼事？
(A) 現場演出
(B) 翻新工程
(C) 商業會議
(D) 教育訓練
解析 4 月這個時間點出現在對話開頭，其中一名女子說到 4 月有飯店翻新工程 (the hotel renovations in April)，故本題正解為選項 (B)。

58. Joanna 想要看什麼？
(A) 一份工作日程
(B) 幾張設計藍圖
(C) 一份預算案
(D) 幾份推薦信
解析 其中一名女子在對話開頭提到另外一名女子是 Joanna(Joanna is on her way now. Oh, here she is.)。被提及的女子在對話最後說自己想看推薦信 (I'd like to take a look at your references before we get started.)，故本題正解為選項 (D)。

Questions 59–61 refer to the following conversation.

M: Gillian, you're in charge of making 59 our gym's exercise class schedule this month, right? No one has been assigned to lead the spinning classes yet.

W: Oh, thanks for reminding me. Would you be willing to lead the classes on Tuesday and Thursday evenings?

M: I'd love to help out, but 60 I attend a class at the local college on those nights. How about asking Catrina to do it?

W: Hmmm... She just started here last week. 61 I'm not sure new workers are ready to lead classes.

M: Well, I did that during my first week.

W: I guess you're right. I'll speak with Catrina and see if she feels comfortable doing that.

男：Gillian，你這個月負責排我們健身房的運動課程表，對吧？目前還沒有人負責上飛輪課。

女：喔，謝謝你提醒我。你可以負責上週二和週四晚上的課嗎？

男：我很想幫忙，但我這幾天的晚上要在當地大學上課。你要不要請 Catrina 負責？

女：嗯…她上週剛來這。我不確定一個新進職員能否有能力獨自帶課程。

男：嗯，我第一週來的時候就那麼做了。

女：你說的沒錯。我會跟 Catrina 談談，看她是否願意做。

59. 說話者們工作的地方是？
(A) 在餐廳
(B) 在健身房
(C) 在大學
(D) 在工廠
解析 男子在對話開頭就說到自己的工作地點是健身房 (our gym)，故本題正解為選項 (B)。

60. 男子為什麼無法幫忙？
(A) 他要去渡假。
(B) 他的身分證不見了。
(C) 他的經驗不足。
(D) 他的行程無法配合。
解析 女子在對話中段詢問男子是否有意願上週二和週四的課，男子說自己那幾天晚上要到當地大學上課 (I attend a class at the local college on those nights.)。由此可知男子的行程無法配合，故本題正解為選項 (D)。

61. 為什麼男子會說「我第一週來的時候就那麼做了」？
(A) 為了解釋自己為什麼夠格
(B) 為了確認截止期限沒問題
(C) 為了否定某個觀點
(D) 為了自願擔任某個角色
解析 女子在對話中段說到不確定一個新進職員能否有能力獨自帶課程 (I'm not sure new workers are ready to lead classes.)，男子接著回覆

「我第一週來的時候就那麼做了」。男子是要透過這句話表達新進職員也能夠獨自帶課程，用另一種方式表達對女子觀點的不認同，故本題正解為選項 (C)。

Questions 62–64 refer to the following conversation and sign.

W: Marty, our CEO has requested that we purchase some new laptop computers from this year's technology trade show.

M: Yes, he told me this morning. By the way, 62 did you see that the event has been moved to the Burnley Convention Center?

W: Oh, really? Well, I'm glad they chose a different venue this year. That means there will be more space for a wider range of merchandise.

M: The CEO specifically mentioned that 63 he wants us to buy Photon branded laptops. He thinks they're the most suitable for our workers.

W: Good choice. Are we the only ones going there?

M: No, we need to take someone from Accounting, too. So, 64 don't forget to ask the Accounting manager to choose a staff member.

The 7th Technology Trade Show

Main Hall-Vendors

Display Zone A—Digitech

Display Zone B—Photon

Display Zone C—Trident

Display Zone D—Quasar

女：Marty，我們的執行長要求我們從今年的技術貿易博覽會購入一些新的筆記型電腦。

男：是，他今天早上有告訴我。順帶一提，你有看到活動改到 Burnley 會展中心了嗎？

女：喔，真的嗎？嗯，我很開心聽到他們今年換了新會場。這意味著將有更多的空間能夠容納更多不同的業者了。

男：執行長特別提到要我們買 Photon 的筆記型電腦。他認為他們最適合我們的職員。

女：很棒的選擇。只有我們兩個要去嗎？

男：不，我們還要帶會計部的職員一起去。所以，別忘了請會計部經理挑一個人跟我們一起去。

第七屆技術貿易博覽會

本館——販賣業者

展區 A——Digitech

展區 B——Photon

展區 C——Trident

展區 D——Quasar

---

62. 根據說話者們的對話，今年的技術貿易博覽會有什麼不同？
(A) 開始時間
(B) 會場
(C) 登錄費用
(D) 活動期間

解析　男子在對話前半部詢問對方知不知道活動改到 Burnley 會展中心舉行 (did you see that the event has been moved to the Burnley Convention Center?)。由此可知今年的會場改變了，故本題正解為選項 (B)。

63. 請參照圖表，說話者們應該會去哪個展區？
(A) 展區 A
(B) 展區 B
(C) 展區 C
(D) 展區 D

解析　男子在對話中段說到執行長要他們買 Photon 的筆記型電腦 (he wants us to buy Photon branded laptops)。從圖表可知 Photon 這個品牌所在的展區為 "Display Zone B"，故本題正解為選項 (B)。

64. 男子提醒女子做什麼事？
(A) 安排住宿
(B) 確認支出費用
(C) 購買活動門票
(D) 和某主管談話

解析　男子在對話末段要對方別忘了請會計部經理挑一個人跟他們一同前往 (don't forget to ask the Accounting manager to choose a staff member)，故本題正解為選項 (D)。

Questions 65–67 refer to the following conversation and instruction manual.

W: Hi. I heard that 65 you called down to the front desk because you can't connect to the Wi-Fi in your room.

M: That's right. I didn't realize that I'd have to pay for Internet connection here. Anyway, I started trying to connect, but then I got a little confused.

W: No problem. Do you mind showing me your phone? Ah, I see... 66 the next step is to choose the amount of data you think you'll need. The different options are charged at different rates.

M: Oh, now I understand. Thanks. Oh, and I have one more question. Is it possible to make the air conditioner run a little colder? It's so hot in here.

W: Hmm... It should be working perfectly. 67 I'll get in touch with one of our maintenance workers and have him come up and take a look at it for you.

Step 1. Connect to our Wi-Fi
Step 2. Enter your credit card details
Step 3. Select data amount and rate
Step 4. Click "Confirm"

女：嗨。我聽說你打給前臺，因為房間裡連不到無線網路。

男：沒錯。我無法理解為什麼在這裡連個網路還要付錢。總之，我試著要連上網路，但接著我有些困惑。

女：沒問題。可以讓我看一下你的手機嗎？啊，我知道了…下一步要選你可能需要用到的傳輸量。不同的選項會有不同的費率。

男：喔，我現在了解了。謝謝。喔，我還有一個問題。你可以幫我把冷氣的溫度調低一些嗎？這裡太熱了。

女：嗯…冷氣應該是沒有問題才對。我會連絡我們的一位維修部門人員並請他上來幫你檢查一下。

第一步、連上我們的無線網路
第二步、輸入你的信用卡資訊
第三步、選擇你需要的傳輸量與費率
第四步、點「確認」鍵

---

65. 對話的地點應該是哪？
(A) 在機場
(B) 在辦公室
(C) 在飯店
(D) 在電子用品商店

解析 女子在對話開頭說到對方因為在房間裡連不到無線網路，曾打電話到前臺 (you called down to the front desk because you can't connect to the Wi-Fi in your room)。由此可知說話者們對話的地方為飯店，故本題正解為選項 (C)。

66. 請參照圖表。男子接下來要做的是第幾個步驟？
(A) 第一步
(B) 第二步
(C) 第三步
(D) 第四步

解析 女子在對話中段提到下一步要選擇所需的傳輸量，不同的選項會有不同的費率 (the next step is to choose the amount of data you think you'll need. The different options are charged at different rates)。對照圖表可知選擇傳輸量和費率的步驟為 "Step 3. Select data amount and rate"，故本題正解為選項 (C)。

67. 女子接下來可能會做什麼？
(A) 連絡同事
(B) 換某項物品
(C) 提供密碼
(D) 做示範動作

解析 女子在對話末段說自己會連絡維修部門人員 (I'll get in touch with one of our maintenance workers)。由此可知女子將連絡同事，故本題正解為選項 (A)。

Questions 68–70 refer to the following conversation and hotel invoice.

W: Thanks for calling the Beaumont Hotel. How can I help you?

M: Hello. I just checked the invoice from my recent stay at your hotel, and **69** the charge from July 14 should not be on there. I'd like to have it removed.

W: Oh, I'll take a look at that for you, sir. **68** Can you tell me the number on the top of the invoice?

M: Yes, it's 548971.

W: OK, I'm looking at a copy of the document now. I see you were charged for room service on July 14.

M: Yes. I ordered some food to eat in my room, but then I canceled the order and decided to eat in the restaurant downstairs, where I paid in cash.

W: I see. In that case, **70** you'll need to call our guest services number and file an official complaint with them. I'm sorry for the inconvenience.

Date	Hotel Service	Fee
July 12	Dry Cleaning	$35.00
July 13	Pay-Per-View Movie	$11.50
July 14	Room Service	$27.98
July 15	Late Check Out	$40.00

女：感謝你致電 Beaumont 飯店。有什麼我可以幫你的嗎？

男：你好。我剛剛確認了一下最近在你們飯店的收費明細，7 月 14 日不應該有那筆費用。希望你可以幫我刪掉它。

女：喔，先生，我幫你查詢一下。你可以告訴我收費明細上端的編號嗎？

男：好，編號是 548971。

女：好的，我正在看這份明細的複本。我看到你 7 月 14 日有一筆客房服務的費用。

男：對。我原本點了一些食物要在房間內吃，但後來我取消了這筆訂單並決定到樓下的餐廳用餐，我在那裡使用現金付款。

女：我了解了。這種狀況下，你必須打給我們的客服部門，提出正式的客訴。很抱歉造成你的不便。

日期	飯店服務	費用
7 月 12 日	乾洗	35 美元
7 月 13 日	單次付費電影	11.5 美元
7 月 14 日	客房服務	27.98 美元
7 月 15 日	延遲退房	40 美元

68. 男子被要求提供什麼資訊？
(A) 房號
(B) 他的姓氏
(C) 他的信用卡資訊
(D) 收費明細的編號

解析 關於男子被要求的事項在對話中段，女子向男子詢問了收費明細上端的編號 (Can you tell me the number on the top of the invoice?)，故本題正解為選項 (D)。

69.
請參照圖表，男子說要刪除的費用是多少錢？
(A) 35 美元
(B) 11.5 美元
(C) 27.98 美元
(D) 40 美元

解析 男子在對話開頭提及自己的需求，指出 7 月 14 日的收費明細有誤，希望那筆費用能被刪除 (the charge from July 14 should not be on there. I'd like to have it removed)。對照圖表可知 7 月 14 日的費用為 27.98 美元，故本題正解為選項 (C)。

70.
女子建議男子做什麼？
(A) 完成表格
(B) 打電話
(C) 寄電子郵件
(D) 變更預約

解析 女子在對話末段建議男子打電話到客服部門，提出正式的客訴 (you'll need to call our guest services number and file an official complaint)，故本題正解為選項 (B)。

Part 4

Questions 71–73 refer to the following broadcast.

Greetings, listeners, and **71** welcome to *Good Health & You*, the radio show that brings you the best news and advice related to health. Our special guest this morning is Maria Morrison, a highly-respected nutritionist. **72** Ms. Morrison travels all over the world speaking at conferences and conventions, and her talks are always well-received. Ms. Morrison is regarded as one of the leading minds when it comes to nutrition. In fact, **73** she's all set to publish her first book on the topic. It will be released through her Web site this spring. Visit www.mariamorrison.net for more details.

各位聽眾好，歡迎收聽 *Good Health & You*，帶給你與健康相關的好新聞與建議的廣播節目。今早的特別來賓是一位高度受人敬重的營養學家 Maria Morrison。Morrison 女士經常到世界各地的會議上演講，她的演講總是受到好評。只要說到營養學，首先會想到的人之中少不了 Morrison 女士。事實上，她即將針對這個主題出版她的第一本書。今年春天就能在她的網站上找到這本書。想了解更多資訊，請上 www.mariamorrison.net。

71.
這個廣播節目的主題為何？
(A) 金融
(B) 職涯
(C) 健康
(D) 育兒

解析 說話者在談話開頭說了歡迎收聽帶給你與健康相關的好新聞與建議的廣播節目 *Good Health & You* (welcome to *Good Health & You*, the

radio show that brings you the best news and advice related to health)，故本題正解為選項 (C)。

72.
根據說話者所說，Morrison 女士到世界各地的理由是什麼？
(A) 為了訓練職員
(B) 為了募款
(C) 為了在活動上演講
(D) 為了創業

解析 Morrison 女士的名字出現在談話中段，說話者說 Morrison 女士經常到世界各地的會議上演講 (Ms. Morrison travels all over the world speaking at conferences and conventions)，故本題正解為選項 (C)。

73.
今年春天將推出什麼？
(A) 一部紀錄片
(B) 一堂課程
(C) 一個新網站
(D) 一本書籍

解析 談話後半部提到 Morrison 女士將在春天出版她的第一本書 (she's all set to publish her first book on the topic. It will be released through her Web site this spring)，故本題正解為選項 (D)。

Questions 74–76 refer to the following telephone message.

Hi, Jeremy. I'd really appreciate it if you could start work early tomorrow. **74** We have so much gardening work to do, and I'd like you to take charge of one of the most important jobs: **74** trimming the hedges that surround Meadow Park. **75** The annual food fair will be held there in two days, and the town council has hired us to make all the trees, bushes, and flowerbeds look beautiful. So, I want you to begin trimming the hedges at around 7 A.M. **76** Once you're finished, give me a quick call, and I'll let you know what task I want you to focus on next. I'll probably ask you to plant new flowers or mow the grass. Thanks.

你好，Jeremy。如果你願意明天早點來上班的話，我會很感謝你。我們有很多園藝工作要做，我也想要你負責最重要的工作之一：修剪圍繞 Meadow 公園的樹籬。那邊兩天後將舉行年度食品展，鎮議會僱用我們整理所有樹木、灌木叢和花壇，讓它們看起來賞心悅目些。所以，我想要你從早上 7 點左右開始修剪樹籬。完成之後請立刻打給我，我會告訴你下一個任務是什麼。我可能會請你去種花，或是修整草坪，謝謝。

74.
說話者應該是誰？
(A) 一位園藝景觀設計師
(B) 一位廚師
(C) 一位市長
(D) 一位活動發起人

解析 説話者在談話前半部説到有很多園藝工作要做 (We have so much gardening work to do)，其中一項是修剪樹籬 (trimming the hedges)。由此可知説話者為園藝景觀設計師，故本題正解為選項 (A)。

75. 説話者在為什麼活動做準備？
(A) 一場演唱會
(B) 一場食品展
(C) 一場大型會議
(D) 一場開幕典禮

解析 説話者在談話中段提到公園的樹籬，並説明那個地方即將舉辦年度食品展 (The annual food fair will be held there in two days)，故本題正解為選項 (B)。

76. 為什麼説話者要聆聽者打電話給他？
(A) 為了要求更多供貨
(B) 為了確認他已經抵達某地
(C) 為了安排某個地方的檢查作業
(D) 為了接收下一步指令

解析 説話者在談話後半部要對方完成任務後立刻打給自己，他會告訴聆聽者接下來該做什麼 (Once you're finished, give me a quick call, and I'll let you know what task I want you to focus on next.)。由此可知説話者要聆聽者打電話給自己，藉此接收下一步的指令，故本題正解為選項 (D)。

Questions 77–79 refer to the following tour information.

Thank you for joining this afternoon's tour of the Ray Wilson Gallery. I'm sure you all enjoyed seeing the exhibition of **77** Mr. Wilson's amazing sculptures. For your information, **78** Mr. Wilson recently created some exclusive sculptures for the new Millennium Museum in the Waterfront District. His pieces can be seen outside the entrance and throughout the interior of the museum. Admission is half-price until the end of the month. Also, you might be interested to hear about **79** an exciting change happening here at the gallery in July. We're starting art classes for all ages and experience levels, at reasonable prices. If you're interested, you can register at the reception desk before you leave today.

感謝你參加今天下午 Ray Wilson 藝廊的導覽。我相信各位都很享受於參觀 Wilson 先生巧奪天工的雕塑作品。提供資訊給各位參考，Wilson 先生最近為了 Waterfront 區新開的 Millennium 博物館創作了獨家展示的雕塑作品。他的作品從入口處外到博物館內部都看得到。門票到這個月底都是半價。此外，各位可能會有興趣聽到藝廊將在 7 月有個令人興奮的變化。我們將開設學費公道的藝術課程給所有年齡層及程度的民眾。如果你有興趣，可以在今天離開藝廊前至服務臺登記。

77. Ray Wilson 是誰？
(A) 一位畫家
(B) 一位導遊
(C) 一位雕塑家
(D) 一位藝術評論家

解析 談話前半部提到 Wilson 先生巧奪天工的雕塑作品 (Mr. Wilson's amazing sculptures.)。由此可知 Wilson 先生是一位雕塑家，故本題正解為選項 (C)。

78. 為什麼説話者説「門票到這個月底都是半價」？
(A) 為稍早造成的不便道歉
(B) 告知聆聽者價格上有誤
(C) 通知藝廊關門的時間
(D) 鼓勵聆聽者們到某個博物館參觀

解析 談話中段提到 Wilson 先生為了新開的 Millennium 博物館創作了幾個獨家展示的雕塑作品，並説明了那些作品的所在位置 (Mr. Wilson recently created some exclusive sculptures for the new Millennium Museum... throughout the interior of the museum.)，接著説「門票到這個月底都是半價」。由此可知説話者是在鼓勵聆聽者們去參觀新開的博物館，故本題正解為選項 (D)。

79. 7 月會發生什麼事？
(A) 將舉辦一場戶外活動。
(B) 將有一場演講。
(C) 一堂藝術課將開課。
(D) 一間公司要遷址。

解析 説話者在談話的後半部説 7 月會有個令人興奮的變化，接著説明該變化時將開設藝術課 (an exciting change happening here at the gallery in July. We're starting art classes)，故本題正解為選項 (C)。

Questions 80–82 refer to the following introduction.

80 As a member of Waterford City Council, I'm delighted to announce that the recipient of this year's Waterford Person of the Year Award is Mr. Scott Bennett, the president of the Golden Wish Foundation. **81** Mr. Bennett established the non-profit organization three years ago and has managed to raise a significant amount of money for the children's charity. Mr. Bennett is a Waterford native and has strong ties to the local community. It's clear that **82** he fully understands what the people of Waterford need and care about. Now, let me hear a warm round of applause as we welcome Mr. Bennett to the stage.

身為 Waterford 市議會的一員，我很開心能宣布今年 Waterford Person 的受獎人是 Scott Bennett 先生，Golden Wish 基金會的董事長。Bennett 先生在 3 年前創立了這個非營利組織並成功地為兒童慈善事業募到金額十分可觀的善款。Bennett 先生是位土生土長的 Waterford 人，與當地社會關係也十分緊密。很明顯地，他很清楚

Waterford 市民需要及關心的是什麼。現在，讓我們給 Bennett 先生溫暖的掌聲並歡迎他上臺。

80. 說話者是誰？
(A) 一間公司的老闆
(B) 一位導遊
(C) 一位受獎人
(D) 一位市府公務員
解析 說話者在談話開始時說到身為 Waterford 市議會
的一員 (As a member of Waterford City Council)，表明了自己的身分，故本題正解為選項 (D)。

81. Bennett 先生 3 年前做了什麼？
(A) 他辭職。
(B) 他開店。
(C) 他搬到一個新國家。
(D) 他創立一個機構。
解析 Bennett 這個名字和 3 年前這個時間點出現在談話的中段，內容提到 Bennett 先生 3 年前創立了非營利組織 (Mr. Bennett established the non-profit organization three years ago)，故本題正解為選項 (D)。

82. 根據說話者所說，Bennett 先生很了解什麼？
(A) 理財
(B) 不動產價格
(C) 社區需求
(D) 消費者趨勢
解析 談話後半部用 he 代指 Bennett 先生，提到 Bennett 先生很清楚 Waterford 市民需要和關心的是什麼 (he fully understands what the people of Waterford need and care about)。由此可知 Bennett 先生很了解社區的需求，故本題正解為選項 (C)。

Questions 83-85 refer to the following talk.

Well done, everyone! 83 You've finally reached the end of this three-day orientation. Now, you should fully understand our company's policies, product ranges, and future goals and be ready for your first proper day of work. 84 I'm sure some of you will still have questions during your first week here. So, don't forget, my office is on the third floor. Additionally, you each have an employee handbook that I'm sure you'll find very helpful. Oh, and a few of you asked about the company's business hours during the upcoming Christmas period. Well, 85 I will be transferring to our branch in London on December 1, so I'm not sure about that. But, the replacement HR manager will certainly let you know.

做得很好，各位！你們終於來到這個 3 日新進職員訓練的最後了。現在，你們都應該充分地了解公司的政策、產品類型和未來遠景，也準備好要正式開

始上班了。我相信在公司上班的第一週，你們之中部分的人還是會有一些疑問。所以別忘了，我的辦公室在 3 樓。此外，你們每個人都有一本職員手冊，你之後會發現它能提供很多幫助。喔，有部分的人問了我不久後的聖誕節期間，上班時間是幾點到幾點。嗯，我 12 月 1 日會被調到倫敦的分公司，所以這點我不太確定。不過，新任人事部經理屆時一定會告訴各位。

83. 說話者在主持什麼活動？
(A) 一場產品演示
(B) 一場工作面試
(C) 一場記者會
(D) 一場新進職員訓練
解析 說話者在談話開頭說到將結束 3 天的新進職員訓練 (You've finally reached the end of this three-day orientation.)，故本題正解為選項 (D)。

84. 說話者說「我的辦公室在 3 樓」代表什麼意思？
(A) 他想到不同的樓層工作。
(B) 他無法參加某項活動。
(C) 他可以提供協助。
(D) 他會發資料給聆聽者們。
解析 說話者在談話中段提到聆聽者們在工作的第一週一定還是會有疑問 (I'm sure some of you will still have questions during your first week here.)，接著說「我的辦公室在 3 樓」。由此可知說話者是要說如果有疑問，可以來向他請求協助，故本題正解為選項 (C)。

85. 說話者說他 12 月會做什麼？
(A) 調到別的分公司
(B) 增聘職員
(C) 修訂公司的手冊
(D) 公布某個季節性工作時程
解析 12 月這個時間點出現在談話的後半部，說話者說自己 12 月 1 日將調到倫敦的分公司 (I will be transferring to our branch in London on December 1)，故本題正解為選項 (A)。

Questions 86-88 refer to the following speech.

It's nice of you to stop by the Entech Systems display booth 86 here at the STA Software Convention. Please allow me to show you our newest product, which won't be available in stores until next month. The Safe Guard Anti-Virus Package keeps your computer completely safe from all known viruses, and 87 users receive free automatic updates every month to ensure the program is working effectively. Safe Guard will be officially launched on May 15, but 88 if you place an advance order right now, you can receive a special 10 percent discount.

謝謝你來 STA 軟體展的 Entech 系統展位。請讓我為你展示我們最新的商品，這個商品下個月才供販售。這款 Safe Guard 防毒軟體讓你的電腦能防所有已知的病毒，使用者們每個月都能享有免費的

自動更新服務來保障你的軟體能有效發揮功效。Safe Guard 將在 5 月 15 日正式上市，如果你現在預訂的話，就能享有九折優惠折扣。

86. 說話者在哪裡？
(A) 在一場盛大的開幕典禮
(B) 在一場軟體展會
(C) 在一個訓練工作坊
(D) 在一場股東會議

解析 說話者在談話開頭就說到這裡是 STA 軟體展 (here at the STA Software Convention)，故本題正解為選項 (B)。

87. 說話者提到商品的什麼特色？
(A) 它可以在網路上購買。
(B) 它有保固。
(C) 它能自動更新。
(D) 它在業界得過獎。

解析 談話中段提到使用者們每個月都能享有免費的自動更新服務 (users receive free automatic updates every month)，故本題正解為選項 (C)。

88. 聆聽者要怎麼做才能享有折扣？
(A) 拿商品型錄
(B) 申辦會員
(C) 提前預訂
(D) 使用禮物券

解析 說話者在談話後半部說到如果現在先預訂的話，就能享有九折優惠折扣 (if you place an advance order right now, you can receive a special 10 percent discount)，故本題正解為選項 (C)。

Questions 89–91 refer to the following recorded message.

Thank you for calling Pro Form Gym. The gym is closed right now, so nobody is available to take your call. 89 Please leave us a message by staying on the line until the end of this recording. We check our telephone messages every morning and will do our best to respond promptly. And, 90 we've just received the Best Fitness Instructors award for the fourth year straight at the Michigan Health & Fitness Awards. To celebrate this achievement, 91 we're offering 20% off all our gym memberships until the end of this month. So, come on over and get in shape at Pro Form Gym!

謝謝你致電 Pro Form 健身房。現在非健身房的營業時間，目前無人能夠接聽。請勿掛斷電話，待此段語音結束後留下你的訊息。我們每天早上都會確認電話留言，盡我們所能及時回覆。並且，我們已經連續 4 年在密西根健康與健身大獎上獲得最佳健身教練獎。為了慶祝這項成就，到這個月底前，所有健身房會員都享有會費八折優惠。所以，快到 Pro Form 健身房練出好身材吧！

89. 根據說話者所說，聆聽者們要如何留訊息？
(A) 瀏覽網站
(B) 打另一支電話
(C) 寄電子郵件
(D) 不掛斷電話

解析 說話者在談話前半部提到要留言的話不要掛斷電話，並等到該段語音結束 (Please leave us a message by staying on the line until the end of this recording.)，故本題正解為選項 (D)。

90. Pro Form 健身房最著名的應該是什麼？
(A) 提供最低的價格
(B) 提供最新的健身器材
(C) 僱用最優秀的教練
(D) 擁有最多分店

解析 談話中段寫到該健身房連續 4 年獲得最佳健身教練獎 (we've just received the Best Fitness Instructors award for the fourth year straight)。由此可知這間健身房以有優秀的教練群著名，故本題正解為選項 (C)。

91. Pro Form 健身房到這個月底前會提供什麼？
(A) 免費運動課程
(B) 免費禮物
(C) 有折扣的器材
(D) 較便宜的會費

解析 說話者在談話的後半部說到這個月底，所有健身房會員都享有會費八折優惠，故本題正解為選項 (D)。

Questions 92–94 refer to the following speech.

Well, I'm sure I speak for all of us when I say that 92 I'm very sad that Joshua Park is retiring, but I'm so glad we could all get together for dinner to bid farewell to him. 93 Joshua has been directing television shows for us here at HBC Broadcasting ever since the company was founded two decades ago. He is renowned in the television industry for helping to 94 create some of the most successful shows in the U.K., many of which have won millions of fans over the years. His biggest drama series... It's still on Channel 7 today. Joshua, it has been a pleasure working with you, and we wish you all the best.

那麼，我想大家應該都和我想說的一樣，我很難過 Joshua Park 要退休了，但同時也很開心我們能一起享用晚餐為他餞別。Joshua 從 20 年前公司創立開始，就一直在 HBC 電視公司執導電視節目。他在電視圈享有盛名，因為他曾協助做出好幾部英國知名的節目，多年來深受百萬觀眾的喜愛。他最成功的影集…現在仍在第 7 臺播出。Joshua，很榮幸能與你共事，祝你一切順心。

92. 這是什麼類型的活動？
(A) 頒獎典禮
(B) 職前訓練
(C) 退休餐敘
(D) 記者會

解析 說話者在談話開頭說對 Joshua Park 的退休感到傷心，並為此聚在一起用餐 (I'm very sad that Joshua Park is retiring, but I'm so glad we could all get together for dinner)，故本題正解為選項 (C)。

93. 誰是 Joshua Park？
(A) 一位演員
(B) 一位導演
(C) 一位攝影師
(D) 一位經紀人

解析 Joshua Park 的名字出現在前半段，其中提及他過去都在執導電視節目 (Joshua has been directing television shows for us here at HBC Broadcasting)，故本題正解為選項 (B)。

94. 為什麼說話者說「現在仍在第七臺播出」？
(A) 想表達這個節目仍然很受歡迎
(B) 提出一個新的企劃案
(C) 建議修改節目播出日程
(D) 對聆聽者們的成功表達祝賀

解析 談話後半部說到 Joshua 做的很多部節目深受百萬觀眾的喜愛，說到他最成功的影集後 (create some of the most successful shows in the U.K., many of which have won millions of fans over the years. His biggest drama series...)，再接著說「現在仍在第七臺播出」。由此可知說話者是想表達這個節目仍舊很受歡迎，故本題正解為選項 (A)。

Questions 95–97 refer to the following telephone message and map.

Hey Betty, it's Roger. I took a look around the downtown area and I saw a vacant commercial space we could rent. I think it would be an ideal spot for 95 our new bakery. It's on a busy street corner, and 96 it's directly opposite a large office building, so we'd probably get business from workers who want to buy some donuts or pastries during their lunch break. Before we schedule a viewing of the property, 97 I think we should ask how much the landlord expects in rent per month. That way, we can figure out if we can afford it. Anyway, please get back to me once you get this message.

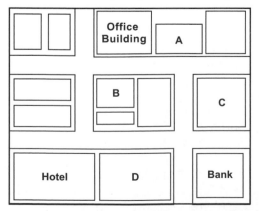

嘿，Betty，我是 Roger。我在市中心看了一下，

並看到一間我們能租的空店面。我想這裡會是我們新烘焙坊最理想的地點。它位在一個熱鬧的街角，正對一棟大型辦公大樓，所以我們午休時間可能會有一些想買些甜甜圈或甜點當下午茶的上班族客群。在約時間去看那個店面之前，我想我們應該要先問房東預期一個月要收多少租金。這樣一來，我們就可以先評估是否能夠負擔。總之，收到訊息後請盡快回覆我。

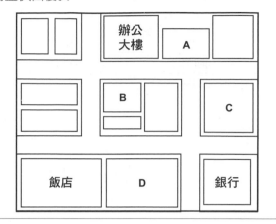

95. 說話者要開什麼樣的店？
(A) 一間服飾店
(B) 一間不動產仲介公司
(C) 一間藝廊
(D) 一間烘焙坊

解析 說話者在談話開頭說到我們的新烘焙坊 (our new bakery)，故本題正解為選項 (D)。

96. 請參照圖表。請問說話者想要的店面地點在哪？
(A) 地點 A
(B) 地點 B
(C) 地點 C
(D) 地點 D

解析 說話者在談話中段提到他想要的地點在大型辦公大樓的正對面 (it's directly opposite a large office building)，並說明了該地點的優點。對照圖表可知大型辦公大樓的對面為地點 B，故本題正解為選項 (B)。

97. 說話者想要弄清楚什麼？
(A) 能不能停車
(B) 大樓的大小
(C) 租金的多寡
(D) 當地交通方式

解析 說話者在談話的最後說到必須詢問房東預期的每月房租是多少錢 (I think we should ask how much the landlord expects in rent per month.)。由此可知說話者想先弄清楚的是租金，故本題正解為選項 (C)。

Questions 98–100 refer to the following telephone message and Web site.

Hi, Steve. This is Chloe. I'm calling because I need to fly out to California to meet with a client, and 98 because you're my department manager, I need your help. I contacted our accounting team, and they gave me some options for flights to California. 99 I'd prefer to

fly with DC Airlines. It's a little more expensive than some of the other airlines, but DC Airlines is less likely to have a delay. The accounting manager is ready to book the flight for me, but he says I need my department manager's authorization. So, **100** I'd appreciate it if you could send me an authorization form by e-mail before the end of today. Thanks a lot.

West Air	$275
Easy Wings	$295
DC Airlines	$300
Smart Jet	$315

你好，Steve。我是 Chloe。我打給你是因為我必須飛去加州跟客戶見面，因為你是我的部門經理，所以我需要你的幫忙。我連絡了我們的會計部，他們給了我飛往加州的幾個航班做選擇。我偏好搭 DC Airlines。它比其他航空公司貴一些，但 DC Airlines 的班機比較少延誤。會計部經理已經準備要幫我訂機票了，但他說這需要經過我的部門經理批准。如果你能在今天之前透過電子郵件寄批准表格給我的話，我會非常感謝你。謝謝。

West Air	275 美元
Easy Wings	295 美元
DC Airlines	300 美元
Smart Jet	315 美元

98. 這則留言是要給誰的？
(A) 一名客戶
(B) 一名主管
(C) 一名航空公司職員
(D) 一名會計師
解析 說話者在談話開頭說到因為對方是自己的部門經理，所以希望他能幫忙 (because you're my department manager, I need your help)，故本題正解為選項 (B)。

99. 請參照圖表。說話者的機票將花費多少錢？
(A) 275 美元
(B) 295 美元
(C) 300 美元
(D) 315 美元
解析 說話者在談話中段說到自己想搭乘 DC Airlines(I'd prefer to fly with DC Airlines.)。對照圖表可知該航空公司的機票為 300 美元 (DC Airlines/$300)，故本題正解為選項 (C)。

100. 說話者要聆聽者寄什麼？
(A) 旅遊行程
(B) 客戶的連絡資訊
(C) 批准表格
(D) 付款收據
解析 說話者在談話的最後說希望對方能透過電子郵件寄批准表格給自己 (I'd appreciate it if you could send me an authorization form by e-mail)，故本題正解為選項 (C)。

Part 5

101.
答案 (A)
譯文 Harrington 主廚喜歡他為飯店客人煮的餐點，但他更想做一些更複雜的料理。
解析
空格位於主詞 Chef Harrington 和動詞 likes 及受詞 the food 構成的完整子句後方，另一個動詞 cooks 直接接在其後，但沒有主詞。這代表從空格到 guests 必須為用來修飾先行詞的關係子句，動詞 cooks 前方的空格必須是這個關係子句的主詞，故主格代名詞選項 (A) he 為本題正解。此外，the food 和空格填入的 he 之間省略了關係代名詞 which 或 that。

102.
答案 (C)
譯文 Luxo 化妝品為了市場調查，正在尋找 18 歲到 35 歲之間的女性顧客。
解析
空格前面的介系詞和 and 為一對，形成 "between A and B" 的結構，故本題正解為選項 (C) and。

103.
答案 (B)
譯文 銀行經理實在太忙了，以致於她的顧客都要等至少一週才能跟她見到面。
解析
空格為被不定冠詞 an 修飾，同時能和介系詞 with 一起使用的名詞，故本題正解為選項 (B) appointment。

104.
答案 (D)
譯文 位於觀光地區的中心點，York 歷史博物館展示了英國最古老的掛毯收藏品。
解析
出現 in the UK 這個範圍代表要進行比較 (在英國最…的)，因此需要形容詞最高級，而用來修飾名詞 collection 的形容詞中「最古老的」最符合博物館收藏品的特性，故本題正解為選項 (D) oldest。

105.
答案 (D)
譯文 那副白色耳機現在是我們 High Street 分店唯一一副庫存。
解析
在 be 動詞 are 的後方，作為主詞 The white earphones 的補語，需要一個能夠和主詞成為同格的單字，故本題正解為能夠代指前方複數名詞的代名詞選項 (D) ones。

106.
答案 (A)
譯文 Burns 先生被贈予一隻黃金腕錶，以感謝他為公司工作 30 年的努力。
解析
空格內須填入能夠和前後方介系詞 in 和 of 一起使用的名詞，能和這兩者一起使用，並帶有「感謝」的意思的選項 (A) recognition 為本題正解。

107.
答案 (B)
譯文 一旦試用期結束，新進職員將在總公司參加績效考核。

解析
空格位在連接詞 Once 和作為主詞使用的名詞子句 probationary period 之間，須填入能夠修飾名詞子句的詞語，故能夠擔任這個角色的所有格選項 (B) their 為本題正解。

108.
答案 (D)
譯文 Astrid 金融服務公司希望透過在歐洲各地設立新的分公司來擴大其事業版圖。

解析
空格後方的動名詞子句「在歐洲各地設立新的分公司」是擴大事業版圖的方法。故用「透過…；靠著…」來表達方法時使用的介系詞選項 (D) by 為本題正解。

109.
答案 (C)
譯文 很多唱片行都倒閉，因為對光碟和其他實體形式的音樂需求有限。

解析
空格位在定冠詞 the 和名詞 demand 之間，必須填入可以修飾名詞的詞語，故能擔任這個角色的過去分詞選項 (C) limited 為本題正解。

110.
答案 (A)
譯文 雙面列印能夠減少需要用到的紙張，也因此減少了垃圾。

解析
空格前方的子句說明雙面列印減少了紙張的使用，空格後方的分詞構句則寫到能減少垃圾。由此可知代表「於是；因此」的副詞 (A) consequently 為本題正解。

111.
答案 (A)
譯文 在搬到紐西蘭辦公室之前，Marlowe 先生花了好幾週的時間訓練接替他的人。

解析
空格位在被所有格代名詞 his 給修飾的名詞位置，故本題正解為選項 (A) replacement。

112.
答案 (B)
譯文 DCA 網路設計提供報價服務給想要強化店家在網路上可見度的老闆。

解析
空格內須填入能夠和意思為價格的名詞 price 構成複合名詞，且必須是能夠提供給業者的東西，故能表達「報價（單）」的選項 (B) estimates 為本題正解。

113.
答案 (B)
譯文 當老闆增加一系列素食選擇時，餐廳的菜單上已經有 75 道菜。

解析
空格位於 be 動詞 were 和名詞子句 75 dishes 之間，因此要從能夠修飾名詞子句的形容詞 (A) every 或能

夠修飾整個句子的 (B) already 之中擇一。(A) every 用來修飾單數名詞，故能夠修飾整個句子的選項 (B) already 為本題正解。

114.
答案 (C)
譯文 為了吸引更多觀光客，傑佛遜山國家公園開發了好幾個涵蓋適合不同運動強度的健行步道。

解析
空格內須填入能夠和介系詞 for 一起使用，並在後方修飾 hiking trails 的形容詞，「適合不同運動強度的健行步道」在語意上最為自然，和 for 一同出現，表達「適合…」的選項 (C) appropriate 為本題正解。

115.
答案 (B)
譯文 Alford 牙醫診所允許患者遲到最多 15 分鐘，超過之後就要重新預約。

解析
連接詞 which 後面只有主詞 the appointment 和空格，由此可知空格內須填入 which 子句的動詞。此外，which 子句的主詞 appointment 需要人去做調整，所以 reschedule 必須是被動語態。該動詞必須和主要子句的動詞 allows 一樣為描述一般事實的現在式，故本題正解為選項 (B) is scheduled。

116.
答案 (D)
譯文 當牆壁在油漆的時候，職員們沒有辦法進去職員休息室。

解析
空格的前後各有一句有著主詞和動詞的子句，可知空格內須填入能夠連接兩個子句的連接詞。在連接詞 (C) although 和 (D) while 之間，能夠表達「牆壁在油漆的時候，無法進去休息室」的選項 (D) while 為本題正解。

117.
答案 (C)
譯文 Gupta 女士建議確認註冊完畢後，就立刻將活動手冊寄給參展的人員。

解析
空格位在連接詞 after 前方，可知空格內須填入能夠強調「…之後；立刻」的副詞，故本題正解為選項 (C) immediately。

118.
答案 (D)
譯文 Arnold Schneider 會在聖誕節期間觀察職員們的出缺勤狀況，並向人資部門的主管報告。

解析
空格後方為名詞子句 employee absences，因此須填入能夠針對職員的出缺勤做些什麼的動詞。後面的句子寫到「向人資部門的主管報告」，為求語意通順，空格內應該要填入有「觀察；監視」等意思的選項 (D) monitoring。

119.
答案 (C)
譯文 離開的租客必須把出入口的卡片鑰匙歸還到大門警衛室。

解析
空格位在作為主詞的名詞 tenants 前方，可知須填入能夠修飾名詞的形容詞，故本題正解為選項 (C) Departing。

120.
答案 (B)
譯文 Dawson 先生從大學畢業後，他就開始在 Raleigh 聯合事務所擔任建築師。

解析
空格後方有兩個以逗點區分，包含主詞與動詞的子句，由此可知空格內須填入連接兩個子句的連接詞，故本題正解為選項中唯一一個連接詞 (B) As soon as。

121.
答案 (C)
譯文 第一個達成本月目標的業務能得到 3 天有薪假的獎勵。

解析
句子中已經有 will be awarded 這個動詞，所以另一個動詞 reach 在空格內必須以動狀詞的形態出現。除此之外，空格前後的名詞子句要構成「第一個達成本月目標的業務」，語意才通順。可知空格內須填入能夠擔任由後方修飾名詞的形容詞角色的詞語，故本題正解為選項 (C) to reach。

122.
答案 (C)
譯文 顧客在 Direct 電子購買筆記型電腦後，公司在六個月內的任何時間都會進行免費維修。

解析
空格後方的 a six-month period 為表期間的名詞子句，故能夠表達「在…期間內」，擺在名詞（句）前方的介系詞選項 (C) during 為本題正解。

123.
答案 (B)
譯文 面試官認為 Howden 女士在亞洲的工作經驗適用於該職位的工作職責和責任。

解析
空格內須填入在 be 動詞 was 的後方，作為 that 子句主詞 Ms. Howden's experience working in Asia 補語的詞語。從語意看來，必須填上能夠點出 Howden 女士在亞洲的工作經驗特性的形容詞，故本題正解為選項 (B) applicable。

124.
答案 (D)
譯文 Lowden 公司強制禁止總公司所有部門使用社群媒體。

解析
空格內須填入適合與後方受詞 its social media ban 擺在一起的動詞。「強制禁止」的語意最為通順，故本題正解為選項 (D) enforces。

125.
答案 (D)
譯文 公司現在聘請了幾名兼職的辦公室助理，我們的工作量變得沒那麼重。

解析
空格位在 be 動詞 is 和作為補語的比較級形容詞

lighter 之間，可知空格內須填入能夠修飾形容詞的副詞，故本題正解為選項 (D) considerably。

126.
答案 (A)
譯文 位在舊城區的飯店因為觀光客湧入，最近突然變得非常受歡迎。

解析
空格為表原因時使用的介系詞 thanks to 的受詞。因此必須填入變得受歡迎的理由，且必須是和觀光客相關的名詞。故本題正解為能夠表達「觀光客湧入」選項 (A) influx。

127.
答案 (A)
譯文 更換網路供應業者後，Moss 先生發現無線網路常常會斷線。

解析
選項中的動詞 switch 如果要在沒有主詞的情況下，直接接在作為介系詞或連接詞使用的 After 後面，必須要是動名詞或是分詞的形態，故本題正解為選項 (A) switching。

128.
答案 (D)
譯文 大部分的零食製造商都會刻意設計出能吸引孩子目光的廣告。

解析
空格內須填入能夠修飾動詞 design 的副詞，且需表達出刻意設計成能吸引孩子目光的語意，故本題正解為選項 (D) purposely。

129.
答案 (A)
譯文 Interior King 家具廣受顧客歡迎，因為其簡單的設計和易於組裝。

解析
空格前方為對等連接詞 and，因此須填入詞性相同的詞語，故和作為 for 受詞的名詞 design 有著同樣詞性的選項 (A) ease 為本題正解。

130.
答案 (C)
譯文 Ironman 營養補給為所有單筆訂單超過 300 美元的顧客提供免運費優惠。

解析
名詞子句 its shipping fee 為受詞，空格內須填入和運費相關的動詞。「為消費超過 300 美元的顧客提供免運優惠」的語意最為通順，故本題正解為選項 (C) waive。

Part 6

請參考以下電子郵件回答**第 131 至 134 題**。

收件人：Feltman 公司職員們 **寄件人：**Lee Durst **主旨：**自助餐廳垃圾 **日期：**6 月 19 日

131.

答案 (C)

解析 空格內須填入能夠連接前後名詞子句 a new policy 和 the serving of food and disposal of trash，並表達「和…相關的新政策」，故本題正解為選項 (C) regarding。

132.

答案 (C)

解析 空格前的主詞 This policy 是代指用不鏽鋼餐盤取代一次性塑膠餐盤這件事，接著空格後方出現關於垃圾量的名詞子句，可知空格內需填入該政策對垃圾量造成什麼影響的動詞。電子郵件下半部提到能夠讓公司變得更環境友善，可知該政策減少了垃圾量，故本題正解為「將…減到最少」的選項 (C) minimize。

133.

答案 (C)

解析 空格前方寫到更換餐盤，後方寫到更換飲料杯。可知此處是在描述兩個有關連性的新政策，因此表「此外，另外」，增加資訊的連接副詞選項 (C) In addition 為本題正解。

134.

答案 (D)

譯文 (A) 請告訴我們你對新菜色的想法。
(B) 翻新工程期間，有些餐點不提供。
(C) 這個案子因為各位的努力非常成功。
(D) 我們會很感謝各位的積極配合。

解析 整封電子郵件都在談為了減少垃圾實行的新政策，因此用 this effort 代指這件事，並對他人的積極配合表達感謝的選項 (D) 為本題正解。

請參考以下信件回答**第 135 至 138 題**。

135.

答案 (C)

解析 選項都是動詞 send 的不同形態，假如 If 子句後面的主要子句沒有主詞，直接要接動詞的話，必須是以原形動詞當開頭的祈使句句型，故本題正解為選項 (C) send。

136.

答案 (D)

譯文 (A) Northern 電力公司最近施行了一個新的支付方式。
(B) Northern 電力公司希望能在某個部門多聘幾個職員。
(C) 這一週電力可能會臨時中斷。
(D) 也請明確地指出你遇到的問題。

解析 空格前的句子要顧客在收到帳單後的三天內提出帳單上的錯誤。接著用 the problem 代指前面曾出現的 any billing errors，表達需要明確指出問題，才有辦法幫忙解決，故本題正解為選項 (D)。

137.

答案 (A)

解析 從空格前方出現的動詞來看，空格內的名詞應為能夠評估和決定的事項。前一句提到如果電費帳單有誤，就要告訴電力公司，後用顧客所要求的事項代指告訴電力公司的問題，評估並針對所有要求做決定的語意較為通順，故意思為「要求 (事項)、主張」的選項 (A) claims 為本題正解。

138.

答案 (B)

解析 從空格前後文意，可知在證明溢收電費後，下一期的帳單會減少某樣東西，故意思為「金額；數量」的選項 (B) amount 為本題正解。

請參考以下備忘錄回答**第 139 至 142 題**。

139.
答案 (A)
解析
空格裡的形容詞必須能和 from the hotel lobby 一同使用，並點出兩間會議廳和飯店大廳的位置關連性，故本題正解為表「能夠接近、能夠使用」等意思的選項 (A) accessible。

140.
答案 (C)
譯文 (A) 許多活動提高了飯店的名聲。
　　　(B) Rita Tennant 做了好幾次商業演示。
　　　(C) 兩間會議廳都要事先預約。
　　　(D) 面試會在 9 月初進行。
解析
空格前講到兩間新會議廳的施工日程、規模和用途，故用 Both rooms 代指會議廳並說明使用方法的選項 (C) 為本題正解。

141.
答案 (C)
解析
空格前面提到 Tennant 女士會暫時負責活動的預約，空格後方則說到她重返原本客服人員的崗位。像這種依現在和未來順序排列的句子之間，要填入能夠表前後關係，表「在那之後」的選項 (C) After that 為本題正解。

142.
答案 (D)
解析
空格內需填入能夠將後方名詞 reservations 當作受詞，同時作為介系詞 for 受詞的動名詞，故本題正解為選項 (D) overseeing。

請參考以下電子郵件回答**第 143 至 146 題**。

> 收件人：pkilroy@amerimail.net
> 寄件人：mwagstaff@marksmotors.com
> 主旨：Bronco Meridian
> 日期：12 月 14 日
>
> Peter 你好：
>
> 謝謝你詢問我們在當地報紙上廣告的 Bronco Meridian 轎車。我很遺憾必須告訴你，我剛剛跟我的業務主管談過，143 看來這臺車在今早已銷售一空。
>
> 如果你願意告訴我一些關於你想買的車款的具體細節，144 我可以幫助你找一些適合你的車款。當你方便時，可以透過電子郵件將預算、想購買的品牌和你喜歡的車子類型，以及其他具體性能傳送給我。145 接著，我會找符合你需求的車輛。
>
> 你也可以選擇接收定期 146 通知。通過註冊這些，你將收到簡訊通知你我們車輛清單中的新內容。若你有興趣，請讓我知道。
>
> 敬祝 順心

Mark Wagstaff
Mark 中古車商

143.
答案 (A)
解析
空格前方說到和業務主管談話，後面寫收件人想要的車輛今天早上已經銷售一空。由此可知空格內需填入從已知資訊推斷結論的詞語，故表「由此看來」，依照某些做推測時使用的選項 (A) apparently 為本題正解。

144.
答案 (B)
解析
空格所在的主要子句是在 If 子句所說的條件被滿足時可能發生的事，故本題正解為包含表可能性的助動詞 can 的選項 (B) can assist。

145.
答案 (D)
譯文 (A) 當然，你必須符合職務要求。
　　　(B) 我週一會在車廠收到這些新車。
　　　(C) 這是最近汽車產業的趨勢。
　　　(D) 接著，我會找符合你需求的車輛。
解析
空格前一句請收件人透過電子郵件提供預算、想購買的品牌和喜歡的車子類型，以及其他具體性能。這些內容都是幫電子郵件收件人尋找想要車輛的必要條件，故本題正解為幫客人尋找符合他需求的選項 (D)。

146.
答案 (A)
解析
從空格後的句子可知答案為能夠以 these 代稱的複數名詞，並提到如果申請這樣東西，就能收到最新資訊。申請定期通知在語意上最為通順，故本題正解為表「通知 (服務)」的選項 (A) notifications。

Part 7

請參考以下資訊回答**第 147 至 148 題**。

> **沒有比用 Air Transnat 預訂航班更簡單的了！**
>
> 在尋找能夠輕鬆預訂航班的方法，但無法快速使用電腦嗎？只要在手機上安裝我們新推出的應用程式，你就可以在幾分鐘內完成所有事情！在應用程式裡，所有航班的價格每 30 秒就會更新一次，所以你看到的資訊總是準確的。
>
> 這還不是全部！147 我們為應用程式用戶們提供與網站用戶們相同的好處。當你訂機票時，你可以選擇你的座位、147 想在飛機上享用的餐點，甚至是要求額外的用品，像是枕頭、毛毯和耳機。
>
> 一旦你的預訂完成後，148 你會收到一組特別的預訂代碼，你可以在出發的一週前用這組代碼更改你所選的座位、餐點。

147. 根據以上資訊，何者為事實？
(A) 可以透過應用程式選擇餐點。
(B) 預訂資訊會透過電子郵件確認。
(C) 航班資訊一小時更新一次。
(D) 網站最近重新設計過。

解析

文章第二段寫到會提供應用程式用戶們與網站用戶們相同的好處 (We offer the same perks to application users that we do to Web site users.)，並說明有哪些好處。在提及的內容中有一項是能選擇想在飛機上享用的餐點 (choose what you would like to eat on the plane)，由此可知用戶能在應用程式上選擇餐點，故本題正解為選項 (A)。

148. 特別代碼的用處是什麼？
(A) 能夠快速辦理登機
(B) 買機票能夠打折
(C) 能夠申請網路服務
(D) 能夠變更預訂內容

解析

特別代碼出現在最後一段，文章內提到能夠用代碼更改所選的座位或餐點 (receive a special reservation code that you can use to make changes to your seat and meal preferences)，由此可知特別代碼是用來變更預訂內容，故本題正解為選項 (D)。

請參考以下產品介紹回答**第 149 至 150 題**。

今天改善你的健康吧！

有著 0.65 公升的容量，這款 149 調理機比起市面上的類似商品能容納更多食材。此機型由電子工程師 Manuel Vega 設計，這項裝置適合家用也適合專業用途。150 1000 瓦特的馬達提供了大馬力和高效率，所以你可以用比以往更快的速度混合食材。並且可分離的不鏽鋼刀片能夠以水平和垂直的方式切開食材！能選擇的顏色有白色、銀色和黑色，149 本產品還會附贈一本食譜和兩個不同尺寸的果汁杯。

149. 這是在描述何種產品？
(A) 軟體包
(B) 施工工具
(C) 廚房用品
(D) 家具

解析

文章開頭就提到該產品是調理機 (blender)，最後寫上會附贈食譜和果汁杯 (a recipe book and two different sizes of juice cups)。由此可知此產品用於食品調理，故本題正解為選項 (C)。

150. 文章裡提到關於產品的何種特性？
(A) 馬力很強。
(B) 重量很輕。
(C) 價格便宜。
(D) 易於使用。

解析

文章中段提到調理機 1000 瓦特的馬達提供了大馬力和高效率 (The 1000-Watt motor provides impressive power and efficiency)，由此可知該產品的馬力很強，故本題正解為選項 (A)。

請參考以下電子郵件回答**第 151 至 152 題**。

收件人：William Stuckman
寄件人：Magdalena Horowitz
日期：4 月 26 日
主旨：更新

William 你好：

我需要你更新我們針對 Marston 國家公園景觀設計合約的提案。客戶剛剛告訴我他們想要在公園裡有一些野餐區，151 所以我希望你能在我們的設計圖上加入幾個潛在的地點，並把它們加入簡報資料裡。我對這些最佳地點有自己的想法，但我想先看看你的選擇。

此外，因為 Matthew Wilkinson 的市府造景工程有些延遲，152 所以他要到 5 月 13 日週一時才能處理 Marston 國家公園的案子，這比我們原先預計的時間還要晚一週。你需要在我們跟客戶報告之前先修正這個資訊。謝謝你的幫忙。

Magdalena

151. Horowitz 女士為什麼要寄這封電子郵件？
(A) 為了接受某個工作機會
(B) 為了修改某個企劃案
(C) 為了提議籌劃一個活動
(D) 為了要簡報資料的複本

解析

電子郵件的第一段寫到客戶對景觀設計合約的提案有其他要求，所以必須拜託收件人在設計圖上增加野餐區 (I'd like you to add some potential sites to our diagram)。由此可知 Horowitz 女士寄這封電子郵件的目的是要修改某個企劃案，故本題正解為選項 (B)。

152. Stuckman 先生被要求做什麼？
(A) 去市政府
(B) 重新安排和客戶開會的日程
(C) 連絡 Wilkinson 先生
(D) 更改開工的日期

解析

電子郵件第二段寫到負責該工程的 Wilkinson 先生要比預計的時間晚一週開工，所以要請 Stuckman 先生做修改 (he'll not be able to take charge at Marston Country Park until Monday, May 13, one week later than we originally scheduled. You'll need to correct this information as well)。由此可知 Stuckman 先生被要求更改開工日期，故本題正解為選項 (D)。

請參考以下線上對話回答**第 153 至 154 題**。

線上聊天 V3.0

Kurt Staley [下午 2:11]	153 感謝你使用 Spark 軟體的線上客服。有什麼我可以幫你的嗎？

Iris Cavalera [下午 2:13]	你好，今早有一位你們的技術人員來過我們 Ritz 雜誌，在我們辦公室的某些電腦上安裝照片編輯套件。但我打開程式時遇到了點困難。
Kurt Staley [下午 2:14]	這就奇怪了。你在打開它時有看到什麼樣的訊息嗎？
Iris Cavalera [下午 2:15]	嗯，它要我輸入產品啟動碼。我打了那位技術人員寫下的 AB469。153 之前跟你們公司買過舊版，但沒遇過這種問題。
Kurt Staley [下午 2:17]	154 喔，我知道問題出在哪了！我很確定那個 "B" 其實是 "8"。啟動碼裡只會有一個英文字母。
Iris Cavalera [下午 2:19]	原來如此。我原本還很擔心要重新安裝。非常感謝你。

153. 文章中提到 Ritz 雜誌的什麼資訊？
(A) 它退了一些瑕疵品回 Spark 軟體。
(B) 它曾經買過 Spark 軟體的產品。
(C) 它需要技術人員去修理設備。
(D) 它要刊登一篇關於圖像設計軟體的文章。

解析
Cavalera 在下午 2 點 15 分寫的訊息中說她們公司曾經在對方公司 (Staley 先生在第一則訊息說到自己在 Spark 軟體任職) 買過舊版軟體 (the previous versions we bought from you)。由此可知該公司曾向對方公司買過產品，故本題正解為選項 (B)。

154. Cavalera 在下午 2 點 19 分寫的訊息中說「原來如此」，她想表達什麼意思？
(A) 她剛剛誤會了 Staley 先生的說明。
(B) 她學到如何在 Spark 軟體訂購產品。
(C) 她知道自己為什麼無法使用軟體了。
(D) 她想和技術人員討論她遇到的問題。

解析
"That explains it" 直譯的話是「這就能說明那件事」，更自然的說法就是「原來如此」。這句話是在回應 Staley 先生在前一句找出了啟動碼無法使用的問題點 (Oh, I've got it! I'm pretty sure the "B" is actually an "8". There should only be one letter in the code.)，故本題正解為選項 (C)。

請參考以下電子郵件回答**第 155 至 157 題**。

收件人：所有業務主管
寄件人：Terence Materazzo，執行長
主旨：公務車
日期：7 月 10 日，週三

早安：

在昨天的董事會中，155 決定我們所有在 Arandell 製造公司工作的人都必須更重視於減少我們對環境的影響。其中一個要實行的方法就是購買靠電力發動且不會排放有害氣體的電動車當新的公務車。這些汽車將提供給所有業務主管，並且應使用在每當

你要四處拜訪客戶時。156 我們知道你們之中部分的人已經將車子換成不靠燃料的車種。假如是這種情況，請繼續使用你自己的車，從週一開始，公司將會負擔所有充電的費用。

157(D) 這些新車將會於週一送到總公司，我希望各位能在下午一點至地下停車場集合。157(C) 更大臺、更高級的車輛會提供給高階主管，而基層主管則會領標準轎車。所有車都是由 Azari 汽車所製，157(B) 並且他們的其中一位代表屆時也會來現場告訴各位怎麼操作和替車輛充電。157(A) 工作時間結束時，你就能自由開你的車回家了。

敬祝 順心

Terence Materazzo
執行長
Arandell 製造公司

155. 為什麼公司會提供公務車？
(A) 慶祝今年事業上的成功。
(B) 希望職員們到更遠的地方拜訪客戶。
(C) 想試著變得更環境友善。
(D) 要送給表現最成功的業務主管。

解析
電子郵件第一段就寫到所有在 Arandell 製造公司工作的人都必須更重視於減少我們對環境的影響 (all of us at Arandell Manufacturing must place greater emphasis on lessening our impact on the environment)，接著說其中一個方法就是購買不會排放有害氣體的汽車。由此可知提供公務車是為了環境友善所做的努力，故本題正解為選項 (C)。

156. 文章內提到關於部分業務主管的什麼資訊？
(A) 他們的工作不用出差。
(B) 他們已經有電動車。
(C) 他們目前收到每月出差津貼。
(D) 他們抱怨過自己開的車。

解析
電子郵件第一段後半部說到部分的收件人已經買了不會排放廢氣的車款 (some of you have already made the switch to a gas-free model)，這邊所指的就是前面提到的電動車，故本題正解為選項 (B)。

157. 下列關於公務車的敘述，何者並非事實？
(A) 必須要停在公司停車場。
(B) 有位汽車公司的職員會來示範怎麼操作。
(C) 會照位階做安排。
(D) 下週會送到總公司。

解析
電子郵件最後一段說到汽車公司會派一名代表來教電動車的操作和充電方式 (one of its representatives will be on hand to show you how to operate the cars and recharge their batteries)，由此可知選項 (B) 正確。從更大臺、更高級的車輛會提供給高階主管，基層主管則會領標準轎車 (Larger, more advanced vehicles will be offered...will receive standard sedans) 這句話則可知選項 (C) 也正確。由這些新車週一會送到總公司 (These new cars will be delivered to our head office on Monday) 的敘述可確認選項 (D) 也正確。而最後一段提到可以把車輛開回家 (you're

free to take your vehicle home with you) 的敘述和
選項 (A) 正好相反，故本題正解為選項 (A)。

請參考以下廣告回答**第 158 至 160 題**。

Gerber 烘焙食品

Gerber 烘焙食品一直以來都以高品質蛋糕與甜點
著名。這間公司於 37 年前由一位經驗老道的烘焙
師傅 Paul Gerber 創立，他原本在多倫多當烘焙
學徒，後來搬到格雷文赫斯特開始自己的事業。

起初，Gerber 先生親自處理每日的運營，除了每
天早上早起做商品外，還為開店做準備和服務客
人。最終，159 烘焙坊變得越來越受歡迎，所以他
不得不向他的妻子、姪子還有他的弟弟請求協助。
儘管 Gerber 先生 160(B) 已經把主要經營業務交
給他的弟弟 Mark，他們所有人還是一直在總店幫
忙。這間店在過去 5 年成長十分快速，160(A) 增
加了供應的商品，160(C) 也在鄰近的城鎮，像是
亨茨維爾和布里斯橋等地開了比較小的分店。

如果你想來一點精緻的甜點，158 停下腳步來
Gerber 烘焙食品試看看。我們的總店位在格雷文
赫斯特 Lakeside 路 347 號，就在 Lloyd 藥局隔壁。
你也可以上 www.gerberbakedgoods.ca 看我們
提供的商品。

---

158. 這個廣告最有可能出現在哪裡？
(A) 商業雜誌
(B) 廚藝學校
(C) 當地刊物
(D) 就業博覽會

解析
廣告第一段和第二段介紹完烘焙坊開店的背景之後，在
最後一段請大家到他們的店裡嚐嚐，還給了店家的地
址 (stop by Gerber Baked Goods to try our products.
Our main store is located at 347 Lakeside Road,
Gravenhurst, just next to Lloyd's Pharmacy)。由此
可知這則廣告是給一般顧客，也就是當地居民看的，
那麼該廣告刊登在當地刊物上的可能性極高，故本題
正解為選項 (C)。

159. 關於 Gerber 烘焙食品的敘述，何者正確？
(A) 創辦人得過獎。
(B) 總店位在亨茨維爾。
(C) 正在找烘焙學徒。
(D) 是個家族事業。

解析
廣告第二段說到 Gerber 先生的妻子、姪子還有他的
弟弟都一直在店裡幫忙，而且已經把主要經營業務交
給他的弟弟 (ask for the help of his wife, his nephew,
and his brother. All of them continue to help out at
the main store, although Mr. Gerber has handed
over senior management duties to his younger
brother, Mark)。由此可知這間烘焙坊是家族事業，
故本題正解為選項 (D)。

160. 下列關於業者所做的改變，何者並未在廣告中
提及？
(A) 增加產品種類

(B) 換人管理
(C) 開了新分店
(D) 降低售價

解析
廣告第二段提到將經營業務交給弟弟 (Mr. Gerber
has handed over senior management duties to
his younger brother, Mark)，可知選項 (B) 正確。
接著從在鄰近城鎮開了較小的分店 (opening smaller
stores in nearby towns such as Huntsville and
Bracebridge)，可知選項 (C) 正確。增加了供應商品
(expanding its range of offerings) 這句話證明選項
(A) 也正確。故本題正解為廣告中未提及的選項 (D)
降低售價。

請參考以下公告回答**第 161 至 164 題**。

必須閱讀！

作家們請注意！ Alderdale 公立圖書館正在為必須
閱讀的新措施籌備一個 161 募款活動，162 為了
當地孤兒院的孩子們買書和漫畫。我們正在尋找不
限年紀和經歷的作家協助我們！

4 月整個月的正常開館時間 (週一到週六早上 10
點到晚上 7 點) 都歡迎來館。163(C) 我們會指定一
位歷史人物給你撰寫。有各式各樣有趣的人可以提
供選擇。

請在調查完該歷史人物後，開始進行他們的生平、
事蹟、寫作。163(A) 別忘了在最後簽上你的名字。

最晚在 4 月 30 日前交到還書櫃臺，以及附上你的
照片。
(請見下方)

這些「人生故事」163(B) 整個 5 月都會展示在圖書
館的牆上。每收到一份稿件，圖書館就會捐 10 美
元到這個募款活動中。164 投稿作家的照片將會展
示在主要閱覽區旁邊的牆面上。

想知道更詳細的資訊，可以直接打 555–2878 到
Alderdale 公立圖書館，或上 www.alderdalelibrary.
co.uk/lifestories。

---

161. 這則公告在鼓勵閱讀的人做什麼？
(A) 來某個活動當志工
(B) 參與募款活動
(C) 幫忙導覽當地圖書館
(D) 捐錢到慈善機構

解析
公告第一段寫到要透過募款活動幫當地孤兒院的孩子
們購買書和漫畫，所以在尋找能夠提供協助的作家們
(organizing a fundraising activity for its Need to
Read initiative, which raises money to purchase...
age groups to lend a hand)。由此可知這則公告是要
鼓勵看到的人參與這次的募款活動，故本題正解為選
項 (B)。

162. 必須閱讀募款活動的目標是什麼？
(A) 為新圖書館的設備籌募資金
(B) 回收舊書並製作新書

(C) 提供孩子們讀物
(D) 舉辦當地書展

解析
公告第一段就提到要募集為當地孤兒院的孩子們買書和漫畫的資金 (Need to Read initiative, which raises money to purchase books and comics for children at the local orphanage)，故本題正解為選項 (C)。

163. 下列關於「人生故事」的敘述，何者為非？
(A) 作者一定要簽名。
(B) 5 月會展示。
(C) 都是不同人的故事。
(D) 會參加某個競賽。

解析
公告第五段提到「人生故事」，這是指作家們寫的文章。關於該文章的資訊，第三段有寫到作者要簽名 (Don't forget to sign your name at the end.)，可知選項 (A) 正確。第五段則提到整個 5 月都會展示 (will be displayed on a wall in the library throughout the month of May)，可知選項 (B) 正確。第二段提到會指定書寫的歷史人物 (We will assign you one historical figure to write about)，可知選項 (C) 也正確。故本題正解為未被提及的選項 (D) 會參加某個競賽。

164. 圖書館的參觀者會在哪裡看到作者們的照片？
(A) 還書櫃臺
(B) 閱覽區附近
(C) 網站上
(D) 圖書館大門

解析
作者們的照片在第五段被提及，並說明會展示在主要閱覽區旁邊的牆上 (Photographs of contributing writers will be posted on the wall next to the main reading area)，故本題正解為選項 (B)。

請參考以下電子郵件回答**第 165 至 167 題**。

> 166 收件人：Woodgrain 家具店全體職員
> 166 寄件人：Philip Downie，店長
> 日期：6 月 11 日
> 主旨：夏季旅遊
>
> 各位職員好：
>
> 我們公司的年度旅遊時間快到了，165 我想詢問各位關於今年我們要去哪裡的意見。此外，我們將會舉辦一個比賽，看誰能提出最棒的渡假地點！全體職員到這個月底前可以提出我們 7 月下旬 3 天之旅的地點。你們可以選出自己認為最棒的三個地點，在 6 月 30 日前交給行政部門的 Ogilvie 女士。提出的建議被我選中的人，將得到 166 我們公司附近轉角的電影院——Galaxy 電影院的兩張電影票。
>
> 提交應使用從辦公室領取的報名表。當看各位提出的意見時，我會就以下幾點做評估：167(C) 能否受到喜好都不同的廣大職員喜愛，167(D) 還有該地點能做的活動 (越多越好！)，並且 167(A) 交通和住宿的費用是否合理。

祝各位好運！

165. 電子郵件的目的是什麼？
(A) 公布某個比賽
(B) 邀請職員參加派對
(C) 描述某個訓練機會
(D) 說明商業企劃的細節

解析
電子郵件第一段就提到要舉辦一場比賽詢問職員們的意見，用以決定旅遊地點 (we will run a contest to find the best suggestion)，故本題正解為選項 (A)。

166. 關於 Galaxy 電影院的敘述，何者正確？
(A) 和另一間公司合併了。
(B) 會提供職員獎勵。
(C) 要舉辦特別活動。
(D) 位在家具店附近。

解析
電子郵件第一段寫到 Galaxy 電影院在公司附近的轉角 (a movie at the theater around the corner from us, Galaxy Movie Theater)。從電子郵件上端的資訊欄 (To: All staff of Woodgrain Furniture Store/ From: Philip Downie, Store Proprietor) 可知寄件人是家具店店長，故本題正解為選項 (D)。

167. 哪一點並未被提及是個好地點的條件？
(A) 旅費不會太貴
(B) 寬敞的飯店房間
(C) 所有職員都能享受其中
(D) 有許多能夠從事的活動

解析
關於好的旅行地點條件出現在最後一段，內容有交通和住宿的費用都合理 (affordability of transportation and accommodation)，可知選項 (A) 正確，從受到喜好不同的職員們喜愛 (appeal to our diverse employees) 可知選項 (C) 正確。而能做的活動越多越好 (the number of activities on offer (the more, the better!)) 說明了選項 (D) 也正確。電子郵件中未提及要有很大的飯店房間，故本題正解為選項 (B)。

請參考以下線上對話回答**第 168 至 171 題**。

> **Lucas Sears [上午 11:25]**
> 早安，各位。我希望你們明天午餐時間過後能排出時間來開會。我們新的產品線賣得不是很理想。我們可能要考慮轉移重心。
> **Emma Harding [上午 11:26]**
> 你有想到些什麼嗎？
> **Lucas Sears [上午 11:29]**
> 168 既然 High Wave 時尚飾品的主要客群是青少年，169 我覺得比起透過印傳單宣傳，把重點放在線上銷售會更恰當。
> **Murray Henney [上午 11:31]**
> 沒錯。171 近來社群媒體和各種網站對消費者是否購買商品的影響力越來越大。
> **Rico Augustus [上午 11:33]**
> 我也同意那個想法。或許我們可以開始嘗試連絡一些社群媒體公司取得報價。
> **Emma Harding [上午 11:35]**
> 好主意。我們也可以試著尋找哪個網站的觸及量最高。

Lucas Sears [上午 11:37]
很好。看來我們的想法都相同。當我們明天見面時,我想要先看一些資料。 170 171 請各位去看一下不同的線上平臺,並確認在上面刊登廣告的費用是多少。接著,我會把這些資料整理好,送到董事會讓他們做評估。

Rico Augustus [上午 11:38]
170 我馬上就開始做。

Lucas Sears [上午 11:39]
謝謝,有任何疑問可以問我。我下午都會待在我的辦公室。

168. High Wave 時尚飾品最近在賣什麼商品?
(A) 電子設備
(B) 流行飾品
(C) 運動器材
(D) 清潔用品

解析
Sears 先生在 11 點 29 分傳送的訊息中提到業者的名稱和特點。從 High Wave 時尚飾品的名字和目標客群是青少年 (target market for High Wave fashion accessories largely consists of teenagers) 這句話中,可判斷這間公司販賣流行飾品,故本題正解為選項 (B)。

169. Sears 先生在 11 點 25 分傳送的訊息中寫到「我們可能要考慮轉移重心」,他指的是什麼意思?
(A) 公司必須要停賣某些商品。
(B) 要到別的地方開會。
(C) 公司必須要採取新的廣告策略。
(D) 會議討論的主題要更多樣化。

解析
Sears 先生說了這句話之後,在 11 點 29 分傳送的訊息中提到比起透過印傳單宣傳,把重點放在線上銷售會更恰當 (targeting consumers online rather than through print media seems like a better fit for us),故本題正解為改變廣告策略的選項 (C)。

170. Augustus 先生接下來可能會做什麼?
(A) 修改行銷預算
(B) 詢價
(C) 寄一些文件給 Sears 先生
(D) 更新公司的網站

解析
Sears 先生在 11 點 37 分傳送的訊息中提到要詢問廣告的費用 (find out how much it costs to run ads),接著 Augustus 先生回了他馬上就開始做 (I'll get right on it)。由此可知 Augustus 先生是要去詢問報價,故本題正解為選項 (B)。

171. Sears 先生會交給董事會成員什麼東西?
(A) 針對新商品的意見
(B) 為了增加網站觸及量的提案
(C) 廣告需要的設計
(D) 社群媒體的資訊

解析
Sears 先生在 11 點 37 分傳送的訊息中要大家去看一下不同的線上平臺,並確認費用,接著他會把資料送到董事會 (Look into the different online platforms...I'll compile the findings and pass them on to the board

for review.)。這邊所指的是 Henney 先生在 11 點 31 分說的社群媒體和各種網站 (Social media and other Web sites) 相關的資料,故本題正解為選項 (D)。

請參考以下文章回答**第 172 至 175 題**。

Spectacular 咖啡館即將開始營業

(倫敦,2 月 12 日)——法國連鎖咖啡品牌 Spectacular 咖啡館計劃於下個月在英國貝德福德郡開第三間咖啡廳。 175 打算要將咖啡廳開在鄧斯特布爾的 Eastlee 大道。–[1]–。

172 「因為鄧斯特布爾這的高級咖啡廳不多,這個城鎮對我們來說是一個開設最新店面的完美地點,」連鎖咖啡業者 Jerome Lemieux 說道。「我們非常興奮能在貝德福德郡增加另一個據點,並且我們很期待提供我們多樣化的優質咖啡給鄧斯特布爾的居民。」–[2]–。

173 總店位在馬賽的連鎖咖啡業者最近也在北愛爾蘭的貝爾法斯特開了咖啡廳。根據 Lemieux 先生所言, 174 他們的下一步是在今年年底再往北拓展,可能會越過邊界到蘇格蘭。–[3]–。就這一點看來,最有可能的地點應該是格拉斯哥和丹狄。–[4]–。

---

172. Lemieux 先生說新店地點有什麼優點?
(A) 店面價格合理
(B) 店面的大小
(C) 沒有什麼競爭者
(D) 居民人數很多

解析
Lemieux 先生的談話出現在第二段,他提到鄧斯特布爾高級的咖啡廳不多 (Because there aren't many high-end coffee houses in Dunstable)。由此可知同業競爭也不多,故本題正解為選項 (C)。

173. Spectacular 咖啡館的總店在哪?
(A) 鄧斯特布爾
(B) 貝爾法斯特
(C) 格拉斯哥
(D) 馬賽

解析
最後一段提到總店位在馬賽 (The Marseilles-based coffee chain),故本題正解為選項 (D)。

174. 根據文章內容,這間公司之後打算做什麼?
(A) 到蘇格蘭拓店
(B) 公布新的咖啡產品
(C) 併購當地咖啡公司
(D) 在貝德福德郡做行銷活動

解析
關於未來的計劃出現在最後一段,業者提到今年年底會再往北拓展,可能會越過邊界到蘇格蘭 (the next step will be to move further north and over the border into Scotland later this year)。由此可知是要到蘇格蘭拓店,故本題正解為選項 (A)。

175. 下面這個句子最適合填入 [1]、[2]、[3]、[4] 之中哪一個位置?
「盧頓和肯普斯頓這兩個城市已經有分店了。」

(A) [1]
(B) [2]
(C) [3]
(D) [4]

解析

這邊用 the other 代表除了已提及的之外的特定事物，所以必須放在和店面地點相關的資訊後面。由此可知這個句子應該填在 [1]，在 Eastlee 大道上開新店的句子後方，語意才會通順，故本題正解為選項 (A)。

請參考以下網頁和電子郵件回答**第 176 至 180 題**。

---

http://www.woolcroftbusinessinstitute.com

| 首頁 | 館內設施 | 全日制課程 | **即將舉辦的研討會** |

提升商業演說自信的系列研討會
提供 Anatolia 餐廳外燴

177(D) Woolcroft 商業學院 (WBI) 很開心地宣布我們 10 月的系列研討會，**176** 這次的研討會是設計給常常需要發表公開商業演說的人，為他們提升自信。所有研討會都會由在商業領域中擁有豐富經驗的講師帶領。每個研討會的空間需求很大，加上我們每一場最多只能收 250 人。有興趣的人請透過線上申請，**177(A)** 或直接撥打電話 555-0127。每場研討會的參加者都能在 **177(B)** 研討會結束後享用美味的自助式餐飲，由當地的土耳其餐廳 Anatolia 提供。

日期	時間	主題	講師	地點
10 月 7 日	下午 12:30–下午 2:00	演講入門介紹	Kenneth Lee	**177(C)** WBI 本館講堂
10 月 14 日	下午 3:00–下午 4:30	了解你的目標聽眾	Vlatko Andonov	**177(C)** WBI 本館講堂
10 月 21 日	下午 4:30–下午 6:00	產出有效的演講	Sheri Renner	**177(C)** WBI 本館講堂
10 月 28 日	下午 6:00–下午 7:30	**178** 在任何面試都能成功	**178** Karisma Kapoor	**177(C)** WBI 本館講堂

收件人：smeadows@estracorp.com
寄件人：registration@wbi.com
日期：10 月 3 日
主旨：研討會登記
附件：Stanmeadows.docx

親愛的 Meadows 先生：

我們連絡你是想確認你登記了我們 10 月系列研討會的其中一場。我確信你在研討會上 **179** 學到的策略與技巧，**178** 日後將能夠幫助你避免掉任何面試時會遇到的問題。

180 請確認一下附件中關於我們學院的詳細資訊的文件，裡面有建築內地圖、設施介紹，以及停車資訊。如果你想看看還有什麼全日制課程，你可以在我們的網站上找到完整的課程表。研討會那天你一抵達學院，請直接到資訊機臺前領取身分標籤。

Woolcroft 商業學院對我們的專業能力開發課程非常有信心。我們很期待能幫助你提升自己的能力。

敬祝 順心

課程登記部門
Woolcroft 商業學院

---

176. 根據網頁內容，他們提供了些什麼？
(A) 能夠增進公開演說技巧的機會
(B) 關於工作機會的資訊
(C) 提供給業主的財務諮詢
(D) 行銷公司間的交流活動

解析

網頁一開始就寫到這次的研討會是設計給常常需要發表公開商業演說的人，為他們提升自信 (is designed to give confidence to those who are often required to speak publicly in the business world)。由此可知答案是增進演說技巧的機會，故本題正解為選項 (A)。

177. 關於研討會的敘述，何者為非？
(A) 它們可以透過電話登記。
(B) 它們會提供餐點和飲品。
(C) 它們在好幾個會場舉辦。
(D) 它們都是由 Woolcroft 商業學院舉辦。

解析

網頁的第一段提到可以透過電話登記 (by calling us directly at 555-0127)，可知選項 (A) 正確。從能夠享用自助式餐飲 (will be able to enjoy a delicious buffet and drinks after the session) 可知選項 (B) 正確。此外，一開始就提到 Woolcroft 商業學院是系列研討會的主辦方 (Woolcroft Business Institute (WBI) is delighted to announce its October seminar series)，可知選項 (D) 也正確。但活動日程表格上的地點全都是 WBI 本館講堂，故本題正解為選項 (C)。

178. 誰會負責 Meadows 先生要參加的那堂研討會？
(A) Lee 先生
(B) Andonov 先生
(C) Renner 女士
(D) Kapoor 女士

解析

寄給 Meadows 先生的電子郵件第一段中，提到該研討會日後能夠幫助他避掉任何面試時會遇到的問題 (help you to avoid any problematic job interviews in the future)。對照網頁的表格後，可知和面試相關的研討會為最後一個 Succeeding in Any Interview Scenario，而該研討會的講師為 Karisma Kapoor，故本題正解為選項 (D)。

179. 與電子郵件第一段第二行的 "pick up" 意思最相近的詞語為_____
(A) 搬運
(B) 選擇
(C) 學習
(D) 分配

解析

這個詞語出現在 you will pick up 裡，負責修飾前方兩個名詞 strategies 和 skills，這兩個名詞的意思是「策略」和「技術」，可知這是收件人 Meadows 先生將透過研討會學到的東西。可推斷 pick up 在這裡

的意思代表「學」，因此有「學習」意思的選項 (C)
acquire 為本題正解。

180. 電子郵件附件是什麼樣的文件？
 (A) 可以上的課程
 (B) 關於學院的介紹
 (C) 登記收據
 (D) 身分標籤

解析
附件出現在第二段，裡面有建築內地圖、設施介紹，以及停車資訊 (including a map of the building, a description of amenities, and details about parking)。由此可知附件是和學院介紹相關的文件，故本題正解為選項 (B)。

請參考以下廣告與電子郵件回答**第 181 至 185 題**。

Cosmo 電腦優化──新年優惠價

電話號碼：0898-555-0126
電子郵件：sales@cosmotuneups.com

為了慶祝新一年的開始，我們決定提供優惠價給在 1 月和 2 月 182 進行電腦優化的客戶。 181 這只提供給先前曾經使用過我們服務的企業用戶。Cosmo 的技師會用我們創新的診斷系統和修復工具透過移除有害軟體、優化作業系統和安裝建議的更新，以最大化電腦的性能。定價和限時優惠價請參考下方表格。

電腦數量	定價 (每臺電腦)	優惠價 (每臺電腦)
1–9 臺	20 美元	17 美元
10–19 臺	18 美元	15 美元
184 20–29 臺	16 美元	184 13 美元
30 臺以上	14 美元	11 美元

額外提供：若在預定服務時，185 在電子郵件主旨寫上優惠廣告碼 "MAT123"，我們在前往貴公司進行電腦優化作業時，會贈送十個 Cosmo 滑鼠墊。

收件人：Bianca Lancaster
<blancaster@romacorp.com>
寄件人：Adam Crenna
<adamc@cosmotuneups.com>
日期：2 月 2 日
185 主旨：回覆：MAT123

親愛的 Lancaster 女士：

感謝你來信預訂 Roma 公司的電腦優化作業。
183 根據你提供的資訊，我幫你安排我們的服務在 2 月 9 日上午 9 點。正如你在電子郵件中提及的，184 你的公司符合新年優惠價的資格。我們的技師在安排的那天會準時抵達，並為你們辦公室的 20 臺電腦做優化。整個作業流程不會超過 3 小時。

如果你有任何疑問，請馬上再次連絡我。我們很期待能夠再次為你和你的公司服務。

敬祝 順心

Adam Crenna
客服部經理
Cosmo 電腦優化

181. 下列關於優惠價的資訊，何者正確？
 (A) 只適用於特定品牌的電腦。
 (B) 提供的期間為 3 個月。
 (C) 只能透過網站預訂。
 (D) 只提供給老客戶。

解析
優惠價出現在廣告的第一段，並說明這個優惠只提供給先前曾經使用過該公司服務的企業用戶 (This offer is only available to business clients who have used our services in the past.)。由此可知優惠價只提供給老客戶，故本題正解為選項 (D)。

182. 與廣告第一段第二行的 "performed" 意思最相近的詞語為_____
 (A) 執行
 (B) 展示
 (C) 改進
 (D) 努力

解析
performed 這個詞語在該句裡是以過去分詞的形態出現，負責修飾前方提到的名詞子句 all computer tune-ups。tune-ups 的意思是系統優化，再加上後面的特定期間一起修飾前方名詞，因此 performed 要是「 (在…期間) 執行」的意思，語意才會通順，故本題正解為同樣表執行的過去分詞，選項 (A) conducted。

183. 這封電子郵件的主要目的是什麼？
 (A) 要求某些資訊
 (B) 確認某項服務
 (C) 調整預約的日程
 (D) 宣傳特殊折扣

解析
電子郵件第一段寫到根據客戶提供的資料，安排 2 月 9 日上午 9 點執行服務 (Based on the information you provided, I've scheduled our service for February 9 at 9 A.M.)，並說明了詳細內容。由此可知這封電子郵件是在確認某個預約好的服務，故本題正解為選項 (B)。

184. Roma 公司每臺電腦做系統優化的價格是多少？
 (A) 11 美元
 (B) 13 美元
 (C) 15 美元
 (D) 20 美元

解析
電子郵件第一段提到新年優惠價，並說要幫客戶公司的 20 臺電腦做優化 (your company qualifies for our special New Year rates....tune up the twenty computers in your offices)。對照第一篇文章的圖表，可知 20 臺電腦的優惠價是 13 美元 (20–29/ Special Rate (per computer)/$13)，故本題正解為選項 (B)。

185. 下列關於 Lancaster 女士的敘述，何者正確？
 (A) 製造商會負責修她的電腦。

(B) 她的公司最近買了新的電腦。
(C) 她曾經是 Cosmo 電腦優化的職員。
(D) 她能夠得到免費的滑鼠墊。

解析
從電子郵件上端的主旨可知這是對方寄給 Lancaster 女士的回信，原本的主旨上寫了 MAT123 (Subject: Re: MAT123)。從第一篇文章的最後一段可知只要在電子郵件的主旨打上該優惠廣告碼，就能得到十個滑鼠墊 (if you write the specific advertisement code "MAT123" in the subject line of your e-mail, we'll provide up to 10 Cosmo mouse mats)。由此可知 Lancaster 女士能得到免費的滑鼠墊，故本題正解為選項 (D)。

請參考以下簡介及兩封電子郵件回答**第 186 至 190 題**。

Brightspark 太陽能板批發商

Brightspark 是歐洲首屈一指的商業用及住宅用太陽能板供應商。我們向全世界最棒的太陽能板製造商進了許多各式各樣的太陽能板。下面，為你介紹其中幾個我們的人氣商品。

188 **Synergy Solar**：可靠且物超所值的單晶太陽能板，適合所有類型的屋頂，無論任何角度。每一片太陽能板有 72 顆電池。
Sol Turbo：和 Synergy Solar 差不多，但太陽能板裡的 60 顆電池都是多晶體，讓太陽能板的成本更划算。
Solar King：這些 60 顆單晶電池的太陽能板，採用經由陽極氧化處理的重型鋁架建造，可以承受強風和大雪。
Sun Catcher：單晶太陽能板，每片有 72 顆電池，比起放在屋頂，此產品是為了放在建築物的垂直牆面而設計。

如果對我們提供的任何太陽能板你有任何疑問，請寄電子郵件至 inquiries@brightspark.co.uk 詢問。

當購買太陽能板時，準確測量太陽能板安裝的表面是非常重要的。測量過後，選擇你想要的太陽能板類型，186 我們的線上計算工具會準確地告訴你需要買多少片太陽能板，才能覆蓋你所要安裝的地點。現在就到 www.brightspark.co.uk/calculator 上自己試試看。

收件人：inquiries@brightspark.co.uk
寄件人：crundgren@smarthomes.com
日期：3 月 17 日
主旨：最近的訂單

親愛的 Brightspark：

我是房屋翻新公司的老闆，也是你們的常客之一。在 3 月 15 日，188 我幫我一位客戶的家訂了 25 片 72 顆電池的單晶太陽能板。我連絡你是因為我的顧客對這些太陽能板有些疑慮。187 188 她有些擔心這些太陽能板安裝到她湖邊小屋的屋頂上後，看起來會不太美觀。我試著向她保證這些太陽能板相對比較小且不顯眼。你可以寄給我任何屋頂上安裝了這個太陽能板的房屋的照片嗎？這樣一來我的

客戶就能放心了。

另外，還有一點。我上次跟你們訂太陽能板的時候，190 我可以自己上網印品質保證書，並提供給我的客戶。但我這次在官網上找不到能列印的地方。如果能告訴我如何得到這個資訊，讓我的客戶更滿意的話，我會非常感激。

謝謝你！

Colin Rundgren

收件人：crundgren@smarthomes.com
寄件人：anna321@brightspark.co.uk
189 日期：3 月 17 日
主旨：回覆：最近的訂單

親愛的 Rundgren 先生：

感謝你最近的詢問。即將寄給你的太陽能板是我們最受歡迎的款式，並且你的客戶無須擔心。我附上了幾張其他客戶很滿意的住家完工照，讓你的客戶可以看一看。如果她不滿意並且 189 想要選別的款式的話，請在今天下午 5 點前告訴我，這樣我才能變更訂單。

關於你詢問的其他問題，190 如果需要更詳細的文件，恐怕你得要直接連絡供應商。

敬祝 順心

Anna Thorn

---

186. 根據簡介的內容，顧客能夠在網站上做什麼？
(A) 比較供應商們提供的價格
(B) 要求諮詢服務
(C) 確認需要多少太陽能板
(D) 閱覽顧客的推薦

解析
簡介的最後一段提到了網站，寫到線上計算工具會準確地告訴你需要買多少片太陽能板 (our online calculation tool will tell you precisely how many panels you will need to buy)，接下來提供了網址並鼓勵讀者自己上去試試看，事先確認需要的太陽能板，故本題正解為選項 (C)。

187. Rundgren 先生的客戶對太陽能板有哪方面的擔憂？
(A) 外觀
(B) 安裝費用
(C) 能源產出量
(D) 耐用度

解析
Rundgren 先生出現在第一封電子郵件的寄件人欄，該封電子郵件的第一段就提及他的客戶有些擔心，並進一步說明是擔心太陽能板安裝到她湖邊小屋的屋頂上後，看起來會不太美觀 (She is worried that the panels will look unattractive)。由此可知他的客戶擔心的是外觀，故本題正解為選項 (A)。

188. Rundgren 先生最可能幫他的客戶訂的是哪種太陽能板？
(A) Synergy Solar
(B) Sol Turbo
(C) Solar King
(D) Sun Catcher

解析

第一封電子郵件的第一段寫到他幫一位客戶的家訂了 25 片 72 顆電池的單晶太陽能板 (I placed an order for 25 of your 72-cell monocrystalline solar panels)，後面又提到要安裝在屋頂上 (once they have been installed on the roof)。簡介中提到安裝在屋頂上，有著 72 顆電池的單晶太陽能板為 Synergy Solar(Synergy Solar: Reliable and cost-effective monocrystalline panels...Each panel is comprised of 72 cells)，故本題正解為選項 (A)。

189. 根據 Thorn 女士所說，為什麼 Rundgren 先生可能會需要在 3 月 17 日再次連絡她？
(A) 收某些文件
(B) 選擇其他太陽能板
(C) 支付最後的款項
(D) 重新安排安裝日期

解析

3 月 17 日這個日期出現在第二封電子郵件的寄件日期，文章第一段寫到想要選別的款式的話，要在今天下午 5 點前告訴她，這樣才能變更訂單 (If she is not satisfied and wishes to select a different type, please inform me by 5 P.M. this afternoon)。由此可知 Rundgren 先生可能會需要再次連絡對方的理由可能是要選擇其他太陽能板。

190. 關於產品品質保證書，可以就文章內容做出什麼推斷？
(A) 最近被修改過。
(B) 在產品的包裝裡。
(C) 會寄給 Rundgren 先生的客戶。
(D) 已經無法在 Brightspark 的網站上取得了。

解析

產品的品質保證書出現在第一封電子郵件的第二段，Rundgren 先生說之前可以在線上列印品質保證書，再交給客戶，現在在網站上卻找不到 (I was able to print out the warranty information online...I can't seem to find it on your site.)。而第二封電子郵件的第二段也與此相關，對方回覆要直接和供應商連絡才拿得到該份文件 (you'll need to contact the supplier directly if you wish to receive the full, detailed document)。由此可知網站上已經無法再取得品質保證書，故本題正解為選項 (D)。

請參考以下廣告、表單及電子郵件回答**第 191 至 195 題**。

191 **替你的職員報名 Gilford 學院吧！**

藉由提供你的職員補強訓練，你可以創建一支適應力強、高效率和凝聚力的勞動力。在 Gilford 學院，我們提供四種高度評價的專業能力開發課程：

有效的領導力——公司提供職員們領導力訓練的課程十分重要，不能只有主管和經理級職員。藉由早期培養職員們的領導力，你可以讓他們具備未來擔任領導者角色時，所有應該要知道的知識。
學員人數上限：40 人。每週一和週二上課。

192 *多樣性的訓練*——近來，工作場所變得比過去更多樣化。因此確保所有職員們都對多樣性的問題有一定程度的了解顯得十分重要。我們的多樣性訓練課程會加強職員們的知識量，讓他們能夠接受職場上的多樣性。
192 學員人數上限：70 人。每週二和週四上課。

時間管理——時間是所有公司最珍貴但最有限的資源。然而，許多職員缺少提高效率的相關知識和訓練。這樣的情況經常會導致錯過截止日期並產出糟糕的工作成果。我們的課程會幫助你的職員每天工作時都變得更有組織、更專注，且生產力變高。
學員人數上限：60 人。每週一和週三上課。

193 *增強溝通能力*——糟糕的溝通會造成低下的生產力及不必要的爭執。不管是面對面還是透過電子郵件，每一位職員都要對溝通的基礎有一定的了解。我們的課程會幫助職員們加強自身在說話和書面上所必須要會的溝通技巧。
學員人數上限：50 人。193 每週二和週三上課。

請寄電子郵件至 inquiries@gilfordinstitute.com 了解更多課程內容、課程時間和註冊相關的資訊。195 所有課程的上課地點都在我們位於 Rutherford 市區的本館。

Gilford 學院——進階商業訓練

課程報名表

公司代表：James Buckner
193 公司名稱：Markley 公司
報名職員人數：33
193 課程名稱：增強溝通能力

註冊日期：4 月 19 日

收件人：Gilford 學院 <inquiries@gilfordinstitute.com>
寄件人：James Buckner <jbuckner@markley.com>
日期：4 月 27 日
主旨：最近註冊的課程

親愛的先生／女士：

我最近有在你的學院替 Markley 公司行銷部門的職員註冊課程。我們都非常 194 熱切地期待課程開始，並從講師們的專業知識中受益。我連絡你是想詢問學院附近是否有能夠停車的地方。195 因為我們是從郊區前往，所以必須幫職員們租巴士過去。因為車輛會很大 (標準 52 人座巴士)，所以我們必須找一個適合停車的地方。可以請你給一些建議，包含地圖和指引嗎？這將會對我們很有幫助。

謹啟

James Buckner
行銷部主管
Markley 公司

191. 廣告的對象是誰？
(A) 剛畢業的學生們
(B) 就業博覽會的參加者們
(C) 課程講師們
(D) 公司老闆們
解析
廣告的開頭就說到替公司的職員報名 Gilford 學院 (Enroll Your Employees at The Gilford Institute!)，可知這個廣告的對象是公司老闆，故本題正解為選項 (D)。

192. 哪一個課程可以容納最多學員？
(A) 有效的領導力
(B) 多樣性的訓練
(C) 時間管理
(D) 增強溝通能力
解析
廣告的第三段寫到「多樣性的訓練」學員人數上限為 70 人 (Maximum class size: 70)，比其他課程的人數還要多，故本題正解為選項 (B)。

193. Markley 公司的職員什麼時候要去 Gilford 學院上課？
(A) 每週一和週二
(B) 每週一和週三
(C) 每週二和週三
(D) 每週二和週四
解析
表單上寫到該公司報名了增強溝通能力的課程 (Company: Markley Corporation/Course: Enhanced Communication)。第一篇文章的課程介紹裡寫明了增強溝通能力課程的上課時間是每週二和週三 (Course runs on Tuesdays and Wednesdays)，故本題正解為選項 (C)。

194. 與電子郵件第一段第二行的 "eager" 意思最相近的詞語為_____
(A) 有耐心的
(B) 令人滿意的
(C) 明顯的
(D) 熱烈的
解析
該句子的前一句說到已經報名了某個課程，eager 後面接 to 不定詞片語，內容為開始上課，並受益於講師的專業知識。由此可判斷 eager 是要表達對課程開始的熱切期盼，故本題正解為帶有「熱烈的」之意的選項 (D) enthusiastic。

195. Buckner 先生針對 Markley 公司說了些什麼？
(A) 公司在 Rutherford 市區外。
(B) 希望修改部分報名細節。
(C) 之前曾經和 Gilford 學院合作過。
(D) 想要 Gilford 學院提供交通方式。
解析
Buckner 先生寄送的電子郵件中段寫到他們是從郊區

前往 (Because we will be coming from out of town)，而廣告的最後一句提到所有課程的上課地點都在位於 Rutherford 市區的本館 (All courses are offered at our main campus building in downtown Rutherford.)。由此可知 Markley 公司位在拉塞福市區外，故本題正解為選項 (A)。

請參考以下電子郵件和估價單回答**第 196 至 200 題**。

收件人：Joe Turner <joeturner@lla.com>
寄件人：Roberta Fleck <rfleck@fleckevents.com>
主旨：估價單
日期：12 月 12 日
附件：飯店清單 .docx

親愛的 Turner 先生：

196 我有收到你最近傳來的電子郵件，關於你不久後預計在 Manchester 這裡舉辦 Lovett 文藝協會頒獎典禮。請你確認一下有適合舉辦這類活動宴會廳的飯店清單。

197 正如你要求的，我已經把位在 Belmont 的那間飯店加到清單裡。雖然我個人沒有參加過任何在那間飯店舉辦的活動，我的同事非常確定地告訴我那裡的設備完善，可以舉辦大型活動。

一旦你決定之後，你必須在 12 月 15 日前先支付 10% 的訂金，以確保保留場地。最近剛好是一年內最難預約活動場地的時間點。我期盼能幫助你順利舉辦活動。

謹啟

Roberta Fleck

活動空間租借估價單				
租借人：**Lovett 文藝協會**		活動時間：**4 小時**		
大略參加人數：**400**		活動日期：**2 月 5 日**		
飯店	地區	其他資訊	每小時費用	總金額
Arlington 飯店	Five Hills	有能舉辦現場音樂表演的設備	250 英鎊	1,000 英鎊
Thames 飯店	Longford	屋頂活動空間及酒吧	300 英鎊	1,200 英鎊
198 Yarrow 飯店	Hampton	198 方便進出並為行動不便人士設計的無障礙坡道	225 英鎊	1,100 英鎊
199 Musgrove 飯店	Dayton	199 剛翻新的多功能宴會廳及舞臺	275 英鎊	199 1,300 英鎊
197 Ascot 飯店	Belmont	提供自助餐或套餐選擇	325 英鎊	1,400 英鎊

收件人：Roberta Fleck <rfleck@fleckevents.com>
寄件人：Joe Turner <joeturner@lla.com>
主旨：回覆：估價單
日期：12 月 15 日
附件：飯店清單 .docx

親愛的 Fleck 女士：

謝謝你為我們的頒獎典禮整理地點清單。你真的非常努力地幫我們籌備每件事。就如你所建議，**199** 我已經先支付了 10% 的訂金，以提前確保我們訂下那間飯店的活動場地。雖然 Thames 飯店的屋頂活動空間聽起來很不錯，**199** 但我覺得還是挑一間最近剛翻新過的飯店比較重要，因為我們想要在一個精緻又迷人的環境下舉辦活動。除此之外，我也不傾向訂屋頂的空間，以防突然下雨。

我第二個考量的點是餐飲。**200** 你能推薦不錯的外燴業者，能在活動上提供餐點嗎？那間飯店的經理建議我找專門替我們這種大型活動提供外燴料理的業者。**200** 我會先看看幾個不同選項，但我會等你回覆再做最終決定。

敬祝 順心

Joe Turner

196. 從文章中能夠得知 Fleck 女士的什麼資訊？
(A) 她在 Manchester 的飯店工作。
(B) 她入圍了某個獎項。
(C) 她正在籌劃一個特別的典禮。
(D) 她住在 Belmont 附近。

解析
Fleck 女士在第一封電子郵件的第一段提到自己收到對方的電子郵件，內容是不久後預計在 Manchester 舉辦 Lovett 文藝協會頒獎典禮，並請收件人確認有宴會廳的飯店清單 (I received your recent e-mail about your upcoming Lovett Literary Association awards show,...Please find a list of hotels that have suitable function rooms)。由此可知 Fleck 女士正在幫忙籌劃一場典禮，故本題正解為選項 (C)。

197. Fleck 女士因 Turner 先生的要求，加入了哪間飯店？
(A) Arlington 飯店
(B) Thames 飯店
(C) Musgrove 飯店
(D) Ascot 飯店

解析
第一封電子郵件的第二段寫到因為對方的要求，在清單上加入了位在 Belmont 的飯店 (Just like you asked, I have made sure to add a hotel situated in Belmont)。對照估價單所列的飯店清單可知位在 Belmont 的飯店為 Ascot 飯店 (Ascot Hotel/Belmont)，故本題正解為選項 (D)。

198. 從文章中能夠得知 Yarrow 飯店的什麼資訊？
(A) 有輪椅的出入口。
(B) 活動空間相對而言較小。

(C) 能提供現場音樂表演。
(D) 客人們能夠享用自助式餐點。

解析
估價單上關於 Yarrow 飯店的其他資訊中寫到有為行動不便人士所設計方便進出的無障礙坡道 (Yarrow Hotel/Easy access and ramps for those with disabilities)。這個無障礙坡道即是為坐輪椅的客人所設計，故本題正解為選項 (A)。

199. Turner 先生租借活動場地總共要支付多少錢？
(A) 1,000 英鎊
(B) 1,200 英鎊
(C) 1,300 英鎊
(D) 1,400 英鎊

解析
第二封電子郵件的第一段寫到已經支付了 10% 的訂金，且點出自己選擇了最近剛翻新過的飯店 (I have paid a 10 percent deposit...it was more important to choose a venue that has recently undergone modifications)。對照估價單中的飯店清單，可知最近剛翻新過的飯店是 Musgrove 飯店，總金額為 1,300 英鎊 (Musgrove Hotel/Newly renovated function room and stage/ £1,300)，故本題正解為選項 (C)。

200. 根據第二封電子郵件的內容，Turner 先生接著會做什麼？
(A) 連絡飯店經理
(B) 思考要選什麼樣的現場表演
(C) 安排和 Fleck 女士開會
(D) 比較外燴業者

解析
Turner 先生在第二封電子郵件的第二段請對方推薦能在活動上提供餐食的外燴業者，接著說自己也會看看其他選項 (Can you recommend a good caterer to provide food at the event?...I'll take a look at some different options)。由此可知他是要比較外燴業者，故本題正解為選項 (D)。

揮別厚重，迎向高分！
最接近真實多益測驗的模擬題本

特色 **1** 單回成冊

揮別市面多數多益題本的厚重感，單回裝訂仿照真實測驗，提前適應答題手感。

特色 **2** 錯題解析

解析本提供深度講解，針對正確答案與誘答選項進行解題，全面掌握答題關鍵。

特色 **3** 誤答筆記

提供筆記模板，協助深入了解誤答原因，歸納出專屬於自己的學習筆記。

Name	
Registration Number	

TOEIC

Test of English for International Communication

TEST 2

三民書局

LISTENING TEST

In the Listening test, you will be asked to demonstrate how well you understand spoken English. The entire Listening test will last approximately 45 minutes. There are four parts, and directions are given for each part. You must mark your answers on the separate answer sheet.

Do not write your answers in your test book.

PART 1

Directions: For each question in this part, you will hear four statements about a picture in your test book. When you hear the statements, you must select the one statement that best describes what you see in the picture. Then find the number of the question on your answer sheet and mark your answer. The statements will not be printed in your test book and will be spoken only one time.

Statement (D), "They are taking photographs," is the best description of the picture, so you should select answer (D) and mark it on your answer sheet.

1.

2.

GO ON TO THE NEXT PAGE ➡

3.

4.

5.

6.

PART 2

Directions: You will hear a question or statement and three responses spoken in English. They will not be printed in your test book and will be spoken only one time. Select the best response to the question or statement and mark the letter (A), (B), or (C) on your answer sheet.

7. Mark your answer on your answer sheet.

8. Mark your answer on your answer sheet.

9. Mark your answer on your answer sheet.

10. Mark your answer on your answer sheet.

11. Mark your answer on your answer sheet.

12. Mark your answer on your answer sheet.

13. Mark your answer on your answer sheet.

14. Mark your answer on your answer sheet.

15. Mark your answer on your answer sheet.

16. Mark your answer on your answer sheet.

17. Mark your answer on your answer sheet.

18. Mark your answer on your answer sheet.

19. Mark your answer on your answer sheet.

20. Mark your answer on your answer sheet.

21. Mark your answer on your answer sheet.

22. Mark your answer on your answer sheet.

23. Mark your answer on your answer sheet.

24. Mark your answer on your answer sheet.

25. Mark your answer on your answer sheet.

26. Mark your answer on your answer sheet.

27. Mark your answer on your answer sheet.

28. Mark your answer on your answer sheet.

29. Mark your answer on your answer sheet.

30. Mark your answer on your answer sheet.

31. Mark your answer on your answer sheet.

PART 3

Directions: You will hear some conversations between two or more people. You will be asked to answer three questions about what the speakers say in each conversation. Select the best response to each question and mark the letter (A), (B), (C) or (D) on your answer sheet. The conversations will not be printed in your test book and will be spoken only one time.

32. Where is the conversation most likely taking place?
(A) In a taxi
(B) In an airplane
(C) In a bus station
(D) In a hotel

33. What did Olivia give to the woman?
(A) Event tickets
(B) Meal vouchers
(C) A travel budget
(D) A city map

34. Why will the man call a conference center?
(A) To cancel a talk
(B) To ask for directions
(C) To hire equipment
(D) To check a schedule

35. Where do the men most likely work?
(A) At a bank
(B) At a bookstore
(C) At a conference hall
(D) At a radio station

36. What did the woman recently do?
(A) Designed a product
(B) Launched a business
(C) Wrote a book
(D) Directed a film

37. What will the woman do next?
(A) Introduce a product
(B) Discuss her career
(C) Ask questions
(D) Offer some tips

38. What do the speakers say about Regina?
(A) She has been promoted.
(B) She is absent.
(C) She won an award.
(D) She is retiring.

39. What does the woman ask about?
(A) A work schedule
(B) A reservation
(C) A bonus
(D) A new policy

40. What does the man say he will do this afternoon?
(A) Purchase a gift
(B) Attend a staff meeting
(C) Make a reservation
(D) Eat a meal

41. What is the man disappointed about?
(A) A venue is unavailable.
(B) A room is too expensive.
(C) A client cannot attend an event.
(D) A hotel has gone out of business.

42. What does the man want approval to do?
(A) Arrange transportation
(B) Reschedule an event
(C) Increase a budget
(D) Extend his trip

43. What does the woman ask the man to do next?
(A) Print an itinerary
(B) Make a payment
(C) Send a design
(D) Review some figures

GO ON TO THE NEXT PAGE

44. Who most likely is the woman?
    (A) A marketing director
    (B) A financial consultant
    (C) A safety inspector
    (D) A customer service agent

45. What does the man mean when he says, "I just bought it a few days ago"?
    (A) A package has not been delivered yet.
    (B) A bill was sent to the wrong person.
    (C) A purchase does not need to be made.
    (D) A product should be in perfect condition.

46. What will the man most likely do next?
    (A) Check a receipt
    (B) Replace a part
    (C) Press a switch
    (D) Read a manual

47. Where do the speakers work?
    (A) At a post office
    (B) At a medical clinic
    (C) At a factory
    (D) At a library

48. What does the woman offer the man?
    (A) Additional training
    (B) Management experience
    (C) Extra vacation leave
    (D) Higher pay

49. What does the man ask about?
    (A) A workshop location
    (B) A bus timetable
    (C) A ticket cost
    (D) A registration process

50. What is the conversation mainly about?
    (A) A landscaping project
    (B) A community event
    (C) A building renovation
    (D) A business merger

51. What did the men do this morning?
    (A) Purchased materials
    (B) Tidied up a work site
    (C) Reviewed designs
    (D) Interviewed job applicants

52. What would Mike like to change?
    (A) A deadline
    (B) A budget
    (C) A location
    (D) A supplier

53. What does the man want to discuss?
    (A) A promotion strategy
    (B) A business relocation
    (C) A safety procedure
    (D) A staff incentive plan

54. What problem does the man mention about the part-time workers?
    (A) They are not busy.
    (B) They require extra training.
    (C) They were hired recently.
    (D) They have received complaints.

55. According to the woman, why were employees unhappy?
    (A) They wanted higher wages.
    (B) Their work shifts were too long.
    (C) They experienced bad weather.
    (D) Their vacation leave was reduced.

56. What is indicated about the library?
    (A) It has changed its business hours.
    (B) It has moved to a new location.
    (C) It was recently remodeled.
    (D) It is hiring new staff.

57. What does the man say he used to do?
    (A) Read during lunchtime
    (B) Eat at a cafeteria
    (C) Write magazine articles
    (D) Visit a nearby restaurant

58. What does the woman advise the man to do?
    (A) Visit a bakery
    (B) Skip lunch
    (C) Attend an event
    (D) Leave work early

59. What are the speakers mainly discussing?
    (A) Promotional flyers
    (B) Staff training
    (C) Work uniforms
    (D) A Web site design

60. What does the man imply when he says, "We have until Friday to confirm the order"?
    (A) There is still time to make changes.
    (B) They will finish a task ahead of schedule.
    (C) Additional employees are required.
    (D) The number of items should be increased.

61. What does the man suggest doing?
    (A) Visiting a business
    (B) Sending an e-mail
    (C) Making a phone call
    (D) Canceling a meeting

Comment Card
(Please indicate a score out of 10)
1. Cleanliness : ⬚
2. Service : ⬚
3. Amenities : ⬚
4. Additional Comments : _____
_____
_____
_____

62. Who is the comment card for?
    (A) Restaurant diners
    (B) Airline passengers
    (C) Hotel guests
    (D) Event attendees

63. How did the woman choose the scoring method on the comment card?
    (A) She read a magazine article.
    (B) She asked for customer feedback.
    (C) She consulted her supervisor.
    (D) She copied a competitor's.

64. Look at the graphic. Which item will be removed from the comment card?
    (A) Item 1
    (B) Item 2
    (C) Item 3
    (D) Item 4

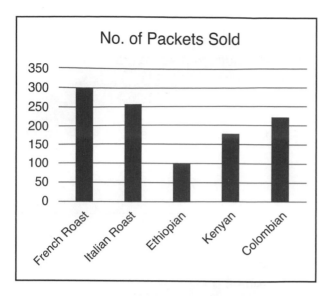

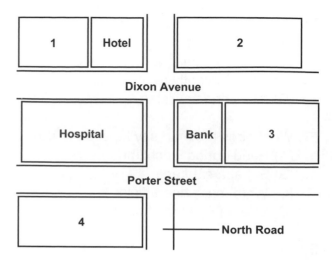

65. What did the speakers do last month?
(A) They hosted a special event.
(B) They opened a new business.
(C) They hired additional staff.
(D) They renovated a coffee shop.

66. Look at the graphic. Which coffee variety will be sold at a lower price in August?
(A) Italian Roast
(B) Ethiopian
(C) Kenyan
(D) Colombian

67. Why does the man think more customers will come to the coffee shop?
(A) A new range of products is available.
(B) A seasonal sale will be held.
(C) A new advertisement was launched.
(D) A membership plan is being offered.

68. Where do the speakers most likely work?
(A) At a law office
(B) At a real estate agency
(C) At a marketing company
(D) At a catering firm

69. Look at the graphic. Which building will the speakers go to on Monday?
(A) Building 1
(B) Building 2
(C) Building 3
(D) Building 4

70. What does the man offer to do?
(A) Send the woman a document
(B) Reschedule a meeting
(C) Give the woman a ride
(D) Cancel a dentist appointment

Directions: You will hear some talks given by a single speaker. You will be asked to answer three questions about what the speaker says in each talk. Select the best response to each question and mark the letter (A), (B), (C), or (D) on your answer sheet. The talks will not be printed in your test book and will be spoken only one time.

71. What type of product is being advertised?
    (A) A sleeping bag
    (B) A pair of boots
    (C) A tent
    (D) A backpack

72. What does the speaker say is a surprising thing about the product?
    (A) Its weight
    (B) Its durability
    (C) Its appearance
    (D) Its price

73. What should listeners do to receive a discount?
    (A) Sign up for a membership
    (B) Attend a grand opening
    (C) Spend a specific amount
    (D) Make an online purchase

74. What is the speaker writing a report about?
    (A) Ways to recruit skilled employees
    (B) The benefits of advertising online
    (C) Methods for reducing waste
    (D) Ideas for increasing sales

75. According to the speaker, what has changed?
    (A) An e-mail address
    (B) A project deadline
    (C) A marketing campaign
    (D) A trip itinerary

76. Why does the speaker say, "You know Steve at the head office, right"?
    (A) To suggest inviting Steve to a meeting
    (B) To confirm that a project has been approved
    (C) To recommend that the listener apply for a position
    (D) To request that the listener contact a colleague

77. Who is being introduced?
    (A) A retiring director
    (B) An award recipient
    (C) A new board member
    (D) A company client

78. What is mentioned about an advertisement?
    (A) It was for a range of cell phones.
    (B) It was less successful than expected.
    (C) It was seen all over the world.
    (D) It has been aired for 15 years.

79. What is suggested about Jeremy Lee?
    (A) He is active.
    (B) He enjoys reading.
    (C) He founded a business.
    (D) He will be promoted.

80. What is the speaker calling about?
    (A) A business proposal
    (B) An upcoming sale
    (C) A job application
    (D) A project deadline

81. What problem does the speaker mention?
    (A) A schedule conflict has occurred.
    (B) Some information is missing.
    (C) Some guidelines are incorrect.
    (D) An event has been postponed.

82. What does the speaker ask the listener to do?
    (A) Visit a business
    (B) Attend an interview
    (C) Return the call
    (D) Send an e-mail

83. According to the speaker, why is St. Mark's Cathedral popular?
(A) It hosts special events.
(B) Its architecture is unique.
(C) It does not charge an entry fee.
(D) It contains many artworks.

84. What does the speaker mean when she says, "that's why I'm here!"?
(A) She is recommending a specific attraction.
(B) She wants the listeners to follow her.
(C) She is apologizing for arriving late.
(D) She will be happy to answer questions.

85. What does the speaker remind the listeners about?
(A) A parking permit
(B) A special discount
(C) A bus number
(D) A departure time

86. What is the broadcast mainly about?
(A) Employment opportunities
(B) Leisure facilities
(C) Community awards
(D) Upcoming events

87. According to the speaker, what field does Karen Gosford have experience in?
(A) Entertainment
(B) Finance
(C) Marketing
(D) Science

88. What does the speaker invite the listeners to do?
(A) Ask questions
(B) Attend a ceremony
(C) Share their opinions
(D) Cast a vote

89. What service does the company provide?
(A) Home improvements
(B) Financial advice
(C) Event planning
(D) Travel packages

90. Why is the speaker not available?
(A) She is in a board meeting.
(B) She is on sick leave.
(C) She is leading a course.
(D) She is on vacation.

91. What should the listeners do if they have an urgent problem?
(A) Call a different number
(B) Visit the speaker's office
(C) Send an e-mail
(D) Review a document

92. Where do the listeners work?
(A) At a travel agency
(B) At a bank
(C) At a supermarket
(D) At a coffee shop

93. What does the speaker imply when he says, "Many employees will want this day off"?
(A) A business will be closing temporarily.
(B) A company event will need to be postponed.
(C) The listeners should consult a work schedule.
(D) The listeners should make a request soon.

94. What does the speaker encourage the listeners to do?
(A) Request overtime hours
(B) Pick up a uniform
(C) Submit a payment
(D) Check an employee handbook

Friday	Saturday	Sunday	Monday
⛈	🌧	🌬	☀

95. Look at the graphic. When will the outdoor concert take place?
(A) Friday
(B) Saturday
(C) Sunday
(D) Monday

96. What does the speaker say he is looking forward to?
(A) A singer
(B) A fireworks display
(C) A parade
(D) A comedian

97. What does the speaker advise the listeners to do?
(A) Enter a competition
(B) Request a gift voucher
(C) Send an e-mail
(D) Visit a Web site

Meeting Schedule		
9:15	Introduction	
9:30	Stacey Naylor	Product Design Manager
10:15	Phil Meeks	R&D Manager
10:45	Rosie Fisher	Personnel Manager
11:15	Abdul Singh	Marketing Manager

98. Who most likely are the listeners?
(A) Company shareholders
(B) Preferred customers
(C) Potential clients
(D) New employees

99. What type of products does the company make?
(A) Appliances
(B) Clothing
(C) Furniture
(D) Vehicles

100. Look at the graphic. Who will speak next?
(A) Stacey Naylor
(B) Phil Meeks
(C) Rosie Fisher
(D) Abdul Singh

This is the end of the Listening test. Turn to Part 5 in your text book.

READING TEST

In the Reading test, you will read a variety of texts and answer several different types of reading comprehension questions. The entire Reading test will last 75 minutes. There are three parts, and directions are given for each part. You are encouraged to answer as many questions as possible within the time allowed. You must mark your answers on the separate answer sheet. Do not write your answers in your test book.

PART 5

Directions: A word or phrase is missing in each of the sentences below. Four answer choices are given below each sentence. Select the best answer to complete the sentence. Then mark the letter (A), (B), (C), or (D) on your answer sheet.

101. Guests can have their poolside drink orders ------- charged to their hotel bill.
(A) automatically
(B) automatic
(C) automates
(D) automate

102. The east wing of Huxtable Art Museum will be closed to visitors until further -------.
(A) alert
(B) regard
(C) notice
(D) admission

103. There are many vitamins and supplements in our health store that can help ------- to lose weight.
(A) you
(B) your
(C) yourself
(D) yourselves

104. It is ------- that customers be informed about our new business hours before they go into effect.
(A) frequent
(B) critical
(C) potential
(D) actual

105. The painting by Fernando Boleo has been ------- at less than 75 percent of its expected value.
(A) appraiser
(B) appraise
(C) appraised
(D) appraisal

106. The marketing department will work late this week ------- problems with the new advertising campaign.
(A) while
(B) whereas
(C) as for
(D) due to

107. It is recommended that audience members take their seats at least 10 minutes before the singer's ------- performance time.
(A) schedules
(B) schedule
(C) scheduling
(D) scheduled

108. Trey Nispel's regular newspaper column, Sports Breakdown, is ------- every Saturday in The Richmond Times.
(A) competed
(B) published
(C) determined
(D) attributed

109. To avoid work delays, the ------- of Crawley Castle will be carried out by a team of 25 experts.
(A) restore
(B) restorative
(C) restored
(D) restoration

110. Please note that opening times for the swimming area at Sadler Lake are subject to change ------- in accordance with the seasons.
(A) lightly
(B) quarterly
(C) properly
(D) barely

111. New employees at BAS Accounting should provide two forms of ------- on their first day of work.
(A) recognition
(B) categorization
(C) identification
(D) acceptance

112. Katherine Brewer has the ------- necessary to supervise training of all newly-hired staff at our factory in Pontianak.
(A) limitation
(B) profitability
(C) experience
(D) decision

113. According to the ------- of this lease, you must vacate the apartment by October 31 at the latest.
(A) signatures
(B) terms
(C) properties
(D) reviews

114. Restaurant staff who are ------- in working overtime this summer should speak directly to the owner.
(A) interest
(B) interests
(C) interested
(D) interesting

115. The waiting room at Hillside Dental Clinic contains many magazines that are ------- to health and nutrition.
(A) definite
(B) completed
(C) relevant
(D) focused

116. Mr. Rundle had to turn off the factory's cutting machine ------- because of a potentially dangerous malfunction.
(A) quickly
(B) quicken
(C) quicker
(D) quickest

117. The dishes served at Rainbow Restaurant are made from many imported ingredients, even some ------- farms in India.
(A) up
(B) from
(C) upon
(D) between

118. At Regent Chemicals Inc., you may apply to join the staff safety committee if you have ------- one year of first aid training.
(A) assumed
(B) completed
(C) expected
(D) allowed

119. The use of bicycles for transportation is ------- even though gas prices have slightly declined.
(A) expand
(B) expands
(C) expanded
(D) expanding

120. The management is delighted to announce that ------- will merge with Iridium Software on the new video game project.
(A) we
(B) our
(C) us
(D) ourselves

121. For shuttle buses to become a popular service, the buses must run ------- on time throughout the day.
(A) exacted
(B) exactness
(C) exact
(D) exactly

122. Many rainforests in Brazil are expected to shrink by 30% ------- the next two decades.
(A) about
(B) within
(C) toward
(D) following

123. The CEO asked Ms. Spencer to buy another issue of the magazine that -------.
(A) misplaces
(B) misplacing
(C) misplaced
(D) was misplaced

124. During her vacation, Ms. Theakston will let her assistant handle all issues except for those that require her ------- attention.
(A) sturdy
(B) fluent
(C) easy
(D) urgent

125. Please fill out a comment card ------- management can evaluate staff performance effectively.
(A) so that
(B) in order to
(C) because of
(D) as well as

126. The first Monday of every month is ------- the outside windows of the office building are cleaned.
(A) how
(B) for
(C) when
(D) what

127. Although his books use some difficult vocabulary, Jim Wallis believes young readers will ------- find them enjoyable.
(A) still
(B) quite
(C) too
(D) ever

128. ------- you have passed the initial interview phase, we will ask you to take a written test to demonstrate your knowledge of electrical engineering.
(A) Then
(B) Next
(C) Once
(D) Always

129. File folders ------- with red stickers are for employees who are yet to complete the full customer service training course.
(A) marked
(B) marking
(C) that mark
(D) are marked

130. Our scuba diving classes will help you prepare for any obstacles you may ------- underwater.
(A) surprise
(B) refine
(C) encounter
(D) occupy

PART 6

Directions: Read the texts that follow. A word, phrase, or sentence is missing in parts of each text.

Four answer choices for each question are given below the text. Select the best answer to complete the text. Then mark the letter (A), (B), (C) or (D) on your answer sheet.

Questions 131–134 refer to the following e-mail.

To: Frank Edgar <fedgar@robocorp.com>

From: Eloise Dunn <eloisedunn@estinc.com>

Subject: Information

Date: May 4

Dear Mr. Edgar,

You were the keynote speaker at the recent Artificial Intelligence Conference in Berlin, and I was lucky to be in the ----- for your talk. I found the things you said about the future
131.
of robotics in the vehicle manufacturing industry extremely enlightening. -----, it made me
132.
consider making some major changes at my company. The introduction of advanced robots in our factory could greatly improve our production efficiency! Would you mind meeting with me and my company's president? -----. I've attached a schedule ----- some suitable dates
133. **134.**
for a meeting this month. I hope to hear from you soon.

Regards,

Eloise Dunn

Chief Operating Officer

EST Motors Inc.

---

131. (A) brochure
(B) presentation
(C) company
(D) audience

132. (A) In fact
(B) On the contrary
(C) Meanwhile
(D) Lastly

133. (A) He was very impressed with the way you solved the problem.
(B) Once again, I apologize for the postponement of the event.
(C) Your knowledge of robotics will be of great interest to him.
(D) The project should take no longer than two months to complete.

134. (A) is providing
(B) that provides
(C) provided those
(D) having provided

Questions 135–138 refer to the following notice.

At Four Points Amusement Park, we treat visitor ＿＿＿ as a very serious matter. In the event
135.
of inclement weather, we keep an eye on the conditions minute-to-minute. If conditions
become severe, such as strong winds or heavy rains, it may be necessary to close specific
rides, certain park areas, or even the entire park itself.

Park Supervisors will communicate updates to visitors in person and via the public
announcement system. ＿＿＿. Visitors ＿＿＿ a free pass for a future visit to the park if they
136. **137.**
need to leave due to poor weather. Once employees have helped escort all visitors out of
the park, they should return ＿＿＿ immediately and continue shutting down all areas of the
138.
park. To find out more about our bad weather procedures, speak with your supervisor.

135. (A) safety
(B) attraction
(C) compensation
(D) accommodation

136. (A) Live performances are held at an
outdoor stage inside the park.
(B) Opening times are subject to change
depending on weather conditions.
(C) This policy will be implemented
sometime next year.
(D) It's our priority to ensure all visitors
are kept informed.

137. (A) received
(B) will receive
(C) have received
(D) had been receiving

138. (A) to work
(B) working
(C) worked
(D) the work

Questions 139–142 refer to the following e-mail.

To: All festival organizers
From: Roy Hatton, Head Organizer
Subject: Rock World Music Festival

This year's Rock World Music Festival will take place on Saturday, July 19th from 10 A.M. to 11 P.M. at a site on the banks of Lake Marlin. We are confident that the performers and audience members alike will enjoy this scenic _____. The event will end with an impressive
139.
fireworks display, but your work shifts will finish beforehand so that all of you _____.
140.

Festival tickets will go on sale tomorrow through our Web site and various vendors. Employees will be able to purchase tickets at a discounted rate for themselves and their friends and family. _____, tickets are limited to three per person.
141.

_____
142.

139. (A) building
(B) setting
(C) presentation
(D) device

140. (A) participation
(B) participating
(C) can participate
(D) who participated

141. (A) However
(B) In conclusion
(C) Therefore
(D) For example

142. (A) Many tour groups are expected to visit Lake Marlin this year.
(B) Thank you for your interest in performing at the event.
(C) We will be hosting several concerts this summer.
(D) Let's work hard to make this the best festival yet.

Questions 143–146 refer to the following review.

I have good things and bad things to say about Splendid Catering. They provide a diverse range of foods and their prices are very reasonable. However, I ------ them my business
143.
again. My recent order contained several items that were not fresh. It seemed like the staff didn't bother checking the ------ of the sandwiches they delivered to the event I was
144.
hosting. ------. None of them looked like the pictures advertised on the Web site. But did the
145.
company agree to replace them with new ones? No, they didn't. Next time I will choose a catering firm that will let me ------ items that don't meet basic expectations.
146.

143. (A) did not give
(B) will not be giving
(C) might not have given
(D) could not have given

144. (A) size
(B) quality
(C) price
(D) brand

145. (A) More than half of them were too odd to eat.
(B) Most of my guests were impressed with the food.
(C) The firm offers discounts on bulk orders.
(D) We did not have enough ingredients to fill the order.

146. (A) exchange
(B) purchase
(C) view
(D) store

Directions: In this part you will read a selection of texts, such as magazine and newspaper articles, e-mails, and instant messages. Each text or set of texts is followed by several questions. Select the best answer for each question and mark the letter (A), (B), (C), or (D) on your answer sheet.

Questions 147–148 refer to the following receipt.

RENTAL RECORD
DATE: July 26
NAME: STEVEN CHAMBERS

RENTAL DETAILS	ITEMS
To help me complete a renovation project I will lead in Sawyer City from August 4 to August 29(the conversion of the old Latimer Theater into apartment units).	Sledgehammer (x 2) Cement Mixer Safety Goggles (x 4) Power Drill (x 2)

I confirm receipt of the above items.

Signature *Steven Chambers*

147. What will Mr. Chambers do in Sawyer City in August?
(A) Lead a training class
(B) Hire new workers
(C) Sign a property lease
(D) Renovate a building

148. What does Mr. Chambers confirm?
(A) Receiving equipment
(B) Purchasing a vehicle
(C) Accepting a job offer
(D) Repairing a device

Questions 149–150 refer to the following notice.

Cooper Dental Practice
Amazing discounts available at
our Astrid Mall location!

Cooper Dental is celebrating 10 years of business!

Make your smile the best it can possibly be!

We are offering high-quality implants

and teeth whitening treatments for 15% off.

Other selected treatments are available for up to 30% off.

Offers begin on February 1 and end on March 31.

We are open from 9 A.M. to 7 P.M., Monday through Saturday;

You can find us on the second floor of the building–

just at the top of the escalators once you come in the main entrance.

Appointments can be made by visiting www.cooperdental.co.uk
or by calling 555-0171.

149. Who most likely posted the notice?
(A) A business owner
(B) A human resources manager
(C) A health inspector
(D) A Web site designer

150. What is suggested about Cooper Dental?
(A) It is moving to a larger location.
(B) It runs a different promotion each month.
(C) It recently purchased new equipment.
(D) It has a clinic in a shopping center.

Earnshaw Textiles Inc. guide for completing an accident report

* Describe the incident, including the name of the employee(s) involved.
* If a machine has been turned off as a result of the accident, check the box labeled "Shut Down" and provide details.
* Reports must be filled out immediately when an accident takes place.
* Date the report and submit it to the administration office. Reports that are undated will be returned to the submitter.
* Ensure that work areas are safe and secure.

The repair of tools or machines will be scheduled whenever necessary as soon as the report has been submitted.

---

151. According to the instructions, what must appear on every accident report?
(A) A contact number
(B) An employee's name
(C) A business address
(D) An incident date

152. What is indicated about Earnshaw Textiles Inc.'s administration office?
(A) It runs a regular health and safety training session.
(B) It makes arrangements to have equipment fixed.
(C) It publishes an accident report on a monthly basis.
(D) It issues replacement work tools upon request.

Questions 153–155 refer to the following advertisement.

See the World!

Let The Pacifica Take Your Breath Away!

Recipient of the "Best Mid-price Cruise Liner" award at this year's Global Travel Awards.

The Pacifica offers the following:

Wonderful Views! See spectacular mountains and coastlines from the decks of our vessel. Watch as dolphins and whales leap in the waters surrounding you.

Amazing Entertainment! In the evening, enjoy a wide variety of entertainment options such as comedy shows, magic shows, live music and theater performances.

World-class Amenities! When the weather is nice, take part in some yoga classes, or use our brand new badminton courts! Three excellent restaurants can be found on board, but if you feel like relaxing, you can just order food using the phone in your cabin.

All entertainment and activities on The Pacifica are included in our cruise price with the exception of theater productions. Tickets for live performances should be purchased on board.

153. What most likely is The Pacifica?
(A) A cruise ship
(B) A restaurant
(C) A theater
(D) A hotel

154. What is indicated about The Pacifica?
(A) It has recently been renovated.
(B) It has been internationally recognized.
(C) It offers guided tours to guests.
(D) It can be booked for private events.

155. What is offered at an extra cost?
(A) Comedy shows
(B) Exercise classes
(C) Catered meals
(D) Theater shows

Questions 156–158 refer to the following e-mail.

From:	Ryan Kane
To:	All Staff
Date:	May 16
Subject:	Elevator Changes

Hi, everyone,

Please take note that the main elevators in our building will be unavailable from May 21 to May 24 while they undergo urgent maintenance. We hope that they will be available again for use on the morning on May 25. Employees are advised to use the stairs in the meantime, and they can talk with their supervisors about the possibility of temporarily working on one of the lower floors. Please note that a limited number of keycards are available for those who wish to use the service elevator, which will be unaffected by the repair work.

Also, I'm sure you will all be interested to learn that the main elevators will feature voice recognition technology once the work has been completed. We will send you another e-mail on May 24 detailing how to use this technology effectively.

Ryan Kane

156. According to the e-mail, what can employees discuss with their managers?
(A) The changes to a work schedule
(B) The possibility of working on a different floor
(C) The best way to reach an office building
(D) The option of attending a different training class

157. What is suggested about the service elevator?
(A) It requires a keycard to use.
(B) It was recently repaired.
(C) It will be closed on May 21.
(D) It only stops on lower floors.

158. What does Mr. Kane mention about the main elevators?
(A) They will be energy efficient.
(B) They are more than ten years old.
(C) They can only access certain floors.
(D) They will utilize new technology.

GO ON TO THE NEXT PAGE

Questions 159–160 refer to the following text message.

Jeff Sanderson 2:54 P.M.
I just got a call from one of our clients at Marx Advertising. The client asked us to book a return flight to Germany for him, from August 4 to August 9, but he wants to change the return date to August 12, as his business meetings have been rescheduled.

Muhammed Anita 2:57 P.M.
I see. Well, even when using our travel agency, clients will still most likely need to pay a fee to change the date of a flight. But sometimes an airline will waive the charge of its regular passengers. Are you going to call the airline and see if they'll make an exception?

Jeff Sanderson 3:01 P.M.
It's worth a try. The client is Clinton Mulgrew, and he takes trips using Rheine Air several times a year.

Muhammed Anita 3:03 P.M.
Yes, and he is normally a Business Class passenger, so the airline might be more understanding.

Jeff Sanderson 3:05 P.M.
Right. I'll let you know how I get on.

159. What does the client want to do?
(A) Reschedule a business meeting
(B) Reserve accommodations in Germany
(C) Check in early for a flight
(D) Return from a business trip later

160. At 3:01 P.M., what does Mr. Sanderson most likely mean when he writes, "It's worth a try"?
(A) He agrees that a charge is too high.
(B) He thinks a client will agree to an itinerary change.
(C) He is willing to contact an airline representative.
(D) He would prefer to use a different airline.

Jim Finnigan
45 Ides Road
Feltham, Middlesex
TW14 8HA

Dear Mr. Finnigan,

Yesterday, you received your last shipment of produce from Penman Berries. We have yet to receive any notification from you about whether you would like us to continue in our role as your supplier. –[1]–. Since our founding, Penman Berries has become widely regarded as the leading producer of strawberries, raspberries, and blackberries in the United Kingdom. –[2]–. We believe that our goods are tremendously valuable to your business. For example, we know that your fruit pies have received a high amount of praise from your diners. –[3]–. Please take the time to read the revised business agreement that I have enclosed. As you'll note, we are willing to lower the standard price per month should you decide to remain our client. I would appreciate it if you would seriously consider this special offer. –[4]–. You may get back to me in writing or by calling me at 555-0198.

Best regards,

Radha Longoria
Client Services
Penman Berries

161. Where does Mr. Finnigan probably work?
(A) In a factory
(B) At a restaurant
(C) At a financial institute
(D) At a supermarket

162. What does Ms. Longoria offer?
(A) A sample of a product
(B) An incentive program
(C) An employment opportunity
(D) A reduced monthly rate

163. In which of positions marked [1], [2], [3], and [4] does the following sentence best belong?
"We hope that the reason is simply that you have been too busy of late."
(A) [1]
(B) [2]
(C) [3]
(D) [4]

```
E-mail Message
```

To: <Undisclosed Recipients>
From: abigailjordan@usmail.net
Subject: Festival Cancelation
Date: Wednesday, May 7

Dear Performers,

With regret, I must tell you that the Solstice Music Festival, scheduled for this Saturday at NY Art Center, will not be going ahead as planned. This unfortunate news is a result of flooding in the building and a lack of alternative spaces. I'm afraid we have no option but to cancel the event.

Late yesterday, I was informed by the curator of the NY Art Center and Recreation Department that the space we had planned to use, Gallery A, will not be available for the event, as it is closed for renovations following recent flood damage. I was told that we could use the vacant Gallery B on the second floor, but it is a fraction of the size of Gallery A. There's simply no chance that even half of the ticket holders would be able to squeeze in to see the bands perform.

I hope that you will all understand the situation and accept that the decision is out of our hands. We have searched elsewhere for similar event spaces, but nothing is available at such short notice.

To apologize for this late cancelation, the gallery curator has offered to provide each of you with a complimentary ticket for the gallery's main exhibition. These typically cost $30, so it is a kind gesture, and I hope it makes up for the disappointment you must feel.

Best wishes,

Abigail Jordan

164. Who most likely is Ms. Jordan?
(A) A gallery curator
(B) An event organizer
(C) An art exhibitor
(D) A concert performer

165. What is suggested about Gallery B at NY Art Center?
(A) It is currently hosting an art exhibition.
(B) It is not equipped with adequate lighting.
(C) It cannot accommodate large crowds.
(D) It will need to undergo structural repairs.

166. The word "accept" in paragraph 3, line 1, is closest in meaning to
(A) obtain
(B) prefer
(C) enter
(D) recognize

167. What will Solstice Music Festival performers receive?
(A) A full reimbursement
(B) An event ticket
(C) An information pack
(D) An updated concert schedule

Questions 168-171 refer to the following online chat discussion.

Claire Sheldon (10:02 A.M.)
Hi, everyone. Did we hear anything back from Chavez Hotel yet?

Leo Goodman (10:04 A.M.)
Well, when I spoke with Mr. Chavez on Monday, he told me that he'd let me know his decision by e-mail this morning. But, I'm still waiting.

Claire Sheldon (10:06 A.M.)
We're running out of time here. If we don't order the carpet cleaner and stain remover by the end of today, we won't be able to get those tasks done by the deadline they quoted, even if we've already done the vacuuming and dusting.

Tom Bernstein (10:07 A.M.)
Oh... Actually, I already placed the order yesterday.

Claire Sheldon (10:09 A.M.)
That's potentially a bad move, Tom. If we don't get the contract with Mr. Chavez, we'll lose money on those items that we won't use. How much did you spend on them?

Tom Bernstein (10:10 A.M.)
I just thought we would surely get the contract. Hmmm... I'll find out.

Claire Sheldon (10:12 A.M.)
Leo, perhaps I should send Mr. Chavez another message to see what's happening.

Tom Bernstein (10:14 A.M.)
It was just over $100, but fortunately, we can cancel and have our money returned as long as we do it today.

Leo Goodman (10:15 A.M.)
Don't bother, Claire. Ms. Leiper just got in touch with me. She said that Mr. Chavez apologizes, but he's chosen Evergleam Company for this particular job.

Claire Sheldon (10:18 A.M.)
Well, at least we know what's going on. Let's focus on the other big jobs we have coming up.

168. What kind of business do the writers most likely work for?
(A) Catering
(B) Interior design
(C) Cleaning
(D) Landscaping

169. At 10:10 A.M., what does Mr. Bernstein indicate he will do when he says, "I'll find out"?
(A) Check a payment amount
(B) Ask about a delivery time
(C) Look for an alternative product
(D) Provide directions to a location

170. What information did Ms. Leiper provide?
(A) How to get in touch with Mr. Chavez
(B) Where to order the required equipment
(C) Why Mr. Chavez accepted a business proposal
(D) Who will provide a service to Chavez Hotel

171. What will Mr. Bernstein most likely do next?
(A) Cancel an order
(B) Go to a work site
(C) Send an e-mail to Mr. Chavez
(D) Contact Evergleam Company

GO ON TO THE NEXT PAGE

Saturn Set to Change Strategy at OTC

SYDNEY (September 19)—Computer manufacturer Saturn Electronics announced yesterday that it will not be unveiling its newest laptops and tablets at this year's five-day Oceania Technology Convention (OTC) in December. –[1]–.

The OTC was once regarded as the most notable event of the year for the technology industry in Australia, where the country's leading tech firms would demonstrate their upcoming gadgets to thousands of technology enthusiasts. In addition to tech fans, the event would often attract significant media attention. However, the impact that the event has on a company's sales and profile has become increasingly weak in recent years. –[2]–.

Speaking to reporters at the company's head office, Saturn CEO Howard Markley explained that, even though the firm will not give a full demonstration of its new products, it will still be involved with the OTC in a less public manner. –[3]–. "We apologize to fans of our products who had hoped to see the new devices unveiled onstage. Instead of a full-scale public presentation, we have something more intimate and exciting in store for our fans," Markley said. "Throughout the OTC, we will be operating a display booth where a limited number of lucky individuals will have a chance to get hands-on experience with the new laptops and tablets."

Mr. Markley elaborated on the company's new approach, saying that Saturn would prefer to get valuable feedback directly from consumers, as some products are still in development and may yet be modified based on the reactions from fans. Also, by not officially unveiling and demonstrating its devices at the OTC, Saturn will discourage consumers from paying attention to early, inaccurate reviews printed by technology Web sites and magazines. "We would prefer that consumers make up their own minds about the quality of our products," Markley added. –[4]–.

172. The word "notable" in paragraph 2, line 1, is closest in meaning to
(A) repetitive
(B) important
(C) recorded
(D) convenient

173. According to the article, what will Saturn Electronics do during the OTC?
(A) Give a presentation on trends in the technology industry
(B) Provide reviews of its competitors' products
(C) Hold a press conference with local reporters
(D) Allow attendees to try out new devices

174. What is one reason mentioned in the article why Saturn Electronics has changed its OTC plans?
(A) It is planning to launch an advertising campaign.
(B) It has a business deal with various magazines.
(C) It wants consumers to ignore online opinions.
(D) It will unveil its products at a different event.

175. In which of the positions marked [1], [2], [3], and [4] does the following sentence best belong?
"Saturn's decision was therefore no huge shock to those who follow the tech industry closely."
(A) [1]
(B) [2]
(C) [3]
(D) [4]

Questions 176–180 refer to the following notice and e-mail.

City of Bridgewell
Winter Ice Festival (January 18)

The city council is organizing its first ever Winter Ice Festival, which will be held in Forbes Park and the surrounding streets and businesses. If the festival proves to be as popular as anticipated, the city council will consider making it a regular event.

Several fun and exciting events will take place during the festival, and we encourage all local residents to come along and take part in the celebrations. In addition to the scheduled events listed below, there will be food vendors, face painting, a sledding hill, and various souvenir stalls.

The main festival events are as follows:

9:30 A.M.–10:30 A.M.	Ice sculpture display and demonstration
10:30 A.M.–11:30 A.M.	Children's build-a-snowman competition
11:30 A.M.–2:00 P.M.	Barbecue lunch at the picnic area ($10 per head)
2:00 P.M.–4:00 P.M.	Live performances by various local musicians
4:00 P.M.–5:30 P.M.	Fireworks display and complimentary hot chocolate

Admission is free for all although donations are welcome at the main entrance. Any proceeds from the event will be put toward future town festivals and community events. We hope to see you all at the Winter Ice Festival!

To:	Bridgewell City Council <contact@bridgewell.gov>
From:	Mark Lincoln <mlincoln@newmail.com>
Date:	January 23
Subject:	Winter Ice Festival

To whom it may concern,

I am a local resident of Bridgewell, and I was very excited when I first saw the notices around town for the Winter Ice Festival. Although my two sons had an enjoyable time at the festival, I think there are a few things you should do differently if you plan to hold the event again. Firstly, the assigned parking area was far too small. I arrived promptly at 9:30 A.M., but an event organizer informed me that the parking area was already full. I ended up having to park several blocks away from the festival site and arriving much later than planned. Fortunately, we got there just in time for the snowman building competition, which my boys really enjoyed. Secondly, ten dollars was far too high a price for the food that was on offer. Attendees were limited to a choice of either one burger or one hot dog, and nothing to accompany it. I hope you take my ideas into consideration and use them when planning future events.

Regards,

Mark Lincoln

176. Where will the event take place?
    (A) In a park
    (B) At City Hall
    (C) In a sports stadium
    (D) In a restaurant

177. What is implied about the event?
    (A) It is held every year.
    (B) It will likely boost tourism.
    (C) It is expected to be well-attended.
    (D) It will raise funds for a local charity.

178. When will event attendees most likely receive a free beverage?
    (A) At 10:30 A.M.
    (B) At 11:30 A.M.
    (C) At 2:00 P.M.
    (D) At 4:00 P.M.

179. What is the main purpose of Mr. Lincoln's e-mail?
    (A) To thank event organizers for their efforts
    (B) To complain about incorrect information
    (C) To suggest improvements to an event
    (D) To inquire about upcoming events

180. What part of the event did Mr. Lincoln miss?
    (A) The ice sculpture demonstration
    (B) The build-a-snowman contest
    (C) The barbecue lunch
    (D) The musical performances

GO ON TO THE NEXT PAGE

To: Department Staff
From: Larry Gambon, Department Supervisor
Date: January 21
Subject: Painting work

Hi, colleagues,

As you know, our department will be painted on Wednesday, January 27, from 1 P.M. to 4 P.M. This work will be fairly disruptive to our entire team. When the sales, marketing, and customer service departments were painted last week, a lot of employees complained about the noise as well as the fumes from the paint.

Therefore, I have obtained permission from head office for all of us to take the afternoon off during the painting work. Please make sure that you finish any urgent tasks by noon on that day and then vacate our department so that the decorating team can enter and get prepared. You can return to work as normal the following morning. I know many of you are working on next year's budget. Make sure that you do not leave any information lying around. It should be locked securely in a file cabinet. If you have any questions and I'm not around, please send me a brief e-mail.

Thanks,

Larry Gambon

E-mail Message

To: lgambon@baracaeng.com
From: loxley@baracaeng.com
Subject: Staff payroll
Date: January 22

Dear Mr. Gambon,

I received the memo you circulated around the department yesterday, and it just occurred to me that the plan you suggested may cause a problem. As you know, the day of the painting is the day that I should be processing the employee payroll. Normally, I receive all of the information I need in the afternoon, and then calculate staff pay between 2 P.M. and 5 P.M. You suggested that I do it a day late, but I'm sure a lot of our workers will be disappointed, so would it be okay to do it a day earlier instead? If so, I'll need you to ask the other department managers to send me the necessary data early as well. Also, I just wanted to remind you that I'll be away from the office tomorrow afternoon as I'll be attending my nephew's wedding reception.

Thanks,

Lucy Oxley

181. What is the purpose of the memo?
(A) To seek ideas for the decorating of a workspace
(B) To request that employees make less noise
(C) To instruct staff to take some time off
(D) To inform employees about an upcoming installation

182. In what department does Mr. Gambon most likely work?
(A) Customer service
(B) Sales
(C) Marketing
(D) Accounting

183. Why does Ms. Oxley want to reschedule a task?
(A) She does not want to upset employees.
(B) She has a particularly heavy workload.
(C) She does not have access to some information.
(D) She has another appointment in her schedule.

184. What date does Ms. Oxley wish to reschedule her task for?
(A) January 26
(B) January 27
(C) January 28
(D) January 29

185. What is Ms. Oxley planning to do on January 23?
(A) Assign tasks to staff
(B) Attend a family event
(C) Calculate staff wages
(D) Meet with Mr. Gambon

GO ON TO THE NEXT PAGE

HanPro Software Inc.
Harvey Kim's Trip to China, March 12–16

Date	Time	Details	Hotel
Sunday, March 12	7:15 P.M.	Arrive at Pudong International Airport Collect car from Zhou Rental Facility	Sha Tan Hotel Shanghai, China
Monday, March 13	10:30 A.M.–1:30 P.M.	Drive to Suzhou Lunch meeting with CEO of Sunburst Games Company	Jade Flower Hotel Suzhou, China
	3:00 P.M.–5:00 P.M.	Meeting with President of Cheng Computer Systems Inc.	
Tuesday, March 14	9:30 A.M.–11:30 A.M.	Interview with Video Gaming Monthly Magazine	Jade Flower Hotel Suzhou, China
	1:30 P.M.–4:00 P.M.	Presentation to E-Soft Distribution marketing managers	
Wednesday, March 15	10:00 A.M.–6:00 P.M.	Drive to Shanghai HanPro product launch and talk at Asian Technology Expo	Golden Gate Hotel Shanghai, China
Thursday, March 16	11:00 A.M.	Return car to Zhou Rental Facility Depart from Pudong International Airport	

To:	Harvey Kim
From:	Alice Lee
Date:	March 7
Subject:	China Business Trip

Dear Mr. Kim,

As you requested, I have finalized your itinerary, which you should have received via fax earlier today. I'm still compiling a selection of maps and suggested driving routes so that you can reach all of your destinations by car without any major difficulties. I'll forward these to you before the end of the week.

At each hotel, make sure that you use the company credit card, as I have negotiated a significant corporate discount for your rooms. As is standard in China, foreign visitors typically receive free gifts upon arrival, so you will be presented with a basket of fruit and other items when you check in to the Sha Tan Hotel in Shanghai.

If you have any questions, or need further assistance, please don't hesitate to get in touch.

Regards,

Alice Lee

To:	Alice Lee
From:	Harvey Kim
Date:	March 7
Subject:	Re: China Business Trip

Hi Alice,

I really appreciate all the hard work you have put into organizing my trip to China. I've been thinking about my plans and there is one more thing that I'd appreciate your help with. Can you get in touch with all of our board members and schedule a teleconference? I'd like to speak with them all immediately after my meeting with the marketing managers from E-soft Distribution. I'm sure all of them will want to know right away about all of the advertising strategies that will be discussed at the meeting.

Thanks again for your help!

Sincerely,

Harvey Kim

186. What is indicated about Mr. Kim in the itinerary?
(A) He will arrive in Shanghai in the morning.
(B) He will stay in Shanghai for the duration of his trip.
(C) He will use a hired vehicle during his visit.
(D) He will board a connecting flight in Suzhou.

187. What is Mr. Kim NOT scheduled to do in China?
(A) Discuss a new product
(B) Participate in a magazine interview
(C) Take a tour of a company's office
(D) Meet with a chief executive

188. What will Ms. Lee send to Mr. Kim?
(A) Discount coupons for hotels
(B) Directions to locations
(C) A corporate credit card
(D) A list of client contact details

189. When will Mr. Kim receive some complimentary items?
(A) On March 12
(B) On March 13
(C) On March 14
(D) On March 15

190. At what time of day does Mr. Kim plan to hold a teleconference?
(A) 1:30 P.M.
(B) 4:00 P.M.
(C) 5:00 P.M.
(D) 6:00 P.M.

Questions 191–195 refer to the following Web page, form, and e-mail.

www.technologynow.com/article2918/topstreaming/page1

Technology NOW! Your online guide to the latest developments in technology!
TOP TV/MOVIE STREAMING SERVICES THIS YEAR

Editor's Top Pick: Youphoria

Youphoria is the most convenient, affordable, and reliable way to stream newly-released and past television shows and films on your computer or smart phone. Youphoria has been available as a TV-streaming service for almost five years, but it only recently became popular over the last 18 months since introducing movies to its online selection.

When subscribers stream any content through their devices, Youphoria automatically logs it in their viewing history and makes further recommendations based on their viewing habits. The service also allows subscribers to join chat rooms and leave comments and ratings for any television show or movie they have streamed. Incentives are offered in return for comments and ratings. Any subscriber who rates or reviews at least 10 shows or films in a month will be able to stream extra content above their fixed limit in the following month. A basic Casual service starts at $15 per month, but it only allows subscribers to stream 15 TV episodes and 10 movies per month. Other packages have higher limits, for a slightly increased price.

Welcome to the Youphoria streaming service!

To complete the subscription process, please provide the required information below. You will receive a confirmation e-mail within 24 hours. Please click the link in the e-mail to confirm your identity, and then you can begin using our services. If you have a friend or family member who is interested in subscribing to Youphoria, you can personally refer them by logging into our service and visiting the "Refer a Friend" page. For each friend you refer, you'll receive an additional free movie per month.

Subscriber Details

Name: *Reed Randolph*
E-mail: *rrandolph@homenet.com*
Phone number: *656-555-0196*

How often do you watch TV shows/movies online? *Every day*
What device do you normally use to stream TV/movies? *My smart phone*
Favorite TV shows: *Criminal Intent, Suburbia Tales, Carfax Abbey*
Favorite films: *A Song to Remember, Erased Memories, Storm City*

What level of service do you require?

Casual: $15/month ( )
Pro: $20/month ( )
Extreme: $25/month (✓)
Addict: $30/month ( )

To:	rrandolph@homenet.com
From:	subscriberservices@youphoria.com
Date:	January 16
Subject:	New update

Dear Youphoria subscriber,

Please be advised that we will be making some changes to our services starting from February 1. By slightly raising some prices, we will be able to bring you a larger selection of shows and movies, and for the first time, we will be able to offer them at the highest quality: 4K Ultra HD. Also, this will allow us to increase the size of our call center workforce, which means that we will be able to assist our customers more quickly and efficiently. All of these benefits help us stay one step ahead of our competitors. Extreme and Addict service subscribers will also receive special early access to our Classic Film archive before it launches in April. The new prices are as follows:

Service Level	Monthly Streaming Limit	Cost Per Month
Casual	20 TV episodes + 15 Movies	$15
Pro	30 TV episodes + 20 Movies	$20
Extreme	50 TV episodes + 30 Movies	$30
Addict	Unlimited	$35

If you hold a subscription to Extreme and Addict services, you will receive two complimentary tickets to see a movie of your choice at your local Cine-Galaxy Cinema. If you have any inquiries, you can reach us at help@youphoria.com.

191. According to the Web page, what does the Youphoria service allow subscribers to do?
(A) Download the latest music
(B) Watch new film releases online
(C) View photographs on a Web site
(D) Receive discounts on cinema tickets

192. What is suggested about the Youphoria service?
(A) It recently began offering television shows.
(B) It can only be accessed through cell phones.
(C) It has been successful for the past five years.
(D) It suggests suitable content to users.

193. Why is Mr. Randolph eligible to receive a pair of movie tickets?
(A) He did not exceed his monthly streaming limit.
(B) He signed up for Youphoria's Extreme service.

(C) He took part in Youphoria's online survey.
(D) He referred a family member to Youphoria.

194. What is NOT mentioned in the e-mail as a reason for the change in price?
(A) Improving customer service
(B) Expanding the amount of content
(C) Merging with a competitor
(D) Offering higher quality videos

195. What specific change is being made to the Casual service?
(A) The streaming limit is being increased.
(B) The monthly cost is going up.
(C) The subscription payment date will be changed.
(D) Subscribers are gaining access to the Classic Film archive.

GO ON TO THE NEXT PAGE

Questions 196–200 refer to the following invoice, policy information, and e-mail.

OMEGA HEALTH PRODUCTS

Order ID: *773678* Date: *February 15*
Client: *Mr. Jean-Paul Jolie* Deliver to: *580 Porter Street, Regina, SK S4M 0A1*

Product Code	Quantity	Product Details	Per Unit Price	Total Price
#3348	10	Peanut Energy Bar	$2.69	$26.90
#2929	1	Atlas Protein Powder (1 kg, Strawberry)	$60.00	$60.00
#4982	1	Green Tea Gift Set	$75.00	$75.00
#4982		Preparation	$15.00	$15.00
			Sub-total	$176.90
			Member's discount (15%)	-$26.54
			Delivery fee	$20.00
			Total Cost	$170.36

Omega Health Products
Ordering and Return Policies

When ordering our products, whether it be online, by phone, or at our physical location, customers may request gift wrapping for selected items. This additional service will be indicated as "Preparation" on your order invoice and is a flat-fee per item. All orders are guaranteed to arrive at the delivery destination within 5 days of the original ordering date. In the case where a last-minute change is made to an order, please allow an additional 1 or 2 days.

In order for returns to be accepted and a full or partial refund provided, certain conditions must be met. Generally, only damaged products will be accepted for return. This includes damage sustained during transportation and manufacturer defects. Requests to change the size or flavor of an item, however, may be honored with any difference in price handled as outlined below. The original receipt is not strictly necessary when returning defective goods, as long as you can provide the order ID as stated on your invoice. All returned items shall be subject to quality control and assessment to confirm their condition. In the case of foods, beverages, vitamins, and supplements, if these have been consumed at all, they will not be eligible for return or refund.

When acceptable changes are made to an order and the total cost is increased, customers must send the outstanding payment as outlined below:
◆ For payments of $50 or more, send the amount via bank transfer to our account at RBU Bank (Account No.: 5837939390).
◆ For payments of less than $50, you may either give it to us in cash at our physical location, or hand it over to the courier who delivers your order.

From: jpjolie@maplemail.com
To: customerservice@omegahealth.com
Date: February 19
Subject: Recent order

Greetings,

I'd like to make an adjustment to an order I placed through your Web site last week. As part of the order, I selected the Atlas Protein Powder in strawberry flavor. After some discussion with my personal trainer, I would like the same strawberry protein powder, but in a 2 kg bag instead of 1 kg. According to the order tracker feature on your site, my order has not left your distribution facility yet, so I hope you will be able to accommodate my request.

I'm sorry if this causes any inconvenience. Please let me know how I should pay the additional amount of $51.

Best wishes,

Jean-Paul Jolie

196. What is indicated about Omega Health Products?
(A) It has a branch in Regina.
(B) It runs a membership program.
(C) It is having a seasonal sale.
(D) It was recently established.

197. Why most likely was Mr. Jolie charged for "Preparation"?
(A) He wanted an item gift wrapped.
(B) He requested expedited shipping.
(C) His order was difficult to source.
(D) His order was larger than expected.

198. When will product return requests be rejected?
(A) When an item is damaged in transit
(B) When an original receipt is not provided
(C) When the wrong product is included in an order
(D) When an item has been partially used

199. What did Mr. Jolie's personal trainer probably recommend doing?
(A) Trying a different flavor of a product
(B) Changing the size of a product
(C) Comparing two different brands
(D) Increasing the frequency of an order

200. What is probably true about Mr. Jolie?
(A) He will receive his order next month.
(B) He will need to visit the business in person.
(C) He will be required to make a bank transfer.
(D) He will give an amount in cash to a courier.

Stop! This is the end of the test. If you finish before time is called, you may go back to Parts 5, 6, and 7 and check your work.

NO TEST MATERIAL ON THIS PAGE

ANSWER SHEET

姓名　　　測驗回數　　　日期

LISTENING COMPREHENSION (PART 1~4)

NO	ANSWER A B C D	NO	ANSWER A B C D	NO	ANSWER A B C D	NO	ANSWER A B C D	NO	ANSWER A B C D
1	ⓐⓑⓒⓓ	21	ⓐⓑⓒⓓ	41	ⓐⓑⓒⓓ	61	ⓐⓑⓒⓓ	81	ⓐⓑⓒⓓ
2	ⓐⓑⓒⓓ	22	ⓐⓑⓒⓓ	42	ⓐⓑⓒⓓ	62	ⓐⓑⓒⓓ	82	ⓐⓑⓒⓓ
3	ⓐⓑⓒⓓ	23	ⓐⓑⓒⓓ	43	ⓐⓑⓒⓓ	63	ⓐⓑⓒⓓ	83	ⓐⓑⓒⓓ
4	ⓐⓑⓒⓓ	24	ⓐⓑⓒⓓ	44	ⓐⓑⓒⓓ	64	ⓐⓑⓒⓓ	84	ⓐⓑⓒⓓ
5	ⓐⓑⓒⓓ	25	ⓐⓑⓒⓓ	45	ⓐⓑⓒⓓ	65	ⓐⓑⓒⓓ	85	ⓐⓑⓒⓓ
6	ⓐⓑⓒⓓ	26	ⓐⓑⓒⓓ	46	ⓐⓑⓒⓓ	66	ⓐⓑⓒⓓ	86	ⓐⓑⓒⓓ
7	ⓐⓑⓒⓓ	27	ⓐⓑⓒ	47	ⓐⓑⓒⓓ	67	ⓐⓑⓒⓓ	87	ⓐⓑⓒⓓ
8	ⓐⓑⓒⓓ	28	ⓐⓑⓒⓓ	48	ⓐⓑⓒⓓ	68	ⓐⓑⓒⓓ	88	ⓐⓑⓒⓓ
9	ⓐⓑⓒⓓ	29	ⓐⓑⓒⓓ	49	ⓐⓑⓒⓓ	69	ⓐⓑⓒⓓ	89	ⓐⓑⓒⓓ
10	ⓐⓑⓒⓓ	30	ⓐⓑⓒⓓ	50	ⓐⓑⓒⓓ	70	ⓐⓑⓒⓓ	90	ⓐⓑⓒⓓ
11	ⓐⓑⓒⓓ	31	ⓐⓑⓒ	51	ⓐⓑⓒⓓ	71	ⓐⓑⓒⓓ	91	ⓐⓑⓒⓓ
12	ⓐⓑⓒⓓ	32	ⓐⓑⓒⓓ	52	ⓐⓑⓒⓓ	72	ⓐⓑⓒⓓ	92	ⓐⓑⓒⓓ
13	ⓐⓑⓒⓓ	33	ⓐⓑⓒⓓ	53	ⓐⓑⓒⓓ	73	ⓐⓑⓒⓓ	93	ⓐⓑⓒⓓ
14	ⓐⓑⓒⓓ	34	ⓐⓑⓒⓓ	54	ⓐⓑⓒⓓ	74	ⓐⓑⓒⓓ	94	ⓐⓑⓒⓓ
15	ⓐⓑⓒⓓ	35	ⓐⓑⓒⓓ	55	ⓐⓑⓒⓓ	75	ⓐⓑⓒⓓ	95	ⓐⓑⓒⓓ
16	ⓐⓑⓒⓓ	36	ⓐⓑⓒⓓ	56	ⓐⓑⓒⓓ	76	ⓐⓑⓒⓓ	96	ⓐⓑⓒⓓ
17	ⓐⓑⓒⓓ	37	ⓐⓑⓒⓓ	57	ⓐⓑⓒⓓ	77	ⓐⓑⓒⓓ	97	ⓐⓑⓒⓓ
18	ⓐⓑⓒⓓ	38	ⓐⓑⓒⓓ	58	ⓐⓑⓒⓓ	78	ⓐⓑⓒⓓ	98	ⓐⓑⓒⓓ
19	ⓐⓑⓒⓓ	39	ⓐⓑⓒⓓ	59	ⓐⓑⓒⓓ	79	ⓐⓑⓒⓓ	99	ⓐⓑⓒⓓ
20	ⓐⓑⓒⓓ	40	ⓐⓑⓒⓓ	60	ⓐⓑⓒⓓ	80	ⓐⓑⓒⓓ	100	ⓐⓑⓒⓓ

READING COMPREHENSION (PART 5~7)

NO	ANSWER A B C D	NO	ANSWER A B C D	NO	ANSWER A B C D	NO	ANSWER A B C D	NO	ANSWER A B C D
101	ⓐⓑⓒⓓ	121	ⓐⓑⓒⓓ	141	ⓐⓑⓒⓓ	161	ⓐⓑⓒⓓ	181	ⓐⓑⓒⓓ
102	ⓐⓑⓒⓓ	122	ⓐⓑⓒⓓ	142	ⓐⓑⓒⓓ	162	ⓐⓑⓒⓓ	182	ⓐⓑⓒⓓ
103	ⓐⓑⓒⓓ	123	ⓐⓑⓒⓓ	143	ⓐⓑⓒⓓ	163	ⓐⓑⓒⓓ	183	ⓐⓑⓒⓓ
104	ⓐⓑⓒⓓ	124	ⓐⓑⓒⓓ	144	ⓐⓑⓒⓓ	164	ⓐⓑⓒⓓ	184	ⓐⓑⓒⓓ
105	ⓐⓑⓒⓓ	125	ⓐⓑⓒⓓ	145	ⓐⓑⓒⓓ	165	ⓐⓑⓒⓓ	185	ⓐⓑⓒⓓ
106	ⓐⓑⓒⓓ	126	ⓐⓑⓒⓓ	146	ⓐⓑⓒⓓ	166	ⓐⓑⓒⓓ	186	ⓐⓑⓒⓓ
107	ⓐⓑⓒⓓ	127	ⓐⓑⓒⓓ	147	ⓐⓑⓒⓓ	167	ⓐⓑⓒⓓ	187	ⓐⓑⓒⓓ
108	ⓐⓑⓒⓓ	128	ⓐⓑⓒⓓ	148	ⓐⓑⓒⓓ	168	ⓐⓑⓒⓓ	188	ⓐⓑⓒⓓ
109	ⓐⓑⓒⓓ	129	ⓐⓑⓒⓓ	149	ⓐⓑⓒⓓ	169	ⓐⓑⓒⓓ	189	ⓐⓑⓒⓓ
110	ⓐⓑⓒⓓ	130	ⓐⓑⓒⓓ	150	ⓐⓑⓒⓓ	170	ⓐⓑⓒⓓ	190	ⓐⓑⓒⓓ
111	ⓐⓑⓒⓓ	131	ⓐⓑⓒⓓ	151	ⓐⓑⓒⓓ	171	ⓐⓑⓒⓓ	191	ⓐⓑⓒⓓ
112	ⓐⓑⓒⓓ	132	ⓐⓑⓒⓓ	152	ⓐⓑⓒⓓ	172	ⓐⓑⓒⓓ	192	ⓐⓑⓒⓓ
113	ⓐⓑⓒⓓ	133	ⓐⓑⓒⓓ	153	ⓐⓑⓒⓓ	173	ⓐⓑⓒⓓ	193	ⓐⓑⓒⓓ
114	ⓐⓑⓒⓓ	134	ⓐⓑⓒⓓ	154	ⓐⓑⓒⓓ	174	ⓐⓑⓒⓓ	194	ⓐⓑⓒⓓ
115	ⓐⓑⓒⓓ	135	ⓐⓑⓒⓓ	155	ⓐⓑⓒⓓ	175	ⓐⓑⓒⓓ	195	ⓐⓑⓒⓓ
116	ⓐⓑⓒⓓ	136	ⓐⓑⓒⓓ	156	ⓐⓑⓒⓓ	176	ⓐⓑⓒⓓ	196	ⓐⓑⓒⓓ
117	ⓐⓑⓒⓓ	137	ⓐⓑⓒⓓ	157	ⓐⓑⓒⓓ	177	ⓐⓑⓒⓓ	197	ⓐⓑⓒⓓ
118	ⓐⓑⓒⓓ	138	ⓐⓑⓒⓓ	158	ⓐⓑⓒⓓ	178	ⓐⓑⓒⓓ	198	ⓐⓑⓒⓓ
119	ⓐⓑⓒⓓ	139	ⓐⓑⓒⓓ	159	ⓐⓑⓒⓓ	179	ⓐⓑⓒⓓ	199	ⓐⓑⓒⓓ
120	ⓐⓑⓒⓓ	140	ⓐⓑⓒⓓ	160	ⓐⓑⓒⓓ	180	ⓐⓑⓒⓓ	200	ⓐⓑⓒⓓ

聽力測驗 Part1 & Part 2

冊次	TEST 1 ☑ TEST 2 ◯ TEST 3 ◯
題號	1
頁數	45
	(A) The man is hanging up a poster. (B) The woman is taking a picture. (C) The man is pointing at something. (D) They are looking at each other.

錯誤原因

圖中的兩個人正看著某個東西，不能因為聽到「在看」就確定答案！
一定要確定受詞！
Something 也有可能是答案！

重要字彙	hang up 掛 point at 指向 look at each other 看著對方

1. 將答錯及用猜的題目寫下來！
2. 用螢光筆將不知道意思或讀音的單字畫起來！
3. 彙整用螢光筆標示起來的單字及文句！
4. 錯誤原因：(1) 將表「動作」（be being p.p）誤解成表「狀態」。
　　　　　　(2) 不知道 schedule 的英式發音 [ˈʃɛdjul] 與美式發音 [ˈskɛdʒu] 唸法不同。

誤答筆記 聽力測驗 Part1 & Part 2

冊次	TEST 1 ◯　TEST 2 ◯　TEST 3 ◯
題號	
頁數	
錯誤原因	

冊次	TEST 1 ◯　TEST 2 ◯　TEST 3 ◯
題號	
頁數	
錯誤原因	

重要字彙	

＊請將本頁表格剪下，複印後使用。

找出 Part 5 & Part 6 錯誤的原因

冊次	TEST 1 ☐　TEST 2 ☑　TEST 3 ☐	
題號	101	我選擇的答案 B
頁數	67	**錯誤原因**

我選擇的答案 B

錯誤原因

不知道 [there is/are+ 名詞]
看到 has been 就急忙認定是 P.P
需要看完文句的整體結構！

~ there has been much _____
in agriculture, with ~.
(A) develop
(B) developed
(C) developing
(D) development

答案 D

正確原因

there is 句型 → 空格才是主語！
範例中，只有身為名詞的 development
能擔任主語，雖然 there 這個副詞在
主語的位置上，但並不是真正的主語。
實際上真正的主語是接在 be 動詞後的
名詞！

★找出我的弱點！
問題類型　　(文法) 句子的結構
　　　　　　　 詞彙

重要字彙	there is N　有 ~ develop　發展 agriculture　農業

1. 不用把所有的題目都抄起來！只需要寫下會影響正解的部分，其他以連接號「~」代替！
2. 不要將正解寫在問題裡，需要另外標示！
3. 掌握為什麼答錯才是最重要的！
4. 簡要解釋不懂的部分！
5. 快速掌握題型的話，解題的速度也會提升！確認錯誤的題目屬於什麼類型！
6. 一定要整理題目裡不懂的單字！

誤答筆記　找出 Part 5 & Part 6 錯誤的原因

冊次	TEST 1 ◯　　TEST 2 ◯　　TEST 3 ◯
題號	我選擇的答案
頁數	錯誤原因
	答案 正確原因
★找出我的弱點！ 問題類型　　文法 　　　　　　詞彙	

冊次	TEST 1 ◯　　TEST 2 ◯　　TEST 3 ◯
題號	我選擇的答案
頁數	錯誤原因
	答案 正確原因
★找出我的弱點！ 問題類型　　文法 　　　　　　詞彙	

重要字彙	

* 請將本頁表格剪下，複印後使用。

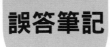

Part 3 & Part 4 & Part 7
Paraphrasing 整理

more detailed report 更詳細的報告	→	a revised document 修訂的文件
drop off your report 留下你的報告	→	turn in an assignment 提交作品
later today 今天稍晚	→	this afternoon 今天下午
	→	
	→	

請整理對話或短文中的線索，再次確認其線索是如何變成正確答案的！

整理對話、短文中的線索是如何變成正確答案的，盡可能精簡。如果將冗長的文句都寫下來，很容易感到厭倦。準備多益最重要的是「跑完全程」。

→	→
→	→
→	→
→	→
→	→
→	→
→	→
→	→
→	→
→	→

＊請將本頁表格剪下，複印後使用。

　屬於我的多益單字表

學習時遇到不會的單字，記得整理起來（特別是句子填空題中出現在選項的單字）。

另外，如果在文句中出現跟該單字搭配使用的搭配詞／慣用語，最好也一起寫下來。

也別忘了記下 Part 3、4、7 的文句及選項中影響判斷的單字！

	Sample
sign up 報名；註冊；簽約 sign up for the seminar 報名研討會 = register for	
rarely 很少；不常見 = not often highly 非常 = very	

＊請將本頁表格剪下，複印後使用。

揮別厚重，迎向高分！
最接近真實多益測驗的模擬題本

特色 **1** 單回成冊

揮別市面多數多益題本的厚重感，單回裝訂仿照真實測驗，
提前適應答題手感。

特色 **2** 錯題解析

解析本提供深度講解，針對正確答案與誘答選項進行解題，
全面掌握答題關鍵。

特色 **3** 誤答筆記

提供筆記模板，協助深入了解誤答原因，歸納出專屬於自己
的學習筆記。

TOEIC
Test of English for International Communication

TEST 2

答案與解析

三民書局

TEST 2

PART 1

1. (B) 2. (A) 3. (C) 4. (A) 5. (D) 6. (A)

PART 2

7. (B) 8. (C) 9. (A) 10. (C) 11. (C) 12. (C) 13. (B) 14. (A) 15. (B) 16. (A) 17. (A) 18. (A) 19. (B) 20. (A) 21. (B) 22. (B) 23. (A) 24. (B) 25. (C) 26. (B) 27. (C) 28. (B) 29. (C) 30. (A) 31. (C)

PART 3

32. (A) 33. (A) 34. (D) 35. (D) 36. (C) 37. (D) 38. (D) 39. (C) 40. (C) 41. (A) 42. (C) 43. (C) 44. (D) 45. (D) 46. (C) 47. (D) 48. (A) 49. (A) 50. (A) 51. (C) 52. (C) 53. (A) 54. (A) 55. (C) 56. (C) 57. (A) 58. (A) 59. (C) 60. (A) 61. (A) 62. (C) 63. (A) 64. (D) 65. (C) 66. (B) 67. (A) 68. (D) 69. (A) 70. (C)

PART 4

71. (C) 72. (A) 73. (D) 74. (D) 75. (A) 76. (D) 77. (C) 78. (C) 79. (A) 80. (C) 81. (B) 82. (C) 83. (D) 84. (D) 85. (D) 86. (C) 87. (D) 88. (C) 89. (B) 90. (D) 91. (C) 92. (C) 93. (D) 94. (A) 95. (C) 96. (D) 97. (D) 98. (D) 99. (C) 100. (C)

PART 5

101. (A) 102. (C) 103. (A) 104. (B) 105. (C) 106. (D) 107. (D) 108. (B) 109. (D) 110. (B) 111. (C) 112. (C) 113. (B) 114. (C) 115. (C) 116. (A) 117. (B) 118. (B) 119. (D) 120. (A) 121. (D) 122. (B) 123. (D) 124. (D) 125. (A) 126. (C) 127. (A) 128. (C) 129. (A) 130. (C)

PART 6

131. (D) 132. (A) 133. (C) 134. (B) 135. (A) 136. (D) 137. (B) 138. (A) 139. (B) 140. (C) 141. (A) 142. (D) 143. (B) 144. (B) 145. (A) 146. (A)

PART 7

147. (D) 148. (A) 149. (A) 150. (D) 151. (D) 152. (B) 153. (A) 154. (B) 155. (D) 156. (B) 157. (A) 158. (D) 159. (D) 160. (C) 161. (B) 162. (D) 163. (A) 164. (B) 165. (C) 166. (D) 167. (B) 168. (C) 169. (A) 170. (D) 171. (A) 172. (B) 173. (D) 174. (C) 175. (B) 176. (A) 177. (C) 178. (D) 179. (C) 180. (A) 181. (C) 182. (D) 183. (A) 184. (A) 185. (B) 186. (C) 187. (C) 188. (B) 189. (A) 190. (B) 191. (B) 192. (D) 193. (B) 194. (C) 195. (A) 196. (B) 197. (A) 198. (D) 199. (B) 200. (C)

Part 1

1.

(A) She's washing the dishes.
(B) She's cooking some food.
(C) She's tying her apron.
(D) She's carrying a plate.

(A) 她在洗碗盤。
(B) 她在煮一些食物。
(C) 她在綁圍裙。
(D) 她在端盤子。

解析 照片內僅有一人時，須留意該人物的動作、姿勢及與其有關連性的事物。
(A) 女子並未有洗碗盤的動作，故非正解。
(B) 女子做出煮菜的動作，故為正解。
(C) 女子沒有在綁圍裙，已經是穿好的狀態，故非正解。
(D) 女子並未有端盤子的動作，故非正解。

2.

(A) Some people are walking through an archway.
(B) Some people are entering a building.
(C) Some people are looking into a store window.
(D) Some people are crossing a street.

(A) 有些人正在穿越拱門。
(B) 有些人正在走進建築內。
(C) 有些人正在看商店的窗戶。
(D) 有些人正在過馬路。

解析 照片內出現多個人物時，須留意人物們的動作、姿勢及周邊事物。
(A) 照片內的人物正在穿越拱門，故為正解。
(B) 照片內沒有人正在進入建築，故非正解。
(C) 照片內沒有人正在看商店的窗戶，故非正解。
(D) 照片內沒有人正在過馬路，故非正解。

3.

(A) She's hanging an artwork.
(B) She's distributing some pamphlets.
(C) She's reading in a library.
(D) She's arranging books on the bookshelf.

(A) 她正在掛一個藝術品。
(B) 她正在發放一些小冊子。

(C) 她正在圖書館裡閱讀。
(D) 她正在排書櫃上的書籍。

解析 照片內僅有一人時，須留意該人物的動作、姿勢及與其有關連性的事物。
(A) 女子並未做出掛藝術品的動作，故非正解。
(B) 女子並未做出發放小冊子的動作，故非正解。
(C) 女子正在閱讀，故為正解。
(D) 女子並未有整理書櫃上書籍的動作，故非正解。

4.

(A) Some packages are piled on a cart.
(B) Some machines are being repaired.
(C) A courier is opening the trunk of a vehicle.
(D) A man is locking a garage.

(A) 一些物品被擺到推車上。
(B) 一些機器正在被修理。
(C) 快遞員正在打開車廂。
(D) 一位男子正在鎖倉庫。

解析 照片內僅有一人時，須留意該人物的動作、姿勢及與其有關連性的事物。
(A) 推車上堆放了物品，故為正解。
(B) 照片內沒有修理機器的動作，故非正解。
(C) 照片內沒有快遞員開車廂的動作，故非正解。
(D) 照片內沒有男子正在鎖倉庫，故非正解。

5.

(A) Some machines are being dusted off.
(B) They're facing each other.
(C) An audio system is being packed into a case.
(D) A man is adjusting some equipment.

(A) 有些機器正在被除塵。
(B) 他們面對面看著對方。
(C) 音響被裝到箱子裡。
(D) 一位男子正在調整設備。

解析 照片內出現兩人時，須留意兩位人物共同的動作、姿勢及人物們周邊的事物。
(A) 照片內沒有人在清潔機器上的灰塵，故非正解。
(B) 照片內的人物並非面對面，故非正解。
(C) 照片內沒有包裝音響的動作，故非正解。
(D) 兩位男子中的一位正在調整設備，故為正解。

6.

(A) A few screens have been positioned side by side.
(B) Several pens have been placed on a desk.
(C) Some papers are spread out on the floor.
(D) Blinds have been pulled closed in the office.
(A) 有幾個螢幕被並排擺在一起。
(B) 有一些筆被放在桌上。
(C) 有一些紙張散落在地板上。
(D) 辦公室裡的百葉窗被關起來了。

解析 照片內僅有物品時，必須留意物品的名稱和所在位置。
(A) 照片內有幾個螢幕被並排擺在一起，故為正解。
(B) 桌子上並沒有筆，故非正解。
(C) 地板沒有散落的紙張，故非正解。
(D) 辦公室的百葉窗並未關上，故非正解。

Part 2

7. Where is the expense report?
(A) It wasn't expensive.
(B) In my drawer.
(C) Every Friday.
支出報告在哪裡？
(A) 那個不貴。
(B) 在我的抽屜。
(C) 每週五。

解析 本題為詢問支出報告在哪的 Where 疑問句。
(A) 用和 expense 發音相近的 expensive 混淆考生，故非正解。
(B) 用位置回答 Where 疑問句，故為正解。
(C) 此為針對 How often 疑問句，告知頻率的回答，故非正解。

8. When will the cooking contest begin?
(A) It's a new restaurant.
(B) Sure, anyone can enter.
(C) At 3 P.M.
料理比賽何時會開始？
(A) 那是新開的餐廳。
(B) 當然，每個人都可以參加。
(C) 下午 3 點。

解析 本題為詢問料理比賽何時開始的 When 疑問句。
(A) 用聽到 cooking 容易聯想到的 restaurant 混淆考生，故非正解。
(B) 用聽到 contest 容易聯想到的 enter 混淆考生，故非正解。
(C) 用特定時間回覆 When 疑問句，故為正解。

9. What bus should I take to Mayfair Hotel?
(A) Number 32.

(B) About 30 minutes.
(C) Two tickets, please.
要去 Mayfair 飯店該搭哪臺公車？
(A) 32 號。
(B) 大概 30 分鐘。
(C) 請給我兩張票。

解析 本題為詢問該搭哪臺公車到 Mayfair 飯店的 What 疑問句。
(A) 用特定公車號碼回答 What bus 的疑問，故為正解。
(B) 此為針對 How long 疑問句，告知所需時間的回答，故非正解。
(C) 此為針對 How many 疑問句，告知數量的回答，故非正解。

10. Who should I send these catalogs to?
(A) The new product range.
(B) In all of our branches.
(C) To our new customers, please.
我該把這些型錄寄給誰？
(A) 新的產品類別。
(B) 在我們所有分店。
(C) 請寄給我們的新客戶。

解析 本題為詢問該將型錄寄給誰的 Who 疑問句。
(A) 用聽到 catalog 容易聯想到的 product range 混淆考生，故非正解。
(B) 此為針對 Where 疑問句，告知地點的回答，故非正解。
(C) 用特定對象回答 Who 疑問句，故為正解。

11. May I see the menu again, please?
(A) I'm afraid he's busy all day.
(B) Yes, I'll have the steak.
(C) Certainly. Here you are.
請問，我可以再看一次菜單嗎？
(A) 我猜他整天應該都很忙。
(B) 對，我想要點牛排。
(C) 當然。給你。

解析 本題為詢問是否能再看一次菜單的請求疑問句。
(A) 回答無法得知對象是誰的 he，故非正解。
(B) 用聽到 menu 容易聯想到的 steak 混淆考生，故非正解。
(C) 用 Certainly 表允許後，接著說給對方物品時常用的句子，故為正解。

12. Where should we hand out our brochures?
(A) Thanks, I got one.
(B) At least 500 copies.
(C) Liz has already picked a spot.
我們該去哪發小冊子？
(A) 謝謝，我有一個了。
(B) 至少 500 份。
(C) Liz 已經找好地點了。

解析 本題為詢問該去哪發小冊子的 Where 疑問句。
(A) 表感謝的句子並未回答到問題，故非正解。
(B) 此為針對 How many 疑問句，告知數量的回答，故非正解。
(C) 告訴對方 Liz 已經找好地點，來回應要去哪發放小冊子的疑問，故為正解。

13. Excuse me, what sizes do these shoes come in?
(A) Come in anytime you like.
(B) We only have them in a 9.
(C) They look great on you.
不好意思，這鞋子有什麼尺寸？
(A) 你什麼時候想來都可以。
(B) 我們只有 9 號。
(C) 你穿起來真好看。

解析 本題為詢問鞋子有什麼尺碼的 What 疑問句。
(A) 此為針對 When 疑問句，告知大概時間點的回答，故非正解。
(B) 用現有的特定尺碼回答疑問，故為正解。
(C) 誇獎對方穿起來很好看的回答與問題無關，故非正解。

14. Who made the most sales this month?
(A) We're still going over the figures.
(B) It's 20 percent off right now.
(C) In the third quarter.
誰這個月的業績最好？
(A) 我們仍在計算中。
(B) 現在打八折。
(C) 在第 3 季。

解析 本題為詢問誰這個月業績最好的 Who 疑問句。
(A) 用能夠確認誰業績最好的方法回答問題，故為正解。
(B) 用聽到 sales 容易聯想到的折數混淆考生，故非正解。
(C) 此為針對 When 疑問句，告知特定時間點的回答，故非正解。

15. You met Mr. Selleck at the staff orientation, didn't you?
(A) I'll be sure to let him know.
(B) Yes, we were introduced.
(C) Around twenty new employees.
你在新進職員訓練見過 Selleck 先生，對吧？
(A) 我一定會讓他知道。
(B) 對，我們打過招呼了。
(C) 大概 20 位新進職員。

解析 本題為確認對方是否在新進職員訓練見過 Selleck 先生的疑問句。
(A) 傳遞消息的回答與是否見過面的問題無關，故非正解。
(B) 用 Yes 表肯定後，用已經打過招呼表達已經見過對方，故為正解。
(C) 用聽到 staff orientation 容易聯想到的 new employees 混淆考生，故非正解。

16. Have you seen the schedule for tomorrow's training workshop?
(A) I didn't receive one.
(B) At 9 A.M. sharp.
(C) His train arrived late.
你看過明天訓練工作坊的行程了嗎？
(A) 我沒有拿到。
(B) 早上 9 點整。
(C) 他搭的火車誤點了。

解析 本題為確認對方是否看過隔天訓練工作坊行程的疑問句。

(A) 用 one 代指 schedule，表達自己因為沒有拿到，所以尚未看過行程，故為正解。
(B) 此為針對 When 疑問句，告知特定時間點的回答，故非正解。
(C) 回答無法得知對象是誰的 His，故非正解。

17. Which employee should we send to represent us at the convention?
(A) The one with the most experience.
(B) She forgot to register for the event.
(C) I found the presentation informative.
該派哪位職員代表我們去參加會議？
(A) 經驗最多的那位。
(B) 她忘記報名那個活動了。
(C) 那場演講讓我受益良多。

解析 本題為詢問該派哪位職員代表參加會議的 Which 疑問句。
(A) 用 one 代指 employee，提出該代表的條件必須是有最多經驗的人，故為正解。
(B) 回答無法得知對象是誰的 She，故非正解。
(C) 問題的未來時態 (should we) 和本選項的過去時態 (found) 不符，故非正解。

18. Do you like walking or riding a bike by the river?
(A) I prefer jogging.
(B) Let's use the bridge.
(C) Sure, I'll give you a ride.
你喜歡在河邊散步或是騎腳踏車嗎？
(A) 我比較喜歡慢跑。
(B) 讓我們走橋。
(C) 當然，我載你一程。

解析 本題為詢問對方比較喜歡在河邊散步還是騎腳踏車的選擇疑問句。
(A) 用喜歡慢跑表達自己的喜好，故為正解。
(B) 關於移動路徑的回答與問題無關，故非正解。
(C) 用 ride 的另一個意思 (載某人一程) 混淆考生，故非正解。

19. Is there a way to adjust the speed of this photocopier?
(A) Copies of the meeting agenda.
(B) Yes, but let me check the manual first.
(C) You take lovely photographs.
有任何調整影印機速度的辦法嗎？
(A) 會議議程的複本。
(B) 可以，但讓我先看一下使用說明書。
(C) 你真會拍照。

解析 本題為確認是否能調整影印機速度的疑問句。
(A) 用和 photocopier 部分發音相近的 copies 混淆考生，故非正解。
(B) 用 Yes 表肯定後，說明了能夠找出方法的條件，故為正解。
(C) 用和 photocopier 發音相近的 photographs 混淆考生，故非正解。

20. None of the shipments arrived this morning, right?

(A) I'll check with the receptionist.
(B) We needed more supplies.
(C) By 11 A.M., please.
今天早上沒有任何貨物送來，對吧？
(A) 我會跟接待人員確認一下。
(B) 我們需要更多物資。
(C) 請在早上 11 點前。

解析 本題為確認今天早上是否沒送任何貨物來的附加問句。
(A) 回答了能夠確認問題的方法，故為正解。
(B) 未回答貨品送達與否，僅說明下訂的目的，與問題無關，故非正解。
(C) 此為針對 When 疑問句，告知期限的回答，故非正解。

21. Didn't Sally interview a job candidate yesterday?
(A) A position in our call center.
(B) She did, but he wasn't qualified.
(C) The deadline for submission is this Friday.
昨天 Sally 不是面試了一位應徵者嗎？
(A) 我們客服中心的職位。
(B) 她做了，但他無法勝任。
(C) 提交的截止日期是這週五。

解析 本題為詢問 Sally 是否面試了一位應徵者的否定疑問句。
(A) 用聽到 interview 容易聯想到的 position 混淆考生，故非正解。
(B) 用 She 代指 Sally 加上助動詞 did，接著再用 he 代指應徵者，表達 Sally 和應徵者的確進行了面試，故為正解。
(C) 截止日期的回答與面試與否的問題無關，故非正解。

22. Tim hasn't booked the hotel rooms for our trip yet.
(A) I enjoyed my stay.
(B) He'd better do it soon.
(C) Three days in London.
Tim 還沒替我們的旅行訂飯店房間。
(A) 我的住宿經驗很棒。
(B) 他最好快點做。
(C) 在倫敦待 3 天。

解析 本題為說明 Tim 尚未訂旅行要住的飯店的敘述句。
(A) 說話者個人經驗相關的回答與問題無關，故非正解。
(B) 用 He 代指 Tim，表達他最好快點訂飯店，故為正解。
(C) 關於住宿期間的回答和是否已預訂無關，故非正解。

23. Are you going to create the new employee handbook this month or next month?
(A) I'll be too busy this month.
(B) You can get a copy from HR.
(C) Thanks for your help.
你這個月會做新的職員手冊，還是下個月？
(A) 這個月我會太忙。
(B) 你可以到人資部門拿複本。

(C) 謝謝你的幫忙。

解析 本題為詢問對方要在這個月還是下個月做新職員手冊的選擇疑問句。
(A) 用這個月太忙的話表達自己下個月才會做，故為正解。
(B) 回答取得的方法，而非職員手冊製作的時間，故非正解。
(C) 向對方表達感謝的話與問題無關，故非正解。

24. How do you like your new apartment?
(A) A studio downtown.
(B) I'm moving in this weekend.
(C) Thanks, I'm pleased with it too.
你覺得你的新公寓如何？
(A) 一間在市中心的套房。
(B) 我這週末要搬進去。
(C) 謝謝，我也很滿意。

解析 本題為詢問對方對新公寓想法的 How do you like 疑問句。
(A) 此為針對 Where 疑問句，告知位置的回答，故非正解。
(B) 用這週末要搬進去表達他很滿意新公寓，故為正解。
(C) 此為當對方對某件事物感到滿意，表達自己同意的時候說的句子，故非正解。

25. When did you buy your tablet computer?
(A) OK, you can borrow it.
(B) Well, you got a great deal.
(C) Actually, it belongs to my husband.
你什麼時候買平板電腦的？
(A) 好，你可以借走。
(B) 嗯，你買的價錢很划算。
(C) 其實，這是我丈夫的。

解析 本題為詢問何時購買了平板電腦的 When 疑問句。
(A) 允許對方借走物品的話與問題無關，故非正解。
(B) 並未回答何時購買了該物品，故非正解。
(C) 說明該物品是丈夫的，表達自己並未購買，故為正解。

26. I will buy tickets for the 8 P.M. movie.
(A) At Grand Movie Theater.
(B) There are no seats left.
(C) A new comedy film.
我會買晚上 8 點那場電影的票。
(A) 在 Grand 電影院。
(B) 已經沒有座位了。
(C) 一部新的喜劇電影。

解析 本題為告知自己要買 8 點電影票的敘述句。
(A) 此為針對 Where 疑問句，告知地點的回答，故非正解。
(B) 用已經沒有座位表達無法購買電影票，故為正解。
(C) 電影類型的回答與問題無關，故非正解。

27. Why haven't you set up the window displays yet?
(A) Our summer clothing collection.

(B) You can set it down over there.
(C) Some stock still hasn't arrived.
為什麼你還沒布置櫥窗展示品？
(A) 我們的夏季時裝系列。
(B) 你可以放在那邊。
(C) 部分存貨還沒送到。

解析 本題為詢問對方為何尚未布置櫥窗展示品的 Why 疑問句。
(A) 關於產品類型的回答與問題無關，故非正解。
(B) 此為針對 Where 疑問句，告知位置的回答，故非正解。
(C) 用存貨尚未送到說明無法布置展示品的理由，故為正解。

28. Would you like an appetizer before your main course?
(A) I'll bring you a menu.
(B) Do you have any soup?
(C) Yes, it was delicious.
主餐前想來點開胃菜嗎？
(A) 我拿菜單給你。
(B) 你們有湯嗎？
(C) 是，它很好吃。

解析 本題為確認對方是否要在主餐前吃點開胃菜的疑問句。
(A) 此為餐廳職員會說的話，故非正解。
(B) 用是否能喝點湯來回應 appetizer，故為正解。
(C) 用 Yes 表肯定後，用和問題不同時態的過去式回答，故非正解。

29. Isn't this year's Christmas party being held on the third floor?
(A) No, it's in December.
(B) All staff are invited.
(C) It's usually on the fourth.
今年的聖誕派對不是要在 3 樓舉辦嗎？
(A) 不，在 12 月。
(B) 所有職員都被邀請參加。
(C) 通常都在 4 樓。

解析 本題為確認聖誕派對是否在 3 樓舉辦的否定疑問句。
(A) 回答舉辦的時間點，而非舉辦地點，故非正解。
(B) 回答受邀人員，而非舉辦地點，故非正解。
(C) 用通常會在某個地點舉辦來表達對方得知的資訊有誤，故為正解。

30. Why don't we offer new gym members some complimentary gifts?
(A) That's a nice idea.
(B) I got a free towel.
(C) A six-month membership.
我們何不送一些禮物給健身房的新會員呢？
(A) 這個想法很不錯。
(B) 我拿到了一條免費的毛巾。
(C) 6 個月的會籍。

解析 本題為詢問對方對於送健身房新會員禮物有什麼想法的疑問句。
(A) 用這個想法很不錯向對方的提議表達同意，

故為正解。
(B) 收到禮物的不是健身房會員而是回答者，故非正解。
(C) 用和 member 部分發音相近的 membership 混淆考生，故非正解。

31. Are you taking the clients for dinner, or to the theater?
(A) The new clients from Japan.
(B) You can buy tickets online.
(C) Both, if that's okay.
你要帶客戶們去吃晚餐，還是去電影院？
(A) 從日本來的新客戶。
(B) 你可以在網路上買票。
(C) 如果情況允許就都去。

解析 本題為詢問對方要帶客戶去用晚餐還是要去電影院的選擇疑問句。
(A) 回答客戶從哪裡來，而非將前往的地點，故非正解。
(B) 票券購買方式的回答與問題無關，故非正解。
(C) 表明兩個地方都會去，並說明先決條件，故為正解。

Part 3

Questions 32–34 refer to the following conversation.

W: Alex, 32 don't forget your briefcase in the trunk of the car.
M: I won't. I just hope we get to our hotel soon so we can take a rest.
W: Yeah. At least 32 this driver seems to know the fastest route. We should have time to rest and go over our speeches before the conference this afternoon.
M: By the way, 33 you did get our event passes from someone at the office, right?
W: Yes, 33 Olivia gave them to me just before we left. We'll need to show the passes at the main entrance.
M: Actually, 34 I'm going to call the conference center once we check in to our rooms. We'd better make sure that the schedule hasn't been changed.

女：Alex，別忘了你放在後車廂的公事包。
男：我不會忘的。我只是希望我們能快點到飯店，這樣我們就能休息了。
女：是的。至少這位司機看起來知道最快的路線。我們應該會有時間休息並在今天下午會議開始前順過一次演講內容。
男：順帶一提，你有從辦公室的某人那裡拿我們的活動通行證，對吧？
女：有，Olivia 在我們離開前拿給我了。我們到大門口必須出示通行證。
男：事實上，我打算我們一登記入住我們的房間時就打去會議中心。我們最好確認一下時程有沒有變動。

32. 說話者們對話的地點應該是哪裡？
(A) 在計程車上
(B) 在飛機上
(C) 在公車站
(D) 在飯店裡

解析 女子在對話開頭就要男子別忘了在後車廂的公事包(don't forget your briefcase in the trunk of the car)，接著又說到司機 (this driver)，由此可知說話者們在計程車上，故本題正解為選項 (A)。

33. Olivia 給了女子什麼東西？
(A) 活動通行證
(B) 餐券
(C) 出差預算
(D) 市區地圖

解析 男子在對話中段詢問對方是否有到辦公室拿活動通行證 (you did get our event passes from someone at the office, right?)，女子接著回答 Olivia 有拿給她 (Olivia gave them to me)，故本題正解為選項 (A)。

34. 男子為什麼要打去會議中心？
(A) 取消演講
(B) 詢問方向
(C) 租借設備
(D) 確認時程

解析 男子在對話最後說到最好打個電話去會議中心確認時程是否有變動 (I'm going to call the conference center once we check in to our rooms. We'd better make sure that the schedule hasn't been changed)，故本題正解為選項 (D)。

Questions 35–37 refer to the following conversation with three speakers.

M1: 35 You're listening to *Money Matters* on the WKRM Breakfast Show with me, Lee Walters, and my co-host Martin Shaw.
M2: Hi, everyone.
M1: This morning, 36 we have a guest in the studio who has recently published a book on financial management. Thanks for coming in today, Sarah.
W: No problem. It's a pleasure to be here.
M2: So, what made you want to write a book on managing money?
W: Well, to be honest, I found that most of the information available online was either incorrect, or too complicated for the average person. So, I wanted to simplify it.
M2: That's a great idea. Well, 37 I'm sure our listeners would love to hear some tips on handling their finances. Would you mind?
W: No, I'd love to help.

- -

男 1：你正在收聽的是 WKRM 早餐秀的節目 *Money Matters*，與我本人，Lee Walters，以及我的共同主持人 Martin Shaw。

男 2：你好，大家。
男 1：今天早上，我們有一位最近出版了一本財務管理書籍的來賓要加入節目。Sarah，謝謝你今天來上節目。
女：不客氣。很榮幸能來這裡。
男 2：所以，是什麼讓你想寫有關財務管理的書呢？
女：嗯，老實說，我發現網路上大部分的資訊不是不正確，就是對一般民眾而言太複雜。所以，我想要簡化它。
男 2：這真是個很棒的想法。嗯，我想我們的聽眾一定很想聽你分享財務管理的小技巧。你介意嗎？
女：不會，我很樂意幫忙。

35. 男子應該是在哪裡工作？
(A) 在銀行
(B) 在書店
(C) 在會議中心
(D) 在廣播電臺

解析 其中一名男子在對話開頭說歡迎收聽 WKRM 的早餐秀 *Money Matters*(You're listening to *Money Matters* on the WKRM Breakfast Show with me)，由此可知男子是在廣播電臺工作，故本題正解為選項 (D)。

36. 女子最近做了什麼？
(A) 設計了一項產品
(B) 開始某個生意
(C) 寫了一本書
(D) 執導了一部電影

解析 其中一名男子在對話前半段介紹了節目的女來賓，點出她最近出了一本關於財務管理的書 (we have a guest in the studio who has recently published a book on financial management)，故本題正解為選項 (C)。

37. 女子接下來會做什麼？
(A) 介紹某個產品
(B) 談論自己的職涯
(C) 詢問問題
(D) 提供一些小技巧

解析 其中一名男子在對話最後告訴女子，聽眾們一定很想聽她談談財務管理的小技巧，並請她分享 (I'm sure our listeners would love to hear some tips on handling their finances. Would you mind?)，故本題正解為選項 (D)。

Questions 38–40 refer to the following conversation.

W: James, 38 isn't November 30 the day of Regina's final shift?
M: That's right. 38 I still can't believe she's retiring. She's been here ever since the factory opened.
W: I know! So, 39 did you make sure to add a bonus to her final pay? That's standard company policy.
M: Yeah, she'll receive an extra 50 percent for her final pay. And should we organize some kind of event for her?

W: Definitely. I was thinking we could book a table at the new Italian restaurant on Jensen Street.

M: Nice idea. **40** I'll make the booking later this afternoon.

女：James，11 月 30 日是 Regina 最後一天上班對吧？

男：沒錯。我還是無法相信她要退休了。她從工廠啟用後就在這工作了。

女：我知道！所以，你有替她的最後一筆薪水加上獎金吧？這是公司的一貫的政策。

男：是的，她最後一筆薪水會多 50%。我們應該要幫她辦個什麼活動嗎？

女：當然。我在想我們可以訂 Jensen 街上那間新開的義大利餐廳。

男：很棒的想法。我今天下午會訂位。

38. 説話者們提到 Regina 的什麼事？
(A) 她要升遷了。
(B) 她缺席。
(C) 她得獎了。
(D) 她要退休了。

解析　女子在對話開頭詢問某天是不是 Regina 最後一天上班 (isn't November 30 the day of Regina's final shift?)，男子接著回答自己無法相信她要退休了 (I still can't believe she's retiring)，故本題正解為選項 (D)。

39. 女子在詢問什麼？
(A) 工作日程表
(B) 預約
(C) 獎金
(D) 新政策

解析　女子在對話中段詢問男子是否有替 Regina 的最後一筆薪水加上獎金 (did you make sure to add a bonus to her final pay?)，故本題正解為選項 (C)。

40. 男子今天下午會做什麼？
(A) 買禮物
(B) 參加職員會議
(C) 訂位子
(D) 用餐

解析　今天下午這個時間點出現在對話的末段，男子説自己下午會訂位 (I'll make the booking later this afternoon.)，故本題正解為選項 (C)。

Questions 41–43 refer to the following conversation.

M: Ms. Park, I've been planning our company's end-of-year banquet, and I have some disappointing news. **41** I just received a call from the manager of The Belmont Hotel, and it turns out their ballroom is no longer available for our event.

W: Really? What was the problem?

M: A double booking, apparently. So, **42** I

was considering booking a hall at the Grand Eagle Hotel instead. However, I'll need to raise our budget a little to cover the cost. Is that fine with you?

W: Okay, go ahead. It's been a successful year, and I want the event to be memorable. Oh, and **43** can you e-mail me a copy of the design you made for the invitations? I'd like to see it before you print them.

男：Park 女士，我一直在籌備我們公司的年終盛宴，但我有一些壞消息。我剛剛接到 Belmont 飯店經理的電話，結果是他們的宴會廳沒辦法讓我們辦活動了。

女：真的嗎？出了什麼問題？

男：看來是重複預約。所以，我在想要不要改訂 Grand Eagle 飯店的宴會廳。但是，我將會需要稍微增加預算才能支付那筆費用。你覺得可以嗎？

女：好，就這麼做吧。今年是成功的一年，我希望這場活動會讓人印象深刻。喔，你可以用電子郵件寄你設計的邀請函給我嗎？我想在你印出來前先看過。

41. 男子對什麼感到失望？
(A) 某個會場無法使用。
(B) 房間太貴了。
(C) 有一位客戶無法參加活動。
(D) 某間飯店停業了。

解析　男子在對話剛開始就説自己接到 Belmont 飯店經理的電話，對方説宴會廳無法供他們使用 (I just received a call from the manager of The Belmont Hotel, and it turns out their ballroom is no longer available for our event.)，故本題正解為選項 (A)。

42. 男子想要徵求什麼許可？
(A) 安排交通
(B) 調整活動日期
(C) 增加預算
(D) 延長出差行程

解析　男子在對話中段提出他在考慮是否要改訂 Grand Eagle 飯店的宴會廳，但需要增加預算才能支付那筆費用 (I was considering booking a hall at the Grand Eagle Hotel instead. However, I'll need to raise our budget a little to cover the cost. Is that fine with you?)，接著詢問女子是否可行。由此可知男子是想請女子批准提高預算，故本題正解為選項 (C)。

43. 女子要男子下一步做什麼？
(A) 影印日程表
(B) 支付費用
(C) 寄某個設計
(D) 覆核某些數值

解析　女子在對話的最後要男子用電子郵件寄他設計的邀請函給自己 (can you e-mail me a copy of the design you made for the invitations?)，故本題正解為選項 (C)。

Questions 44–46 refer to the following conversation.

W: Thanks for calling Toy Kingdom. My name is Rhonda. How can I help you?

M: Hi. `44` `45` I'm calling about the remote-controlled car I bought for my son recently. It worked fine at first, but now the car doesn't respond when we try to make it move. Both my son and I are very upset about it. After all, I just bought it a few days ago.

W: I'm really sorry to hear that. Can I suggest some possible solutions? For example, did you try replacing the batteries in the controller?

M: Yes, of course I tried that. It didn't solve anything, though.

W: I see. And, did you make sure the car is set to remote control, instead of manual? `46` You can press a switch under the car's steering wheel.

M: Oh, I wasn't aware that I could change that. That might be the problem. `46` I'll change it and see if that works.

女：感謝你致電 Toy Kingdom。我是 Rhonda。有什麼我可以幫你的嗎？

男：你好。我打來是為了我最近買給我兒子的遙控車。一開始都沒有問題，但現在我們要讓它動的時候，車子都沒有反應。我跟我的兒子都非常失望。畢竟，我幾天前才買而已。

女：我對此深表遺憾。我可以建議你幾個解決方法嗎？舉例來說，你有試過換遙控器的電池嗎？

男：有，我當然試過。但這沒有解決我的問題。

女：我了解了。那你有確認過車子設定為無線遙控模式，而不是手動模式嗎？你可以試著按遙控車方向盤下方的開關。

男：喔，我不知道可以轉換模式。問題可能就是出在這。我會切換模式，看是否能使用。

---

44. 女子最有可能是誰？
(A) 行銷總監
(B) 財務顧問
(C) 安全檢查員
(D) 客服中心職員

解析 男子在對話前半段說遙控車一開始還能用，但現在要它動都沒反應 (I'm calling about the remote-controlled car I bought for my son recently. It worked fine at first, but now the car doesn't respond)，表達了對商品的不滿。由此可知女子應為客服中心職員，故本題正解為選項 (D)。

45. 男子說「我幾天前才買而已」，是想表達什麼意思？
(A) 某個包裹還沒送到。
(B) 帳單寄給錯的人了。
(C) 沒有必要的消費。
(D) 商品應該要完好如初。

解析 男子在對話前半段說遙控車一開始還能用，但現在要它動都沒反應 (I'm calling about the remote-controlled car I bought for my son recently. It worked fine at first, but now the car doesn't respond)，表達了對商品的不滿，並說出「我幾天前才買而已」。男子說這句話的意思是商品才剛買沒幾天，不應該會有故障的情形發生，故本題正解為選項 (D)。

46. 男子接下來應該會做什麼？
(A) 確認收據
(B) 更換零件
(C) 按下開關
(D) 閱讀說明書

解析 女子在對話中段要男子試著按遙控車的方向盤下方的開關 (You can press a switch under the car's steering wheel.)，男子說他不知道可以換模式，並表示會嘗試看看，看是否能使用 (I'll change it and see if that works.)。由此可知男子接著會去按開關，故本題正解為選項 (C)。

Questions 47–49 refer to the following conversation.

W: Derek, I want to speak with you about your role and responsibilities `47` here at the library. `48` Are you still interested in receiving some extra training?

M: Yes, I'd love to learn more.

W: Good. In that case, `48` I'd like to send you to a computer skills workshop this weekend. The workshop will teach you how to use a wide variety of computer programs. When you return, you'll be ready to do some shifts in the IT Lounge upstairs.

M: That sounds great! `49` Is the workshop being held at the local college?

W: Actually, no. You'll need to travel to Ashville Community Center, but we'll cover your bus fare.

M: Thanks a lot. I'm looking forward to it.

女：Derek，我想談談你在這個圖書館裡擔任的職位和責任。你仍然有興趣接受額外訓練嗎？

男：是的，我想要多學一些。

女：很好。這樣的話，我這週末想派你去參加一個電腦技巧工作坊。這個工作坊會教你如何使用各式各樣的電腦軟體。當你回來後，你就能準備到樓上的資訊科技部值班了。

男：聽起來很棒！工作坊在社區大學裡舉辦嗎？

女：其實不是。你必須到 Ashville 社區中心去，但我們會負責你的公車費用。

男：非常感謝。我非常期待。

---

47. 說話者們在哪裡工作？
(A) 在郵局
(B) 在診所
(C) 在工廠
(D) 在圖書館

解析 女子在對話開頭就提到這裡是圖書館 (here at the library)。由此可知兩人在圖書館工作，故本題正解為選項 (D)。

48. 女子提供男子什麼？
(A) 額外的訓練
(B) 管理的經驗
(C) 額外的休假
(D) 更高的薪資

解析 女子在對話開頭詢問男子是否還有興趣接受額外訓練 (Are you still interested in receiving some extra training?)，表示自己要送男子去參加培養電腦能力的工作坊 (I'd like to send you to a computer skills workshop)，故本題正解為選項 (A)。

49. 男子問了什麼問題？
(A) 工作坊的地點
(B) 公車時刻表
(C) 票價
(D) 申請流程

解析 男子在對話中段詢問工作坊是否在社區大學舉辦 (Is the workshop being held at the local college?)，可知男子對工作坊的地點有疑問，故本題正解為選項 (A)。

Questions 50–52 refer to the following conversation with three speakers.

M1: Hi, Ms. Moxley. Thanks for agreeing to meet with us here today.

W: No problem. **50** I'm looking forward to making a start on the landscaping plans for the park.

M1: Great. This is the project manager and park administrator, Mike Fairchild. He has joined us for this meeting to review your landscaping proposal.

W: **52** Hi, Mike. Were you pleased with the ideas I submitted for the park?

M2: Yes, **51** we looked at your designs this morning and we were both very impressed. But, there's one thing I'd like you to change.

W: Sure, what is it?

M2: Well, I noticed that **52** you positioned the water fountain near the main entrance of the park, but I'd prefer to move it to the middle of the rose garden. Would that be okay?

男 1：你好，Moxley 女士。謝謝你今天答應和我們在此見面。
女：不客氣。我很期待開始執行公園的造景企劃。
男 1：太好了。這位是專案經理及公園管理人 Mike Fairchild。他會加入我們這個會議，討論你的造景企劃案。
女：你好，Mike。你對我針對公園所做的規劃還滿意嗎？
男 2：是的，我們今天早上看過你的設計，令我們兩人都印象深刻。但是，我想麻煩你修改一個地方。

女：沒問題，要改哪裡呢？
男 2：嗯，我發現你將噴水池擺在公園的正門附近，但我想把它移到玫瑰園的中間。這樣可以嗎？

---

50. 對話主要是關於什麼內容？
(A) 造景企劃
(B) 社區活動
(C) 建築翻新
(D) 企業合併

解析 女子在對話前半段說自己很期待開始執行公園的造景企劃 (I'm looking forward to making a start on the landscaping plans for the park.)，後面提及的也都是和造景工程相關的內容，故本題正解為選項 (A)。

51. 男子們今天早上做了什麼事？
(A) 購買材料
(B) 打掃工作現場
(C) 審閱設計圖
(D) 面試應徵者

解析 今天早上這個時間點出現在對話中段，其中一名男子說今天早上看了設計圖 (we looked at your designs this morning)，故本題正解為選項 (C)。

52. Mike 想要修改什麼？
(A) 截止日期
(B) 預算
(C) 位置
(D) 供應商

解析 女子在對話中段稱呼其中一名男子 Mike，而該男子在對話最後說想把預計擺在公園正門附近的噴水池移到玫瑰園的中間 (you positioned the water fountain near the main entrance of the park, but I'd prefer to move it to the middle of the rose garden)。由此可知 Mike 想要修改的是位置，故本題正解為選項 (C)。

Questions 53–55 refer to the following conversation.

M: Melissa, if you have some free time, **53** I'd like to talk about a strategy we could use to promote the restaurant and attract new customers.

W: I'd love to hear your ideas. It's about time we took a new approach to promoting the business.

M: Well, **54** during the day, we don't have many customers, so our part-time workers don't have much work to do. I was thinking we could send them outside to distribute flyers and menus to potential customers on the street.

W: Actually, we tried that strategy a couple of years ago, and **55** the employees weren't happy because it was sometimes raining or snowing while they were outside.

男：Melissa，如果你有時間的話，我想跟你討論一下可以用來宣傳餐廳且吸引新顧客的策略。

女：我很樂意聽你的想法。的確是時候採取新方法來宣傳了。

男：嗯，因為白天的客人不多，所以我們的兼職人員沒什麼工作需要做。我在想可以叫他們去外面發傳單和菜單給街上的潛在顧客。

女：事實上，我們幾年前試過這個方法，但職員們不是很開心，因為他們到外面的時候偶爾會遇到下雨或下雪。

53. 男子想討論什麼？
(A) **宣傳策略**
(B) 遷店
(C) 安全程序
(D) 職員獎勵計劃

解析 男子在對話開頭就提出想要討論宣傳餐廳，吸引新顧客的策略 (I'd like to talk about a strategy we could use to promote the restaurant and attract new customers.)，故本題正解為選項 (A)。

54. 男子提到兼職人員的什麼問題？
(A) **他們不忙碌。**
(B) 他們需要多加訓練。
(C) 他們最近才被聘僱。
(D) 他們收到客訴。

解析 男子在對話中段提到白天客人不多，所以兼職人員沒什麼工作需要做 (during the day, we don't have many customers, so our part-time workers don't have much work to do)，故本題正解為選項 (A)。

55. 根據女子所說，職員們之前為什麼不開心？
(A) 他們想要更高的薪資。
(B) 他們的工時太長了。
(C) **他們經歷了壞天氣。**
(D) 他們的休假被減少了。

解析 職員們之前不開心的理由出現在對話後半段，他們出去宣傳時偶爾會下雨或下雪，所以感到不開心 (the employees weren't happy because it was sometimes raining or snowing while they were outside)，故本題正解為選項 (C)。

Questions 56–58 refer to the following conversation.

M: Hi, Deanna. Do we still have a photocopier here in the library? It used to be right here at the circulation desk, but 56 everything has been moved around now.

W: On the second floor, I think. You know, 56 the remodeling of the library is good for all our members, but it's going to take us a while to get used to it.

M: Yeah, that's for sure. The old layout was very convenient. 57 I used to grab a magazine to read while I ate lunch in the staff room, but now all the magazines are on the third floor, so I don't bother.

W: Oh, by the way, 58 do you know about the new bakery that just opened across the street? You should go and try their sandwiches and cakes during lunchtime today.

男：你好，Deanna。圖書館裡還有影印機嗎？它原本在借還書櫃臺這裡，但現在所有東西的位置都變了。

女：我想它是在 2 樓。你知道的，圖書館整修對我們所有人來說都是好事，不過我們需要一點時間適應。

男：是的，這是肯定的。原本的配置真的很方便，我之前在職員休息室吃午餐的時候會拿本雜誌看，但現在所有雜誌都移到 3 樓，我就不那麼做了。

女：喔，順帶一提，你知道對街那間新開的烘焙坊嗎？你今天午餐時間一定要去試試他們的三明治和蛋糕。

56. 從對話中能夠得知圖書館的什麼資訊？
(A) 它更改了營業時間。
(B) 它搬到新的地點。
(C) **它最近剛整修過。**
(D) 它在招聘新職員。

解析 男子在對話開始說到所有東西都被移動過 (everything has been moved around now)，女子接著點出圖書館經過整修 (the remodeling of the library is good for all our members)，故本題正解為選項 (C)。

57. 男子說他之前常做什麼？
(A) **在午餐時間閱讀**
(B) 在職員餐廳用餐
(C) 撰寫雜誌文章
(D) 到附近的餐廳吃飯

解析 男子在對話中段提到自己在職員休息室吃午餐時，常常會拿雜誌去讀 (I used to grab a magazine to read while I ate lunch in the staff room)，故本題正解為選項 (A)。

58. 女子建議男子去做什麼？
(A) **去一間烘焙坊**
(B) 不要吃午餐
(C) 參加某個活動
(D) 提早下班

解析 女子在對話的最後問男子知不知道對街新開的那間烘焙坊，並建議他去吃吃看那邊的三明治和蛋糕 (do you know about the new bakery that just opened across the street? You should go and try their sandwiches and cakes)，故本題正解為選項 (A)。

Questions 59–61 refer to the following conversation.

W: Bobby, 59 I need to speak with you about the uniforms we ordered for our employees. The supplier just sent me some samples and I really don't like the design.

Our company logo is too small, and the colors are too dark. But, **60** I'm afraid it's too late to ask for changes.

M: We have until Friday to confirm the order. Have you spoken to the supplier about it?

W: Not yet, but I guess I could give them a call after the staff meeting today.

M: Hmm... in order to save time, **61** why don't you go to the supplier today and speak with them in person? That way, you can easily explain what you want them to do.

女：Bobby，我必須跟你談談我們要訂給職員的制服。供應商剛剛寄了一些樣品來，但我不太喜歡這種設計。我們公司的商標太小了，並且顏色太暗。但是，我擔心現在要修改已經太晚了。

男：我們週五前確認訂單就好。你跟供應商提過這個問題了嗎？

女：還沒，但我想我可以在今天職員會議後打給他們。

男：嗯…為了節省時間，你何不親自去找供應商面對面談呢？這樣的話，你可以很輕易地解釋你想要他們做什麼。

---

59. 説話者們主要在討論什麼？
(A) 宣傳單
(B) 職員訓練
(C) 公司制服
(D) 網站設計

解析 女子在對話開頭表示必須和男子談談要訂給職員的制服 (I need to speak with you about the uniforms we ordered for our employees.)，後續也提及該制服設計的缺點，故本題正解為選項 (C)。

60. 男子説「我們週五前確認訂單就好」意味著什麼意思？
(A) 還有修改的時間。
(B) 他們會比計劃還提前完成任務。
(C) 需要增加職員人數。
(D) 物品的數量應該要增加。

解析 女子在對話中段説擔心現在要修改已經太晚了 (I'm afraid it's too late to ask for changes.)，男子接著回「我們週五前確認訂單就好」。由此可知男子是在告訴對方還有時間，故本題正解為選項 (A)。

61. 男子建議做什麼？
(A) 拜訪業者
(B) 寄電子郵件
(C) 打電話
(D) 取消會議

解析 男子在對話最後建議對方直接去找供應商面對面談 (why don't you go to the supplier today and speak with them in person?)，故本題正解為選項 (A)。

Questions 62–64 refer to the following conversation and comment card.

M: Hi, Loretta. **62** Did you have a chance to create the comment cards yet? The ones that we plan to leave in the rooms for our guests to fill out.

W: Yes, and I have a sample with me now. Would you like to take a look?

M: Sure, let me see. Well, they look great to me. **63** I see you've decided to ask for a score out of ten. Why did you choose that method?

W: Well, **63** I read an article in a marketing magazine and it recommended this method. It can give us more information than other methods.

M: I see. I'd like to make one suggestion, though. **64** I don't think it's necessary to ask guests to leave additional comments. We might not have time to read them all. Let's just keep it simple.

W: **64** You might be right. I'll remove that item and let you see the finished version later today.

```
Comment Card
(Please indicate a score out of 10)
1. Cleanliness : [        ]
2. Service :     [        ]
3. Amenities :   [        ]
4. Additional Comments : _____
_____
_____
_____
```

男：你好，Loretta。你有機會做意見卡了嗎？我們計劃要放在房間裡讓客人填的那個。

女：有，而且我現在身上就有範本。你要看看嗎？

男：當然，讓我看一下。嗯，我覺得很好看。看來你打算用滿分 10 分來問意見。為什麼你選擇這種方法呢？

女：嗯，我在行銷雜誌上讀過一篇文章，那篇文章推薦了這個方式。比起其他方法，這個能給我們的資訊更多。

男：我了解了。然而我想要給一個建議。我覺得沒必要請顧客留其他意見。我們可能沒時間讀完全部內容。保持簡單就好了。

女：也許你説得對。我會把它移除掉，今天晚一點會讓你看完成版。

```
意見卡（請以滿分 10 分打分數）
1. 整潔： [        ]
2. 服務： [        ]
3. 設施： [        ]
4. 其他意見： _____
_____
_____
_____
```

62. 意見卡是要給誰填的？
(A) 餐廳客人
(B) 飛機乘客
(C) 飯店客人
(D) 活動參加者

解析 男子在對話開頭詢問對方是否做了意見卡，且說明那是要放在房間裡讓客人填的 (Did you have a chance to create the comment cards yet? The ones that we plan to leave in the rooms for our guests to fill out)。由此可知意見卡的對象是飯店的客人，故本題正解為選項 (C)。

63. 女子是怎麼選擇意見卡上評分方式的？
(A) 她讀了雜誌文章。
(B) 她問了顧客意見。
(C) 她和上司討論過。
(D) 她抄了競爭者的方式。

解析 男子在對話中段說到意見卡上的評分方式為滿分 10 分 (I see you've decided to ask for a score out of ten.)，女子說這是雜誌文章推薦的方式 (I read an article in a marketing magazine and it recommended this method.)，故本題正解為選項 (A)。

64. 請參考圖表。意見卡上的哪一個項目將去除？
(A) 第 1 項
(B) 第 2 項
(C) 第 3 項
(D) 第 4 項

解析 男子在對話後半段說他覺得沒必要請顧客留其他意見 (I don't think it's necessary to ask guests to leave additional comments.... Let's just keep it simple.)，接著女子對男子的意見表達同意 (You might be right.)。對照圖表可知其他意見為第 4 項，故本題正解為選項 (D)。

Questions 65–67 refer to the following conversation and bar graph.

W: Vincent, here's the data for the pre-packaged coffee we sold at our coffee shop last month. Our French Roast coffee variety has proven to be really popular. I didn't expect to sell so many packets.
M: Well, `65` the new employees we hired last month really worked hard to push sales of the pre-packaged coffee. They've done a great job. But, I'm a little disappointed that `66` we only sold 100 packets of this coffee.
W: Me too. `66` Let's slightly reduce the price for that one, starting from August 1.
M: Yes, that should boost its popularity. Also, I think `67` we'll see a rise in the number of customers thanks to the range of coffee mugs we've just started selling.

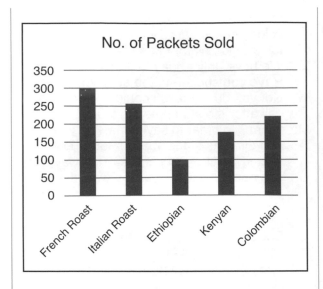

女：Vincent，這是我們咖啡廳上個月所賣的咖啡包數據。我們的法式烘焙咖啡被證明很受歡迎。我沒想過能賣這麼多包。
男：嗯，我們上個月聘的新職員們非常努力推動咖啡包的銷售，他們做得很好。但我對這種咖啡只賣 100 包感到有些失望。
女：我也是。我們從 8 月 1 日起，稍微降低這包的價格。
男：好，這樣應該能讓它賣得更好。此外，我想我們的顧客數量會有顯著的成長多虧於我們剛開始銷售的系列馬克杯。

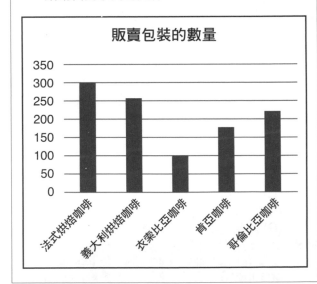

65. 說話者們上個月做了什麼？
(A) 他們舉辦了一個特別活動。
(B) 他們開了一間新店。
(C) 他們多聘了職員。
(D) 他們裝修了咖啡廳。

解析 上個月這個時間點出現在對話中段，男子說到上個月聘了新的職員 (the new employees we hired last month)，故本題正解為選項 (C)。

66. 請看圖表。什麼種類的咖啡 8 月會賣得比較便宜？
(A) 義大利烘焙咖啡
(B) 衣索比亞咖啡

(C) 肯亞咖啡
(D) 哥倫比亞咖啡

解析 男子在對話中段提到只有賣 100 包的商品 (we only sold 100 packets of this coffee.)，接著女子就說試著從 8 月 1 日起稍微降低價格 (Let's slightly reduce the price for that one, starting from August 1.)。對照圖表可知販賣數量為 100 包的商品是衣索比亞咖啡，故本題正解為選項 (B)。

67. 男子為什麼認為會有更多顧客光臨？
(A) 可以買到新類型的商品。
(B) 即將舉辦換季特賣。
(C) 推出了新廣告。
(D) 推出了會員計劃。

解析 男子在對話的最後提到多虧最近剛開始賣的馬克杯，顧客應該會明顯增加 (we'll see a rise in the number of customers thanks to the range of coffee mugs we've just started selling)，故本題正解為提到新商品的選項 (A)。

Questions 68–70 refer to the following conversation and map.

M: Hi, Marion, it's Alan. I'm calling because a previous client of ours, EDP Corporation, **68** wants us to cater another large event for them.

W: Oh, that's good news. Is it another staff training workshop, just like last time?

M: Yes. They want us to attend a meeting at their new premises on Monday at 11A.M. **69** Their headquarters are now located in the Globe Building, just opposite the hospital, on Dixon Avenue.

W: Ah, right. I know that place. The problem is that I have a dentist appointment that morning, and then I'll need to take the subway to the EDP Corporation meeting. I might be a little late.

M: Well, **70** why don't I pick you up in my car after your appointment? That would save us some time.

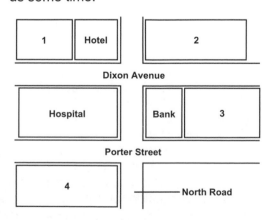

男：你好，Marion，我是 Alan。我打這通電話是因為之前的客戶 EDP 公司，想要我們再為他們另一場大型活動提供外燴服務。
女：喔，這真是個好消息。跟上次一樣是職員訓練嗎？
男：對。他們想要我們週一上午 11 點到他們的新

辦公室參加會議。他們的公司總部現在位於 Dixon 大道上，醫院正對面的 Globe 大廈。
女：啊，對。我知道那個地方。問題是我那天早上有牙科預約，結束後再搭地鐵去 EDP 公司開會，我可能會稍微晚到一些。
男：那麼，何不在你門診後我去載你？那樣能幫我們省一些時間。

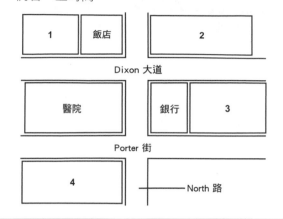

68. 説話者們工作的地點應該是哪裡？
(A) 法律事務所
(B) 不動產仲介公司
(C) 行銷公司
(D) 外燴公司

解析 男子在對話中說客戶想要他們提供外燴服務 (wants us to cater another large event for them)，故本題正解為選項 (D)。

69. 請看圖表。説話者們週一要到哪棟建築物？
(A) 建築 1 號
(B) 建築 2 號
(C) 建築 3 號
(D) 建築 4 號

解析 男子在對話中段說明了客戶公司的位置，該公司總部在 Dixon 大道上，醫院正對面的 Globe 大廈 (Their headquarters are now located in the Globe Building, just opposite the hospital, on Dixon Avenue.)。對照圖表可知位在 Dixon 大道上，又在醫院對面的建築為 1 號，故本題正解為選項 (A)。

70. 男子説他要做什麼？
(A) 寄文件給女子
(B) 重新安排會議時間
(C) 載女子一程
(D) 取消牙科預約

解析 男子在對話最後詢問是否要載對方一程 (why don't I pick you up in my car after your appointment?)，故本題正解為選項 (C)。

Part 4

Questions 71–73 refer to the following advertisement.

Attention, all adventurers! Do you love going camping? Do you like to spend the night in the great outdoors, but need a certain level of comfort and reliable protection from bad weather? **71**

We're pleased to introduce the Explorer 500, a top-of-the-range tent that accommodates up to six people. The surprising thing about it is how light it is! **72** Thanks to the lightweight frame and material, you'll barely notice it when you are carrying it! In addition, until the end of this month, **73** we're offering a 10 percent discount on the Explorer 500, but only to those who purchase it through our Web site at www.hikersworld.com.

請注意，所有冒險者們！你喜歡露營嗎？你喜歡在美好的戶外度過夜晚，但需要一定程度的舒適度和能夠抵擋壞天氣的遮蔽物嗎？我們很開心地向你介紹最多能夠容納 6 人的高級帳篷 Explorer 500。最驚人的是它非常輕！由於它輕量化的框架與材質，你在搬帳篷時幾乎感覺不到它的存在！此外，到這個月底前，Explorer 500 都享有九折的優惠，但這個折扣只提供給在我們的網站 www.hikersworld.com 購買的顧客。

up with ways to boost profits? Well, I've written a report on strategies for driving up sales, but I'm not sure how to submit it to the CEO. Apparently, **75** he has a new e-mail address, because the old one is no longer working. I promised I'd send the report to him by 5 P.M. today, and he's overseas on a business trip right now. **76** Can you help me find out the contact information for our CEO? You know Steve at the head office, right? **76** Perhaps he can help. Thanks in advance.

你好，Greg，我是 Sanjeet。你記得執行長要我們想辦法增加收益嗎？嗯，我寫了一份關於提高銷售量策略的報告，但我不確定要怎麼交給執行長。看來，他應該是換了新電子郵件地址，因為舊的那個已經無法用了。我答應他今天下午 5 點要把報告寄給他，而他現在在海外出差。你可以幫我找執行長的連絡方式嗎？你知道總部辦公室的 Steve 吧？或許他幫得上忙。先跟你說謝謝。

71. 哪種類型的產品正在被宣傳？
(A) 睡袋
(B) 一雙靴子
(C) 帳篷
(D) 背包

解析 談話前半段說明完背景後，就開始介紹最多能容納 6 人的高級帳篷 Explorer 500(We're pleased to introduce the Explorer 500, a top-of-the-range tent)，故本題正解為選項 (C)。

72. 說話者說商品的哪一點令人驚訝？
(A) 它的重量
(B) 它的耐久度
(C) 它的外觀
(D) 它的價格

解析 談話中段提到帳篷使用輕量化的框架與材質，在搬帳篷時幾乎感覺不到它的存在 (Thanks to the lightweight frame and material, you'll barely notice it when you are carrying it!)，說明了帳篷的特點，故本題正解為選項 (A)。

73. 聆聽者們要怎麼做才能得到折扣？
(A) 申請會員
(B) 參加開幕活動
(C) 消費滿特定金額
(D) 在網路上購買

解析 談話後半段點出只有在該公司網站上購買的客戶才能享有九折優惠 (we're offering a 10 percent discount on the Explorer 500, but only to those who purchase it through our Web site at www.hikerworld.com.)，故本題正解為選項 (D)。

Questions 74–76 refer to the following telephone message.

Hi, Greg, this is Sanjeet calling. Do you remember that the **74** CEO asked us to come

74. 說話者的報告是關於什麼的？
(A) 招募經驗豐富職員的方式
(B) 在線上打廣告的優點
(C) 減少垃圾的方法
(D) 增加銷售量的點子

解析 說話者在談話開頭說執行長要他們想能增加收益的方法，而他寫了關於提高銷售量策略的報告 (CEO asked us to come up with ways to boost profits? Well, I've written a report on strategies for driving up sales)，故本題正解為選項 (D)。

75. 根據說話者所說，什麼東西有變動？
(A) 電子郵件地址
(B) 專案截止期限
(C) 行銷活動
(D) 旅遊行程

解析 說話者在談話中段用 he 代指執行長，說他的電子郵件有變，原本的那個已經不能用了 (he has a new e-mail address, because the old one is no longer working.)。由此可知變動的是電子郵件地址，故本題正解為選項 (A)。

76. 為什麼說話者會說「你知道總部辦公室的 Steve 吧」？
(A) 為了建議對方邀 Steve 參與會議
(B) 為了確認某個專案被批准了
(C) 為了推薦聆聽者申請某個職位
(D) 為了請聆聽者連絡某位同事

解析 說話者在談話最後請聆聽者幫自己找能連絡執行長的方式，接著說「你知道總部辦公室的 Steve 吧？」(Can you help me find out the contact information for our CEO?)，並說明那個人或許可以幫得上忙 (Perhaps he can help.)。由此可知他要聆聽者連絡那個人，從那邊得到協助，故本題正解為選項 (D)。

Questions 77–79 refer to the following introduction.

Good afternoon, everyone. 77 I'll start this meeting by telling you about the newest member of the board, Jeremy Lee, who has just joined us as our new marketing director. Many of you will probably already know that Jeremy had been working for Shazam Electronics for the past 15 years. He was responsible for 78 Shazam's highly successful tablet computer advertisement, which was shown throughout the entire world. Also, 79 Jeremy is keen to start up some activity clubs for our staff here, as he enjoys playing a wide range of sports and hiking in his spare time. Anyway, Jeremy, I'll let you tell the other members about yourself!

各位下午好。會議開始的同時，我要先告訴各位新的董事會成員 Jeremy Lee，他會以新行銷總監的身分與我們一起工作。你們之中很多人可能已經知道 Jeremy 過去 15 年都在 Shazam 電子工作。他負責的是 Shazam 最成功的平板電腦的廣告，那個廣告在全世界播出。此外，Jeremy 很想要為職員們創立一些活動社團，因為他本身在閒暇時間就很愛做各種運動和健行。總之，Jeremy，讓你跟其他成員們介紹一下自己！

77. 被介紹的人是誰？
(A) 一位退休的董事
(B) 一位受獎人
(C) 一位新的董事會成員
(D) 一位公司的客戶
解析 說話者在談話開頭說要在會議開始的同時，為大家介紹新的董事會成員 Jeremy Lee(I'll start this meeting by telling you about the newest member of the board, Jeremy Lee)，故本題正解為選項 (C)。

78. 談話中提到關於廣告的什麼資訊？
(A) 它適用於一系列的手機。
(B) 它比想像中還要不成功。
(C) 它被全世界看見。
(D) 它播了 15 年。
解析 廣告出現在談話中段，提到 Shazam 公司最成功的平板電腦廣告在全世界播出 (Shazam's highly successful tablet computer advertisement, which was shown throughout the entire world)，故本題正解為選項 (C)。

79. 談話中提到關於 Jeremy Lee 的什麼資訊？
(A) 他很活躍。
(B) 他很愛閱讀。
(C) 他創立了一間公司。
(D) 他即將升官。
解析 談話後半段提到 Jeremy 想為職員們成立活動社團，他閒暇時間也很愛做各種運動及健行 (Jeremy is keen to start up some activity clubs for our staff here, as he enjoys playing a wide range of sports and hiking)。由此可知 Jeremy 是個活躍的人，故本題正解為選項 (A)。

Questions 80–82 refer to the following telephone message.

Hello, I'm leaving this message for Ms. Burton. 80 This is Angus calling from Jolly Food Company about your application for the sales manager position. I'm reviewing your documents now, but 81 it seems that you forgot to add the names and contact details of the two job references we require. That section of your form is completely blank. I'm afraid I won't be able to invite you for an interview until we receive those details. So, 82 would you mind getting back to me at this phone number at your earliest possible convenience? Thank you.

你好，我要留言給 Burton 女士。我是 Jolly 食品公司的 Angus，這通電話是關於你應徵銷售經理一職之事。我現在正在看你的文件，但你似乎忘了附上我們要求的兩位推薦人的姓名和連絡方式。你表格上的那個欄位完全是空白的。在我們還沒收到那些資訊前，我恐怕無法邀請你來面試。所以，能不能請你儘速回撥這個電話號碼給我？謝謝。

80. 說話者打電話的理由是什麼？
(A) 商業提案
(B) 即將舉辦的折扣活動
(C) 應聘工作相關事項
(D) 專案的截止日期
解析 談話開頭就說到這通電話是關於聆聽者應徵銷售經理一職之事 (This is Angus calling from Jolly Food Company about your application for the sales manager position.)，故本題正解為選項 (C)。

81. 說話者提到什麼問題？
(A) 日程重疊。
(B) 少了某些資訊。
(C) 有些指導原則是錯的。
(D) 活動被延期了。
解析 談話中段說到對方似乎忘了附上兩位推薦人的姓名和連絡方式 (it seems that you forgot to add the names and contact details of the two job references)。由此可知對方漏了某些資訊，故本題正解為選項 (B)。

82. 說話者向聆聽者做了什麼要求？
(A) 拜訪某間公司
(B) 參加一場面試
(C) 回電話
(D) 寄電子郵件
解析 說話者在談話後段請聽者盡快回自己電話 (would you mind getting back to me at this phone number at your earliest possible convenience?)，故本題正解為選項 (C)。

Questions 83–85 refer to the following tour information.

Good morning, and welcome to the Old Town district of York City. We'll begin today's tour by visiting St. Mark's Cathedral. **83** This is one of the most popular historical sites in the city because it contains a large number of valuable paintings and sculptures. Many of these works are culturally significant, so people come from all over the world to see them. **84** While looking around, you might have some questions about them—that's why I'm here! But **85** please remember to be back in the parking lot by 11A.M. We will need to board the bus promptly to set off for our next destination.

早安，歡迎來到約克市的舊城區。我們今天行程的一開始要參觀 St. Mark 大教堂。這是這個城市最受歡迎的歷史景點之一，因為裡面有非常多珍貴的畫作與雕像。裡面很多作品都有重大的文化意義，所以人們從世界各地來欣賞。在四處參觀時，你們可能會對這些藝術品有些疑問——這就是為什麼我在這！但請記得在上午 11 點前回到停車場。我們要準時搭上巴士前往下個景點。

83. 根據說話者所說，為什麼 St. Mark 大教堂很受歡迎？
    (A) 那裡舉辦了特別的活動。
    (B) 那裡的建築風格很獨特。
    (C) 那裡不收門票。
    (D) 那裡有很多藝術品。
解析 談話開頭說到 St. Mark 大教堂是很著名的歷史景點，裡面有很多珍貴的畫作和雕像 (This is one of the most popular historical sites in the city because it contains a large number of valuable paintings and sculptures.)，故本題正解為選項 (D)。

84. 說話者說「這就是為什麼我在這！」意味著什麼意思？
    (A) 她在推薦一個特有的景點。
    (B) 她要聆聽者們跟著她。
    (C) 她為遲到道歉。
    (D) 她很樂意回答疑問。
解析 說話者在談話中段說到，在參觀的時候，聆聽者可能會對藝術品有疑問 (While looking around, you might have some questions about them)，接著說「這就是為什麼我在這」。由此可知她很樂意回答疑問，故本題正解為選項 (D)。

85. 說話者提醒了聆聽者什麼？
    (A) 停車證
    (B) 特別折扣
    (C) 公車號碼
    (D) 出發時間
解析 說話者在談話最後提醒聆聽者上午 11 點前回停車場，才能準時上車前往下個景點 (please remember to be back in the parking lot by 11 A.M. We will need to board the bus promptly to set off for our next destination)，故本題正解為選項 (D)。

Questions 86–88 refer to the following broadcast.

You're listening to Josh on Milford Radio 94.5 FM, and I'm here with a local news story. **86** The annual People of Milford Awards were presented yesterday, and Karen Gosford was named as the community's Person of the Year. **87** Ms. Gosford is a leading scientific researcher at the Milford Agricultural Center and has been praised for her work in developing GM foods and pesticide-free farming practices. Before joining her current research team, she worked with local environmental groups to clean up the region's lakes and rivers. **88** I'd like to hear what you, our listeners, have to say about Ms. Gosford's contributions to our city. Call in at 555-8378 to let us know what you think.

你現在收聽的是 FM94.5 Milford 電臺 Josh 的節目，我在這裡為各位傳達當地新聞消息。年度 Milford 大人物獎昨天頒發了，Karen Gosford 被選為社區年度大人物。Gosford 女士是 Milford 農業中心的精英科學研究員，她開發基因改造食品和無農藥農業的成果獲得許多讚美。在加入她現在所在的研究團隊之前，她和當地環境保護團體一同就當地的湖泊及河流進行清潔。我想要聽聽各位聽眾們對於 Gosford 女士對我們城市的貢獻有什麼話想說。撥打 555-8378，讓我們知道你的想法吧。

86. 廣播節目主要的內容是什麼？
    (A) 就業機會
    (B) 休閒設施
    (C) 社區獎項
    (D) 即將舉辦的活動
解析 談話一開始就提到頒發了年度 Milford 大人物獎，並提及得獎人的名字 (The annual People of Milford Awards were presented yesterday, and Karen Gosford was named as the community's Person of the Year.)，故本題正解為選項 (C)。

87. 根據說話者所說，Karen Gosford 有哪個領域的經驗？
    (A) 演藝
    (B) 金融
    (C) 行銷
    (D) 科學
解析 Gosford 女士是科學研究員的描述出現在談話的中段 (Ms. Gosford is a leading scientific researcher)，故本題正解為選項 (D)。

88. 說話者邀請聽眾們做什麼？
    (A) 提問
    (B) 參加一場典禮
    (C) 分享他們的意見
    (D) 投票
解析 說話者在談話後半段說想要知道聽眾想對得獎人說什麼，並請他們撥電話過去 (I'd like to

hear what you, our listeners, have to say about Ms. Gosford's contributions to our city. Call in at 555-8378)。由此可知說話者在鼓勵聽眾分享意見，故本題正解為選項 (C)。

Questions 89–91 refer to the following recorded message.

Hi. Thank you for calling me, Lisa Finnigan, an advisor at Silverado Investments. I'm sorry that I'm unable to take your call right now, but you are welcome to leave a message. **89** At Silverado Investments, we are dedicated to providing our clients with the best professional advice regarding their finances. **90** I am currently overseas for a week-long family holiday and will return on May 12. I will return your call as soon as I get back to the office. However, **91** if you are an existing client and have an urgent issue, you may e-mail me at lisa@silverado.net. Thank you.

你好。感謝你的來電，我是 Silverado 投資公司的顧問 Lisa Finnigan。抱歉我現在無法接聽你的電話，但是歡迎你留言。在 Silverado 投資公司，我們致力於提供客戶們與財務管理有關的專業建議。我目前和家人在海外過一週的長假，5 月 12 日會回來。我一回到辦公室就會立刻回電給你。然而，如果你已經是我們的客戶，且有急事需要協助，可以寄電子郵件到 lisa@silverado.net 連絡我。謝謝。

89. 這間公司提供什麼服務？
(A) 住宅改造
(B) 財務諮詢
(C) 活動企劃
(D) 套裝旅遊行程
解析 談話中段說到公司致力於提供客戶們最專業的財務建議 (At Silverado Investments, we are dedicated to providing our clients with the best professional advice regarding their finances.)，故本題正解為選項 (B)。

90. 為什麼說話者無法通話？
(A) 她在開董事會。
(B) 她請病假。
(C) 她正在講課。
(D) 她正在休假。
解析 談話中段提到說話者跟家人到海外度假，5 月 12 日會回來 (I am currently overseas for a week-long family holiday and will return on May 12)，故本題正解為選項 (D)。

91. 聆聽者們如果遇到緊急狀況該怎麼做？
(A) 打另一支電話號碼
(B) 到說話者的辦公室
(C) 寄送電子郵件
(D) 審閱文件
解析 談話後半段說如果有急事需要協助，可以寄電子郵件給說話者 (if you are an existing client

and have an urgent issue, you may e-mail me at lisa@silverado.net)，故本題正解為選項 (C)。

Questions 92–94 refer to the following excerpt from a meeting.

Well, we have finally come to the end of **92** our supermarket's orientation session. Before you all go to your departments, there's one last thing to mention. As I'm sure you all know, the city will be hosting a festival to celebrate its 500th birthday on Saturday, June 16. A lot of popular bands and singers will be performing on Main Street. This will be an exciting event, and we understand that many of you will want to attend. **93** You can request leave at the HR office, starting today. Take note, many employees will want this day off. Also, **94** don't forget, you can ask the HR manager for extra hours if you want to make some more money.

嗯，終於到了我們超市新進職員培訓的尾聲。在各位到所屬的部門之前，我還有最後一件事要說。我想各位都知道，這個城市在本週六 6 月 16 日，即將舉辦一場慶典來慶祝它 500 歲的生日。很多知名樂團和歌手都會到主街表演。這將會是一場讓人感到興奮的活動，我們也了解你們之中很多人都想去參加。從今天開始，你們可以到人資部辦公室請假。需要留意的是，應該很多職員都想在這天請假。此外，也別忘了，如果你想多賺點錢，可以向人資經理要求加班。

92. 聆聽者們在哪工作？
(A) 在旅行社
(B) 在銀行
(C) 在超市
(D) 在咖啡廳
解析 說話者在談話開頭就點明工作的地方是超市 (our supermarket)，故本題正解為選項 (C)。

93. 說話者說「應該很多職員都想在這天請假」，是想表達什麼意思？
(A) 業者即將暫時停業。
(B) 某個公司活動必須延期。
(C) 聆聽者們必須要參考工作日程表。
(D) 聆聽者們必須快點提出要求。
解析 說話者在談話後半段說到從今天開始可以到人資部辦公室請假，接著說需要注意一點 (You can request leave at the HR office, starting today. Take note)，再馬上接著表示「應該很多職員都想在這天請假」。由此可知說話者是要大家盡快請假，故本題正解為選項 (D)。

94. 說話者鼓勵聆聽者們做什麼？
(A) 要求加班
(B) 領制服
(C) 支付費用
(D) 查看職員手冊
解析 說話者在談話的最後說如果想多賺點錢可以向

人資經理要求加班 (don't forget, you can ask the HR manager for extra hours if you want to make some more money)，故本題正解為選項 (A)。

Questions 95–97 refer to the following news report and forecast.

Now let's take a look at the upcoming weather. The good news is that it looks like the rain will stop before the outdoor concert takes place in Bishop Park. 95 It'll be cloudy and windy, but at least the concertgoers won't get wet. There will be several musical performances, but 96 I'm mostly looking forward to seeing Joe Whitman, my favorite comedian. If you have any interest in comedy, make sure you catch his set on the second stage. And, don't forget, 97 tickets for the event are cheaper if you purchase them online, so head on over to the official concert Web site to take advantage of a 20 percent discount.

Friday	Saturday	Sunday	Monday
⛈	🌧	🌬	☀

現在讓我們來看一下接下來幾天的天氣。好消息是看來雨會在 Bishop 公園舉辦的戶外演唱會開始前就停。那天多雲有風，但至少參加演唱會的人不會被淋濕。屆時會有許多音樂表演，但我最期待的是能見到 Joe Whitman，我最喜歡的喜劇演員。如果你對喜劇有興趣，記得到第 2 舞臺觀賞他的表演。此外，別忘了，在線上買活動門票會比較便宜，快到演唱會官方網站上享受八折優惠吧。

週五	週六	週日	週一
⛈	🌧	🌬	☀

95. 請參照圖表。戶外演唱會何時舉辦？
(A) 週五
(B) 週六
(C) 週日
(D) 週一
解析 談話前半段提到活動當天的天氣是多雲有風，但不會被雨淋濕 (It'll be cloudy and windy, but at least the concertgoers won't get wet.)。對照圖表可知這樣的天氣是 Sunday，故本題正解為選項 (C)。

96. 說話者說他很期待什麼？
(A) 一位歌手
(B) 一場煙火
(C) 一場遊行
(D) 一位喜劇演員
解析 說話者期待的事出現在談話中段，他說自己很期待能見到最喜歡的喜劇演員 Joe Whitman(I'm mostly looking forward

to seeing Joe Whitman, my favorite comedian.)，故本題正解為選項 (D)。

97. 說話者建議聆聽者們做什麼？
(A) 參加某個比賽
(B) 要求禮券
(C) 寄電子郵件
(D) 上某個網站
解析 談話的最後提到線上購買門票比較便宜，請聆聽者到演唱會官方網站使用這個八折優惠 (tickets for the event are cheaper if you purchase them online, so head on over to the official concert Web site to take advantage of a 20 percent discount.)，故本題正解為選項 (D)。

Questions 98–100 refer to the following excerpt from a meeting and agenda.

Good morning, everyone. As the general affairs manager, 98 it's my pleasure to welcome you all to our team here at Desner Designs. During this morning's session, you'll hear from several managers here at 99 our innovative furniture design company. By the time we're done, you should have a firm understanding of how our departments collaborate to produce our unique desks, chairs, and other furnishings. The original plan was for Stacey Naylor to speak next, but she's been held up in a product design meeting. Instead, 100 let's hear from our personnel manager about company policies.

Meeting Schedule		
9:15	Introduction	
9:30	Stacey Naylor	Product Design Manager
10:15	Phil Meeks	R&D Manager
10:45	Rosie Fisher	Personnel Manager
11:15	Abdul Singh	Marketing Manager

各位早安。身為總務部經理，能夠迎接各位來到 Desner 設計是我的榮幸。今天早上的環節中，各位會聽到我們的創新家具設計公司中各部門經理的演講。結束之後，各位就能夠更加了解各部門是如何合作，做出我們獨特的桌子、椅子和其他家具。原本下一位要發言的是 Stacey Naylor，但她在開產品設計會議。作為替代，就請人事部經理來談談公司的政策。

會議時程		
9:15	開場	
9:30	Stacey Naylor	產品設計經理
10:15	Phil Meeks	研究開發經理
10:45	Rosie Fisher	人事經理
11:15	Abdul Singh	行銷經理

98. 聆聽者們應該是誰？
(A) 公司股東們
(B) 貴賓客戶們
(C) 潛在顧客們
(D) 新進職員們

解析 說話者在談話開頭對加入 Desner 設計的聆聽者們表達歡迎 (it's my pleasure to welcome you all to our team here at Desner Designs.)。這應該是會對新進職員們說的話，故本題正解為選項 (D)。

99. 該公司做什麼產品？
(A) 家電用品
(B) 衣物
(C) 家具
(D) 交通工具

解析 說話者在談話前半段說到我們的創新家具設計公司 (our innovative furniture design company.)，故本題正解為選項 (C)。

100. 請參照圖表，接下來是誰會發言？
(A) Stacey Naylor
(B) Phil Meeks
(C) Rosie Fisher
(D) Abdul Singh

解析 談話的最後說到人事部經理要來談談公司的政策 (let's hear from our personnel manager about company policies.)。對照圖表可知人事經理是 Rosie Fisher(Rosie Fisher/Personnel Manager)，故本題正解為選項 (C)。

Part 5

101.
答案 (A)
譯文 客人們在泳池周邊點飲料可以自動併入飯店帳單內。
解析 「have+ 受詞 + 過去分詞」的結構中，位在受詞和過去分詞中間的空格須填入能夠修飾過去分詞的副詞，故本題正解為選項 (A) automatically。

102.
答案 (C)
譯文 Huxtable 美術館東側在有進一步的通知前，禁止遊客參觀。
解析 空格內須填入被形容詞 further 修飾，同時這個名詞又可以作為介系詞 until 的受詞。因為句子與結束閉館的時間點有關，「有進一步的通知前」的語意最為通順，故本題正解為選項 (C) notice。

103.
答案 (A)
譯文 我們的健康食品專賣店有很多可以幫助你減重的維他命和補充劑。
解析 空格位在動詞 help 和不定詞 to 之間，須填入能夠作為 help 受詞的詞語，故本題正解為受格代名詞選項 (A) you。

104.
答案 (B)
譯文 在即將實行前通知顧客我們的新營業時間很重要。
解析 「It is...that 子句」It 當虛主詞取代真主詞的句型中，位在 is 和 that 子句之間的空格須填入能作為補語使用的形容詞，故本題正解為選項 (B) critical。

105.
答案 (C)
譯文 Fernando Boleo 的畫作被評為比預計價值的 75% 還要低。
解析 空格內須填入能和 be 動詞的現在完成式 has been 搭配使用的詞語，且要是能夠表達主詞 painting 的評估已結束的過去分詞，故本題正解為選項 (C) appraised。

106.
答案 (D)
譯文 因為新廣告的問題，行銷部門這週會工作到很晚。
解析 空格內須填入能將後方名詞片語當作受詞的介系詞。而為了要表達因為廣告的問題要工作到很晚的原因，故本題正解為能表達「因為…」的介系詞 (D) due to。

107.
答案 (D)
譯文 建議觀眾們最好在歌手預計表演時間的 10 分鐘前就座。
解析 空格位在一般名詞所有格和名詞片語 performance time 之間，因此須填入能夠修飾名詞片語的詞語。由此可推斷要從現在分詞和過去分詞中擇一，「表演時間」這個時程是由人來決定的，故本題正解為能夠表被動意思的過去分詞 (D) scheduled。

108.
答案 (B)
譯文 Trey Nispel 的定期報紙專欄，Sports Breakdown，每週六都會刊載在 The Richmond Times 上。
解析 空格內須填入能表達專欄 (column) 和出版品 (The Richmond Times) 之間關係的過去分詞，故本題正解為有「刊載；出刊」意思的選項 (B) published。

109.
答案 (D)
譯文 為了避免工程延遲，Crawley 城堡的整修會由 25 名專家組成的小組負責。
解析 空格位在定冠詞 the 和介系詞 of 之間，必須填入能夠同時被這兩者修飾的名詞，故本題正解為選項 (D) restoration。

110.
答案 (B)
譯文 請留意 Sadler 湖游泳區開放的時間會依照季節中的每個季度改變。
解析 空格內的副詞必須能修飾前方作為動詞使用

的 to 不定詞。而和依照季節 (in accordance with the seasons) 相對應的詞語為「每個季度」，故本題正解為選項 (B) quarterly。

111.
答案 (C)
譯文 BAS 會計事務所的新進職員必須在工作第一天提供兩種身分證明文件。
解析 空格內的名詞要能夠被意思為「兩種」的 two forms 修飾，且要在第一天上班提供給公司。故本題正解為有辦法提供給他人的身分證明文件 (C) identification。

112.
答案 (C)
譯文 Katherine Brewer 擁有必要的經驗來指導我們在坤甸市的工廠中所有新進職員的培訓。
解析 空格內的名詞必須與職員訓練相關，而人所能夠擁有的就是經驗，故本題正解為選項 (C) experience。

113.
答案 (B)
譯文 根據租賃契約的條款，你最晚必須在 10 月 31 日將公寓空出來。
解析 空格內的名詞要能夠被 of this lease 修飾，說明關於合約的內容，且因為作為 According to 受詞的緣故，最晚必須在 10 月 31 日將公寓空出來。故本題正解為表「(契約等的) 條款、條件」的選項 (B) terms。

114.
答案 (C)
譯文 這個夏天有興趣加班的餐廳職員要直接告訴老闆。
解析 空格內須填入能和 be 動詞 are 及介系詞 in 搭配，且能表達「對…有興趣」的形容詞，故本題正解為選項 (C) interested。

115.
答案 (C)
譯文 Hillside 牙醫診所的候診室有很多與健康和營養相關的雜誌。
解析 空格內須填入能和 be 動詞 are 及介系詞 to 搭配，且能表達「與…有相關」的形容詞，故本題正解為選項 (C) relevant。

116.
答案 (A)
譯文 Rundle 先生必須盡快關掉工廠的切割機，因為有發生危險性故障的可能性。
解析 空格位於作為動詞片語 turn off 之受詞的名詞片語 the factory's cutting machine 和介系詞 because 之間，故本題正解為能在後方修飾動詞的副詞 (A) quickly。

117.
答案 (B)
譯文 Rainbow 餐廳提供的料理使用許多進口的食材製造而成，甚至還有從印度農場來的。
解析 even 後面的內容是指前方 many imported

ingredients 的一部分。many imported ingredients 的意思是進口食材，由此可知空格後方點出特定位置農場的名詞片語是在說明其中一個產地。故本題正解為表達出處、出發地時使用的介系詞 (B) from。

118.
答案 (B)
譯文 在 Regent 化學股份有限公司，如果你完成一年的急救訓練後，你就可以申請加入職員安全委員會。
解析 空格所在的 if 子句是要表達加入職員安全委員會的條件，語意上完成一年的急救訓練才會通順。故本題正解為表「結束；完成…」的動詞 complete 的過去分詞選項 (B) completed。

119.
答案 (D)
譯文 儘管油價稍微下跌，越來越多人將腳踏車作為交通工具。
解析 空格內應為能和前方 be 動詞 is 一起使用的過去分詞 (C) expanded 和現在分詞 (D) expanding 的其中之一。expand 可以作為及物動詞，也能作為不及物動詞使用。但「儘管油價下跌，騎腳踏車的人正在增多」的語意最為通順，故本題正解為構成現在進行式的現在分詞選項 (D) expanding。

120.
答案 (A)
譯文 管理層非常開心地宣布我們會就新的電玩專案和 Iridium 軟體進行合併。
解析 that 子句為動詞 announce 的受詞。而空格位在該子句的連接詞 that 和助動詞 will 之間，故本題正解為能當 that 子句主詞的主格代名詞選項 (A) we。

121.
答案 (D)
譯文 接駁公車服務如果要變得更受歡迎，公車整天都必須準時運行。
解析 主詞為 the buses，動詞 run 則為表「運行」的不及物動詞。由此可知位在不及物動詞和介系詞片語之間的空格須為能夠修飾不及物動詞的副詞，故本題正解為選項 (D) exactly。

122.
答案 (B)
譯文 巴西的許多雨林在未來 20 年內預計會減少 30%。
解析 空格後的名詞片語 the next two decades 表期間，故本題正解為能將其當受詞的介系詞選項 (B) within。

123.
答案 (D)
譯文 執行長要求 Spencer 女士再買一期那本被放錯的雜誌。
解析 各選項為動詞 misplace 的各種形態，空格則位於 that 正後方。that 和空格要成為能夠修飾 the magazine 的關係子句，空格則須填入

that 子句的動詞，而 the magazine 的錯放是出於人為，故本題正解應為能表被動語態的 (D) was misplaced。

124.
答案 (D)

譯文 在她的假期間，除了緊急需要她留意的事之外，Theakston 女士會把所有事情交給她的助理處理。

解析 空格所在的 that 子句用來修飾 those。those 作為介系詞 except for 的受詞代指被排除在外的對象。由此可知空格內須填入能夠在 that 子句中和 attention 結合，表達不交給助理處理，需要「緊急留意」的事項，故本題正解為選項 (D) urgent。

125.
答案 (A)

譯文 請填寫意見卡，這樣管理層就能更有效地評估職員的工作表現。

解析 空格前方為命令句結構的子句，後方為包含主詞和動詞的另一個子句。由此可知空格內填入能夠連接兩個子句的連接詞，故本題正解為選項中唯一的連接詞 (A) so that。

126.
答案 (C)

譯文 每個月第一個週一是辦公大樓外面的窗戶都會被打掃乾淨的時候。

解析 空格位在主詞和動詞 is 後面，後面接著有主詞與動詞的子句。空格後面必須是在 is 後作為補語使用的名詞子句，因此空格內須填入名詞子句連接詞，整個句子要表達出打掃窗戶的時間點語意才通順，故本題正解為表「做…的時候」的名詞子句連接詞選項 (C) when。

127.
答案 (A)

譯文 雖然他的書中用了一些比較艱澀的詞彙，Jim Wallis 相信年輕讀者們仍然會覺得很有趣。

解析 空格內須填入助動詞 will 和動詞 find 之間的副詞，「雖然有艱澀的詞彙，年輕讀者們仍然會覺得很有趣」的語意最為通順，故本題正解為表「仍然」的選項 (A) still。

128.
答案 (C)

譯文 一旦你通過第一階段的面試，我們會請你透過筆試來展現你的電機工程知識。

解析 空格後方有兩個各自包含主詞與動詞的子句，並以逗號隔成前後句。由此可知空格內須填入能夠連接兩個句子的連接詞，故本題正解為選項中唯一的連接詞 (C) Once。

129.
答案 (A)

譯文 以紅色貼紙做標記的資料夾是給還沒完成所有客服訓練課程的職員們。

解析 句子中已經有動詞 are，所以另一個動詞 mark 要作為動狀詞，和 with red stickers 一起在 File folders 後方當修飾語。File folders 上貼

貼紙是人為的動作，故本題正解為表被動的過去分詞選項 (A) marked。

130.
答案 (C)

譯文 我們的水肺潛水課將幫助你做好萬全準備去應對在水中可能會碰到的障礙。

解析 關係代名詞 that 被省略，"you may... underwater" 直接修飾位在前方的名詞片語 any obstacles，而空格內應填入和水中障礙物可能會發生什麼狀況的動詞。在這個句子中，obstacles 是透過課程學習如何應對的對象，「在水中可能會碰到的障礙物」在語意上最為自然，故本題正解為表達「碰到…」的選項 (C) encounter。

Part 6

請參考以下電子郵件回答第 131 至 134 題。

收件人：Frank Edgar <fedgar@robocorp.com>
寄件人：Eloise Dunn <eloisedunn@estinc.com>
主旨：資訊
日期：5 月 4 日

親愛的 Edgar 先生：

你最近在柏林舉辦的人工智能大會中擔任主講人，我很幸運地是你講座的其中一位 **131** 聽眾。你對汽車製造業中機器人技術未來的演講讓我有許多啟發。**132** 事實上，這讓我考慮在我的公司進行一些重大改變。引進先進的機器人到我們的工廠應該能大幅提高我們的生產效率！你願意與我和我們公司的負責人見個面嗎？**133** 你對機器人的了解對他來說會很感興趣。我附上了日程表，**134** 提供了這個月適合會面的日期。希望能盡快收到你的消息。

敬祝 順心

Eloise Dunn
營運長
EST 汽車股份有限公司

131.
答案 (D)

解析 空格所在的介系詞片語必須要是 and 子句的主詞 I，也就是電子郵件的寄件人。空格前一句說到對方是人工智能大會的講者，由此可判斷寄件人為演講聽眾之一，故本題正解為表「聽眾，觀眾」的選項 (D) audience。

132.
答案 (A)

解析 空格前方說到寄件人從對方的演講得到啟發，空格後說自己正在思考要做一個大規模的變化。根據文章脈絡，可知後面的句子是針對得到啟發後發生的事情舉例，故本題正解為表「實際上，事實上」，需要舉出具體例子時使用的連接副詞選項 (A) In fact。

133.

答案 (C)

譯文 (A) 他對你解決問題的方式印象深刻。
(B) 我再次為活動延期致歉。
(C) 你對機器人的了解對他來說會很感興趣。
(D) 那個計劃案應該不用花超過兩個月就能完成。

解析 前一句詢問對方是否願意和自己和公司負責人見面，由此可知後一句應該接用 him 代指的公司負責人的反應，故本題正解為選項 (C)。

134.

答案 (B)

解析 空格前的主詞 I 和動詞 have attached，以及受詞 a schedule 構成一個完整子句，由此可知空格後應為修飾語。故本題正解為能夠構成關係子句，修飾空格前方名詞片語 a schedule 的選項 (B) that provides。

請參考以下公告回答**第 135 至 138 題**。

在 Four Points 遊樂園裡，我們將遊客們的 135 安全視為重要的事情。在惡劣的天氣下，我們會時刻留意情況。如果情況變得嚴重，像是有強風或暴雨襲來，我們必須關閉特定的遊樂設施和某些遊樂園的區域，甚至是整座遊樂園。

遊樂園管理者會親自透過公共廣播系統向遊客們傳達最新消息。 136 我們的首要任務就是確保所有遊客都能持續得到最新消息。遊客們 137 將會得到一張日後能再造訪的免費門票，如果他們因為惡劣的天氣必須離園的話。一旦職員們將所有遊客安全送離遊樂園後，必須立刻回到 138 工作崗位，繼續將遊樂園內的所有區域關閉。若想知道更多關於天候不佳的應對程序，請告訴你的上司。

135.

答案 (A)

解析 空格內的名詞要能夠和前方的 visitor 結合成複合名詞，並表達和遊客相關的重要事項。後面的句子提到天候不佳時該如何應對，可知這是與安全相關的內容，故本題正解為能夠表達「遊客安全」的選項 (A) safety。

136.

答案 (D)

譯文 (A) 現場表演在遊樂園的戶外舞臺舉辦。
(B) 開園時間可能會因為天候有所改變。
(C) 這個政策會在明年某個時間點實行。
(D) 我們的首要任務就是確保所有遊客都能持續得到最新消息。

解析 前一句說會透過廣播系統提供遊客們最新消息，由此可知空格內的句子應該與傳達資訊的義務相關，故本題正解為選項 (D)。

137.

答案 (B)

解析 空格後方的 if 子句中出現了現在式動詞 need。假如 if 子句的動詞為現在式，主要子句的動詞必須是未來式，故本題正解為選項 (B) will receive。

138.

答案 (A)

解析 空格所在的主要子句是職員們在將遊客送離遊樂園後要做的事，故能夠與 return(作為不及物動詞時) 結合，表達「回到工作崗位」的介系詞片語選項 (A) to work 為本題正解。

請參考以下電子郵件回答**第 139 至 142 題**。

收件人：所有音樂節籌辦人員
寄件人：主辦人 Roy Hatton
主旨：Rock World 音樂節

今年的 Rock World 音樂節將於 7 月 19 日週六上午 10 點至晚上 11 點在 Marlin 湖畔舉辦。我們相信表演者和觀眾們都會享受於這個景色宜人的 139 環境中。活動會在一場令人讚嘆的煙火表演下落幕，但各位的工作會在那之前結束，所以你們所有人 140 都能夠參加。

音樂節門票明天會開始在我們的網站上和各種通路販賣。職員們能夠以優惠價購買本人、朋友及家人的門票。 141 不過，一個人最多只能買 3 張門票。

142 讓我們一起努力來讓本次活動成為最棒的音樂節。

139.

答案 (B)

解析 空格前的 this 是要指前面提到的特定對象時會使用的詞語，scenic 的意思是「景色宜人」，可知空格內的名詞為之前提到的地點，也就是 a site on the banks of Lake Marlin。故本題正解為表「環境；背景」的選項 (B) setting。

140.

答案 (C)

解析 連接詞 so that 後面接 all of you 和空格。連接詞後方需要有主詞和動詞，all of you 為主詞，可知空格內須填入動詞才能形成正確的結構。故本題正解為包含助動詞在內的動詞型態選項 (C) can participate。

141.

答案 (A)

解析 空格前面提到職員們能夠以優惠價購買本人、朋友及家人的門票，後面則是說明一個人最多只能買 3 張。可知本段為「購買的可能性」和「購買數量限制」相對照的內容，故本題正解為意思是「但是；不過」，用來表達對照或反對的選項 (A) However。

142.

答案 (D)

譯文 (A) 預計今年會有許多旅遊團造訪 Marlin 湖。
(B) 感謝你有意願在活動中表演。
(C) 我們這個夏天會舉辦好幾場演唱會。
(D) 讓我們一起努力來讓本次活動成為最棒的音樂節。

解析 從文章最前面可知這是一封活動主辦人傳給籌辦人員的電子郵件，整封電子郵件都在寫關於

Rock World 音樂節的日程和職員優惠票等相關資訊。而作為電子郵件中的最後一個句子，最適合填入的應該是説明活動籌辦人員該做的事，也就是努力讓活動成功的選項 (D)。

請參考以下評語回答**第 143 至 146 題**。

> 關於 Splendid 外燴，我有優點和缺點要説。他們提供多樣化的餐點種類且價格也十分合理。然而，我 143 將不會再跟他們做生意。我最近一次的訂單中有幾樣食物不新鮮。看來職員並沒有花心思檢查他們送來我活動上三明治的 144 品質。 145 一半以上都太奇怪以致於無法吃。沒有一個看起來跟他們網站上打廣告的照片一樣。那麼業者有答應幫忙換新的嗎？不，他們沒有。下次我會選一間如果不符合基本預期的品質，願意讓我 146 交換的外燴公司。

143.
答案 (B)

解析 空格後方説明了撰寫者自身過去的經驗，最後一句話的動詞用了未來式 will choose，整段文字表達因為過往的經驗，未來會做某種選擇。由此可知空格所在的句子要是未來不會再跟這個業者配合，文意上才通順，故本題正解為包含 will 的選項 (B) will not be giving。

144.
答案 (B)

解析 空格內須填入動名詞 checking 的受詞，且表達沒有確認某項與三明治相關的東西。前面的句子提到有些食物不新鮮，所以此處填入未確認三明治品質最為恰當。故本題正解為有「品質」之意的選項 (B) quality。

145.
答案 (A)

譯文 **(A)** 一半以上都太奇怪以致於無法吃。
(B) 我大部分的客人都對餐點印象深刻。
(C) 那間公司提供大量訂單折扣。
(D) 我們沒有足夠食材能完成訂單。

解析 前面已經提到有些食物不新鮮，還有三明治品質的問題，可知此處應該填入符合負面情形的句子才通順。故用 them 代指 sandwiches，表明一半以上都不新鮮，因為太奇怪了所以無法吃的選項 (A) 為本題正解。

146.
答案 (A)

解析 空格所在的 that 子句負責修飾撰寫者説自己未來要選擇的 a catering firm。從前一個句子説到該業者並沒有幫忙換成新的餐點來看，撰寫者未來應該是會選餐點有問題時，會幫忙換的業者才合理。故本題正解為表「交換…」的選項 (A) exchange。

Part 7

請參考以下簽收單回答**第 147 至 148 題**。

```
                租賃紀錄
             日期：7 月 26 日
           姓名：STEVEN CHAMBERS
```

租賃詳細資訊	品項
為了幫助我完成 147 從 8 月 4 日至 8 月 29 日在索耶市進行的改建工程 (將老舊的 Latimer 電影院改建成公寓)。	大鐵鎚 (x 2) 水泥攪拌機 護目鏡 (x 4) 電鑽 (x 2)

148 確認已收到上列物品。
簽名 *Steven Chambers*

147. Chambers 先生 8 月會在索耶市做什麼？
(A) 帶領訓練課程
(B) 聘僱新職員
(C) 在租賃建築物的合約上簽名
(D) 改建建築物

解析 索耶市出現在租賃詳細資訊內，該欄提到 8 月 4 日至 8 月 29 日將在索耶市進行的改建工程 (a renovation project I will lead in Sawyer City from August 4 to August 29)，故本題正解為選項 (D)。

148. Chambers 先生確認了什麼事項？
(A) 收到裝備
(B) 購入一臺汽車
(C) 接受某個工作機會
(D) 修理某個機器

解析 簽收單下方寫確認已收到上列物品處 (I confirm receipt of the above items.) 有 Chambers 先生的簽名，故本題正解為選項 (A)。

請參考以下公告回答**第 149 至 150 題**。

```
           Cooper 牙醫診所
  149 150 在我們的 Astrid 購物中心分院提供驚人
           的大折扣！

  149 Cooper 牙醫診所正在慶祝開業 10 週年！
        讓你的笑容盡可能地最美！
  我們現在提供高品質的植牙及牙齒美白療程享有
            八五折的優惠。
    其他精選療程最多有高達 7 折的折扣。
      折扣從 2 月 1 日至 3 月 31 日為止。
  我們的營業時間是週一到週六上午 9 點至晚上 7 點。
  150 你可以在建築物的 2 樓找到我們，
     從大門口進來後搭乘電梯上來就會看到。

  預約請上 www.cooperdental.co.uk，或撥打
            555-0171。
```

149. 誰最可能張貼此公告？
(A) 業者
(B) 人資經理

(C) 衛生稽查員
(D) 網站設計師

解析 公告開頭寫到為了慶祝開業 10 週年提供折扣 (Amazing discounts available...Cooper Dental is celebrating 10 years of business!)。由此可知這份公告應該是該業者張貼的，故本題正解為選項 (A)。

150. 從公告中能夠得知 Cooper 牙醫診所的什麼資訊？
(A) 它要搬去更大的地方。
(B) 它每個月都會有不同的促銷活動。
(C) 它最近剛購入新設備。
(D) 它有一間診所在購物中心裡。

解析 公告開頭就提到位於 Astrid 購物中心的分院 (our Astrid Mall location)，後半段說能在建築物的 2 樓找到這間診所 (You can find us on the second floor of the building)。由此可知該分院位在購物中心內部，故本題正解為選項 (D)。

請參考以下指南回答**第 151 至 152 題**。

Earnshaw 紡織股份有限公司事故報告書寫指南

* 描述事件，包括有涉及的職員姓名。
* 假設機器因事故而關閉，請在標「關閉」的格子內打勾，並説明細節。
* 事故一發生就要立刻填寫報告。
* 151 報告標上日期後交到 152 行政辦公室。未標上日期將退回給繳交者。
* 確保工作地點安全無虞。

152 器具或機器的維修作業將在事故報告繳交後立刻安排修理的日期。
---

151. 根據指南內容，所有事故報告上都要有什麼？
(A) 連絡電話
(B) 職員姓名
(C) 公司地址
(D) 事故發生日期

解析 第 4 項提到報告標上日期後要交到行政辦公室，如未標上日期，將退回給繳交者 (Date the report and submit it...Reports that are undated will be returned to the submitter.)。由此可知事故報告上一定要寫明事故日期，故本題正解為選項 (D)。

152. 從指南中能夠得知 Earnshaw 紡織股份有限公司行政辦公室的什麼資訊？
(A) 定期會舉行健康與安全訓練。
(B) 負責安排設備維修。
(C) 每個月公布事故報告。
(D) 作業所需工具需要替換時會負責提供。

解析 第 4 項寫到要把事故報告交到行政辦公室 (submit it to the administration office)，接著又在最後説器具或機器的維修作業將在事故報告繳交後立刻安排修理的日期 (The repair of tools or machines will be scheduled...as soon as the report has been submitted.)。由此可知行政辦公室負責處理設備維修相關事宜，故本題正解為選項 (B)。

請參考以下廣告回答**第 153 至 155 題**。

看見世界！
153 讓 *Pacifica* 帶給你無比驚奇！
153 154 榮獲本年度全球旅行獎「中價位最佳郵輪獎」。

Pacifica 提供以下服務：

絕妙的景色！ 從郵輪的甲板上能夠看到壯觀的山景與海岸線。還能夠看見圍繞著郵輪的海豚和鯨魚在眼前跳躍。

超棒的遊樂設施！ 晚上會有許多有趣的娛樂活動，像是喜劇秀、魔術秀、現場音樂表演和劇場表演。

世界級的設施！ 當天氣好的時候，能夠上瑜伽課，或使用我們新的羽球場！郵輪上有三間美味的餐廳，但如果你想要更舒適地用餐，也可以在船艙內打電話訂餐點。

155 除了舞臺劇表演外，Pacifica 的所有娛樂設施和節目都已經含在郵輪費用中。現場表演的門票則須在郵輪上購買。
---

153. Pacifica 最有可能是什麼？
(A) 郵輪
(B) 餐廳
(C) 劇場
(D) 飯店

解析 Pacifica 這個名稱第一次是出現在廣告開頭，説明它曾得過郵輪獎 (Recipient of the "Best Mid-price Cruise Liner" award)，故本題正解為選項 (A)。

154. 從廣告中能夠得知 Pacifica 的什麼資訊？
(A) 它最近翻新過。
(B) 它受到國際的認可。
(C) 它提供旅客導覽行程。
(D) 它可以預約舉辦私人活動。

解析 廣告開頭説 Pacifica 在全球旅行獎中得到最佳郵輪獎 (Recipient of the "Best Mid-price Cruise Liner" award at this year's Global Travel Awards.)。由此可知 Pacifica 受到國際的認可，故本題正解為選項 (B)。

155. 什麼活動需要付額外費用？
(A) 喜劇秀
(B) 運動課程
(C) 餐飲服務
(D) 劇場表演

解析 最後一段註明除了劇場表演外，Pacifica 的所有娛樂設施和節目都已經含在郵輪費用中 (All entertainment and activities on The Pacifica are included in our cruise price with the exception of theater productions.)。由此可知想觀賞劇場表演必須額外付費，故本題正解為選項 (D)。

請參考以下電子郵件回答**第 156 至 158 題**。

寄件人：Ryan Kane
收件人：全體職員
日期：5 月 16 日
主旨：電梯更換

大家好：

請留意我們這棟建築的主要電梯將從 5 月 21 日到 5 月 24 日止，因為緊急維修無法使用。我們希望 5 月 25 日早上就能再使用它們。在此期間建議各位職員走樓梯，**156** 也可以跟所在部門主管討論是否能暫時到低樓層辦公的可能性。**157** 請注意我們有提供限量門禁卡給想要搭乘貨梯的人，這樣一來就不會被維修工程影響。

此外，我想各位應該會很有興趣知道 **158** 這次維修工程結束後，主要電梯將會增加語音辨識技術。我們 5 月 24 日會再傳電子郵件詳細描述如何有效運用這個技術。

Ryan Kane

156. 根據電子郵件內容，職員們能夠和部門經理討論什麼？
(A) 工作時間的更動
(B) 到其他樓層辦公的可能性
(C) 到辦公大樓最好的方法
(D) 參加其他訓練課程的選擇權

解析 和部門經理討論的敘述出現在電子郵件第一段，文中寫到可以跟所在部門經理討論是否能暫時到低樓層辦公 (can talk with their supervisors about the possibility of temporarily working on one of the lower floors)，故本題正解為選項 (B)。

157. 從郵件中能夠得知職員電梯的什麼資訊？
(A) 它有門禁卡才能搭乘。
(B) 它最近修理過。
(C) 它 5 月 21 日會關閉。
(D) 它只停低樓層。

解析 貨梯出現在第一段的最後一句，說明提供限量門禁卡給想要搭乘貨梯的人 (a limited number of keycards are available for those who wish to use the service elevator)，故本題正解為選項 (A)。

158. 關於主要電梯，Kane 先生說了些什麼？
(A) 它們會變得更節省能源。
(B) 它們已經建超過 10 年了。
(C) 它們只能到特定樓層。
(D) 它們會使用新技術。

解析 最後一段與主要電梯相關的內容中，Kane 先生提到會增加語音辨識技術 (feature voice recognition technology)，意同使用新技術，故本題正解為選項 (D)。

請參考以下簡訊回答**第 159 至 160 題**。

Jeff Sanderson　　　　　　　　　下午 **2:54**
159 我剛接到一位 Marx 廣告裡的客戶打來的電話。這位客戶之前要我們幫他訂 8 月 4 日到 8 月 9 日德國的來回機票，但因為他工作上的會議日程有變，所以想把回程日期改成 8 月 12 日。

Muhammed Anita　　　　　　　　下午 **2:57**
我知道了。嗯，雖然是透過我們旅行社訂票，客戶要改班機時間還是必須要付手續費。不過 **160** 航空公司有時候不會向經常搭乘的乘客收取這筆費用。你要不要打給航空公司，看他們會不會以特例處理？

Jeff Sanderson　　　　　　　　　下午 **3:01**
我覺得值得一試。那名客戶名叫 Clinton Mulgrew，他一年會搭好幾次 Rheine 航空的班機出國。

Muhammed Anita　　　　　　　　下午 **3:03**
對，而且他通常都是坐商務艙，我想航空公司應該更能諒解。

Jeff Sanderson　　　　　　　　　下午 **3:05**
沒錯。我會告訴你後續消息。

159. 這位客戶想要做什麼？
(A) 更改商務會議的時間
(B) 預訂德國的住宿
(C) 提早辦理登機手續
(D) 晚點從出差地點回國

解析 Sanderson 先生傳送的第一則訊息提到客戶打了一通電話給他，並說明客戶因為工作上的會議日程有變，所以想把回程日期從 9 日改成 12 日 (book a return flight to Germany for him, from August 4 to August 9...as his business meetings have been rescheduled)。由此可知客戶想比預計的日期還要晚回國，故本題正解為選項 (D)。

160. Sanderson 先生在下午 3 點 01 分傳送的訊息中，「我覺得值得一試」代表什麼意思？
(A) 他同意收費太高了。
(B) 他認為客戶會同意更改行程。
(C) 他有意願連絡航空公司職員。
(D) 他偏好搭另一間航空。

解析 這個句子的意思是「我覺得值得一試」。Anita 在 2 點 57 分傳送的訊息說到航空公司有時候不會向經常搭乘的乘客收取這筆費用，並詢問對方是否要打給航空公司，看他們會不會以特例處理 (sometimes an airline will waive the charge of its regular passengers. Are you going to call the airline and see if they'll make an exception?)，Sanderson 先生接著就用這句話回答。由此可知他說這句話是表達自己有意願連絡航空公司，故本題正解為選項 (C)。

請參考以下信件回答**第 161 至 163 題**。

Jim Finnigan
Ides 路 45 號
費爾特姆，密德薩斯
TW14 8HA

親愛的 Finnigan 先生：

昨天，你已經收到 Penman 莓果所寄的最後一批農產品。 163 我們目前還沒收到關於你是否要繼續讓我們當你供應商的消息。–[1]–。自從我們公司創立以來，Penman 莓果在英國一直都是草莓、覆盆子和黑莓首屈一指的供應商。–[2]–。相信我們的產品能為你的生意帶來相當大的益處。舉例來說， 161 我們知道到你那邊用餐的客人都對你的水果派讚譽有加。–[3]–。請花點時間讀一下我隨信附上的修正版商務合約。你也會知道 162 假如你願意繼續當我們的客戶，我們也有意願降低每個月的標準價格。如果你願意仔細思考一下這個提議，我們會十分感激。–[4]–。你可以透過信件或是撥打 555-0198 和我連絡。

敬祝 順心

Radha Longoria
客戶服務部
Penman 莓果

---

161. Finnigan 先生應該是在哪工作？
(A) 在工廠
(B) 在餐廳
(C) 在金融機構
(D) 在超級市場

解析 信件上半部寫了 Dear Mr. Finnigan，可知 Finnigan 先生為收件人。信件中段用 your 代指 Finnigan 先生，並提到那邊用餐的客人都對水果派讚譽有加 (your fruit pies have received a high amount of praise from your diners)。由此可推斷 Finnigan 先生是在餐廳工作的人，故本題正解為選項 (B)。

162. Longoria 女士提供了什麼？
(A) 產品樣品
(B) 獎勵計劃
(C) 工作機會
(D) 月費折扣

解析 信件後半段寫到「假如你願意繼續當我們的客戶，我們也有意願降低每個月的標準價格」(we are willing to lower the standard price per month should you decide to remain our client)。意同提供月費折扣，故本題正解為選項 (D)。

163. 下面這個句子最適合填入 [1]、[2]、[3]、[4] 之中哪一個位置？
「我們希望原因只是因為你最近太忙了。」
(A) [1]
(B) [2]
(C) [3]
(D) [4]

解析 該句子用 the reason 代指先前提及的某件事的理由，並推測是因為對方太忙才造成某個情況，因此這個句子應該放在對方沒做某件事的句子後方，語意上才會自然。由此可知該句應擺在還沒收到對方是否要他們當供應商的消息的後方，也就是 [1] 所在的位置，故本題正解為選項 (A)。

請參考以下電子郵件回答**第 164 至 167 題**。

收件人：<匿名收件人>
寄件人：abigailjordan@usmail.net
主旨：音樂節取消
日期：5 月 7 日，週三

167 親愛的表演者們：

164 很遺憾地，我必須告訴各位原本預計於這週六在 NY 藝術中心舉辦的 Solstice 音樂節將無法如期舉行。這不幸的消息是因為該建築淹水，且沒有可替代的空間。因此我們不得不取消這場音樂節。

昨天稍晚，NY 藝術中心負責人和娛樂部門通知我原本我們要用的藝廊 A 已經無法用來舉辦活動，受到最近淹水災情的影響，目前已經關閉進行整修。 165 雖然他們說可以用位在 2 樓空的藝廊 B，但它的規模跟藝廊 A 比起來非常小。即使是一半有門票的人也根本沒有機會擠進去看樂隊表演。

我希望各位能諒解這個情況，且能 166 接受做出這樣的決定並不是我們能控制的。我們也嘗試過尋找差不多規模的活動場地，但事發突然，實在找不到能使用的場地。

167 為了就在最後一刻取消活動致歉，藝術中心負責人會給各位各一張場館主要展覽的免費門票。一般是 30 美元一張，這充分地展現了他們的誠意，我希望這能稍微補償各位失望的感受。

敬祝 順心

Abigail Jordan

---

164. Jordan 女士應該是誰？
(A) 一位藝術中心負責人
(B) 一位活動籌劃人
(C) 一位藝術品參展者
(D) 一位演唱會表演者

解析 從信件上半部可知 Jordan 女士是寄件人，而第一段剛開始就說到這週六在 NY 藝術中心舉辦的 Solstice 音樂節無法如期舉行 (the Solstice Music Festival, scheduled for this Saturday at NY Art Center, will not be going ahead as planned)。從傳遞的訊息內容來看，Jordan 女士應為負責籌劃活動的人，故本題正解為選項 (B)。

165. 從信件中能夠得知 NY 藝術中心藝廊 B 的什麼資訊？
(A) 它最近在舉辦藝術展。
(B) 它沒有合適的照明設備。

(C) 它無法容納太多人。

(D) 它構造必須要重整。

解析 藝廊 B 出現在電子郵件第二段,並説明它的規模跟藝廊 A 比起來非常小,有門票的觀眾中,能擠進去那個空間看樂團表演的人甚至不到一半 (I was told that we could use the vacant Gallery B...even half of the ticket holders would be able to squeeze in)。由此可知藝廊無法容納太多人,故本題正解為選項 (C)。

166. 與電子郵件第三段第一行的 "accept" 意思最相近的詞語為_____

(A) 得到

(B) 偏好

(C) 進入

(D) 認可

解析 出現 accept 的句子前方表達希望對方能夠理解目前的情況,而 accept 的受詞 that 子句説明了該決定超出自己能控制的範圍。由此可知 accept 的意思是請求對方接受該情況不可控,故本題正解為同樣對某件事表達認可的選項 (D) recognize。

167. Solstice 音樂節表演者們會得到什麼?

(A) 全額退費

(B) 活動入場券

(C) 一捆資料冊

(D) 更新過的演唱會行程

解析 從開頭寫了 Dear Performers 就能知道這是一封寄給表演者們的電子郵件,最後一段用 each of you 代指表演者們,並説明為了就在最後一刻取消活動致歉,藝術中心負責人會給他們各一張場館主要展覽的免費門票 (the gallery curator has offered to provide each of you with a complimentary ticket for the gallery's main exhibition),故本題正解為選項 (B)。

請參考以下線上聊天訊息回答**第 168 至 171 題**。

Claire Sheldon (上午 10:02)

大家好。有人收到 Chavez 飯店的回覆了嗎?

Leo Goodman (上午 10:04)

嗯,我週一和 Chavez 先生談的時候,他説他今天早上會透過電子郵件告訴我他的決定。但我還在等消息。

Claire Sheldon (上午 10:06)

我們快沒時間了。 168 如果我們沒在今天之前訂地毯清潔劑和去漬劑,即使我們已經用吸塵器吸過,也把灰塵掃乾淨了,還是沒辦法趕在他們要求的時間完成任務。

Tom Bernstein (上午 10:07)

喔…其實,我昨天已經下訂單了。

Claire Sheldon (上午 10:09)

Tom,這樣做不太好。 171 如果我們沒取得跟 Chavez 先生的合約, 169 我們就會因為那些用不上的物品而虧損。你一共花了多少錢?

Tom Bernstein (上午 10:10)

我只是想説反正一定能成功簽約。嗯…我要查一下。

Claire Sheldon (上午 10:12)

Leo,或許我應該傳另一個訊息給 Chavez 先生確認發生什麼事。

Tom Bernstein (上午 10:14)

大概 100 美元多一點,但幸好, 171 只要我們在今天取消的話,還可以把錢拿回來。

Leo Goodman (上午 10:15)

不用麻煩了,Claire。 170 Leiper 女士剛剛連絡我了。 171 她説 Chavez 先生感到很抱歉,但他決定把這個工作交給 Evergleam 公司來做。

Claire Sheldon (上午 10:18)

嗯,至少我們知道結果了。那就把重心放在即將到來的大案子上吧!

---

168. 傳訊息的人從事的應該是什麼行業?

(A) 外燴

(B) 室內設計

(C) 清潔

(D) 造景

解析 Sheldon 女士在 10 點 6 分傳送的訊息寫到他們職業的特性,例如需要地毯清潔劑和去漬劑,還有已經用吸塵器吸過,也把灰塵掃乾淨兩件事 (If we don't order the carpet cleaner and stain remover...even if we've already done the vacuuming and dusting.)。由此可知他們從事的是清潔業,故本題正解為選項 (C)。

169. Bernstein 先生在上午 10 點 10 分傳送的訊息説「我要查一下。」,是指他要做什麼事?

(A) 找出花了多少錢

(B) 詢問配送的時間

(C) 找替代產品

(D) 提供到某個地點的方法

解析 該句子所在的前一句,Sheldon 女士説會因為用不上的物品而虧損,並詢問 Bernstein 先生花了多少錢 (we'll lose money on those items that we won't use. How much did you spend on them?)。由此可知 Bernstein 先生是要查出花費的金額,故本題正解為選項 (A)。

170. Leiper 女士提供了什麼資訊?

(A) 如何與 Chavez 先生連絡

(B) 到哪裡訂需要的物品

(C) Chavez 先生接受提案的理由

(D) 誰將為 Chavez 飯店提供服務

解析 Goodman 先生在 10 點 15 分的訊息中提到 Leiper 女士,透過她得知 Chavez 先生選擇了 Evergleam 公司 (Ms. Leiper just got in touch with me. She said that Mr. Chavez apologizes, but he's chosen Evergleam Company)。Leiper 女士告知 Chavez 先生選擇了其他公司,並告知提供服務的業者名稱,故本題正解為選項 (D)。

171. Bernstein 先生接下來最有可能會做什麼？
(A) 取消訂單
(B) 到工作現場
(C) 寄電子郵件給 Chavez 先生
(D) 連絡 Evergleam 公司

解析 Bernstein 先生在上午 10 點 14 分傳送的訊息的最後一句寫到今天取消的話可以退費 (we can cancel and have our money returned)。這是針對 Sheldon 女士在 10 點 9 分時寫到如果沒能跟 Chavez 先生簽約的話會有虧損問題的解決方法 (If we don't get the contract with Mr. Chavez, we'll lose money)。Goodman 先生在 10 點 15 分的訊息中説 Chavez 先生選擇了其他公司 (he's chosen Evergleam Company)，可知 Bernstein 先生應該要取消訂單才不會有虧損，故本題正解為選項 (A)。

請參考以下報導回答**第 172 至 175 題**。

Saturn 將改變在 OTC 的策略

雪梨 (9 月 19 日)——電腦製造商 Saturn 電子昨天宣布，他們不會在今年 12 月舉辦為期 5 天的 Oceania 科技大會 (OTC) 上，公開其最新的筆記型電腦和平板電腦。–[1]–。

OTC 曾經是澳洲科技業界 `172` 最重大的年度大會，全國知名的科技業者都會在此向上千名科技產品愛好者們演示他們即將推出的商品。除了科技迷之外，這個活動通常也會吸引媒體的高度關注。`175` 然而，最近幾年這個活動對業者銷售量和知名度的影響越來越小。–[2]–。

Saturn 的執行長 Howard Markley 在自己公司的總部向記者説明，雖然公司不會做新產品的完整演示，但依然會以一個不那麼公開的方式參與 OTC。–[3]–。「我們要向想看我們的新產品在舞臺上公開的支持者們致歉。比起大規模的公開發表會，我們決定用更親近，也更讓人興奮的方式向支持者們演示新產品，」Markley 説。「OTC 期間，我們將會擺演示展位，`173` 只有在人數限制內的幸運兒有機會直接操作新的筆記型電腦和平板電腦。」

Markley 先生仔細地説明了公司的新方式，並表示 Saturn 想要直接從顧客身上得到珍貴的反饋，因為部分產品還在開發中，可能會根據支持者們的反應進行修正。此外，因為沒有要在 OTC 公開或演示公司的新產品，`174` Saturn 將阻止消費者們關注科技網站和雜誌上過早下定論且不正確的評價。「我們希望消費者們能夠自己評斷我們產品的品質，」Markley 補充道。–[4]–。

---

172. 與第二段第一行的 "notable" 意思最相近的詞語為_____
(A) 反覆的
(B) 重要的
(C) 紀錄的
(D) 便利的

解析 notable 修飾的 event 特點出現在 where 子句內，説明這是個全國知名的科技業者都會在此

演示即將推出的商品的活動。從各大公司和眾多參觀者來看，可知這是一場盛事，故本題正解為表「重要」的選項 (B) important。

173. 根據報導內容，Saturn 電子會在 OTC 做什麼？
(A) 針對科技業趨勢進行演講
(B) 提供競爭者產品的評價
(C) 和當地記者們開記者會
(D) 讓參加者試他們的新電子設備

解析 Saturn 電子要在 OTC 期間做的事出現在第三段的最後一句。Markley 執行長説只有在人數限制內的幸運兒有機會直接操作新的筆記型電腦和平板電腦 (a limited number of lucky individuals will have a chance to get hands-on experience with the new laptops and tablets)，故本題正解為選項 (D)。

174. 下列何者是報導中提及 Saturn 電子改變在 OTC 的計劃的其中一個理由？
(A) 它打算要開始推出廣告行銷計劃。
(B) 它和好幾間雜誌社有商業合約。
(C) 它想要消費者無視網路上的評論。
(D) 它想要在別的活動公開它的產品。

解析 最後一段説到 Saturn 電子不希望消費者們關注科技網站和雜誌上過早下定論，且不正確的評價 (Saturn will discourage consumers from paying attention to early, inaccurate reviews printed by technology Web sites and magazines.)。由此可知它的目的是要消費者們無視其他意見，故本題正解為選項 (C)。

175. 下面這個句子最適合填入 [1]、[2]、[3]、[4] 之中哪一個位置？
「Saturn 電子的決定對一直有在關注科技業的人來説並不感到特別意外。」
(A) [1]
(B) [2]
(C) [3]
(D) [4]

解析 該句子裡有講結果的時候會用的 therefore，表達 Saturn 電子的決定帶來的衝擊並不是非常大，因此這個句子應該放在 Saturn 電子的決定以及其原因的句子後方，語意才會自然。報導第一段説明 Saturn 電子的決定之後，第二段的最後説到 OTC 這個活動的影響力變得越來越小，由此可知該句應該填在説完原因和結果的 [2] 才會通順，故本題正解為選項 (B)。

請參考以下公告和電子郵件回答**第 176 至 180 題**。

Bridgewell 市

Winter Ice 節 (1 月 18 日)

`176` 市議會正在籌備初次舉辦的 Winter Ice 節，這個活動會在 Forbes 公園和鄰近街道與營業場所舉辦。`177` 假如本次活動和預期的一樣受歡迎，市議會將考慮把它變成定期舉辦的活動。

一些有趣且刺激的活動將會在節慶期間舉行，並且我們也鼓勵所有當地居民一起參與慶祝活動。除了

下方所列的活動之外，還會有路邊攤、臉部彩繪、滑雪橇及各式各樣的紀念品攤販。

慶典主要活動如下：
180 上午 9:30– 上午 10:30 冰雕展示與演示會
上午 10:30– 上午 11:30 兒童堆雪人比賽
上午 11:30– 下午 2:00 野餐區享用燒烤午餐 (一人 10 美元)
下午 2:00– 下午 4:00 當地許多音樂家們的現場演出
178 下午 4:00– 下午 5:30 煙火及免費熱可可

所有人都可以免費入場，但歡迎在大門入口捐款。本次所有活動收益將用在未來舉辦城市慶典和社區活動上。我們希望能在 Winter Ice 節上見到各位！

收件人：Bridgewell市議會 <contact@bridgewell.gov>
寄件人：Mark Lincoln <mlincoln@newmail.com>
日期：1 月 23 日
主旨：Winter Ice 節

敬啟者：

我是一名 Bridgewell 當地的居民，我第一次在市區裡看到 Winter Ice 節公告時感到非常興奮。雖然我兩個兒子在慶典中玩得很開心，179 但我覺得如果之後還要舉辦的話，有幾個地方可以改變作法。首先，指定的停車空間實在太少了。180 我準時在上午 9 點 30 分抵達，但活動籌辦人員告訴我停車場已經滿了。導致我最終必須將車停在離活動現場的幾個街區外，比預計的時間還晚抵達現場許多。幸好，我們剛好趕上堆雪人比賽，我的兒子們玩得非常開心。其次，餐點要價 10 美元實在太貴了。參加者們只能選一個漢堡或一個熱狗，也沒搭其他東西。我希望你在規劃之後的活動時，能夠將我的想法列入考量中。

敬祝 順心

Mark Lincoln

---

176. 這個活動會辦在哪裡？
(A) 在公園
(B) 在市政府
(C) 在體育場
(D) 在餐廳
解析 公告的第一段寫到會在 Forbes 公園和鄰近街道與營業場所舉辦 (Winter Ice Festival, which will be held in Forbes Park and the surrounding streets and businesses.)，故本題正解為提及活動場地之一的公園的選項 (A)。

177. 從文章中能夠得知活動的什麼資訊？
(A) 它會每年舉辦。
(B) 它可能會帶動觀光。
(C) 它預計會有很多人參加。
(D) 它會幫當地慈善團體募資金。
解析 公告第一段說到市議會正在籌備初次舉辦的

Winter Ice 節 (The city council is organizing its first ever Winter Ice Festival)，可知選項 (A) 非正解，文中沒有關於觀光的內容，可知選項 (B) 也非正解。最後提到本次所有活動收益將用在未來舉辦城市慶典和當地活動上 (Any proceeds from the event will be put toward future town festivals and community events.)，可知為當地慈善團體募資金的選項 (D) 也非正解。同一篇公告的第一段說到「假如本次活動和預期的一樣受歡迎」，可知預計會有很多人參加這個活動，故本題正解為選項 (C)。

178. 活動參加者應該什麼時候會拿到免費飲料？
(A) 上午 10 點 30 分
(B) 上午 11 點 30 分
(C) 下午 2 點
(D) 下午 4 點
解析 公告的時間表上寫著下午 4 點會提供免費熱可可 (4:00 P.M.-5:30 P.M. Fireworks display and complimentary hot chocolate)，故本題正解為選項 (D)。

179. Lincoln 先生傳這封電子郵件的主要目的是什麼？
(A) 感謝活動策畫人員的努力
(B) 抱怨錯誤的資訊
(C) 就活動提出可改進的建議
(D) 詢問即將舉辦的活動
解析 Lincoln 先生所傳的電子郵件前段說到如果之後還要舉辦的話，有幾點可以改變作法 (I think there are a few things you should do differently if you plan to hold the event again.)，並具體指出可以改進的事項，故本題正解為選項 (C)。

180. Lincoln 先生錯過了什麼活動？
(A) 冰雕演示會
(B) 堆雪人比賽
(C) 燒烤午餐
(D) 音樂表演
解析 電子郵件中段說到雖然 Lincoln 先生在上午 9 點 30 分抵達，但因為停車問題，最後正好在堆雪人比賽時抵達 (Fortunately, we got there just in time for the snowman building competition)。從公告的時間表可知堆雪人比賽的前一個活動是上午 9:30 到上午 10:30 的冰雕展示與演示會 (9:30 A.M.-10:30 A.M. Ice sculpture display and demonstration)。由此可知 Lincoln 先生錯過了這個活動，故本題正解為選項 (A)。

請參考以下公司備忘錄及電子郵件回答**第 181 至 185 題**。

---

182 收件人：部門全體職員
182 寄件人：Larry Gambon，部門主管
日期：1 月 21 日
主旨：油漆作業

各位同仁好：

正如各位所知，184 我們部門將於 1 月 27 日，週三下午 1 點至 4 點進行油漆作業。這項作業會為我們全團隊帶來相當大的不便。上週營業部、行銷部和客服部在油漆辦公室時，有許多職員抱怨過程中製造了不少噪音和油漆的氣味。

因此，181 總公司已經批准我們部門可以在油漆作業進行的那個下午休假。希望各位同仁能在當天上午將較緊急的工作完成，將我們的部門空間空出來，讓室內裝修團隊能進入並做準備。你可以在隔天早上正常上班。182 我知道各位之中有很多人都在忙明年的預算案。請確保你沒有將任何資料隨意擺放。它需要被安全地鎖在檔案櫃中。如果有任何問題，在辦公室裡又找不到我的話，請透過電子郵件連絡我。

謝謝各位

Larry Gambon

收件人：lgambon@baracaeng.com
寄件人：loxley@baracaeng.com
主旨：薪資給付問題
185 日期：1 月 22 日

Gambon 先生你好：

昨天有收到你發給部門全體職員的公告，想告知你當天下午休息可能會造成一些問題。你應該也知道，184 油漆作業當天我必須處理職員們的薪資。一般來說，我會在那天下午拿到所有需要的資料，接著在下午 2 點至 5 點間計算薪水。183 184 雖然你建議我延後一天處理，但我確信一定會有許多職員會感到失望，所以想詢問你我是否能提前一天計算薪資？如果這樣的話，我需要你要求其他部門的經理也盡早向我發送必要的資料。此外，185 我想提醒你我明天下午不會在辦公室，因為要參加我姪子的婚宴。

謝謝你

Lucy Oxley

---

181. 公司內部公告的目的為何？
(A) 徵求如何裝修辦公空間的意見
(B) 要求職員們要保持安靜
(C) 指示職員們休假
(D) 通知職員們將進行安裝作業
解析 備忘錄的第一段簡單地說明了狀況，接著在第二段告知總公司已經批准該部門能在油漆作業進行的那天下午休假 (I have obtained permission from head office for all of us to take the afternoon off during the painting work.)，最後再補充職員們需要配合的事項。由此可知此內部公告的目的是指示職員們休假，故本題正解為選項 (C)。

182. Gambon 先生有可能是在哪個部門工作？
(A) 客服部

(B) 營業部
(C) 行銷部
(D) 會計部
解析 備忘錄的第一段，可以知道這是部門主管 Gambon 發給部門全體職員的公告。第二段寫到部門職員們最近都在忙明年的預算案 (I know many of you are working on next year's budget.)。預算案是會計部的業務範圍，故本題正解為選項 (D)。

183. 為何 Oxley 女士想調整處理某項工作的時間？
(A) 她不想讓職員們失望。
(B) 她的工作量特別大。
(C) 她無法拿到某些資料。
(D) 她那天有別的事要忙。
解析 在 Oxley 女士寄出的電子郵件中段，她詢問是否能提早一天處理某項業務，並提到職員們可能會因此失望 (I'm sure a lot of our workers will be disappointed, so would it be okay to do it a day earlier instead?)，故本題正解為選項 (A)。

184. Oxley 女士希望將工作重新安排在哪一天？
(A) 1 月 26 日
(B) 1 月 27 日
(C) 1 月 28 日
(D) 1 月 29 日
解析 電子郵件的前半段寫到油漆作業進行的那天必須處理薪資 (the day of the painting is the day that I should be processing the employee payroll)，中間又詢問是否能夠提早一天處理 (would it be okay to do it a day earlier instead?)。第一封電子郵件的開頭點出漆油漆的日子是 1 月 27 日 (our department will be painted on Wednesday, January 27)。由此可知 Oxley 女士想在這天的前一天，也就是 1 月 26 日處理這項業務，故本題正解為選項 (A)。

185. Oxley 女士 1 月 23 日要做什麼？
(A) 指派工作給職員們
(B) 參與家庭活動
(C) 計算職員的薪資
(D) 和 Gambon 先生見面
解析 電子郵件上方的寄件日期為 1 月 22 日 (January 22)，最後一句則提到隔天下午不會在辦公室 (I'll be away from the office tomorrow afternoon)，由此可知 Oxley 女士 1 月 23 日有事情要做。電子郵件中也寫出她不在的理由是為了參加姪子的婚宴 (as I'll be attending my nephew's wedding reception)，故本題正解為選項 (B)。

請參考以下行程表及兩封電子郵件回答**第 186 至 190 題**。

HanPro 軟體股份公司
Harvey Kim 的中國出差之旅，3 月 12 日～ 16 日

日期	時間	內容	飯店
189 3 月 12 日，週日	下午 7:15	抵達浦東國際機場 **186** 至 Zhou 租車取車	**189** Sha Tan 飯店 **189** 中國上海
3 月 13 日，週一	上午 10:30– 下午 1:30	開車前往蘇州 **187(D)** 和 Sunburst 遊戲公司代表進行午餐會議	Jade Flower 飯店 中國蘇州
	下午 3:00– 下午 5:00	與 Cheng 電腦股份公司代表開會	
3 月 14 日，週二	上午 9:30– 上午 11:30	**187(B)** 接受 Video Gaming 月刊採訪	Jade Flower 飯店 中國蘇州
	190 下午 1:30– 下午 4:00	**190** 向 E-Soft 分銷商行銷部門主管們做報告	
3 月 15 日，週三	上午 10:00– 下午 6:00	開車前往上海參加於亞洲技術博覽會舉辦的 **187(A)** HanPro 新產品上市發表會及演講活動	Golden Gate 飯店 中國上海
3 月 16 日，週四	上午 11:00	**186** 至 Zhou 租車還車於浦東國際機場離境	

收件人：Harvey Kim
寄件人：Alice Lee
日期：3 月 7 日
主旨：中國出差

Kim 先生你好：

根據你的需求，出差日程都已安排完成，稍早你應該已經透過傳真收到行程表了。 **188** 我仍然在編製精選的地圖和建議的行車路線，這樣一來你可以毫無困難地開車抵達所有目的地。我預計這個週末可以給你。

請確保在各飯店消費時都要使用公司卡，我們已經為你的房間談好企業優惠折扣。通常在中國， **189** 外國旅客抵達時都會收到免費的禮物，所以你在上海 Sha Tan 飯店辦理入住時，會拿到一個裝有水果和其他禮品的籃子。

如果有任何問題或者需要幫助，可以直接跟我連絡。

敬祝 順心

Alice Lee

收件人：Alice Lee
寄件人：Harvey Kim
日期：3 月 7 日
主旨：回覆：中國出差

Alice 你好：

謝謝你這麼用心替我安排中國的出差行程。我仔細

看過行程後，希望你能再幫我安排一件事。 **190** 可以替我連絡公司的董事會成員們，並安排視訊會議嗎？我希望能在和 E-soft 分銷商的行銷部門主管們開完會後立即進行。我想董事們一定會想立刻知道我們在會議上討論的所有廣告策略。

感謝你的幫忙！

祝好

Harvey Kim

---

186. 從行程表中可得知關於 Kim 先生的何種資訊？
(A) 他將在上午抵達上海。
(B) 他出差期間都會待在上海。
(C) 他出差期間將以租賃車代步。
(D) 他將在蘇州轉機。

解析 行程表上的第一天 3 月 12 日寫到要去 Zhou 租車取車 (Collect car from Zhou Rental Facility)，最後一天 3 月 16 日則必須歸還車輛 (Return car to Zhou Rental Facility)。由此可知 Kim 先生將使用租賃車輛代步，故本題正解為選項 (C)。

187. Kim 先生不會做下列哪件事？
(A) 討論新產品
(B) 接受雜誌採訪
(C) 參觀公司辦公室
(D) 與公司代表見面

解析 行程表中寫到 3 月 13 日和 Sunburst 遊戲公司代表有午餐會議 (Lunch meeting with CEO of Sunburst Games Company)，可知選項 (D) 正確。從 3 月 14 日接受 Video Gaming 月刊採訪的行程 (Interview with Video Gaming Monthly Magazine)，可知選項 (B) 正確。接著從 3 月 15 日有 HanPro 新產品上市發表會及演講 (HanPro product launch and talk) 的行程看來，可知選項 (A) 也正確。內文中並未提及參觀辦公室的行程，故本題正解為選項 (C)。

188. Lee 女士將寄什麼東西給 Kim 先生？
(A) 飯店折價券
(B) 到各個地點的指引
(C) 公司卡
(D) 客戶連絡資訊清單

解析 第一封電子郵件的第一段寫到 Lee 女士還在整理地圖和建議的行車路線，預計這個週末能傳給 Kim 先生 (I'm still compiling a selection of maps and suggested driving routes...I'll forward these to you before the end of the week.)。由此可知 Lee 女士會提供 Kim 先生到各個地點的方法，故本題正解為選項 (B)。

189. Kim 先生什麼時候會拿到免費的禮物？
(A) 3 月 12 日
(B) 3 月 13 日
(C) 3 月 14 日
(D) 3 月 15 日

解析 第一封電子郵件的第二段提到一般而言，外國旅客都會在抵達當天收到免費禮物，Kim 先生

則會在 Sha Tan 飯店辦理入住時收到 (foreign visitors typically receive free gifts upon arrival...when you check in to the Sha Tan Hotel in Shanghai)。從行程表上可知抵達 Sha Tan 飯店的日期為 3 月 12 日，故本題正解為選項 (A)。

190. Kim 先生打算幾點開視訊會議？
(A) 下午 1 點 30 分
(B) 下午 4 點
(C) 下午 5 點
(D) 下午 6 點

解析 第二封電子郵件的中段提到要安排視訊會議，希望能在和 E-soft 分銷商的行銷部門主管們開完會後，和董事會的成員們聊聊會議內容 (all of our board members and schedule a teleconference?...immediately after my meeting with the marketing managers from E-soft Distribution)。從行程表可知和 E-soft 分銷商的行銷部門主管們開會的時間是 3 月 14 日下午 1 點半到 4 點 (1:30 P.M. - 4:00 P.M. / Presentation to E-Soft Distribution marketing managers)，由此可知 Kim 先生打算在下午 4 點會議結束時進行視訊會議，故本題正解為選項 (B)。

請參考以下網頁、表格及電子郵件回答**第 191 至 195 題**。

科技時代！你體驗科技最新發展的線上嚮導！
今年最強的電視 / 電影播放服務

編輯首選：Youphoria

191 Youphoria 是用電腦或智慧型手機播放最新上映或過去的電視節目及電影的串流服務中，最方便、價格最合理，也最值得信賴的一個。Youphoria 在電視節目播放服務上已耕耘了 5 年，過去 18 個月才因為於線上服務增加電影後開始受到大眾歡迎。

當用戶透過各自的設備播放影片，**192** Youphoria 會自動記錄觀看紀錄，並依照觀看習慣推薦其他影片。這個服務還能讓用戶能夠加入聊天室、留言和為觀看過的影片評分。留言和評分還能得到獎勵。任何一位在一個月內評論超過 10 部節目或電影的用戶，下個月就能觀看比限定數量還要多的影片。**195** 最基本的「Casual」方案每月 15 美元，但用戶每個月只能觀看 15 集電視節目和 10 部電影。其他方案用戶只要多付一點錢，就能提高限制的觀看數量。

歡迎使用 Youphoria 串流服務！

想要完成訂閱，請提供以下資訊。你會在 24 小時內收到一封認證電子郵件。請點電子郵件內的連結驗證你的身分，接著你就可以使用我們的服務。如果你有朋友或是家人有興趣訂閱 Youphoria，你可以登入我們的服務，接著到「推薦朋友」的頁面推薦他們加入。你每推薦一位朋友，每個月就能多看一部免費電影。

訂閱用戶資訊
姓名：Reed Randolph
電子郵件：rrandolph@homenet.com
電話號碼：656-555-0196

你多常線上收看電視節目／電影？每天
你通常使用什麼設備收看電視節目／電影？我的智慧型手機
最喜歡的電視節目：*Criminal Intent*, *Suburbia Tales*, *Carfax Abbey*
最喜歡的電影：*A Song to Remember*, *Erased Memories*, *Storm City*

你想訂閱哪一種方案？
Casual：15 美元／月 ( )
Pro: 20 美元／月 ( )
193 Extreme：25 美元／月 (✓)
Addict：30 美元／月 ( )

收件人：rrandolph@homenet.com
寄件人：subscriberservices@youphoria.com
日期：1 月 16 日
主旨：新消息

親愛的 Youphoria 用戶：

謹通知你我們的服務從 2 月 1 日起將會有一些變化。稍微提高費用，**194(B)** 我們會提供你更多類型的電視節目與電影，也是第一次 **194(D)** 我們將以最高畫質提供：4K 超高畫質。此外，我們也在客服中心增員，這表示 **194(A)** 我們能夠更快、更有效率地提供用戶們協助。這些優勢幫助我們總是走在其他競爭者的前面。Extreme 和 Addict 方案的用戶們還能得到我們即將在 4 月推出的「Classic 電影館」的提前使用權。新的費用如下：

方案等級	每月觀賞量	月費
195 Casual	20 集電視節目 + 15 部電影	15 美元
Pro	30 集電視節目 + 20 部電影	20 美元
Extreme	50 集電視節目 + 30 部電影	30 美元
Addict	無上限	35 美元

193 如果你已經訂閱 Extreme 或 Addict 方案，你會收到兩張免費電影票，可以到你所在地區的 Cine-Galaxy 電影院選擇你想看的電影。如果你有任何疑問，可以透過 help@youphoria.com 連絡我們。

191. 根據網頁內容，Youphoria 串流服務能讓用戶們做什麼？
(A) 下載最新的音樂
(B) 在線上看新上映的電影
(C) 在網站上看照片
(D) 獲得打折的電影票

解析 網頁的第一段介紹了 Youphoria 串流服務，說明它能用電腦或智慧型手機播放最新上映，或過去的電視節目及電影 (Youphoria

is the most convenient, affordable, and reliable way to stream newly-released and past television shows and films on your computer or smart phone.)，故本題正解為選項 (B)。

192. 從網頁內容中能夠得知 Youphoria 串流服務的什麼資訊？
(A) 它最近開始提供電視節目。
(B) 它只能用手機觀看。
(C) 它過去 5 年都很成功。
(D) 它會為用戶推薦適合的影片。
解析　網頁的第二段提到 Youphoria 會自動記錄觀看紀錄，並依照觀看習慣推薦其他影片 (Youphoria automatically logs it in their viewing history and makes further recommendations based on their viewing habits.)。由此可知它會為用戶推薦適合的影片，故本題正解為選項 (D)。

193. Randolph 先生為什麼能夠得到兩張電影票？
(A) 他沒有超過他的每月播放量。
(B) 他訂閱了 Youphoria 的 Extreme 方案。
(C) 他參與了 Youphoria 的線上問卷調查。
(D) 他推薦了一名家庭成員訂閱 Youphoria。
解析　兩張電影票出現在第一封電子郵件的最後一段，提到要得到電影票的條件是有訂閱 Extreme 或 Addict 方案 (If you hold a subscription to Extreme and Addict services, you will receive two complimentary tickets to see a movie...)。Randolph 先生的訂閱資訊在第一封電子郵件的下端，Extreme 方案的格子被打了勾，表示他選擇了這個方案 (Extreme: $25/month (✓)。由此可知 Randolph 先生能獲得電影票的原因，故本題正解為選項 (B)。

194. 電子郵件中並未提到哪種費用變動的理由？
(A) 加強客戶服務品質
(B) 增加影片數量
(C) 與競爭公司合併
(D) 提供畫質更好的影片
解析　提高費用的內容出現在第二封電子郵件的第一段，從我們會提供更多類型的電視節目與電影供你欣賞 (we will be able to bring you a larger selection of shows and movies) 可知選項 (B) 正確，下一句提供最高畫質：4K 超高畫質 (offer them at the highest quality: 4K Ultra HD) 可證明選項 (D) 正確。接著是能夠更快、更有效率地提供用戶們協助 (we will be able to assist our customers more quickly and efficiently)，可知選項 (A) 也正確。只有和競爭公司合併的內容沒有出現在文章中，故本題正解為選項 (C)。

195. Casual 方案有什麼特別的變化？
(A) 播放額度增加了。
(B) 月費增加了。
(C) 訂閱該服務的付款日期將改變。
(D) 該方案用戶能夠使用「Classic 電影館」服務。
解析　從第二封電子郵件的表格中，可知 Casual 方

案能夠看 20 集電視節目和 15 部電影 (20 TV episodes + 15 Movies)。但網頁的第二段寫到該方案每個月能看 15 集電視節目和 10 部電影 (allows subscribers to stream 15 TV episodes and 10 movies per month)。對照下可知觀看量比先前提到的還要多，故本題正解為選項 (A)。

請參考以下發貨單、規定事項及電子郵件回答**第 196 至 200 題**。

OMEGA 健康產品				
訂單編號：773678　　　　　　　　　日期：2 月 15 日				
客戶：Jean-Paul Jolie 先生				
送貨地點：Porter 街 580 號，雷吉納，SK S4M 0A1				
產品代碼	數量	產品明細	單價	總價
#3348	10	花生能量棒	2.69 美元	26.9 美元
#2929	1	Atlas 蛋白粉 (1 公斤，草莓口味)	60 美元	60 美元
#4982	1	綠茶禮盒	75 美元	75 美元
#4982		**197** 準備工作	15 美元	15 美元
			小計	176.9 美元
			196 會員折扣 (15%)	−26.54 美元
			運費	20 美元
			總金額	170.36 美元

Omega 健康產品
訂購與退貨政策

在訂購我們的商品時，不管是在線上、透過電話或在實體店面，**197** 顧客們都能夠要求在指定商品上做禮物包裝服務。這個額外的服務在帳單上會顯示為「準備工作」，每件商品都是收取固定費用。所有訂單都保證會在下訂後的 5 日內送達。如果訂單在最後有修改，請諒解會晚個一兩天。

如果想要退貨，並得到全額或部分退費的話，必須要符合特定條件。一般而言，只有損壞的商品才能退貨。此損傷需發生在運送過程中，或是出自製造商的缺失。要求更換商品大小或口味，則是必須依照下方說明的付款方式處理完價差才能更換。退有瑕疵的商品時，沒有硬性規定要附上發票正本，只要能提供帳單上的訂單編號即可。所有退貨商品都會透過品質管理和評估來確認商品狀態。**198** 在商品是食物、飲料、維他命和營養補充品的情況下，只要有耗損，皆不能退貨或退費。

假如訂單出現可接受的變化，且總金額增加，顧客必須照以下說明支付未付款項：
◆ **200** 50 美元或以上的金額，請以匯款方式匯到我們 RBU 銀行的帳戶 (帳號：5837939390)。

◆ 未滿 50 美元的金額，你可以在實體店面用現金支付，或是直接付給運送商品給你的送貨員。

寄件人：jpjolie@maplemail.com
收件人：customerservice@omegahealth.com
日期：2 月 19 日
主旨：最近的訂單

你好：

我想要修改一下上週在你們網站上下的訂單。訂單中的其中一個品項，我選擇了草莓口味的 Atlas 蛋白粉。**199** 在跟我的私人教練討論過後，我同樣要訂草莓口味的蛋白粉，但想從 1 公斤改成 2 公斤包裝。從你們網站上的訂單追蹤系統，可以看出我的訂單還沒離開你們的物流中心，所以我希望你能接受我的修改。

如果造成你的不便，我很抱歉。**200** 請讓我知道如何支付多出來的 51 美元。

敬祝 順心

Jean-Paul Jolie

196. 從文章中能夠得知 Omega 健康產品的什麼資訊？
(A) 它在雷吉納有分店。
(B) 它有會員制度。
(C) 它正在進行季節性特賣。
(D) 它最近才剛開業。
解析 發貨單下端寫到會員折扣(Member's discount (15%))。由此可知這間店有會員制度，故本題正解為選項 (B)。

197. 為什麼 Jolie 先生會被收取「準備工作」費用？
(A) 他想要將某樣商品包成禮物。
(B) 他要求快速到貨。
(C) 他訂的商品很難取得。
(D) 他訂的商品比預期還大件。
解析 發貨單的下端出現「準備工作」這筆費用，規定事項開頭寫到禮物包裝服務在帳單上會顯示為「準備工作」(customers may request gift wrapping for selected items. This additional service will be indicated as "Preparation")。由此可知 Jolie 先生要求了禮物包裝服務，故本題正解為選項 (A)。

198. 退貨要求在什麼情況下會被拒絕？
(A) 商品在運送過程中損壞
(B) 未提供正本發票
(C) 訂單中有錯誤的物品
(D) 商品的一部分已被使用過
解析 無法退貨的情況出現在規定事項的第二段的最後面，如果產品是食物、飲料、維他命和營養補充品，只要有耗損，皆不能退貨或退費 (if these have been consumed at all, they will not be eligible for return or refund)，這句話就代表商品一旦被使用就無法退，故本題正解

為選項 (D)。

199. Jolie 先生的私人教練建議他做什麼？
(A) 選擇其他口味的產品
(B) 更改產品的尺寸
(C) 比較兩個不同的品牌
(D) 增加下訂單的頻率
解析 電子郵件的第一段寫到 Jolie 先生在跟私人教練討論過後，想把 1 公斤裝的草莓口味的蛋白粉改成 2 公斤裝 (After some discussion with my personal trainer, I would like the same strawberry protein powder, but in a 2 kg bag instead of 1 kg.)。由此可知是要更改產品的大小，故本題正解為選項 (B)。

200. 關於 Jolie 先生，下列何者可能為真？
(A) 他下個月會收到商品。
(B) 他需要親自到這家店。
(C) 他會被要求匯款。
(D) 他會給送貨員一筆現金。
解析 Jolie 先生在電子郵件的第二段請對方告訴自己如何支付多出來的 51 美元 (Please let me know how I should pay the additional amount of $51.)。規定事項下端寫到 50 美元以上的金額，要用匯款的方式匯到 RBU 銀行的帳戶 (For payments of $50 or more, send the amount via bank transfer to our account)。由此可知 Jolie 先生必須要匯款，故本題正解為選項 (C)。

Note

Note

Note

揮別厚重，迎向高分！
最接近真實多益測驗的模擬題本

特色 **1** 單回成冊

揮別市面多數多益題本的厚重感，單回裝訂仿照真實測驗，
提前適應答題手感。

特色 **2** 錯題解析

解析本提供深度講解，針對正確答案與誘答選項進行解題，
全面掌握答題關鍵。

特色 **3** 誤答筆記

提供筆記模板，協助深入了解誤答原因，歸納出專屬於自己
的學習筆記。

Name	
Registration Number	

TOEIC

Test of English for International Communication

TEST 3

三民書局

請掃描左方 QR code 或輸入下方網址進入音檔網站。
https://elearning.sanmin.com.tw/Voice/
1. 於搜尋欄輸入「實戰新多益：全真模擬題本 3 回」或點擊「英文」→「學習叢書」→「Let's
　　TOEIC 系列」尋找音檔。請依提示下載音檔。
2. 若無法順利下載音檔，可至「常見問題」查看相關問題。
3. 若有相關問題，請點擊「聯絡我們」，將盡快為你處理。

三民・東大音檔網

LISTENING TEST

In the Listening test, you will be asked to demonstrate how well you understand spoken English. The entire Listening test will last approximately 45 minutes. There are four parts, and directions are given for each part. You must mark your answers on the separate answer sheet.
Do not write your answers in your test book.

PART 1

Directions: For each question in this part, you will hear four statements about a picture in your test book. When you hear the statements, you must select the one statement that best describes what you see in the picture. Then find the number of the question on your answer sheet and mark your answer. The statements will not be printed in your test book and will be spoken only one time.

Statement (D), "They are taking photographs," is the best description of the picture, so you should select answer (D) and mark it on your answer sheet.

1.

2.

GO ON TO THE NEXT PAGE ➡

3.

4.

5.

6.

7. Mark your answer on your answer sheet.

8. Mark your answer on your answer sheet.

9. Mark your answer on your answer sheet.

10. Mark your answer on your answer sheet.

11. Mark your answer on your answer sheet.

12. Mark your answer on your answer sheet.

13. Mark your answer on your answer sheet.

14. Mark your answer on your answer sheet.

15. Mark your answer on your answer sheet.

16. Mark your answer on your answer sheet.

17. Mark your answer on your answer sheet.

18. Mark your answer on your answer sheet.

19. Mark your answer on your answer sheet.

20. Mark your answer on your answer sheet.

21. Mark your answer on your answer sheet.

22. Mark your answer on your answer sheet.

23. Mark your answer on your answer sheet.

24. Mark your answer on your answer sheet.

25. Mark your answer on your answer sheet.

26. Mark your answer on your answer sheet.

27. Mark your answer on your answer sheet.

28. Mark your answer on your answer sheet.

29. Mark your answer on your answer sheet.

30. Mark your answer on your answer sheet.

31. Mark your answer on your answer sheet.

PART 3

Directions: You will hear some conversations between two or more people. You will be asked to answer three questions about what the speakers say in each conversation. Select the best response to each question and mark the letter (A), (B), (C) or (D) on your answer sheet. The conversations will not be printed in your test book and will be spoken only one time.

32. Where do the speakers work?
(A) At a clothing store
(B) At a fitness center
(C) At a health food shop
(D) At a graphic design firm

33. What will happen this weekend?
(A) A Web site will be launched.
(B) A new product will be revealed.
(C) A discount will be offered.
(D) A new branch will open.

34. What does the man say he has been working on?
(A) A newspaper ad
(B) A product catalog
(C) A poster
(D) A logo design

35. Who most likely is the man?
(A) A sales representative
(B) A repair technician
(C) A recruitment manager
(D) A customer advisor

36. Why is the woman annoyed?
(A) She visited the wrong store location.
(B) She has not received a scheduled delivery.
(C) She was connected to the wrong person.
(D) She purchased a faulty product.

37. What does the man ask the woman to provide?
(A) A product name
(B) A home address
(C) An ID number
(D) A credit card number

38. Who most likely is the man?
(A) An airline employee
(B) A hotel worker
(C) A travel agent
(D) A ticket clerk

39. What problem does the man mention?
(A) There was a booking error.
(B) A special rate is unavailable.
(C) There is a travel delay.
(D) A suitcase has been misplaced.

40. What will Annie do next?
(A) Carry some bags
(B) Speak to a manager
(C) Fill out a form
(D) Pay a deposit

41. What does the man ask the woman about?
(A) Dry cleaning
(B) Home decorating
(C) Vacant properties
(D) Job opportunities

42. What problem does the man have?
(A) A shirt has been damaged.
(B) An interview time was changed.
(C) A vehicle is being repaired.
(D) An appliance has malfunctioned.

43. What does the woman suggest the man do?
(A) Come to her apartment
(B) Contact the building manager
(C) Request a repair service
(D) Visit a clothing store

GO ON TO THE NEXT PAGE →

44. What does the man congratulate the woman for?
   (A) Winning an award
   (B) Receiving a promotion
   (C) Securing a contract
   (D) Founding a business

45. What is the woman looking forward to?
   (A) Developing a product
   (B) Recruiting new workers
   (C) Attending a training workshop
   (D) Working in a foreign country

46. Why does the woman say, "I'm having lunch with the board members"?
   (A) To apologize for a delay
   (B) To reject an invitation
   (C) To request directions
   (D) To ask the man to join her

47. Why are the speakers meeting?
   (A) For a project update
   (B) For a performance review
   (C) For a job interview
   (D) For a sales report

48. What most likely is the woman's profession?
   (A) Marketing director
   (B) Sales team leader
   (C) Recruitment consultant
   (D) Warehouse manager

49. What does the woman say she likes about a company?
   (A) It provides regular training.
   (B) It offers competitive salaries.
   (C) It produces high-quality products.
   (D) It listens to its employees.

50. What type of business does the man most likely work for?
   (A) A supply company
   (B) A library
   (C) A bank
   (D) An Internet provider

51. What new policy does the man tell the woman about?
   (A) The business will close on weekends.
   (B) Customers must confirm their identity.
   (C) Accounts can be opened by phone.
   (D) A Web site requires a password.

52. What does the woman say she will do?
   (A) Visit the business in person
   (B) Make a payment
   (C) Register on a Web site
   (D) Call back later

53. What are the speakers mainly discussing?
   (A) A training workshop
   (B) A company relocation
   (C) A department merger
   (D) A grand opening celebration

54. What does the man mean when he says, "We have a lot going on next month"?
   (A) He would appreciate help with some tasks.
   (B) He doubts an event can be rescheduled.
   (C) He would prefer to push back a deadline.
   (D) He is pleased with the company's success.

55. What does the man offer to do?
   (A) Talk to a colleague
   (B) Call a department meeting
   (C) Post a work schedule
   (D) Reserve a venue

56. What does the woman want to do?
(A) Order office supplies
(B) Organize a staff outing
(C) Create an advertisement
(D) Redesign a Web site

57. What does the man suggest doing?
(A) Reviewing a document
(B) Postponing a team meeting
(C) Comparing some prices
(D) Collaborating with a coworker

58. What will the woman probably do tomorrow?
(A) Attend a product launch
(B) Carry out a survey
(C) Submit a design
(D) Meet with clients

---

59. What are the speakers mainly discussing?
(A) A building renovation
(B) A parking policy
(C) A door entry system
(D) A mobile phone app

60. What will residents receive tomorrow?
(A) A pass code
(B) A keycard
(C) A user name
(D) A manual

61. What does the man say is an advantage of the Apex Gateway?
(A) It is reliable.
(B) It is inexpensive.
(C) It is user friendly.
(D) It is small.

Volunteer Group	Vest Color
Ticket sellers	Orange
Parking attendants	Purple
Information helpers	Blue
Waste collectors	Green

62. What type of event are the speakers discussing?
(A) A convention
(B) A concert
(C) A street parade
(D) A food fair

63. Look at the graphic. Which group of volunteers will begin work in three days?
(A) Ticket sellers
(B) Parking attendants
(C) Information helpers
(D) Waste collectors

64. What will the man do next?
(A) Cancel an order
(B) Revise a schedule
(C) Contact a supplier
(D) Visit the event site

King's Fried Chicken	
8-Piece Bucket	$13.99
12-Piece Bucket	$20.49
16-Piece Bucket	$24.99
20-Piece Bucket	$28.49

65. Who is the man?
(A) An office manager
(B) A director
(C) A singer
(D) A food critic

66. Look at the graphic. How much will the man pay for his order?
(A) $13.99
(B) $20.49
(C) $24.99
(D) $28.49

67. What will the man do next?
(A) Fill out a form
(B) Sample an item
(C) Use a coupon
(D) Provide an address

Merline Toy Store		Black Bean Coffee		Zap Electronics
	Elevator 1		Elevator 2	
Silver Sun Mall – Third Floor				
Elevator 3		Elevator 4		Cherry Clothing
	Sparta Health Foods		Ace Hardware	

68. What department does the man work in?
(A) Maintenance
(B) Customer service
(C) Marketing
(D) Sales

69. What does the man ask the woman to do?
(A) Repair a roof
(B) Order materials
(C) Mop a floor
(D) Put up a sign

70. Look at the graphic. Which elevator is the man referring to?
(A) Elevator 1
(B) Elevator 2
(C) Elevator 3
(D) Elevator 4

Directions: You will hear some talks given by a single speaker. You will be asked to answer three questions about what the speaker says in each talk. Select the best response to each question and mark the letter (A), (B), (C), or (D) on your answer sheet. The talks will not be printed in your test book and will be spoken only one time.

71. What is the topic of the seminar?
(A) Managing finances
(B) Starting a business
(C) Marketing products
(D) Interviewing for jobs

72. Why does the speaker say a skill is crucial?
(A) There is a lot of competition.
(B) Technology is more complicated.
(C) Consumer spending trends are changing.
(D) Many companies are downsizing.

73. What does the speaker ask the listeners to do?
(A) Raise their hands
(B) Complete a form
(C) Read some information
(D) Ask questions

74. Where is the announcement taking place?
(A) At a college
(B) At a hospital
(C) At an airport
(D) At a hotel

75. What new service does the speaker mention?
(A) Exercise classes
(B) Financial advice
(C) Beauty treatments
(D) Free transportation

76. What will the listeners do next?
(A) Attend a seminar
(B) Go to a restaurant
(C) Participate in a tour
(D) Sign up for an event

77. Where do the listeners work?
(A) At a hotel
(B) At a restaurant
(C) At a beach
(D) At a park

78. What does the speaker imply when she says, "the summer holidays are just around the corner"?
(A) Employees should request days off.
(B) A holiday period has been rescheduled.
(C) An area will soon have more visitors.
(D) New businesses are set to open nearby.

79. What does the speaker remind the listeners to do?
(A) Check a schedule
(B) Complete a survey
(C) Bring some notes
(D) Submit a document

80. What is the speaker calling about?
(A) A city map
(B) A mobile phone app
(C) A guidebook
(D) An advertisement

81. Why has the listener been chosen to work on an assignment?
(A) She knows about a specific brand.
(B) She has done similar work before.
(C) She is familiar with an area.
(D) She has free time in her schedule.

82. What does the speaker want to do?
(A) Hire new employees
(B) Visit a business premises
(C) Change a work deadline
(D) Organize a meeting

83. What did the speaker recently do?
   (A) Design a product
   (B) Write a book
   (C) Launch a Web site
   (D) Go on a trip

84. What does the speaker imply when she says, "And I worked as a tour guide in several European cities"?
   (A) She recommends planning a trip to Europe.
   (B) She forgot to include some information on her résumé.
   (C) She is preparing to relocate overseas.
   (D) She is very knowledgeable in her field.

85. What can the listeners receive by entering a code?
   (A) A newsletter
   (B) A free gift
   (C) A discount
   (D) A membership

86. Who is the speaker?
   (A) A TV show host
   (B) A radio broadcaster
   (C) A fitness instructor
   (D) A movie director

87. What inspired the speaker to become a vegetarian?
   (A) Watching a movie
   (B) Speaking with a doctor
   (C) Seeing an advertisement
   (D) Reading an article

88. What will take place next?
   (A) A guest interview
   (B) An exercise routine
   (C) A cooking demonstration
   (D) A product promotion

89. What event is being planned?
   (A) A product launch
   (B) A grand opening
   (C) A career fair
   (D) An orientation

90. According to the speaker, what have volunteers been doing for the event?
   (A) Distributing flyers
   (B) Preparing a room
   (C) Surveying the public
   (D) Setting up booths

91. What does the speaker ask the listeners for?
   (A) Potential event venues
   (B) Advertising expenses
   (C) Web site recommendations
   (D) Ideas for attracting employees

92. Where does the talk take place?
   (A) A city council meeting
   (B) A performance review session
   (C) A professional seminar
   (D) A client presentation

93. Why does the speaker say, "Your employees use the Internet all the time"?
   (A) To suggest restricting Internet access
   (B) To congratulate the listeners on their efforts
   (C) To recommend a different approach
   (D) To request a volunteer to assist him

94. What will the speaker give the listeners?
   (A) A membership card
   (B) A Web site address
   (C) An information pack
   (D) A meal voucher

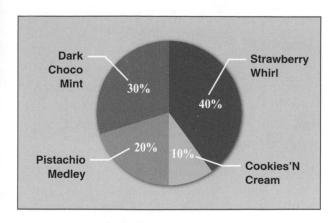

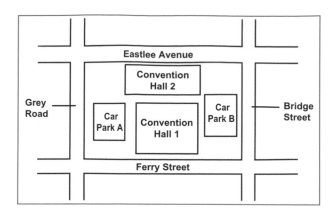

95. Who most likely are the listeners?
(A) Financial consultants
(B) Market researchers
(C) Sales representatives
(D) Product designers

96. Which aspect of the new product will the team discuss in pairs?
(A) Its packaging
(B) Its ingredients
(C) Its cost
(D) Its appearance

97. Look at the graphic. What will be the flavor of the new product?
(A) Strawberry Whirl
(B) Cookies' N Cream
(C) Pistachio Medley
(D) Dark Choco Mint

98. What is the speaker mainly discussing?
(A) A seminar
(B) A concert
(C) A fundraiser
(D) A street parade

99. What should the listeners do when people arrive?
(A) Hand them an event guide
(B) Check their tickets
(C) Give them directions
(D) Offer them refreshments

100. Look at the graphic. Where most likely will the additional merchandise stall be located?
(A) Eastlee Avenue
(B) Grey Road
(C) Bridge Street
(D) Ferry Street

This is the end of the Listening test. Turn to Part 5 in your text book.

READING TEST

In the Reading test, you will read a variety of texts and answer several different types of reading comprehension questions. The entire Reading test will last 75 minutes. There are three parts, and directions are given for each part. You are encouraged to answer as many questions as possible within the time allowed. You must mark your answers on the separate answer sheet. Do not write your answers in your test book.

PART 5

Directions: A word or phrase is missing in each of the sentences below. Four answer choices are given below each sentence. Select the best answer to complete the sentence. Then mark the letter (A), (B), (C), or (D) on your answer sheet.

101. Checking your up-to-date credit score is ------- on the Tempo Tax software.
(A) easy
(B) easily
(C) ease
(D) easing

102. Ms. Kemper's application arrived ------- late for her to be considered for the position.
(A) so
(B) ever
(C) too
(D) already

103. All passengers are ------- to wear life jackets when riding on the boat.
(A) ruled
(B) protected
(C) decided
(D) required

104. Mayor Andrew Jenkins ended the festival by giving a ------- closing speech.
(A) beauty
(B) beautiful
(C) beautify
(D) beautifully

105. ------- June and September, Palm Grove Resort hosts more guests than any other hotel in Vincent Beach.
(A) Against
(B) Between
(C) Along
(D) Below

106. The trailer for Michael Zinn's next action film ------- a lot of publicity.
(A) generate
(B) generating
(C) is generated
(D) has generated

107. After Mr. Lamp's presentation, interested investors are encouraged to stay for a brief -------.
(A) attendance
(B) maintenance
(C) anticipation
(D) discussion

108. The O'Hare Welcome Center provides a free educational pamphlet to help ------- travelers navigate the transit system.
(A) undisclosed
(B) incomplete
(C) unused
(D) inexperienced

109. Mr. Brooks had a conflict with the conference dates since he was ------- scheduled to take his vacation.
(A) already
(B) yet
(C) enough
(D) most

110. Several major entertainment companies are developing virtual reality content ------- growing customer interest.
(A) as a result of
(B) since
(C) only if
(D) provided that

111. Competing firms have ------- been offering partner-track positions to recruit some of the most promising law graduates.
(A) increases
(B) increasing
(C) increased
(D) increasingly

112. For many years, Reilly Plastics has been ------- in organizing community service projects in the Williamsburg area.
(A) active
(B) actively
(C) activists
(D) activities

113. ------- the weekly executive meeting, Ms. Clifford explained the rationale behind reorganizing the office workspace.
(A) Beside
(B) While
(C) During
(D) Among

114. A recent market trends report suggests that most consumers ------- environmentally–safe cleaning products more desirable.
(A) find
(B) feel
(C) take
(D) seem

115. To park in the top level of the parking garage, staff members must present a ------- employee identification card.
(A) valid
(B) gradual
(C) varied
(D) direct

116. Viewers should note that Chef Hawkins shares valuable cooking ------- throughout his recipes.
(A) advice
(B) adviser
(C) advises
(D) advised

117. The film rights for Tony Clark's first novel were sold to Mammoth Studios last week ------- a surprisingly high amount.
(A) from
(B) to
(C) off
(D) for

118. Travel expenses submitted with all necessary documents will be refunded ------- they are reviewed.
(A) due to
(B) as soon as
(C) in addition to
(D) rather than

119. Sweet Bee Grocer's ------- free home delivery service for the past decade.
(A) is offering
(B) has been offering
(C) will be offering
(D) would have been offering

120. Profits soared after our new commercial aired, ------- the marketing team will consider extending the advertising campaign.
(A) so
(B) in which
(C) as if
(D) why

GO ON TO THE NEXT PAGE

121. ------- the new waiting staff has been fully trained, the Huxley Hotel can begin hosting large formal events.
(A) So that
(B) Now that
(C) In order that
(D) In that

122. The main job of the warehouse manager is to maintain orderly ------- of all company products.
(A) store
(B) stored
(C) storage
(D) storable

123. The new Action Life camera from TechWave can ------- a diving depth of 60 meters without losing functionality.
(A) reach
(B) feature
(C) arrive
(D) achieve

124. Although the security cameras are somewhat outdated compared to the latest models, they are still -------.
(A) function
(B) functional
(C) functionally
(D) functioned

125. Regal Travels carefully selects the tour guides who are responsible ------- leading international trips.
(A) of
(B) on
(C) for
(D) in

126. ------- Tracer Industries is able to sell its manufacturing division depends on its performance this quarter.
(A) Even if
(B) Moreover
(C) Whether
(D) What

127. Individuals ------- in organizing a recreational activity should complete a proposal form from the Human Resources Department.
(A) interest
(B) interests
(C) interesting
(D) interested

128. Parkersburg's city council is seeking public ------- on the proposed renovations to Truman Square.
(A) preparation
(B) comment
(C) attendance
(D) complaint

129. Max Burger's health and safety regulations for its restaurants extend ------- those of most fast food franchises.
(A) than
(B) beyond
(C) while
(D) also

130. The community center's new class will help home owners ------- their ability to assess, maintain, and even improve the value of their property.
(A) cover
(B) prepare
(C) progress
(D) evaluate

PART 6

Directions: Read the texts that follow. A word, phrase, or sentence is missing in parts of each text.

Four answer choices for each question are given below the text. Select the best answer to complete the text. Then mark the letter (A), (B), (C) or (D) on your answer sheet.

Questions 131–134 refer to the following Web page.

Situated next to the beautiful Twin Pines National Park, the Sherman Business Development Center is equipped with the facilities required to run highly successful corporate team-building exercises. ----- .
131.
Our programs require groups to participate in a number of ----- . Your employees will work
132.
together to build shelters in the forest, create a bridge over a river using limited resources, and compete against other teams in various races and problem-solving tasks. ----- focus
133.
on strengthening the communication and teamwork skills of the participants involved, and these skills are directly transferable to the workplace. For details about our programs, and to sign up for a team-building session, call: 555-8278. And, don't forget to check out our brand-new Web site at www.sbdc.org/home. You can also find out more ----- our
134.
experienced staff and modern facilities there!

131. (A) Our operators are ready to take your
  call from 9 to 5 every day.
 (B) Your business will benefit from the
  exposure provided by the event.
 (C) You can choose from a wide range
  of catering packages.
 (D) Our instructors know how to get the
  best out of your staff.

132. (A) causes
 (B) professions
 (C) members
 (D) activities

133. (A) You
 (B) We
 (C) Theirs
 (D) I

134. (A) into
 (B) over
 (C) about
 (D) before

Questions 135–138 refer to the following e-mail.

To: inquiries@aceappliances.com
From: mfowler@truemail.net
Subject: Java Press 500
Date: September 14

Dear Sir/Madam,

I would like to _____ an espresso machine called the Java Press 500. My new kitchen
        135.
counter is not as large as I first thought, and I simply don't have enough space for it. I'm

hoping that it will be _____ for me to choose a different item of equal value from your catalog.
                 136.

_____.
137.

Could you recommend a suitable product before September 18? According to your policy, I

will be unable to obtain a refund or a new product after _____.
                                       138.

I look forward to hearing from you.

Meredith Fowler

135. (A) suggest
     (B) return
     (C) repair
     (D) purchase

136. (A) available
     (B) probable
     (C) typical
     (D) possible

137. (A) No such catalog has been delivered
         to me this month.
     (B) I really appreciate your inquiry and
         will respond promptly.
     (C) I have seen it advertised on your
         Web site.
     (D) My preference is to exchange the
         device for a smaller one.

138. (A) one
     (B) then
     (C) that
     (D) what

Questions 139–142 refer to the following article.

COMFLEX UNVEILS NEW MARKETING EXECUTIVE

Edmonton (14 November) – At a press conference yesterday, ComFlex introduced Clive Jenkins as its new Internet Marketing Director. Mr. Jenkins will supervise a division that ----- **139.** social media marketing campaigns to attract new customers.

Dimitri Augustus, founder of the telecommunications company, stated, "We are excited to have Mr. Jenkins join us. His skills and experience will ----- us to reach out further and **140.** more effectively in our efforts to reach potential customers." -----. At his previous company, **141.** TeleNova, he spent 12 years developing and executing a highly effective online marketing strategy.

ComFlex provides a full ----- of telephone, television, and broadband Internet services, and **142.** has recently become the leading provider in Canada.

---

139. (A) has created
(B) is created
(C) created
(D) creates

140. (A) enable
(B) supply
(C) succeed
(D) increase

141. (A) Mr. Jenkins comes to ComFlex with a strong background in the field.
(B) Mr. Jenkins will be honored for his achievements at the Edmonton office.
(C) Mr. Jenkins has been offered a promotion within his department.
(D) Mr. Jenkins is expected to remain at ComFlex if the project is a success.

142. (A) limit
(B) capacity
(C) benefit
(D) range

GO ON TO THE NEXT PAGE

Questions 143–146 refer to the following notice.

Attention Laney's Supermarket Shoppers:

When paying for your items at the checkout, please be aware that you will be charged 50 cents for each plastic bag provided for your groceries. You will see this indicated on your receipt as "Plastic Bag Charge." _____ you inform the checkout operator in advance that you
143.
do not require any plastic bags, he or she will provide them as necessary and charge you the appropriate fee.

Plastic waste can pose a significant threat to our ecosystem, so it is important that plastic bags be disposed of in an environmentally-friendly manner. We have a bin at the main entrance of the store where you can drop off old plastic bags. We will make sure that they are properly _____. The resulting products will be used for other purposes and not discarded
144.
as waste.

Using plastic bags is _____; we would encourage you to instead purchase a $3 durable
145.
canvas shopping bag that can be used repeatedly. _____.
146.

143. (A) So that
(B) Despite
(C) Unless
(D) After

144. (A) recycle
(B) recycles
(C) recycled
(D) recycling

145. (A) recommended
(B) optional
(C) prohibited
(D) simple

146. (A) Just ask one of our checkout operators for one.
(B) We have a wide selection of products available.
(C) Donations are appreciated, but volunteering is even better.
(D) This is why you should check the plastic bags for holes.

PART 7

Directions: In this part you will read a selection of texts, such as magazine and newspaper articles, e-mails, and instant messages. Each text or set of texts is followed by several questions. Select the best answer for each question and mark the letter (A), (B), (C), or (D) on your answer sheet.

Questions 147–148 refer to the following coupon.

Lacey's Salon
Grand Opening Voucher

Bring this voucher with you to your next haircut, manicure, or facial treatment appointment and exchange it for a complimentary head or shoulder rub! This voucher may be redeemed on any day of the week, but only at our new location on Bridge Street.

We can grow with your help!

Tell one of your friends, colleagues, or family members about our salon and the services we provide and get your next treatment for half price!** In order to benefit from this offer, please ensure that the person provides your name when they book their appointment.

** (Be advised that this is a one-time offer.)

---

147. What free service can the voucher be used to obtain?
(A) A facial treatment
(B) A manicure
(C) A haircut
(D) A massage

148. How can a customer receive a 50 percent discount?
(A) By visiting the Bridge Street branch
(B) By attending a grand opening event
(C) By referring a friend to the business
(D) By booking several different appointments

Questions 149–150 refer to the following e-mail.

E-mail Message

To: Felicia Munoz <fmunoz@mymail.com>
From: Curtis Wode <cwode@diamond.com>
Subject: Sleeford Condominiums
Date: November 2

Dear Ms. Munoz,

You expressed interest in renting one of our condominiums last month, but at that time, we did not have any vacant properties. I'm happy to inform you that one of our tenants has just asked to end her lease early, and we are looking for somebody willing to move in by the end of this month. The specific property is on the fifth floor and offers nice views of Garfield Park. I'd appreciate it if you could get back to me regarding this opportunity at your earliest opportunity. If you are no longer interested in moving to Sleeford Condominiums, I'll go ahead and add this unit to our online listings. But, I will hold off on doing that until I hear back from you.

Regards,

Curtis Wode
Diamond Real Estate

---

149. Why does Mr. Wode contact Ms. Munoz?
(A) To notify her about an employment opportunity
(B) To provide details about a real estate company
(C) To announce a vacancy in an apartment building
(D) To confirm some revisions to a property lease

150. What will Mr. Wode wait to do?
(A) Update a listing
(B) Clean an apartment
(C) Contact a tenant
(D) Schedule a viewing

Questions 151–152 refer to the following text message chain.

Gail Weiner [10:21 A.M.]
Hello, Mr. Choi. I'm still waiting to hear from your department about the problems with our online shopping mall. Have you managed to look into that yet?

Arthur Choi [10:23 A.M.]
One of our new programmers is working on it. She's putting the finishing touches to the new search engine and graphics now.

Gail Weiner [10:24 A.M.]
Glad to hear that. A lot of our customers were complaining about the poor search function. Can you let me know once it's ready? The customer service manager and I would like to test it out and check that the issues have been resolved.

Arthur Choi [10:26 A.M.]
No problem. I'll send you a message once we're done. And feel free to get in touch if you have any questions about the new design.

Gail Weiner [10:28 A.M.]
You can count on it. Thanks a lot.

151. In which department does Mr. Choi most likely work?
(A) Web design
(B) Customer service
(C) Marketing
(D) Human resources

152. At 10:28 A.M., what does Ms. Weiner most likely mean when she says, "You can count on it"?
(A) She will make time in her schedule to assist Mr. Choi.
(B) She will ensure that a task is completed this afternoon.
(C) She is certain that customers will be satisfied.
(D) She will contact Mr. Choi if she has any inquiries.

Questions 153–154 refer to the following advertisement.

Knightsbridge International Film Festival (KIFF) (October 3–5)

Since the event was first established 7 years ago, attendance at the KIFF has almost doubled each year, and this year's event is expected to draw its largest crowds yet. Join renowned film producer and KIFF founder Rod Livingstone and several world famous actors for movie premieres, film seminars, and the annual awards show. This year's festival will showcase the work of independent filmmakers more than it ever has before, and several amateur directors such as Lisa Gehrman have been nominated to win our Best New Director award.

This year's KIFF will be held in the Moxley Auditorium, and tickets will be variously priced for different events. A full list of admission prices can be found at www.kiff.com/tickets. As in previous years, KIFF members will receive a 20 percent discount on all event prices. Details about becoming a member can also be found on our Web site.

---

153. What is indicated about the KIFF?
(A) Its admission prices have increased.
(B) It includes filmmaking classes.
(C) It will begin with a welcome speech.
(D) It is attended by movie stars.

154. What information is NOT provided by the advertisement?
(A) The festival location
(B) The price of tickets
(C) An award nominee's name
(D) The amount of discount offered to members

To:	Tomas Verville <tverville@livemail.net>
From:	Carol Koontz <ckoontz@weymouthmuseum.com>
Subject:	Some specifics
Date:	May 1
Attachment:	Directions

Dear Mr. Verville,

On behalf of Weymouth Science Museum, I am very pleased that you accepted the position of tour guide at our institution. Our new premises on the outskirts of the city are almost ready, and we are currently in the process of moving all our permanent exhibits and setting them up.

At 8:30 A.M. on your first day, which will be May 11, our human resources manager, Andy Jackson, will provide you with a tour of the new facility. Afterwards, you will meet with our head of research, Glenda Boone, who will talk to you in more depth about each of our exhibits. It would be a good idea to bring a notepad and pen with you and write things down, as she will most likely provide you with a wealth of important information that you will want to refer to at a later date.

I've attached a map with simple directions that you can use to find the museum. Once you arrive, give your name to the parking attendant and he will waive the visitor parking fee. Later, you will receive an employee parking permit that can be used every day for free parking.

Sincerely,

Carol Koontz
Head Curator
Weymouth Science Museum

155. Why did Ms. Koontz contact Mr. Verville?
(A) To describe some new exhibits
(B) To announce changes to a museum tour
(C) To provide information about a job
(D) To recommend an individual for a position

156. What is indicated about Weymouth Science Museum?
(A) It is relocating to a new building.
(B) It recently hired several new guides.
(C) It has increased its visitor parking fee.
(D) It hosts a different exhibit each month.

157. What is Mr. Verville advised to do?
(A) Take some notes
(B) Use a specific entrance
(C) Contact Ms. Boone in advance
(D) Meet Ms. Koontz in the parking lot

Questions 158–160 refer to the following information.

Telford Logistics Inc.
2nd Annual Company Workshop, May 8–10
Grand Cayman Resort, Cayman Islands

Corporate Discounts

Telford Logistics Inc. is pleased to be holding its workshop here at the Grand Cayman Resort in the beautiful Cayman Islands. Our inaugural workshop proved to be overwhelmingly popular with staff, and we expect this one to be even better. As a workshop participant, you can take advantage of a special discount voucher book, which can be obtained during our welcome meeting in the resort lobby at 9 A.M. on Saturday. When you use these vouchers, a company-issued ID card must also be presented. Vouchers are only valid until the final day of the workshop, and may not be exchanged for cash.

Within the resort, vouchers can be used to obtain discounts in a variety of locations. You can receive a twenty percent discount on scuba diving equipment rental down on the beach, and get half-price beverages in the sports center behind the main lobby building. Additionally, a variety of swimwear and goggles can be bought at a discount in the water park at the eastern end of the resort grounds.

For those venturing outside the resort and into the nearby town, please be advised that these vouchers cannot be redeemed for any local goods or services. Also, make sure that you take your credit card or use the ATM in the lobby before going into town, where ATMs are hard to find. The ATM vestibule in the lobby can be accessed from 8 A.M. to 8 P.M.

158. What is indicated about Telford Logistics Inc.?
(A) It will distribute travel guides to staff members.
(B) It held its first workshop last year.
(C) Its headquarters are based in the Cayman Islands.
(D) It will hold a meeting every morning during the workshop.

159. Where can workshop participants NOT use the discount vouchers?
(A) In the resort lobby
(B) In the water park
(C) In the sports center
(D) On the beach

160. What is true about places to shop outside the resort site?
(A) They prefer to take payments by credit card.
(B) They are offering special promotions.
(C) They will not accept employees' vouchers.
(D) They remain open until 8 P.M.

Dear Staff,

On October 23, Cantor Foods will implement new guidelines related to hand washing practices. Staff members who work in the administration building or in the distribution warehouse will not be affected by this change, but workers who operate the production line and come into direct contact with food products will. They will still be required to clean their hands at the factory entrance before commencing their shifts. However, instead of using hand soap as before, production line workers will now be required to use the special anti-bacterial wipes that will be provided in its place.

If you have any questions regarding this change, please direct them to the factory supervisor, Maurice Chamberlain. I appreciate your cooperation in this effort to improve our sanitary practices.

Jim Hamilton
General Operations Manager
Cantor Foods

161. What is the purpose of the notice?
(A) To announce a staff meeting
(B) To outline a new policy
(C) To remind staff about a deadline
(D) To give details about installation work

162. Who will most likely be affected by the change described in the notice?
(A) Administrative staff
(B) Sales representatives
(C) Production line workers
(D) Warehouse employees

163. What does Mr. Hamilton imply about Cantor Foods?
(A) It plans to close one of its production facilities.
(B) It reviews its health and safety procedures every month.
(C) It has received several complaints from customers.
(D) It will no longer provide hand soap in the factory.

Questions 164–167 refer to the following article.

Medina, AZ, April 23 – WeMOVE Enterprises announced this morning a piece of news that will reshape local industry in the next year. –[1]–. It seems that the company has decided to move its main factory, which provides many residents of Medina with jobs, to a new location.

Derek Ayala, a spokesperson for WeMOVE, announced this morning that the company wanted to thank everyone who has worked at the factory since it opened four decades ago. –[2]–. Mr. Ayala explained that the company could no longer afford to keep the factory open in Medina when a bulk of its customers were coming from Asia. –[3]–.

Ayala was quoted as saying, "WeMOVE will be closing down the factory in July and moving it to Asia." –[4]–. Many of the workers are unsure of what the future will hold, and campaigns have already started with the intention of keeping the company from completing the move.

164. What is the purpose of the article?
(A) To report on new employment opportunities
(B) To inform consumers of a product name change
(C) To announce the relocation of a local company
(D) To explain the risk of a change in suppliers

165. When was the factory in Medina opened?
(A) About 40 years ago
(B) About 30 years ago
(C) About 20 years ago
(D) About 10 years ago

166. What can be inferred from the article?
(A) The company is experiencing a decline in sales.
(B) The factory has already closed its doors.
(C) Some of the workers will retain their positions.
(D) Many employees will be laid off.

167. In which of the positions marked [1], [2], [3], and [4] does the following sentence best belong?
"The precise location of the plant will be announced sometime within the next few weeks."
(A) [1]
(B) [2]
(C) [3]
(D) [4]

💬	▲
Dana Elgort	Rian, Vic, I'm just about to get in my car and go to Korby Inc. to present the design changes we made, but I seem to have forgotten the new blueprint for their headquarters. Did I leave it on my desk? [1:28 P.M.]
Rian Dennehy	Yes, I can see it. But, can't you just describe the modifications we're proposing? [1:30 P.M.]
Dana Elgort	Words aren't as effective. The changes are quite detailed, so they'd have a better chance of understanding if they could see them for themselves. [1:32 P.M.]
Rian Dennehy	In that case, you'd better come back upstairs to the office to collect it. [1:34 P.M.]
Vic Jacoby	Wait, Dana... you don't have to wait for the elevator to come back up here. I can head down to the basement parking garage. [1:36 P.M.]
Dana Elgort	Great! Would you mind meeting me outside the elevator? I'll walk back over there now. [1:37 P.M.]
Vic Jacoby	No problem. Are you on Level B1 or B2? [1:38 P.M.]
Rian Dennehy	Vic, why not just send one of the interns? [1:39 P.M.]
Vic Jacoby	Oh, I wanted to grab my cell phone charger from my car anyway. I was in a hurry this morning and forgot it. [1:40 P.M.]
Dana Elgort	Thanks again, Vic. I'm on Level B2. Will you be here soon? [1:41 P.M.]
Vic Jacoby	I'll see you in a few minutes, Dana. [1:42 P.M.] ▼

168. Who most likely is Ms. Elgort?
(A) A Korby Inc. staff member
(B) A client of Mr. Dennehy
(C) An HR manager
(D) An architect

169. At 1:32 P.M., what does Ms. Elgort most likely mean when she writes, "Words aren't as effective"?
(A) She would prefer to show the client a design.
(B) She is not confident enough to give a presentation.
(C) She thinks a business meeting went poorly.
(D) She believes that the client will agree with some changes.

170. Where is Ms. Elgort?
(A) In her office
(B) In a parking lot
(C) In her car
(D) In an elevator

171. What does Mr. Jacoby offer to do?
(A) Ask an intern to assist Ms. Elgort
(B) Allow Ms. Elgort to borrow a device
(C) Take a document to Ms. Elgort
(D) Accompany Ms. Elgort to a client meeting

Questions 172–175 refer to the following article.

Hakuna Readying New Production Facility

PRETORIA (November 16) — Hakuna Motors, the South African car manufacturer that recently moved its head office to our city, has provided details of the new production plant it has built in Douala, Cameroon. The plant will be supervised by a local management branch of the company, which is called Hakuna CAF, and will open on November 25.

The new factory signifies the company's intention to increase its market share in Central Africa. According to Nelson Aganda, Hakuna's CEO, "Producing automobiles in Douala will allow us to avoid many transportation and distribution costs in the area. –[1]–. As a result, we should be able to compete with our North African rivals who typically dominate the region in terms of sales." Mr. Aganda plans to cut the ribbon at the factory's grand opening event.

Hakuna first attempted to break into the Central African automobile market three years ago. –[2]–. The auto manufacturer widely advertised its Hakuna Solaro model of car throughout the region, emphasizing its reasonable price and impressive fuel efficiency. –[3]–. Unfortunately, sales were slow and unreliable shipping routes meant that customers had to wait several weeks to purchase a car.

Hakuna currently operates production plants in Nairobi, Kenya, and Luanda, Angola. –[4]–. Mr. Aganda noted that the firm has recently contacted members of the Egyptian government to request construction permission for a proposed factory in Alexandria. He hopes to receive confirmation of the project before the end of this year.

172. What is indicated about Hakuna Motors?
  (A) It is preparing to launch a new type of vehicle.
  (B) It was first established three years ago.
  (C) It wants to improve its position in the Central African market.
  (D) It will collaborate on a project with North African auto manufacturers.

173. What is indicated about Mr. Aganda?
  (A) He will take on a management role at the Douala plant.
  (B) He believes the Hakuna Solaro will prove to be a success.
  (C) He spends a lot of time working in Central Africa.
  (D) He intends to travel to Cameroon in November.

174. Where will Hakuna Motors most likely build its next manufacturing plant?
  (A) In South Africa
  (B) In Egypt
  (C) In Angola
  (D) In Kenya

175. In which of the positions marked [1], [2], [3], and [4] does the following sentence best belong?
  "Initial estimates point to a reduction of almost 50 percent of typical shipping expenses."
  (A) [1]
  (B) [2]
  (C) [3]
  (D) [4]

To: Tina Braymer <tbraymer@worldmail.net>
From: Yvonne Gagne <ygagne@evehotels.com>
Subject: Your Room Reservation (#438119)
Date: August 10

Dear Ms. Braymer,

At the end of this month, we will accommodate a large number of presenters and event organizers involved with this year's Skyline Software & Technology Convention. You currently have a room reserved on the second floor, but convention organizers would prefer to book the entirety of that floor for their staff and special guests. Thus, we are contacting you to ask whether you would mind switching to a different room in exchange for a $50 meal coupon. The coupon can be redeemed at any restaurants in any of our hotels, and is valid until the end of this year.

Please look below at the three alternate rooms that we hope you will consider. The first options are the same type of room as you originally reserved, at the same location, but on different floors.

Room 406	Eve Hotel (Porter Road)	Standard Room	Check-in from: 1 P.M., August 28	Check-out by: 11 A.M., August 30
Room 519	Eve Hotel (Porter Road)	Standard Room	Check-in from: 1 P.M., August 28	Check-out by: 11 A.M., August 30

The third option is a Deluxe Room, but this is at our other location, which is a few blocks north from Porter Road. You will be charged at the normal Standard Room rate.

Room 427	Eve Hotel (Clement Street)	Deluxe Room	Check-in from: 2 P.M., August 28	Check-out by: 12 P.M., August 30

If you have no problem with taking one of the suggested rooms, please contact our reservations manager, Harry Henley, at 555-0177. If you wish to keep your originally assigned room, we completely understand. However, we would truly appreciate your cooperation in this matter.

Sincerely,

Yvonne Gagne
Guest Services
Eve Hotel Group

HOTEL BOOKING CONFIRMATION

Reservation #438119) *AMENDED

EVE HOTEL, 387 Clement Street, San Francisco, CA 94105

Guest's Name: *Tina Braymer*

Reservation Details: *Deluxe Room, Check-in: August 28 / Check out: August 30*

Complimentary Breakfast Included

Payment Received: $550 (Credit Card No.: 1867-****-****-2878)

Security Deposit Required Upon Check-In: $100

176. What is the purpose of the e-mail?
- (A) To encourage a guest to change rooms
- (B) To provide a guest with directions to a hotel
- (C) To recommend that guests attend a convention
- (D) To promote a hotel chain's new location

177. What is indicated about the meal coupon?
- (A) It is valid at the Porter Road hotel only.
- (B) It must be used by December 31.
- (C) It can be exchanged for cash.
- (D) It will be mailed to Ms. Braymer.

178. What did Ms. Braymer most likely do after receiving the e-mail?
- (A) Contact an event organizer
- (B) Make a payment
- (C) Respond to the e-mail
- (D) Call Mr. Henley

179. What does the booking confirmation indicate about Ms. Braymer's new room reservation?
- (A) She paid for her room in cash.
- (B) She must pay $550 upon arrival.
- (C) She will receive a free meal.
- (D) She will stay at the hotel for three nights.

180. By what time should Ms. Braymer check out from the hotel?
- (A) 11 A.M.
- (B) 12 P.M.
- (C) 1 P.M.
- (D) 2 P.M.

Questions 181–185 refer to the following advertisement and form.

Upcoming Real Talk Book Readings of Best-sellers

Are you a book lover who wants to listen to some well-known voices reading excerpts from some popular books? If so, tune in to *Real Talk* on 93.1 FM to enjoy our new series of celebrity book readings. We will welcome some popular stars of stage and screen to our studio to read excerpts from some of the most popular novels currently available in bookstores. The readings will be aired live at 2 P.M. on three consecutive Wednesdays in March.

The series consists of three book readings:

- *"Future Proof"*
  - a science fiction novel written by Angus Fring and read by Kenneth Forster
- *"Dark Nights in Cairo"*
  - a thriller/mystery novel written by Jade Levy and read by Alex Knight
- *"The Winding River"*
  - a romance novel written by Angela Masters and read by Margaret Kaye

Have something you'd like to ask the authors? Call *Real Talk*'s host, Anna Hargreaves, at 555-0133 following the readings.

If you plan to listen to any of our readings, please let us know your thoughts via our Web site at www.realtalkradio.com. If they receive a positive response, we'll try to make it a regular fixture in our programming schedule.

---

www.realtalkradio.com/bookreadings/feedback ▼	— ☐ X

We really hope you enjoyed listening to our recent book readings. As with all aspects of our programming, we appreciate the feedback of our listeners. Please take a moment to complete the survey form below.

Name: Frank Mirabito

What did you particularly enjoy about the book readings?

> In my opinion, Mr. Knight's reading was the most enjoyable one. His voice is very expressive and perfectly suited to reading novels. Additionally, the book he read from is easily one of my favorite novels of the last ten years or so. That's the genre I tend to enjoy the most.

How can we improve our book readings in the future?

> During the readings, especially the one that took place on March 27, I felt that the readers were occasionally a little hard to hear. It was as if the microphone or amplification devices were faulty, making the volume inconsistent. It might be worth considering an upgrade for the next time.

181. What is indicated about the book readings?
- (A) They will be held in a bookstore.
- (B) They will be aired on the radio.
- (C) They are intended for aspiring writers.
- (D) They will take place on the same day.

182. According to the advertisement, why should people contact Ms. Hargreaves?
- (A) To enter a competition
- (B) To submit questions
- (C) To recommend an author
- (D) To provide a book review

183. What is implied about the book readers?
- (A) They all have published novels.
- (B) They work for *Real Talk* full-time.
- (C) They are all popular actors.
- (D) They will be interviewed by Ms. Hargreaves.

184. What is suggested about Mr. Mirabito?
- (A) He was unable to listen to one of the readings.
- (B) He has recently purchased *The Winding River*.
- (C) He will participate in the next book reading series.
- (D) He enjoys reading mystery stories.

185. What aspect of the book readings does Mr. Mirabito suggest changing?
- (A) The reading schedule
- (B) The special guests
- (C) The audio equipment
- (D) The types of books

Questions 186–190 refer to the following rental policy, vehicle evaluation, and e-mail.

VERNON'S CAR HIRE - RENTAL POLICY
Torres Megano, B49 VGA

POLICY

This is a seven-day rental, from April 11 to April 17, at a rate of $52 per day, for a total cost of $364. Payment has been received on the first day of the rental period. Late return of the vehicle will incur an additional charge of $75 per day. The rented vehicle comes with a full tank of gas, a CD/DVD player, and TV screen. Device charging cables are not included. A satellite navigation device can be provided for an extra $15 per day. The vehicle must be picked up at our Bayfield Avenue branch and returned to the same location.

DAMAGE COVERAGE

A damage coverage payment of $500 was also received on April 11. This will be returned to the renter in part or in full following an inspection of the returned vehicle. Vernon's Car Hire performed a full evaluation of the car prior to its release, and a copy of the evaluation report was provided to the renter.

VERNON'S CAR HIRE – PRELIMINARY VEHICLE EVALUATION

Date: April 11
Vehicle type: Sedan
Vehicle model: Torres Megano
License plate number: B49 VGA

Evaluation notes:
The electronics, braking and steering mechanisms, and engine have all been fully checked and were found to be in perfect working order. However, there are a slight rip in the upholstery of the vehicle's back seats, and a minor crack in the lower left corner of the windshield. Vernon's Car Hire is aware of the defects and will take full responsibility for them.

Vernon Mason	Elsa Buchanan
Company President	Vehicle Renter

E-mail Message

To: vmason@vernonscarhire.com
From: ebuchanan@ecity.net
Subject: Damage coverage payment
Date: April 19
Attachment: evaluationB49VGA.pdf

Dear Mr. Mason,

I returned a Torres Megano to your business a couple of days ago, and I just received a partial refund of the deposit I paid for damage coverage. I was surprised to find out that you have taken a charge of $200 from my initial payment. I knew that a deduction of $75 would be made in accordance with your rental policy, but there was no reason to deduct the extra $125. Apparently, this is for the tear that was already present when I picked up the car. This is explained in the attached evaluation report. When I picked up the car, your agent even pointed out the rip to me. I hope you will admit that you have made a mistake and return the $125 that I was wrongly charged.

Sincerely,

Elsa Buchanan

---

186. What is indicated in the rental policy?
(A) The vehicle should be brought back with a full tank of gas.
(B) The vehicle will be rented at a rate of $75 per day.
(C) The business owner recently changed the terms.
(D) The renter must use his or her own charging cables.

187. What is implied about Vernon's Car Hire?
(A) It has more than one premises.
(B) It recently added new cars to its fleet.
(C) It provides incentives to returning customers.
(D) It specializes in renting sports cars.

188. In the evaluation report, the word "order" in paragraph 1, line 2, is closest in meaning to
(A) request
(B) condition
(C) shipment
(D) command

189. Why did Ms. Buchanan receive a $75 penalty?
(A) She dropped off the car at the wrong location.
(B) She got into a road accident while driving the car.
(C) She misplaced some vehicle accessories.
(D) She returned the car a day late.

190. What argument does Ms. Buchanan make?
(A) The windshield crack was caused by accident.
(B) The damage to the seats is not her responsibility.
(C) The vehicle's performance was unsatisfactory.
(D) The rental agent gave her the wrong information.

GO ON TO THE NEXT PAGE

Questions 191–195 refer to the following Web page, form, and message board post.

British Bird Watching Message Board
Image Upload Guidelines

1. Please keep your message under 70 words in accordance with our message board policy. This ensures that information is presented concisely and accurately, with no irrelevant details.

2. Image descriptions should adhere to a "Bird species – time – site" format. Our members are all avid bird watchers, so they are particularly interested in being able to quickly scan for details of the images without any fuss. We have a separate page for unidentified bird images.

   Please add a description such as: "Pied Flycatcher – 6 A.M. – At Spurn Point, Yorkshire"

   Please avoid adding vague descriptions such as: "Small brown bird in the countryside"

3. As this is primarily a message board for sharing images, your post should contain at least one image of a bird, and that image must have been taken by you. We will not permit the sharing of images that were not taken personally by you.

British Bird Watching Message Board
New Member Registration Form

Name: Arthur Bedford   E-mail: abedford@homenet.com
Years spent bird watching: 10 years
Current employer: Natural World Weekly
Preferred camera: Zenon 650

I am interested in hearing about the quarterly gatherings that are hosted for British Bird Watching members. YES (✓) NO ( )

Terms of Image Use:
Please be advised that images uploaded to the message board may be added to the Gallery section of our Web site. Although we reserve the right to use uploaded pictures, we will not permit other companies to use them.

British Bird Watching Message Board

MESSAGE BOARD MEMBER: Arthur Bedford

Image description: Lesser spotted woodpecker – 5:45 A.M. – Kirby Forest, Cumbria

Date: May 15

Message: Some of you asked for some pictures of the lesser spotted woodpeckers that are rumored to live in the forest near my new house. Well, I was fortunate enough to capture a picture of one of them while out walking my dogs this morning. Although I only saw one, my neighbors have told me that several have been seen locally in recent weeks. I'll keep my eyes open and my camera ready! (72 words)

Image file attached: Lesser_spotted_woodpecker_05.15

191. What does the Web page indicate about the message board?
   (A) It is used by experienced bird watchers.
   (B) It requires members to pay an annual fee.
   (C) Members can create their own image gallery.
   (D) Videos of certain lengths are permitted.

192. What does the British Bird Watching Message Board promise to its members?
   (A) It will not publish images in its Web gallery.
   (B) It provides tips on photographing birds.
   (C) It holds an event for members once per month.
   (D) It does not share images with other businesses.

193. Why did Mr. Bedford post on the message board?
   (A) To seek recommendations for bird watching locations
   (B) To comment on a member's uploaded image
   (C) To respond to requests from other members
   (D) To request assistance in identifying a bird

194. How did Mr. Bedford fail to follow the message board rules?
   (A) His image description is not detailed enough.
   (B) He did not upload the required number of images.
   (C) He posted in the wrong section of the board.
   (D) His message exceeded a word limit.

195. What is probably true about Mr. Bedford?
   (A) He recently moved to a new home.
   (B) He just started a new job at a magazine.
   (C) He is a moderator of a message board.
   (D) He recently purchased a new camera.

Questions 196–200 refer to the following job advertisement, information, and e-mail.

Job title: *Swimming Pool Activity Coordinator*

Area: *West Los Angeles*

Eagle Condominiums, situated in the foothills of Santa Monica in the Westside part of Los Angeles, is seeking an outgoing individual to create and lead a fun pool activity for children. The instructor must be available to lead a weekend pool activity before the pool opens for regular use at 9:30 A.M.

Suitable payment will be negotiated during the interview with the condominium manager, Mr. Torrance. The activity coordinator is free to create his or her own program for the pool session, but this must be approved by Mr. Torrance.

If you are interested in applying for this role, please send an e-mail to management@eaglecondos.com, and type "Pool Activity Coordinator" in the subject line.

In the e-mail, make sure you describe any relevant experience you have and attach a recent photograph.

Eagle Condominiums

Swimming Pool

Pool Activities Schedule

The swimming pool is open for general use from 9:30 A.M. to 7:30 P.M., except on Tuesdays and Fridays, when it will open at 10:30 A.M. after cleaning. The following activities are available to children and will take place outside normal pool hours. Any child can participate, as long as he or she is a competent swimmer. Parents are welcome to spectate from the side of the pool.

Time	Activity	Coordinator
8:30 A.M.–9:30 A.M. (Mondays, Wednesdays, and Fridays)	Diving for Objects	Steven Chappelle
7:30 P.M.–8:30 P.M. (Mondays, Wednesdays, and Fridays)	Water Aerobics	Kate Underwood
8:30 A.M.–9:30 A.M. (Saturdays and Sundays)	Swimming Races	Louis Simpson
7:30 P.M.–8:30 P.M. (Saturdays and Sundays)	Water Polo	Natalie Liman

All children currently living in Eagle Condominiums may turn up for any session without prior reservations. Children living in the adjacent Livewell and Agostino condo buildings may also attend our pool activity sessions, as long as their parents make arrangements in advance at our reception desk.

E-mail Message

To: Betty Adams, Administration Manager
From: Neil Torrance, Condominium Manager
Date: Friday, August 12
Subject: Re: New swimming pool activities

Hi Betty,

Thanks for letting me know how things are going with our new children's activities in the swimming pool. It seems like the children and their parents are delighted with the new activities we have arranged. However, at the residents meeting yesterday, somebody complained about the noise during our midweek morning activity. So, I'd like you to have a word with the activity coordinator and ask him to come up with a different, less noisy activity. Thanks for your help.

Regards,

Neil Torrance
Condominium Manager
Eagle Condominiums

196. According to the job advertisement, what will the coordinator decide?
(A) What kind of activity to provide
(B) What time a session will begin
(C) How many children may participate
(D) Where an activity will take place

197. Who most likely is the newest pool activity coordinator?
(A) Mr. Chappelle
(B) Ms. Underwood
(C) Mr. Simpson
(D) Ms. Liman

198. What is indicated on the schedule?
(A) Children must be accompanied by a parent at all times.
(B) Children from Eagle Condominiums should register in advance.
(C) Children from other housing locations may use the pool.
(D) Children are encouraged to bring specific equipment.

199. According to the e-mail, with whom did Mr. Torrance speak on August 11?
(A) A job candidate
(B) A condominium manager
(C) A pool activity coordinator
(D) A building resident

200. What pool activity will most likely be changed?
(A) Diving for Objects
(B) Water Aerobics
(C) Swimming Races
(D) Water Polo

Stop! This is the end of the test. If you finish before time is called, you may go back to Parts 5, 6, and 7 and check your work.

NO TEST MATERIAL ON THIS PAGE

ANSWER SHEET

姓名　測驗回數　日期

LISTENING COMPREHENSION (PART 1~4)

NO	ANSWER A B C D	NO	ANSWER A B C D	NO	ANSWER A B C D	NO	ANSWER A B C D	NO	ANSWER A B C D
1	a b c d	21	a b c d	41	a b c d	61	a b c d	81	a b c d
2	a b c d	22	a b c d	42	a b c d	62	a b c d	82	a b c d
3	a b c d	23	a b c d	43	a b c d	63	a b c d	83	a b c d
4	a b c d	24	a b c d	44	a b c d	64	a b c d	84	a b c d
5	a b c d	25	a b c d	45	a b c d	65	a b c d	85	a b c d
6	a b c d	26	a b c d	46	a b c d	66	a b c d	86	a b c d
7	a b c d	27	a b c d	47	a b c d	67	a b c d	87	a b c d
8	a b c d	28	a b c d	48	a b c d	68	a b c d	88	a b c d
9	a b c d	29	a b c d	49	a b c d	69	a b c d	89	a b c d
10	a b c d	30	a b c d	50	a b c d	70	a b c d	90	a b c d
11	a b c d	31	a b c d	51	a b c d	71	a b c d	91	a b c d
12	a b c d	32	a b c d	52	a b c d	72	a b c d	92	a b c d
13	a b c d	33	a b c d	53	a b c d	73	a b c d	93	a b c d
14	a b c d	34	a b c d	54	a b c d	74	a b c d	94	a b c d
15	a b c d	35	a b c d	55	a b c d	75	a b c d	95	a b c d
16	a b c d	36	a b c d	56	a b c d	76	a b c d	96	a b c d
17	a b c d	37	a b c d	57	a b c d	77	a b c d	97	a b c d
18	a b c d	38	a b c d	58	a b c d	78	a b c d	98	a b c d
19	a b c d	39	a b c d	59	a b c d	79	a b c d	99	a b c d
20	a b c d	40	a b c d	60	a b c d	80	a b c d	100	a b c d

READING COMPREHENSION (PART 5~7)

NO	ANSWER A B C D	NO	ANSWER A B C D	NO	ANSWER A B C D	NO	ANSWER A B C D
101	a b c d	121	a b c d	141	a b c d	161	a b c d	181	a b c d
102	a b c d	122	a b c d	142	a b c d	162	a b c d	182	a b c d
103	a b c d	123	a b c d	143	a b c d	163	a b c d	183	a b c d
104	a b c d	124	a b c d	144	a b c d	164	a b c d	184	a b c d
105	a b c d	125	a b c d	145	a b c d	165	a b c d	185	a b c d
106	a b c d	126	a b c d	146	a b c d	166	a b c d	186	a b c d
107	a b c d	127	a b c d	147	a b c d	167	a b c d	187	a b c d
108	a b c d	128	a b c d	148	a b c d	168	a b c d	188	a b c d
109	a b c d	129	a b c d	149	a b c d	169	a b c d	189	a b c d
110	a b c d	130	a b c d	150	a b c d	170	a b c d	190	a b c d
111	a b c d	131	a b c d	151	a b c d	171	a b c d	191	a b c d
112	a b c d	132	a b c d	152	a b c d	172	a b c d	192	a b c d
113	a b c d	133	a b c d	153	a b c d	173	a b c d	193	a b c d
114	a b c d	134	a b c d	154	a b c d	174	a b c d	194	a b c d
115	a b c d	135	a b c d	155	a b c d	175	a b c d	195	a b c d
116	a b c d	136	a b c d	156	a b c d	176	a b c d	196	a b c d
117	a b c d	137	a b c d	157	a b c d	177	a b c d	197	a b c d
118	a b c d	138	a b c d	158	a b c d	178	a b c d	198	a b c d
119	a b c d	139	a b c d	159	a b c d	179	a b c d	199	a b c d
120	a b c d	140	a b c d	160	a b c d	180	a b c d	200	a b c d

聽力測驗 Part1 & Part 2

冊次	TEST 1 ☑ TEST 2 ◯ TEST 3 ◯
題號	1
頁數	45
	(A) The man is hanging up a poster. (B) The woman is taking a picture. (C) The man is pointing at something. (D) They are looking at each other.

錯誤原因

圖中的兩個人正看著某個東西，不能因為聽到「在看」就確定答案！
一定要確定(受詞)！
Something 也有可能是答案！

重要字彙	hang up　掛 point at　指向 look at each other　看著對方

1. 將答錯及用猜的題目寫下來！
2. 用螢光筆將不知道意思或讀音的單字畫起來！
3. 彙整用螢光筆標示起來的單字及文句！
4. 錯誤原因：(1) 將表「動作」（be being p.p）誤解成表「狀態」。
　　　　　　 (2) 不知道 schedule 的英式發音 [ˈʃɛdjul] 與美式發音 [ˈskɛdʒu] 唸法不同。

誤答筆記 聽力測驗 Part1 & Part 2

冊次	TEST 1 ◯ TEST 2 ◯ TEST 3 ◯
題號	
頁數	

錯誤原因	

冊次	TEST 1 ◯ TEST 2 ◯ TEST 3 ◯
題號	
頁數	

錯誤原因	

重要字彙	

＊請將本頁表格剪下，複印後使用。

找出 Part 5 & Part 6 錯誤的原因

冊次	TEST 1 ◯　TEST 2 ☑　TEST 3 ◯	
題號	101	**我選擇的答案** B
頁數	67	**錯誤原因**

~ there has been much _____ in agriculture, with ~.
(A) develop
(B) developed
(C) developing
(D) development

★找出我的弱點！
問題類型　　（文法）句子的結構
　　　　　　詞彙

我選擇的答案 B

錯誤原因
不知道 [there is/are+ 名詞]
看到 has been 就急忙認定是 P.P
需要看完文句的整體結構！

答案 D
正確原因
there is 句型 → 空格才是主語！
範例中，只有身為名詞的 development
能擔任主語，雖然 there 這個副詞在
主語的位置上，但並不是真正的主語。
實際上真正的主語是接在 be 動詞後的
名詞！

重要字彙	there is N　有 ~ develop　發展 agriculture　農業

1. 不用把所有的題目都抄起來！只需要寫下會影響正解的部分，其他以連接號「~」代替！
2. 不要將正解寫在問題裡，需要另外標示！
3. 掌握為什麼答錯才是最重要的！
4. 簡要解釋不懂的部分！
5. 快速掌握題型的話，解題的速度也會提升！確認錯誤的題目屬於什麼類型！
6. 一定要整理題目裡不懂的單字！

誤答筆記　找出 Part 5 & Part 6 錯誤的原因

冊次	TEST 1 ◯　　TEST 2 ◯　　TEST 3 ◯	
題號		我選擇的答案 錯誤原因
頁數		
		答案 正確原因
★找出我的弱點！ 問題類型　　文法 　　　　　　詞彙		

冊次	TEST 1 ◯　　TEST 2 ◯　　TEST 3 ◯	
題號		我選擇的答案 錯誤原因
頁數		
		答案 正確原因
★找出我的弱點！ 問題類型　　文法 　　　　　　詞彙		

重要字彙	

＊請將本頁表格剪下，複印後使用。

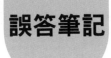

Part 3 & Part 4 & Part 7
Paraphrasing 整理

more detailed report 更詳細的報告	→	a revised document 修訂的文件
drop off your report 留下你的報告	→	turn in an assignment 提交作品
later today 今天稍晚	→	this afternoon 今天下午
	→	
	→	

請整理對話或短文中的線索，再次確認其線索是如何變成正確答案的！

整理對話、短文中的線索是如何變成正確答案的,盡可能精簡。如果將冗長的文句都寫下來,很容易感到厭倦。準備多益最重要的是「跑完全程」。

→	→
→	→
→	→
→	→
→	→
→	→
→	→
→	→
→	→
→	→

＊請將本頁表格剪下,複印後使用。

單字表　屬於我的多益單字表

學習時遇到不會的單字，記得整理起來（特別是句子填空題中出現在選項的單字）。

另外，如果在文句中出現跟該單字搭配使用的搭配詞／慣用語，最好也一起寫下來。

也別忘了記下 Part 3、4、7 的文句及選項中影響判斷的單字！

sign up 報名；註冊；簽約 sign up for the seminar 報名研討會 = register for	**Sample**
rarely 很少；不常見 = not often highly 非常 = very	

＊請將本頁表格剪下，複印後使用。

揮別厚重，迎向高分！
最接近真實多益測驗的模擬題本

特色 1 單回成冊

揮別市面多數多益題本的厚重感，單回裝訂仿照真實測驗，提前適應答題手感。

特色 2 錯題解析

解析本提供深度講解，針對正確答案與誘答選項進行解題，全面掌握答題關鍵。

特色 3 誤答筆記

提供筆記模板，協助深入了解誤答原因，歸納出專屬於自己的學習筆記。

TOEIC

Test of English for International Communication

TEST 3

答案與解析

三民書局

TEST 3

PART 1

1. (D) 2. (C) 3. (A) 4. (B) 5. (C) 6. (B)

PART 2

7. (A) 8. (C) 9. (A) 10. (A) 11. (C) 12. (B) 13. (A) 14. (B) 15. (B) 16. (A) 17. (A) 18. (C) 19. (B)
20. (C) 21. (C) 22. (B) 23. (A) 24. (A) 25. (A) 26. (B) 27. (A) 28. (C) 29. (A) 30. (B) 31. (A)

PART 3

32. (A) 33. (A) 34. (A) 35. (D) 36. (C) 37. (C) 38. (B) 39. (A) 40. (D) 41. (A) 42. (D) 43. (A) 44. (C)
45. (D) 46. (B) 47. (B) 48. (D) 49. (A) 50. (C) 51. (C) 52. (D) 53. (A) 54. (B) 55. (A) 56. (C) 57. (D)
58. (A) 59. (C) 60. (A) 61. (B) 62. (B) 63. (D) 64. (C) 65. (B) 66. (D) 67. (D) 68. (B) 69. (C) 70. (D)

PART 4

71.(D) 72. (A) 73. (A) 74. (B) 75. (A) 76. (C) 77. (C) 78. (C) 79. (C) 80. (C) 81. (C) 82. (D) 83. (C)
84. (D) 85. (C) 86. (A) 87. (D) 88. (C) 89. (C) 90. (A) 91. (C) 92. (C) 93. (C) 94. (C) 95. (D) 96. (D)
97. (A) 98. (B) 99. (C) 100. (B)

PART 5

101. (A) 102. (C) 103. (D) 104. (B) 105. (B) 106. (D) 107. (D) 108. (D) 109. (A) 110. (A) 111. (D)
112. (A) 113. (C) 114. (A) 115. (A) 116. (A) 117. (D) 118. (B) 119. (B) 120. (A) 121. (B) 122. (C)
123. (A) 124. (B) 125. (C) 126. (C) 127. (D) 128. (B) 129. (B) 130. (D)

PART 6

131. (D) 132. (D) 133. (B) 134. (C) 135. (B) 136. (D) 137. (D) 138. (C) 139. (D) 140. (A) 141. (A)
142. (D) 143. (C) 144. (C) 145. (B) 146. (A)

PART 7

147. (D) 148. (C) 149. (C) 150. (A) 151. (A) 152. (D) 153. (D) 154. (B) 155. (C) 156. (A) 157. (A)
158. (B) 159. (A) 160. (C) 161. (B) 162. (C) 163. (D) 164. (C) 165. (A) 166. (D) 167. (D) 168. (D)
169. (A) 170. (B) 171. (C) 172. (C) 173. (D) 174. (B) 175. (A) 176. (A) 177. (B) 178. (D) 179. (C)
180. (B) 181. (B) 182. (B) 183. (C) 184. (D) 185. (C) 186. (D) 187. (A) 188. (B) 189. (D) 190. (B)
191. (A) 192. (D) 193. (C) 194. (D) 195. (A) 196. (A) 197. (C) 198. (C) 199. (D) 200. (A)

Part 1

1.

(A) She's resting on a sofa.
(B) She's clearing off the table.
(C) She's arranging the bookshelves.
(D) She's sweeping the floor.
(A) 她在沙發上休息。
(B) 她在清理桌子。
(C) 她在整理書櫃。
(D) 她在掃地。

解析 照片內僅有一人時，須留意該人物的動作、姿勢及與其有關連性的事物。
(A) 女子並未在沙發上休息，故非正解。
(B) 女子並非在清理桌子，故非正解。
(C) 女子並非在整理書櫃，故非正解。
(D) 女子拿著掃把在掃地，故為正解。

2.

(A) She's displaying baked goods.
(B) She's wrapping a box of cookies.
(C) She's looking into a glass case.
(D) She's walking into a shopping mall.
(A) 她在陳列烘焙產品。
(B) 她在包一盒餅乾。
(C) 她在看玻璃櫃。
(D) 她正走進一間購物中心。

解析 照片內僅有一人時，須留意該人物的動作、姿勢及與其有關連性的事物。
(A) 女子並非在陳列烘焙產品，故非正解。
(B) 女子並未包裝餅乾，故非正解。
(C) 女子正往玻璃櫃裡看，故為正解。
(D) 女子並未走進購物中心，故非正解。

3.

(A) A man is pointing at a computer screen.
(B) One of the women is writing on some chart paper.
(C) Some chairs are stacked in a corner.
(D) A door has been left open.
(A) 一名男子指著電腦螢幕。
(B) 其中一名女子正在填記錄紙。
(C) 有些椅子堆在角落。
(D) 有扇門敞開著。

解析 照片內出現多個人物時，須留意人物們的動作、姿勢及周邊事物。

(A) 男子正指著電腦螢幕，故為正解。
(B) 照片中沒女子在寫東西，故非正解。
(C) 照片中沒有堆在角落的椅子，故非正解。
(D) 照片中沒有敞開的門，故非正解。

4.

(A) One of the women is putting on a jacket.
(B) One of the women is holding a piece of paper.
(C) A man is making a pot of coffee.
(D) A man is distributing notepads.
(A) 其中一位女子正在穿外套。
(B) 其中一位女子拿著一張紙。
(C) 一位男子在煮一壺咖啡。
(D) 一位男子在發便條紙。

解析 照片內出現多個人物時，須留意人物們的動作、姿勢及周邊事物。
(A) 照片中沒有正在穿外套的女子，故非正解。
(B) 其中一位女子手裡拿著一張紙，故為正解。
(C) 男子並非在煮咖啡，故非正解。
(D) 男子並未發放便條紙，故非正解。

5.

(A) Some people are buying flowers.
(B) Some flowerpots are being moved.
(C) Some plants are on display.
(D) Some potted plants are being watered.
(A) 有些人在買花。
(B) 有些花盆正被移動。
(C) 有些植物被展示。
(D) 有些盆栽植物正被澆水。

解析 照片內僅有物品時，必須留意物品的名稱和所在位置。
(A) 照片中並未出現人物，故非正解。
(B) 照片中的花盆並未被移動，故非正解。
(C) 照片中的植物是被陳列展示的狀態，故為正解。
(D) 照片中沒有替植物澆水的動作出現，故非正解。

6.

(A) One of the men is driving a truck.
(B) Some men are standing on a dock.
(C) There are boats approaching the shore.
(D) Some workers are unloading containers from the ship.

(A) 其中一名男子在開貨車。
(B) 幾位男人站在碼頭。
(C) 幾艘小船正在接近海岸。
(D) 幾位工人正從船上卸下貨櫃。

解析 照片內出現兩人時，須留意兩位人物共同的動作、姿勢及人物們周邊的事物。
(A) 照片中沒有開著貨車的男子，故非正解。
(B) 男子們正站在碼頭邊，故為正解。
(C) 照片中沒有朝海岸靠近的小船，故非正解。
(D) 照片中沒有從船上卸下貨櫃的人，故非正解。

Part 2

7. Who's responsible for the annual bonuses?
(A) The payroll manager.
(B) 500 dollars.
(C) In December.
誰負責年終獎金？
(A) 薪酬經理。
(B) 500 美元。
(C) 12 月。

解析 本題為詢問誰負責年終獎金的 Who 疑問句。
(A) 以特定職位的人回覆 Who 疑問句，故為正解。
(B) 此為針對 How much 疑問句，告知費用的回答，故非正解。
(C) 此為針對 When 疑問句，告知時間點的回答，故非正解。

8. Do you prefer taking the bus or the train?
(A) The station on Main Street.
(B) It's a direct route.
(C) I like buses.
你比較喜歡搭公車還是火車？
(A) 在主街的車站。
(B) 這是直達路線。
(C) 我喜歡搭公車。

解析 本題為詢問公車和火車間比較想要搭哪一個的選擇疑問句。
(A) 此為針對 Where 疑問句，告知地點的回答，故非正解。
(B) 移動路線的特徵與問題無關，故非正解。
(C) 在兩個選項中選擇了公車，故為正解。

9. When will the next company newsletter be sent out?
(A) In August.
(B) No, at this company.
(C) Make sure I get a copy.
公司下一期的電子報什麼時候會發出？
(A) 8 月。
(B) 不，在這間公司。
(C) 要確保我會拿到一份複本。

解析 本題為詢問公司下一期電子報何時會發出的 When 疑問句。
(A) 用特定時間點回覆 When 疑問句，故為正解。
(B) 用 No 回答疑問詞問句，故非正解。
(C) 回話者要對方給自己一份複本的回答與問題無關，故非正解。

10. How long is tomorrow's seminar?
(A) Three hours, I think.
(B) Sure, I can attend.
(C) At least 100 people.
明天的研討會時間多長？
(A) 我想是 3 小時。
(B) 當然，我可以參加。
(C) 至少 100 人。

解析 本題為詢問明天舉辦的研討會時間多長的 How long 疑問句。
(A) 用一段持續的時間回答 How long 疑問句，故為正解。
(B) 用 Sure 回答疑問詞問句，故非正解。
(C) 此為針對 How many 疑問句，告知人數的回答，故非正解。

11. Doesn't this bakery sell drinks?
(A) That's not too expensive.
(B) A wide range of bread.
(C) There's a coffee shop next door.
這間烘焙坊沒賣飲料嗎？
(A) 那沒有很貴。
(B) 很多種類的麵包。
(C) 隔壁有一間咖啡廳。

解析 本題為確認烘焙坊是否沒賣飲料的否定疑問句。
(A) 未回答是否販賣飲料，只回答價格高低，故非正解。
(B) 麵包種類很多的回答與問題無關，故非正解。
(C) 用隔壁有咖啡廳間接表達這間店沒賣飲料，故為正解。

12. Can we have another look at the menu, please?
(A) Yes, it was delicious.
(B) I'll be right back.
(C) I can see that.
請問我們可以再看一下菜單嗎？
(A) 是，非常美味。
(B) 我馬上就回來。
(C) 我可以看到那個。

解析 本題為詢問是否能再看一次菜單的請求疑問句。
(A) 用過去式 (was) 指過去發生的事，而不是對未來的要求，故非正解。
(B) 用馬上回來表達自己要去拿菜單過來給對方看，故為正解。
(C) 用聽到 look 容易聯想到的 see 混淆考生，故非正解。

13. Why didn't the box of product catalogs arrive yesterday?
(A) Because of a shipping error.
(B) I like the new merchandise.
(C) Next day delivery, please.
為什麼那箱產品型錄昨天沒送到？
(A) 因為有運送錯誤。
(B) 我喜歡新商品。
(C) 請幫我隔日到貨。

解析 本題為詢問產品型錄還沒到的理由的 Why 疑問句。

(A) 用能夠用來回覆 Why 疑問句的 Because of 表達運送上出了問題，故為正解。
(B) 用聽到 product 容易聯想到的 merchandise 混淆考生，故非正解。
(C) 用聽到 product 和 arrive 容易聯想到的 Next day delivery 混淆考生，故非正解。

14. Who requested to swap work shifts this Saturday?
(A) It's our busiest day.
(B) I'll check the schedule.
(C) You'll need authorization.
誰要求這週六要換班？
(A) 是我們最忙的一天。
(B) 我會確認班表。
(C) 你需要得到批准。

解析 本題為詢問誰這週六要換班的 Who 疑問句。
(A) 關於特定工作日特性的回答與問題無關，故非正解。
(B) 回答了能夠確認問題中資訊的方法，故為正解。
(C) 用聽到 requested to swap work shifts 容易聯想到的 authorization 混淆考生，故非正解。

15. Should I finish this before lunchtime, or can it wait until later?
(A) The restaurant across the road.
(B) This afternoon's fine.
(C) No, I got here on time.
我要在午餐時間前完成，還是可以等晚一點？
(A) 對街的餐廳。
(B) 今天下午也可以。
(C) 不，我準時到這。

解析 本題為詢問某件事是否必須在午餐時間前完成，還是可以往後延一些的選擇疑問句。
(A) 用聽到 lunchtime 容易聯想到的 restaurant 混淆考生，故非正解。
(B) 用今天下午也可以來表達可以稍微延後一些，故為正解。
(C) 抵達的時間點與問題中的工作完成時間點無關，故非正解。

16. Where can I sign up for the marketing workshop?
(A) You can sign up right here.
(B) Anyone can attend.
(C) A new farmers' market.
哪裡可以報名參加行銷工作坊？
(A) 你可以在這報名。
(B) 任何人都能參加。
(C) 一個新的農產品市場。

解析 本題為詢問哪裡可以申請參加行銷工作坊的 Where 疑問句。
(A) 用表位置的 here 來回答 Where 疑問句，說明能夠申請的地點，故為正解。
(B) 此為回答申請資格，而非地點，故非正解。
(C) 用和 marketing 部分發音相同的 market 混淆考生，故非正解。

17. You know the supervisor of the graphic design department, don't you?
(A) Yes, he's a friend of mine.
(B) Several designer vacancies.
(C) This one's my favorite.
你認識平面設計部門的主管，對吧？
(A) 對，他是我一個朋友。
(B) 好幾個設計師職位空缺。
(C) 這個是我的最愛。

解析 本題為確認對方是否認識平面設計部門主管的附加問句。
(A) 用 Yes 表肯定，並說明兩人是什麼關係，故為正解。
(B) 用和 design 發音和意思都相似的 designer 混淆考生，故非正解。
(C) 說明自己的喜好與問題無關，故非正解。

18. Isn't Ms. Findlay's car in the parking lot?
(A) The parking fee is 5 dollars.
(B) I parked across the street.
(C) I didn't see it there.
Findlay 女士的車不是在停車場嗎？
(A) 停車費是 5 美元。
(B) 我把車停在對街。
(C) 我在那裡沒看到。

解析 本題為確認 Findlay 女士的車是否在停車場的否定疑問句。
(A) 停車費的回答與問題無關，故非正解。
(B) 未提及 Findlay 女士的車，而是回答自己的車停在哪，故非正解。
(C) 用 it 代指 Ms. Findlay's car，再用 there 代指 parking lot，表達自己在停車場沒看到她的車，故為正解。

19. How do I apply for a store membership?
(A) All twenty branches.
(B) You need to visit our Web site.
(C) That position has been filled.
我要怎麼申請成為商店會員？
(A) 總共 20 間分店。
(B) 你必須瀏覽我們的網站。
(C) 那個職位被補上了。

解析 本題為詢問如何成為商店會員的 How 疑問句。
(A) 此為針對 How many 疑問句，告知分店數量的回答，故非正解。
(B) 用瀏覽他們的網站指出申請會員的方法，故為正解。
(C) 用聽到 apply 容易聯想到的 position 和 filled 混淆考生，故非正解。

20. I'm going to the concert at AGS Music Hall tonight.
(A) Lots of great musicians.
(B) Sure, I'd love to.
(C) Hasn't it been canceled?
我今天晚上要去在 AGS 音樂廳舉辦的音樂會。
(A) 有很多很棒的音樂家。
(B) 當然，我很樂意。
(C) 那個不是被取消了嗎？

解析 本題為描述今晚要去在 AGS 音樂廳舉辦的音樂會的敘述句。

(A) 用聽到 concert 和 Music Hall 容易聯想到的 musicians 混淆考生，故非正解。
(B) 此為向對方的提議表示同意時使用的句子，故非正解。
(C) 用 it 代指 concert 並反問活動不是已經取消了，故為正解。

21. What do you think about this hotel?
(A) A single room, please.
(B) No, we're fully booked.
(C) I love staying here.
你覺得這間飯店如何？
(A) 請給我一間單人房。
(B) 不，我們都訂滿了。
(C) 我喜歡住在這。
解析 本題為詢問對方對特定飯店想法的 What 疑問句。
(A) 此為要求特定房型時說的話，與問題無關，故非正解。
(B) 用 No 回答疑問詞問句，故非正解。
(C) 用 here 代指 this hotel，表達自己喜歡住在這，故為正解。

22. Why don't we go to the food fair in Waterside Park?
(A) Yes, it's delicious.
(B) Sounds great to me.
(C) Around 30 vendors.
我們何不去水岸公園的食品展呢？
(A) 是，很美味。
(B) 我覺得很棒。
(C) 大概 30 個攤販。
解析 本題為詢問去參加食品展如何的提議疑問句。
(A) 用聽到 food 容易聯想到的 delicious 混淆考生，故非正解。
(B) 此為接受提議時使用的句子，故為正解。
(C) 參與業者的規模與問題無關，故非正解。

23. 8 A.M. isn't the best time for a staff meeting, is it?
(A) You're right. It's too early.
(B) For all full-time employees.
(C) In the upstairs conference room.
早上 8 點不是開職員會議最好的時間，對吧？
(A) 你說的對。太早了。
(B) 適合所有正職職員。
(C) 在樓上的大會議廳。
解析 本題為確認早上 8 點是否不是最好的開會時間的附加問句。
(A) 表達同意後，說明覺得早上 8 點開會不恰當的理由，故為正解。
(B) 並未回答所問的會議時間，而是會議參加者，故非正解。
(C) 此為針對 Where 疑問句，告知地點的回答，故非正解。

24. I haven't applied for the head librarian job yet.
(A) The closing date is this Friday.
(B) I don't think I'm qualified.
(C) Mark was the right choice.

我還沒申請圖書館館長一職。
(A) 截止日是本週五。
(B) 我不認為我符合資格。
(C) Mark 是最好的選擇。
解析 本題為描述自己尚未申請圖書館館長職位的敘述句。
(A) 用截止日勸對方快點申請，故為正解。
(B) 未回覆對方申請與否的問題，而是說明自己的資格，故非正解。
(C) 未回覆對方申請與否的問題，而是說自己認為最適合的人選，故非正解。

25. Which restaurant should I take Mr. Cheng to?
(A) Alice can recommend one.
(B) He's one of our new clients.
(C) Thanks, but I already had dinner.
我該帶鄭先生去哪間餐廳？
(A) Alice 可以推薦一間。
(B) 他是我們其中一位新客戶。
(C) 謝謝，但我已經用過晚餐了。
解析 本題為詢問該帶鄭先生去哪間餐廳的 Which 疑問句。
(A) 用 one 代指 restaurant，回答有人能為他推薦餐廳，故為正解。
(B) 並未提及餐廳，而是回答客戶的相關事項，故非正解。
(C) 已經用過晚餐的回答與問題無關，故非正解。

26. Would you like to become a member of our gym?
(A) It costs 30 dollars per month.
(B) I already have a membership here.
(C) The weights are next to the entrance.
你願意成為我們健身房的會員嗎？
(A) 一個月的費用是 30 美元。
(B) 我已經是這裡的會員了。
(C) 重量訓練器材在入口旁邊。
解析 本題為向對方提議是否要成為健身房會員的疑問句。
(A) 未回答是否要加入會員，而是說明與問題無關的費用，故非正解。
(B) 用是會員來表達自己已經加入，故為正解。
(C) 未回答是否要加入會員，而是說明運動器材的位置，故非正解。

27. Are the product samples being sent out today or tomorrow?
(A) Michael already delivered them.
(B) Our new range of camping supplies.
(C) Yes, it was simple to use.
產品的樣品是今天會寄出還是明天？
(A) Michael 已經寄送出去了。
(B) 我們新的露營系列用品。
(C) 對，使用上很容易。
解析 本題為詢問今天還是明天會寄送產品樣品的選擇疑問句。
(A) 用 them 代指 product samples，告知已經送出，故為正解。
(B) 未回答寄送時間點，而是回答產品類型，

故非正解。

(C) 用和 sample 發音類似的 simple 混淆考生，故非正解。

28. When is the retirement party for the general manager?
(A) Everyone had a great time.
(B) David will replace him.
(C) I wasn't invited to that.
總經理的退休派對是什麼時候？
(A) 所有人都度過了愉快的時間。
(B) David 會取代他。
(C) 我沒有被邀請參加。

解析 本題為詢問總經理退休派對何時舉辦的 When 疑問句。
(A) 回答為過去式 (had)，與問題的時態不符，故非正解。
(B) 此為針對 Who 疑問句，告知接任的人是誰的回答，故非正解。
(C) 用 that 代指 retirement party，用沒被邀請表達自己不知道派對何時舉辦，故為正解。

29. Does this bus seem too small for all the tour group members?
(A) No, it should be fine.
(B) Thanks, I'd love to participate.
(C) There are several sites to visit.
旅行團全團要搭的這臺巴士不會太小嗎？
(A) 不，應該坐得下。
(B) 謝謝，我想要參加。
(C) 有好幾個景點可以參觀。

解析 本題為詢問對整團旅行團來說，這臺巴士是否太小的疑問句。
(A) 用帶有否定之意的 No 表不同意對方的想法，故為正解。
(B) 用聽到 tour 容易聯想到的 participate 混淆考生，故非正解。
(C) 用聽到 tour 容易聯想到的 sites to visit 混淆考生，故非正解。

30. Why will the Web site be offline this afternoon?
(A) I don't know the address.
(B) Didn't you read the notice?
(C) At around 3 P.M.
為什麼網站今天下午會斷線？
(A) 我不知道地址。
(B) 你沒看公告嗎？
(C) 大概下午 3 點。

解析 本題為詢問今天下午網站為何斷線的 Why 疑問句。
(A) 用聽到 Web site 容易聯想到的 address 混淆考生，故非正解。
(B) 透過反問對方是否沒看公告，點出能夠確認相關資訊的方法，故為正解。
(C) 此為針對 When 疑問句，告知時間點的回答，故非正解。

31. How can we attract more customers to our store?

(A) Paul's going to hand out flyers.
(B) You can store it here for now.
(C) Yes, it's really boosted our profits.
要怎麼吸引更多顧客來我們的店？
(A) Paul 會去發傳單。
(B) 你可以先存放在這。
(C) 對，這真的增加了我們的收益。

解析 本題為詢問如何吸引更多顧客光臨店裡的 How 疑問句。
(A) 回答了發傳單這個能吸引更多顧客的方法，故為正解。
(B) 利用 store 的另一個意思 (保存) 混淆考生，故非正解。
(C) 用 Yes 回答疑問詞問句，故非正解。

Part 3

Questions 32–34 refer to the following conversation.

W: I'm so happy that 32 our sportswear store is already making a good profit, Chris. There seems to be a high demand for the range of running shoes, T-shirts, and shorts we carry.

M: Yes, and 33 when we finally launch our Web site this weekend, we can expect even more shoppers to come to the store.

W: I agree. Oh, by the way, 34 are you still designing an advertisement that we can run in the local newspaper?

M: 34 Yes, I'm almost done with it. It should be ready by the end of the week.

女：Chris，我很開心我們的運動服飾店已經獲得很好的利潤。看來我們有的運動鞋、T 恤和短褲的需求量很大。
男：沒錯，而且當我們終於在這週末上線網站後，我們預計會有更多消費者來我們店。
女：我同意。喔，順帶一提，你還在設計我們要刊在當地報紙上的廣告嗎？
男：對，我快要完成了。應該這週末會準備好。

32. 說話者們在哪裡工作？
(A) 在服飾店
(B) 在健身中心
(C) 在健康食品商店
(D) 在平面設計公司

解析 女子在對話開頭說到我們的運動服飾店 (our sportswear store)，點出他們工作的地點，故本題正解為選項 (A)。

33. 這週末會發生什麼事？
(A) 網站會正式上線。
(B) 新產品要公開。
(C) 將會提供折扣。
(D) 新分店要開幕。

解析 這個週末出現在對話中段，男子說這週末網站要上線 (when we finally launch our Web site this weekend)，故本題正解為選項 (A)。

34. 男子說他在處理什麼工作？
(A) 報紙廣告
(B) 產品型錄
(C) 海報
(D) 商標設計

解析 女子在對話後半段詢問男子是否還在設計要刊在當地報紙上的廣告 (are you still designing an advertisement that we can run in the local newspaper?)，男子接著回覆已經快完成了，故本題正解為選項 (A)。

Questions 35–37 refer to the following conversation.

M: **35** You've reached the customer service department at Pulsar Telecom. You're speaking to Zara. What can I do for you today?

W: It's about time. **36** I was put through to the wrong department earlier. I'm becoming quite annoyed. This happened the last few times I called, too.

M: I'm sorry about that, ma'am. We've had a problem with our switchboard, and some calls are being put through to the wrong extension numbers. We're doing our best to fix the problem. Now, before I can help you today, **37** would you mind giving me your customer identification number? I'll need that to access your account details.

男：你撥打的是 Pulsar 電信公司的客戶服務部門。我是 Zara。今天有什麼可以為你服務的嗎？
女：終於。我稍早被轉接到錯誤的部門。這讓我很煩躁。我之前打電話的時候也發生過幾次。
男：我對此感到很抱歉，女士。我們的接線總機有點問題，有些電話會被接到錯誤的分機上。我們正在努力解決這個問題。現在，在我今天為你提供協助之前，可以請你提供你的顧客確認碼嗎？我需要這個來查看你的顧客詳細資訊。

35. 男子應該是誰？
(A) 業務代表
(B) 維修技師
(C) 招聘經理
(D) 顧客顧問

解析 男子在對話開頭說這裡是 Pulsar 電信公司客戶服務部 (You've reached the customer service department at Pulsar Telecom.)，故本題正解為選項 (D)。

36. 女子為什麼感到煩躁？
(A) 她去了錯誤的分店。
(B) 她沒收到預計要送達的包裹。
(C) 她被轉接給錯誤的人。
(D) 她買到有瑕疵的產品。

解析 女子在對話前半段說自己被轉接到錯誤的部門，這讓她很煩躁 (I was put through to the wrong department earlier. I'm becoming quite annoyed.)，故本題正解為選項 (C)。

37. 男子要女子提供什麼？
(A) 產品名稱
(B) 家裡的地址
(C) 身分證明號碼
(D) 信用卡號碼

解析 男子在對話最後請女子提供顧客確認碼 (would you mind giving me your customer identification number?) 故本題正解為選項 (C)。

Questions 38–40 refer to the following conversation with three speakers.

W1: Excuse me, sir. **38** My sister and I were wondering whether we can check in to our room a little early. We know that the check-in time is supposed to be 2 P.M. It's under the name Williams.

M: Let's see... Ah, yes, Williams. **39** I'm afraid there's a small problem. We accidently double booked the twin room you wanted, and we already have a guest in there now. However, the manager has offered to upgrade you to a suite at no extra cost. **40** You just need to pay a $100 security deposit.

W2: That sounds great! **40** Annie, can you handle that for us?

W1: **40** Sure, I'll put it on my card.

女 1：不好意思，先生。我和我的妹妹在想我們能不能早點辦理入住房間。我知道入住時間應該是下午 2 點。訂房的名字是 Williams。
男：我看看⋯啊，對，Williams。恐怕出了點小問題。我們不小心重複訂了你要的雙床房，而這間房裡面已經有客人入住了。然而，經理決定免費幫你升級為套房。你只需要付 100 美元的訂金。
女 2：聽起來太棒了！Annie，你可以幫我們處理費用嗎？
女 1：當然，我會用我的信用卡支付。

38. 男子最有可能是誰？
(A) 航空公司職員
(B) 飯店職員
(C) 旅行社職員
(D) 售票員

解析 其中一名女子在對話開頭詢問是否能早點登記入住 (My sister and I were wondering whether we can check in to our room a little early.)。這是在飯店才會出現的對話內容，故本題正解為選項 (B)。

39. 男子提到了什麼問題？
(A) 出現了訂房錯誤。
(B) 無法享有優惠價。
(C) 有交通延遲的問題。
(D) 行李箱遺失了。

解析 男子在對話中段提到出了點小問題，女子的房間被重複預訂 (I'm afraid there's a small

problem. We accidentally double booked the twin room you wanted,)，故本題正解為選項 (A)。

40. Annie 接著會做什麼？
(A) 拿一些袋子
(B) 跟經理說話
(C) 填寫表格
(D) 付訂金
解析 男子在對話後半段請女子們支付 100 美元的訂金 (You just need to pay a $100 security deposit.)。接著其中一名女子叫了 Annie，並請她處理這筆費用 (Annie, can you handle that for us?)，另一名女子表示同意 (Sure, I'll put it on my card.)，故本題正解為選項 (D)。

Questions 41–43 refer to the following conversation.

M: Hey, Ursula, **41** do you know if there's a dry cleaner near our apartment building?
W: Actually, I'm not sure. Why do you ask?
M: Well, **42** my washing machine has broken down. I really need to clean my favorite shirt and pants before my job interview tomorrow morning.
W: Well, you could try looking online for one, but if there isn't one nearby, **43** you could come to my place and use my machine. You know, I'm in Apartment 5C, just above you.
M: Thanks, I really appreciate it.

- -

男：嘿，Ursula，你知道我們公寓附近有乾洗店嗎？
女：其實，我不確定。你怎麼會問這個？
男：嗯，我的洗衣機故障了。明天早上工作面試前，我必須要洗我最愛的襯衫和褲子。
女：那麼，你可以試著在網路上找一間，但如果附近沒有，你可以到我家用我的洗衣機。你知道，我住在 5C，就在你樓上。
男：謝謝，真的很感謝你。

41. 男子問了女子什麼？
(A) 乾洗
(B) 家中的擺飾
(C) 空著的房產
(D) 工作機會
解析 男子在對話開頭詢問了公寓附近是否有乾洗店 (do you know if there's a dry cleaner near our apartment building?)，故本題正解為選項 (A)。

42. 男子遇到了什麼問題？
(A) 襯衫被損壞了。
(B) 面試時間改了。
(C) 汽車送修了。
(D) 某項家電故障了。
解析 男子在對話前半段提到自家的洗衣機故障 (my washing machine has broken down)，故本

題正解為選項 (D)。

43. 女子建議男子做什麼？
(A) 到她的公寓去
(B) 連絡建築管理者
(C) 要求維修服務
(D) 去服飾店
解析 女子在對話後半段說可以到她家借用洗衣機 (you could come to my place and use my machine)，並告訴男子自己的房間號碼，故本題正解為選項 (A)。

Questions 44–46 refer to the following conversation.

M: Janice, I just heard that **44** your department won the construction contract to collaborate with Cheng Engineering in China. Well done! That's a big deal for everyone here at our firm.
W: Thanks a lot! We have a lot of hard work ahead of us, but **45** I'm really looking forward to working overseas.
M: It will certainly be an amazing experience. **46** If you don't have any plans, I'd love to treat you to lunch today to celebrate. Are you free at noon?
W: I appreciate the offer, but... I'm having lunch with the board members.
M: Oh, no problem! Maybe another time then.

- -

男：Janice，我剛聽說你們部門贏得了跟中國的 Cheng 工程合作的建設合約。做得好！這對我們公司的所有人來說都是很重要的合作。
女：非常感謝你！我們之後還有很多工作，但我非常期待到海外工作。
男：這一定會是個很棒的經驗。如果你沒有其他安排，我今天想請你吃午餐慶祝一下。你今天中午有空嗎？
女：我很感謝你的邀請，但…我要和董事會成員吃午餐。
男：喔，沒問題！或許下次。

44. 男子為了什麼事恭喜女子？
(A) 她得了獎
(B) 她升遷了
(C) 她獲得某個合約
(D) 她自己創業
解析 男子在對話開頭恭喜女子簽到和中國的 Cheng 工程合作的建設合約 (your department won the construction contract to collaborate with Cheng Engineering in China. Well done!)，故本題正解為選項 (C)。

45. 女子在期待什麼事？
(A) 開發產品
(B) 招聘新職員
(C) 參加訓練工作坊
(D) 在國外工作

解析 女子在對話中段説自己非常期待到海外工作 (I'm really looking forward to working overseas.)，故本題正解為選項 (D)。

46. 女子為什麼要説「我要和董事會成員吃午餐」？
(A) 為了某個延遲問題道歉
(B) 為了拒絕某個邀約
(C) 為了詢問方向
(D) 為了要男子和她一起去
解析 男子在對話中段説為了慶祝，今天中午要請女子吃午餐，問她那個時間有沒有空 (If you don't have any plans, I'd love to treat you to lunch today to celebrate. Are you free at noon?)，而女子回覆「我要和董事會成員吃午餐」。由此可知男子的邀約被拒絕了，故本題正解為選項 (B)。

Questions 47–49 refer to the following conversation with three speakers.

M1: Hi, Claire. I'm Craig Collingwood, the personnel manager here at Margate Manufacturing. This is the head of operations, Bill Hendry, and **47** we'll be reviewing your job performance today.
W: Hi, it's great to meet both of you.
M2: It's good to see you, Claire. Now, **48** you've been supervising our warehouse for the past 6 months, and we've been very pleased with your performance. Do you think you've learned a lot in that time?
W: Oh, definitely. **49** I'm very pleased that the company runs training workshops every month. Those have allowed me to gain a lot of new skills that help me perform better in my job.
M1: I'm glad to hear that. It's important to us that our employees always try to learn new skills.

男1：嗨，Claire。我是 Margate 製造的人事經理 Craig Collingwood，這位是營運長 Bill Hendry，我們今天會負責評價你的工作表現。
女：嗨，很高興見到兩位。
男2：很開心見到你，Claire。那麼，你過去 6 個月都負責管理我們的倉庫，而我們非常滿意你的表現。你覺得自己有在那段時間學到許多嗎？
女：喔，那是當然。我對公司每個月都舉辦訓練工作坊感到非常滿意。那讓我學到很多新技能，也協助我能有更好的工作表現。
男1：我很開心聽到你這麼説。職員們常保努力學習新技能的心態對我們來説很重要。

47. 為什麼説話者們會見面？
(A) 為了更新企劃案進度
(B) 為了評價工作表現
(C) 為了面試職員
(D) 為了做銷售報告
解析 其中一名男子在對話前半段説要評價女子的工作表現 (we'll be reviewing your job

performance today)，故本題正解為選項 (B)。

48. 女子的職業應該是什麼？
(A) 行銷總監
(B) 業務組長
(C) 招聘顧問
(D) 倉庫經理
解析 其中一名男子在對話中段提到女子負責管理倉庫 (you've been supervising our warehouse)，故本題正解為選項 (D)。

49. 女子説她很喜歡公司的哪一點？
(A) 提供定期訓練。
(B) 提供有競爭力的薪資。
(C) 製造高品質的產品。
(D) 傾聽職員的聲音。
解析 女子在對話後半段説自己對公司每個月都舉辦訓練工作坊感到非常滿意 (I'm very pleased that the company runs training workshops every month.)，故本題正解為選項 (A)。

Questions 50–52 refer to the following conversation.

M: **50** Thanks for calling the High Street branch of Meadowside Bank. How can I help you?
W: Hi, I'd like to open a savings account online, but I'm having trouble using your Web site. My name is Emma Smith.
M: Okay, do you already have an account with us?
W: Yes. I've had a checking account for a few years.
M: Well, **51** we have a new policy, and you can now open a new account directly over the phone. I'll just need to ask you a few security questions before we get started.
W: Great! But, will it take long? I'm actually in a bit of a hurry. Perhaps I should call back.
M: It should take 10 to 15 minutes to set up the new account.
W: In that case, **52** it's better that I call again later today. Thanks for your help!

男：感謝你致電 Meadowside 銀行 High Street 分行。有什麼我可以幫你的嗎？
女：嗨，我想要在線上開一個儲蓄帳戶，但我在使用你們的網站時遇到了點問題。我的名字是 Emma Smith。
男：好的，你原本就有帳戶了嗎？
女：有。我有支票帳戶好幾年了。
男：嗯，我們有個新規定，你可以直接用手機開一個新帳戶。在開始前我必須先問你幾個安全問題。
女：太好了！但要花很長時間嗎？我其實有點趕時間。或許我該之後再打過去。
男：開新帳戶大概需要 10 到 15 分鐘的時間。
女：這樣的話，我還是今天晚點再打比較好。感謝你的幫忙！

50. 男子應該是在哪工作？
(A) 供應商
(B) 圖書館
(C) 銀行
(D) 提供網路服務的公司

解析 男子在對話開頭說了感謝你致電 Meadowside 銀行 High Street 分行 (Thanks for calling the High Street branch of Meadowside Bank.)，故本題正解為選項 (C)。

51. 男子告訴了女子什麼新規定？
(A) 該業者週末不會營業。
(B) 顧客必須確認他們的身分。
(C) 能夠用電話開新帳戶。
(D) 網站上需要密碼。

解析 男子在對話中段提到新規定，內容是可以直接用手機開一個新帳戶 (we have a new policy, and you can now open a new account directly over the phone)，故本題正解為選項 (C)。

52. 女子說她會怎麼做？
(A) 親自到該營業場所
(B) 支付費用
(C) 在網站上註冊
(D) 晚點再打電話回去

解析 女子在對話的最後說今天晚點再打電話比較好 (it's better that I call again later today)，故本題正解為選項 (D)。

Questions 53–55 refer to the following conversation.

W: Hi, Paul.
M: Hi, Joanne. Do you need something?
W: Well, `53` I was just speaking with our department managers about the company workshop at the end of this month, and, it seems that quite a few of our staff members will not be able to attend the training due to work deadlines. `54` I was wondering if we could postpone the event until the following month.
M: Oh, but...We have a lot going on next month.
W: I know, but, it would be really unfair if some employees were forced to miss out. Everyone has been really looking forward to it.
M: Well, `55` I'll speak with Geraldine in General Affairs. Maybe she can find some space in next month's schedule for us.

女：嗨，Paul。
男：嗨，Joanne。你需要些什麼嗎？
女：嗯，我剛剛在跟我們部門經理討論這個月底要舉辦的公司工作坊，有少部分職員會因為業務上的截止日無法參與這個訓練。我在想能不能把活動延到下個月。
男：喔，但…我們下個月有很多事情。
女：我知道，但如果有些職員被迫因為工作無法參

加就太不公平了。每個人都很期待這個活動。
男：好吧，我會跟總務部門的 Geraldine 談談。或許她可以幫我們找出下個月可以的空間。

53. 說話者們主要在討論什麼？
(A) 訓練工作坊
(B) 公司搬遷
(C) 部門合併
(D) 開幕活動

解析 女子在對話前半段提到自己跟部門經理討論了公司的工作坊 (I was just speaking with our department managers about the company workshop)，後面的對話也在討論工作坊的日程，故本題正解為選項 (A)。

54. 男子說我們「我們下個月有很多事情」，是要表達什麼意思？
(A) 他會很感激某些工作上的協助。
(B) 他對能調整活動日期抱懷疑態度。
(C) 他想要延後截止日期。
(D) 他為公司的成功感到開心。

解析 女子在對話中段說她在想能不能把活動延到下個月 (I was wondering if we could postpone the event until the following month.)，男子就接著說故「下個月有很多事情」。由此可知他是想表達要將活動延期可能有困難，本題正解為選項 (B)。

55. 男子說他要做什麼？
(A) 和同事談談
(B) 開部門會議
(C) 發布工作日程
(D) 預約活動場地

解析 男子在對話最後說自己會跟總務部門的 Geraldine 談談 (I'll speak with Geraldine in General Affairs)。由此可知男子是要跟同事談話，故本題正解為選項 (A)。

Questions 56–58 refer to the following conversation.

W: Colin, do you have a minute? `56` I want to design an advertisement for our new range of fruit smoothies. Do you think it would be a good idea?
M: Definitely. Our new flavors could be a huge success, so the more people who know about them, the better. But, you don't have much experience with advertising, right? `57` Why don't you work on it with James from the graphic design team?
W: Okay. We've actually worked together on some projects in the past.
M: Great. And it might be a good idea if you taste our new smoothie flavors first. `58` Why don't you come with me to the product launch at the Food & Beverage Expo tomorrow?
W: `58` I'd love to! I can't wait to try them.

女：Colin，你有時間嗎？我想要為我們新推出的水果奶昔系列設計一個廣告。你覺得這個想法好嗎？

男：當然。我們的新口味可能會非常成功，所以越多人知道這些商品越好。但你在廣告這塊沒什麼經驗對吧？你何不和平面設計組的 James 合作呢？

女：好。其實我們之前也在別的企劃案上合作過。

男：太好了。你先試喝看看我們的新口味奶昔可能會比較好。你明天何不跟我一起去食品與飲料博覽會上的產品發布會呢？

女：我非常樂意！我迫不及待想試喝了。

56. 女子想做什麼？
(A) 訂購辦公室用品
(B) 籌備職員郊遊活動
(C) 創作廣告
(D) 重新設計網站

解析 女子在對話開頭說自己想要為新推出的水果奶昔系列設計廣告 (I want to design an advertisement for our new range of fruit smoothies)，故本題正解為選項 (C)。

57. 男子建議女子做什麼？
(A) 審查文件
(B) 將小組會議延後
(C) 比較幾個價格
(D) 和同事合作

解析 男子在對話中段提到女子廣告經驗不多，建議她可以和平面設計組的 James 合作 (Why don't you work on it with James from the graphic design team?)，故本題正解為選項 (D)。

58. 女子明天應該會做什麼？
(A) 參加產品發布會
(B) 做調查
(C) 繳交設計圖
(D) 和客戶見面

解析 男子在對話的最後建議女子明天去食品與飲料博覽會上的產品發布會 (Why don't you come with me to the product launch at the Food & Beverage Expo tomorrow?)。而女子的回覆是非常樂意前往 (I'd love to!)，故本題正解為選項 (A)。

Questions 59–61 refer to the following conversation.

M: Hi, Alison. **59** The technician just installed the Apex Gateway, our building's new electronic door security system. Only the residents will be able to use it, so we can prevent any salespeople and other uninvited individuals from entering the building now.

W: Great! So, **60** the residents will just need to enter the correct pass code to open the door?

M: Exactly, so they'll need to stop by the building office **60** some time tomorrow so that I can tell them the door code.

W: Sounds perfect. Do you think we could

install the system on the fitness room door, too?

M: I'm considering that. **61** The Apex Gateway is not very expensive at all, so we could definitely afford to purchase another one.

男：嗨，Alison。技術人員剛安裝好我們大樓新的電子門保全系統，Apex 保全系統。只有住戶能使用這個系統，所以我們就能避免任何推銷員或其他不速之客進入這棟建築了。

女：太好了！所以，住戶只要輸入正確的密碼就可以開門對嗎？

男：沒錯，所以他們明天必須找時間到大樓辦公室一趟，我會告訴他們門的密碼。

女：聽起來相當完美。你覺得我們可以在健身房的門裝同樣的保全系統嗎？

男：我正在考慮這件事。Apex 保全系統一點都不昂貴，所以我們絕對有能力再買一臺。

59. 說話者們主要在討論什麼話題？
(A) 建築改裝工程
(B) 停車規定
(C) 大門出入系統
(D) 手機應用程式

解析 男子在對話開頭提到這棟建築物剛裝好新的電子門保全系統——Apex(The technician just installed the Apex Gateway, our building's new electronic door security system.)，接著繼續談論和該保全系統相關的話題，故本題正解為選項 (C)。

60. 住戶們明天會收到什麼？
(A) 密碼
(B) 門禁卡
(C) 使用者名稱
(D) 使用說明

解析 女子在對話中段詢問是否靠輸入密碼來開門 (the residents will just need to enter the correct pass code to open the door?)。男子回答明天會告訴住戶門的密碼 (some time tomorrow so that I can tell them the door code)，故本題正解為選項 (A)。

61. 男子認為 Apex 保全系統的優點是什麼？
(A) 值得信賴。
(B) 價格低廉。
(C) 人性化設計。
(D) 體積小。

解析 男子在對話後半段提到 Apex 保全系統並不昂貴 (The Apex Gateway is not very expensive at all)，故本題正解為選項 (B)。

Questions 62–64 refer to the following conversation and table.

M: Hi, Phoebe. I'm making sure we have all the equipment and materials we need for the volunteers helping out with **62** the outdoor concert this weekend.

W: I'm pretty sure we have everything we

need. It should be a huge success.

M: Well, as you know, all our volunteers are supposed to wear color-coded vests so that attendees can easily identify them. But, it seems like 63 we don't have enough green vests for the team that will wear them.

W: That's not a big problem. 63 Those volunteers won't be on the event site for another three days. That gives us plenty of time to purchase more vests in that color.

M: I guess you're right. 64 I'll call the supplier now to place an order.

Volunteer Group	Vest Color
Ticket sellers	Orange
Parking attendants	Purple
Information helpers	Blue
Waste collectors	Green

男：嗨，Phoebe。我想確認一下這週末戶外演唱會的志工們需要的裝備和物品是否都準備好了。

女：我很確定所有東西都準備好了。這場演唱會一定會很成功。

男：嗯，你也知道，我們所有的志工都應該要穿上不同顏色的背心來讓參加者們可以輕易地辨識他們。但我發現我們綠色背心的量可能不夠多。

女：這不是什麼大問題。那一組的志工 3 天後才需要過來活動現場，我們有足夠的時間能多購入一些那個顏色的背心。

男：你說的沒錯。我現在就打給供應商下訂單。

志工組別	背心顏色
售票組	橘色
停車組	紫色
資訊服務組	藍色
清潔組	綠色

---

62. 說話者們在討論什麼類型的活動？
(A) 大型會議
(B) 演唱會
(C) 街頭遊行
(D) 食品展
解析 關於活動類型，男子在對話一開始就提及這週末要舉辦戶外演唱會 (the outdoor concert this weekend)，故本題正解為選項 (B)。

63. 請參考表格。哪一組志工 3 天後才會開始工作？
(A) 售票組
(B) 停車組
(C) 資訊服務組
(D) 清潔組
解析 男子在對話中段提到綠色背心的數量不夠給某一組志工穿 (we don't have enough green vests for the team that will wear them)，女子接著說那一組的志工 3 天後才會來到活動現

場 (Those volunteers won't be on the event site for another three days.)。對照表格可知 Green 是 Waste collectors 的背心，故本題正解為選項 (D)。

64. 男子接下來會做什麼？
(A) 取消訂單
(B) 修改日程表
(C) 連絡供應商
(D) 前往活動會場
解析 男子在對話的最後說要打給供應商 (I'll call the supplier now)，故本題正解為選項 (C)。

Questions 65–67 refer to the following conversation and sign.

W: Hello, and welcome to King's Fried Chicken.

M: Hi, 65 I'm the director of a play at the nearby theater, and I'd like to buy some chicken to celebrate our opening night tonight.

W: Oh, I think I saw some advertisements for that play. Well, I have good news for you. We are currently offering a discount on all our chicken buckets. You can take a look at this sign to see our sizes and prices.

M: Thanks. Well, we'll still need a lot of chicken, so 66 twenty pieces should be perfect. But, is it possible to have this delivered to the theater? I have some other errands to run right now. 67 I could give you the address.

W: Sure. Hold on a moment while I grab a pen.

King's Fried Chicken	
8-Piece Bucket	$13.99
12-Piece Bucket	$20.49
16-Piece Bucket	$24.99
20-Piece Bucket	$28.49

女：你好，歡迎光臨 King 的炸雞。

男：嗨，我是附近劇場的舞臺劇導演，我想買些炸雞慶祝今晚開演。

女：喔，我似乎看過那齣舞臺劇的宣傳廣告。那麼，我有個好消息要告訴你。我們的炸雞桶餐最近在打折。你可以看一下這塊板子，上面有寫份量和價格。

男：謝謝。嗯，我們需要滿多炸雞，所以 20 塊應該最合適。但你可以幫我外送到劇場嗎？我現在有其他事情需要處理。我可以給你地址。

女：沒問題。請稍等一下，我去拿支筆。

King 的炸雞	
8 塊炸雞桶	13.99 美元
12 塊炸雞桶	20.49 美元
16 塊炸雞桶	24.99 美元
20 塊炸雞桶	28.49 美元

65. 男子的身分是？
(A) 辦公室經理
(B) 導演
(C) 歌手
(D) 美食評論家

解析 男子在對話開頭就說自己是附近劇場裡的舞臺劇導演 (I'm the director of a play at the nearby theater)，故本題正解為選項 (B)。

66. 請參考表格，男子需要付多少錢？
(A) 13.99 美元
(B) 20.49 美元
(C) 24.99 美元
(D) 28.49 美元

解析 男子在對話中段提到 20 塊炸雞剛剛好 (twenty pieces should be perfect)。對照表格可知 20-Piece Bucket 的價格為 28.49 美元，故本題正解為選項 (D)。

67. 男子接下來會做什麼？
(A) 填寫表格
(B) 試吃產品
(C) 使用折價券
(D) 提供地址

解析 男子在對話後半段說會告訴對方地址 (I could give you the address.)，女子接著說要去拿筆，故本題正解為選項 (D)。

Questions 68–70 refer to the following conversation and floor plan.

W: Silver Sun Mall. This is Carol speaking. You've reached the Maintenance Department. What can I do for you?
M: Hi, Carol. This is Bradley Peters. `68` I work in the Customer Service office here at the mall.
W: Hi, Bradley. Is there something I can help you with?
M: Well, I just used one of the elevators and when I came out I noticed a puddle of water on the floor. I think the roof might be leaking. `69` Could someone come up to the third floor to mop up the water?
W: I'll head up there right away. What number is the elevator?
M: Umm...I'm not sure which number it is.
W: Hmm...can you tell me which shops you see nearby?
M: Okay. Ah, `70` it's right in between Sparta Health Foods and Ace Hardware.
W: Thanks. I'll be there soon.

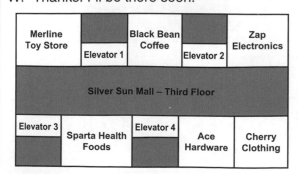

女：Silver Sun 購物中心。我是 Carol。這裡是維修部門。有什麼可以幫你的嗎？
男：嗨，Carol。我是 Bradley Peters。我在這間購物中心的客服部工作。
女：嗨，Bradley。有什麼我可以幫忙的嗎？
男：嗯，我剛剛搭乘其中一臺電梯，出來的時候發現地上有一灘水。我想可能是屋頂漏水了。有人可以到 3 樓把那灘水拖乾淨嗎？
女：我現在就過去。請問那是幾號電梯呢？
男：嗯…我不太清楚是幾號。
女：嗯…那你可以告訴我附近有哪些店家嗎？
男：好。啊，它位在 Sparta 健康食品和 Ace 五金行之間。
女：謝謝。我現在就馬上過去。

68. 男子在哪個部門工作？
(A) 維修部
(B) 客服部
(C) 行銷部
(D) 營業部

解析 男子在對話開頭表明自己在客服部工作 (I work in the Customer Service office here at the mall)，故本題正解為選項 (B)。

69. 男子要女子做什麼？
(A) 修理屋頂
(B) 訂材料
(C) 拖地
(D) 放置標示牌

解析 男子在對話中段表示希望有人過來 3 樓把那灘水拖乾淨 (Could someone come up to the third floor to mop up the water?)，故本題正解為選項 (C)。

70. 請參照圖表。請問男子是在說哪一臺電梯？
(A) 電梯 1
(B) 電梯 2
(C) 電梯 3
(D) 電梯 4

解析 關於出狀況的電梯所在位置的相關資訊出現在對話後半段，男子說它位在 Sparta 健康食品和 Ace 五金之間 (it's right in between Sparta Health Foods and Ace Hardware)。對照圖表可知在這兩間店之間的電梯為「電梯 4」，故本題正解為選項 (D)。

Part 4

Questions 71–73 refer to the following excerpt from a seminar.

Hi, everybody. I'm Tina Underwood, and I'll be leading the seminar this afternoon. A large number of you here today are university undergraduates, which means **71** you will soon be graduating and attending many job interviews. Being able to impress potential employers during interviews is a crucial skill because **72** there is more competition in the job market than ever before. Many positions will attract more than 500 job applicants, and you need to do everything you can to make yourself stand out. Now, before we start, **73** I'd like you to put up your hand if you have ever been rejected for a job. Then we can look at the reasons why.

嗨，大家。我是 Tina Underwood，我將會負責主持今天下午的專題討論。今天來這裡的人大部分都是大學生，也就是說你們即將面臨畢業及參加工作面試。讓可能成為你僱主的人在面試中留下深刻印象是個非常重要的技能，因為現在的求職環境比過去還要更競爭。很多職位會吸引超過 500 名應徵者，所以你必須要讓自己非常突出。那麼在我們開始之前，我想請曾經在面試中被刷掉的人舉個手。接著我們會分析其中的理由。

71. 這個專題討論的主題是什麼？
(A) 財務管理
(B) 創業
(C) 產品行銷
(D) 求職面試
解析 説話者在談話前半段説聆聽者們畢業後必須要面試，並提及在面試中讓人留下深刻印象的重要性 (you will soon be graduating and attending many job interviews. Being able to impress potential employers during interviews is a crucial skill)，故本題正解為選項 (D)。

72. 為什麼説話者説某個技能很重要？
(A) 競爭很激烈。
(B) 技術變得更複雜。
(C) 消費者的消費趨勢在改變。
(D) 許多公司在縮小規模。
解析 談話中段提到了在面試中讓人留下深刻印象的重要性，接著説現在的求職環境比過去還要更競爭 (there is more competition in the job market than ever before)，故本題正解為選項 (A)。

73. 説話者要聆聽者們做什麼？
(A) 舉手
(B) 填寫表格
(C) 閱讀一些資訊
(D) 提問

解析 説話者在談話的後半段請曾經在面試中被刷掉的人舉起手 (I'd like you to put up your hand if you have ever been rejected for a job.)，故本題正解為選項 (A)。

Questions 74–76 refer to the following announcement.

It's nice to see all of you here today for the opening of the new fitness center **74** here at Maryfield Hospital. Thanks to the financial support that you and other investors have provided, our long-term patients will be able to keep fit by using the new gym. **75** They will also be able to attend free fitness classes and receive professional advice from the instructors. **76** Now, I'd like you all to join me for a quick tour of the gym, where you'll see some of the advanced machines and equipment in use. When we are done looking around, let's have some drinks and sandwiches in the lounge.

很開心今天能見到各位來參加 Maryfield 醫院新健身中心的開幕。感謝各位及其他投資者們的財務支援，我們的長期住院患者們能透過運用新的健身中心來維持健康。他們也即將能上免費的健身課程，從教練那得到專業的建議。現在，我想邀各位和我一起做個健身中心的快速導覽，你們會看到許多高級的器材和設備。參觀完之後，我們就到休息室用點飲料和三明治。

74. 這段話是在哪裡説的？
(A) 大學裡
(B) 醫院裡
(C) 機場裡
(D) 飯店裡
解析 説話者在談話開頭就説到這個地方是 Maryfield 醫院 (here at Maryfield Hospital)，故本題正解為選項 (B)。

75. 説話者提到了什麼新服務？
(A) 運動課程
(B) 理財建議
(C) 美容療程
(D) 免費交通工具
解析 説話者在談話中段説到患者們能夠運用健身中心，也能上免費健身課程 (They will also be able to attend free fitness classes)，故本題正解為選項 (A)。

76. 聆聽者們接下來會做什麼？
(A) 參加研討會
(B) 去餐廳
(C) 參與導覽
(D) 申請參加某個活動
解析 説話者在談話後半段請聆聽者們加入健身中心的快速導覽 Now, I'd like you all to join me for a quick tour of the gym，故本題正解為選項 (C)。

Questions 77–79 refer to the following excerpt from a meeting.

I just have a couple of things to mention before 77 we get the beach prepared for visitors this morning. As you know, the summer holidays are just around the corner. So, 78 please let me know if you are prepared to work some extra shifts over the coming months. And another thing..., I just wanted to remind you about our regular lifeguard training session tomorrow morning. 79 Don't forget to bring the presentation notes I gave you last week about medical procedures, as I'll be testing you on some of the most important points.

在我們去為遊客將海灘準備好前，我有幾件事要說。各位都知道，暑假就快要到了。所以，如果有人接下來幾個月想要多排些班，請讓我知道。另外一件事，我想要提醒各位明天早上有定期救生訓練。別忘了帶我上週給你們的醫療程序資料，因為我會就幾個重點對你們進行測驗。

77. 聆聽者們在哪裡工作？
(A) 飯店
(B) 餐廳
(C) 海邊
(D) 公園
解析 說話者在談話開頭將自己和聆聽者們稱做 we，並敘述他們的工作是要去替遊客將海灘準備好 (we get the beach prepared for visitors)，故本題正解為選項 (C)。

78. 說話者說「暑假就快要到了」是想表達什麼意思？
(A) 職員們必須要求休假。
(B) 假期被調整過。
(C) 某個地點會有更多遊客。
(D) 新的商家準備在附近開業。
解析 說話者在談話前半段說了「暑假就快要到了」，接著說如果有人想要多排些班要讓他知道 (please let me know if you are prepared to work some extra shifts over the coming months)，這是因應暑假來臨後，海邊的遊客變多的解決方法，故本題正解為選項 (C)。

79. 說話者提醒聆聽者們做什麼？
(A) 確認日程
(B) 完成問卷調查
(C) 帶某些資料
(D) 繳交文件
解析 說話者在談話後半段要聆聽者們別忘了帶他給的資料 (Don't forget to bring the presentation notes)，故本題正解為選項 (C)。

Questions 80–82 refer to the following telephone message.

Hi, Emma. 80 I'm calling about revisions I'm making to the new edition of our city restaurant guidebook. The editor-in-chief informed me that our section on the Burnside district is very outdated, as many of the restaurants we listed have now closed, and new ones have opened. We need someone to visit the area and compile accurate data about all current restaurants. 81 I'd like to pick you for this assignment because you used to live in Burnside and know your way around there. 82 Let's get together for a meeting to discuss the exact details of what I want you to do. Just get back to me to let me know a suitable time. Thanks.

嗨，Emma。我打給你是為了幾個我將在我們新版的城市餐廳指南裡修訂的事項。總編說 Burnside 區的資料都非常過時，我們列出的餐廳有些已經倒閉了，也開了新餐廳。我們需要派一個人去該地區蒐集所有在營業的餐廳的準確資訊。我想把這個任務交給你去做，因為你之前住過 Burnside 區，比較熟那邊的路。我們開個會，就我想要你做的事做討論。請回撥給我，並讓我知道合適的時間。謝謝。

80. 說話者打電話的原因和什麼有關？
(A) 一張城市地圖
(B) 一個手機應用程式
(C) 一本指南
(D) 一個廣告
解析 說話者在談話開頭就說自己打給對方是為了幾個將在餐廳指南裡修訂的事項 (I'm calling about revisions I'm making to the new edition of our city restaurant guidebook.)，故本題正解為選項 (C)。

81. 為什麼聆聽者被選去完成某個任務？
(A) 她知道一個特定的品牌。
(B) 她先前曾做過類似的工作。
(C) 她對某個地區很熟悉。
(D) 她行程上有空檔。
解析 說話者在談話中段提到要把某個任務交給聆聽者，理由是因為她之前住過那一區，對那邊比較熟 (I'd like to pick you for this assignment because you used to live in Burnside and know your way around there.)，故本題正解為選項 (C)。

82. 說話者想要做什麼？
(A) 想聘僱新職員
(B) 參觀營業場所
(C) 想改某個工作截止日
(D) 想安排會議
解析 說話者在談話後半段提議一起開會 (Let's get together for a meeting)，故本題正解為選項 (D)。

Questions 83–85 refer to the following speech.

83 My new Web site, EuroTravelSource.com, is for anyone interested in taking a trip around Europe. Travelers often search for information

online about accommodations, transportation, and restaurants, but finding the information they need is often time-consuming. My Web site compiles all of this information into one user-friendly database. **84** I also provide my personal sightseeing recommendations to travelers based on their destination. And I worked as a tour guide in several European cities. After my presentation tonight, **85** I'll give each of you a special promo code. You can use this on my site to get 10 percent off selected hotel bookings.

我的新網站 EuroTravelSource.com，是為了想在歐洲旅行的人建立的。旅行者們通常會在網路上搜尋住宿、交通和餐廳，但搜尋所需的資訊通常要花很多時間。我網站裡的所有資訊都整理在一個使用者友善的平臺上。我也會根據旅行者們的目的地，為他們提供我的私房景點。我之前是一位歐洲城市的導遊。在我結束今晚的演講後，我會給你們每個人一個優惠代碼。各位用這個在我的網站上訂飯店，就能得到九折優惠。

83. 説話者最近做了什麼？
(A) 設計產品
(B) 寫書
(C) 啟用網站
(D) 去旅行

解析 説話者在談話開頭説了自己網站的名稱和網站用途 (My new Web site, EuroTravelSource.com, is for anyone interested in taking a trip around Europe)，故本題正解為選項 (C)。

84. 説話者説「我之前是一位歐洲城市的導遊」是想表達什麼意思？
(A) 她建議大家到歐洲旅遊。
(B) 她忘記在履歷上寫某些資訊。
(C) 她在準備移居海外。
(D) 她對自己所在的領域非常了解。

解析 説話者在談話中段説會根據旅行者們的目的地，為他們提供私房景點 (I also provide my personal sightseeing recommendations to travelers based on their destination.)，接著説「我之前是一位歐洲城市的導遊」。由此可知她是要表達自己對這個領域很了解，也有很多經驗，故本題正解為選項 (D)。

85. 聆聽者們輸入某組代碼能得到什麼？
(A) 電子報
(B) 免費禮物
(C) 折扣
(D) 會員資格

解析 關於代碼的內容出現在談話後半段，説話者説只要使用優惠代碼在她的網站上訂飯店，就能得到九折優惠 (I'll give each of you a special promo code. You can use this on my site to get 10 percent off)，故本題正解為選項 (C)。

Questions 86–88 refer to the following broadcast.

---

86 Good evening, viewers. I'm Jerry Chapman, and you're watching *Jerry's Place*, my new chat show on the HTO cable TV network. Just before the commercial break, a member of the audience asked me why I recently decided to become a vegetarian. Well, I had been thinking about stopping eating meat for several years. Then, a few months ago, **87** I picked up a copy of a health & nutrition magazine, and an article on plant-based diets really surprised me. I realized that by changing my diet, I could feel much healthier. And now, **88** I'm going to show you how to cook one of my favorite vegetarian dishes. Let's move to the kitchen area.

觀眾們，晚上好。我是 Jerry Chapman，你正在收看的是 HTO 有線電視臺的新談話節目 *Jerry's Place*。在進廣告休息之前，其中一位觀眾問我為什麼最近決定當個素食主義者。嗯，其實我考慮停止吃肉很多年了。接著，在幾個月前，我拿起了一本健康與營養的雜誌，一篇關於植物性飲食的文章讓我非常驚訝。我發現改變飲食習慣，我會感覺更健康。現在，我要為你們示範如何煮我最愛的一道素食料理。我們移動到廚房。

86. 説話者是誰？
(A) 電視節目主持人
(B) 廣播節目主持人
(C) 健身教練
(D) 電影導演

解析 説話者在談話開頭跟觀眾們打招呼，並説出觀眾目前在收看的電視節目名稱 (Good evening, viewers. I'm Jerry Chapman, and you're watching *Jerry's Place*)，故本題正解為選項 (A)。

87. 是什麼讓説話者決定變成素食主義者？
(A) 看了一部電影
(B) 和醫生的談話
(C) 看到一則廣告
(D) 讀到一篇文章

解析 説話者在談話中段説自己曾看了健康與營養的雜誌，而一篇關於植物性飲食的文章讓他非常驚訝，改變飲食習慣後也感覺更健康了 (I picked up a copy of a health & nutrition magazine, and an article on plant-based diets really surprised me. I realized that by changing my diet, I could feel much healthier.)。由此可知説話者是讀了文章後被啟發，故本題正解為選項 (D)。

88. 接著會發生什麼事？
(A) 採訪來賓
(B) 一組運動
(C) 示範做菜
(D) 產品促銷

解析 説話者在談話最後説要示範如何煮他最愛的一道素食料理，接著説要移動到廚房 (I'm going to show you how to cook one of my favorite vegetarian dishes. Let's move to

the kitchen area.)，故本題正解為選項 (C)。

Questions 89–91 refer to the following excerpt from a meeting.

I'm pleased that you all found time to come to this last-minute managers' meeting. As you know, 89 our company's annual career fair will take place early next month. This year's event is especially important, as we plan to expand our operations and will need to recruit a large number of workers. 90 We already have some volunteers passing out flyers and putting up posters to publicize the event. However, I think we also need to advertise online. So, 91 can anyone recommend some sites that might be suitable for running our advertisement?

我非常開心各位能排出時間來參加這個最後關頭前的經理會議。各位都知道，下個月初就要舉辦我們公司的年度徵才活動。因為我們打算擴大公司的規模，需要招聘非常多的職員，所以今年的活動尤其重要。我們已經找了一些志工幫忙發送傳單，並貼海報宣傳這個活動。不過，我想我們也需要在網路上打廣告。因此，有人可以推薦適合放我們廣告的網站嗎？

89. 目前在籌劃什麼活動？
(A) 產品發表會
(B) 開幕活動
(C) 徵才活動
(D) 說明會
解析 說話者在談話前半段說下個月初就要舉辦公司的年度徵才活動 (our company's annual career fair will take place early next month)，後面也都在描述該活動的籌備事宜，故本題正解為選項 (C)。

90. 根據說話者所說，志工們為活動做了些什麼？
(A) 發傳單
(B) 準備房間
(C) 對民眾做問卷調查
(D) 架設攤位
解析 談話中段提到志工們幫忙發送傳單，並貼海報宣傳這個活動 (We already have some volunteers passing out flyers and putting up posters)，故本題正解為這兩者之一的選項 (A)。

91. 說話者向聆聽者們要了什麼？
(A) 能舉辦活動的場地
(B) 廣告支出費用
(C) 推薦的網站
(D) 能吸引職員們的想法
解析 談話的最後詢問是否有人能推薦適合放公司廣告的網站 (can anyone recommend some sites that might be suitable for running our advertisement?)，故本題正解為選項 (C)。

Questions 92–94 refer to the following talk.

92 It's my pleasure to welcome you all to this year's Web design seminar. As a Web site designer with over twenty years of experience, I have several tips for you on how to build a commercial Web site. Now, most companies employ market research firms to poll consumers and gather feedback about Web site layouts and features, but 93 this process can be time-consuming and a waste of money. Your employees use the Internet all the time. 93 Who better to ask about Web design than your own staff? After all, they are consumers, too. Just make sure that you use an effective information-gathering method. 94 I've listed some of these in the information packs, which I'm going to pass around to each of you now.

非常榮幸能歡迎各位參加今年的網站設計研討會。身為一個經歷超過 20 年的網站設計師，我有一些如何建立商業網站的小技巧要教各位。現在，大部分的公司都會僱市場調查公司對消費者做民意調查，藉此獲得關於網站架構和特色的意見，但這樣的過程可能要花許多時間和金錢。各位的職員們一直在使用網路。需要網站設計的意見，還有比他們更適合詢問的人嗎？畢竟，他們也是消費者。只要確保你用的是有效的資訊蒐集方法。我現在要發給各位的相關資料裡有列出幾項。

92. 這段談話進行的地點是哪裡？
(A) 市議會的會議
(B) 業務能力評估會
(C) 專業研討會
(D) 客戶發表會
解析 說話者在談話開頭歡迎大家來到今年的網站設計研討會 (It's my pleasure to welcome you all to this year's Web design seminar.)，故本題正解為選項 (C)。

93. 說話者為什麼說「各位的職員們一直在使用網路」？
(A) 建議限制網路的使用
(B) 恭喜聽者努力的成果
(C) 推薦另一種方法
(D) 要求志工協助自己
解析 說話者在談話中段提到民意調查要花很多時間和金錢 (this process can be time-consuming and a waste of money)，接著說「各位的職員們一直在使用網路」。後面再補充說明沒有人比職員們更適合詢問，最終他們也是消費者 (Who better to ask about Web design than your own staff? After all, they are consumers, too.)。由此可知說話者是想推薦不同於現有資訊蒐集法的方式，本題正解為選項 (C)。

94. 說話者會給聽者們什麼？
(A) 會員卡
(B) 網站的網址
(C) 相關資料
(D) 餐券

解析 説話者在談話的最後提到相關的資料，且説要發給聽眾們 (I've listed some of these in the information packs, which I'm going to pass around)，故本題正解為選項 (C)。

Questions 95–97 refer to the following excerpt from a meeting and chart.

> **95** Welcome to this morning's product design meeting. We're here to discuss the plans for our first ever ice cream cake, which we plan to sell in our own stores and in other retailers. This product needs to be perfect—if it is a success, we plan to release more cakes using our ice cream in the future. So, **96** I'd like you all to split into pairs and come up with some ideas for how the cake should look. Make sure that it's eye-catching and innovative. By the way, **97** the first cake in our range will use our best-selling flavor of ice cream. You can take a look at this chart to see which flavors sell the most.

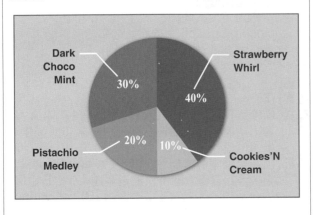

歡迎各位參與今天早上的產品設計會議。今天聚在這是要討論我們要在公司旗下賣場和其他零售商販賣的第一個冰淇淋蛋糕。這個產品必須要完美無缺──假如成功了，我們計劃日後要用我們的冰淇淋做更多口味的蛋糕。所以，我希望各位分成兩兩一組，想想蛋糕的外觀要怎麼呈現。一定要能吸引目光，且夠創新。順帶一提，這個系列的第一個蛋糕會用我們賣得最好的冰淇淋口味下去做。各位可以看一下這張圖表，找出哪個口味賣得最好。

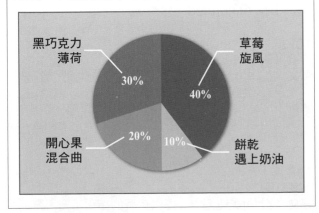

95. 聆聽者們應該是誰？
(A) 財務顧問們
(B) 市場調查員們

(C) 業務們
(D) 產品設計師們

解析 説話者在談話開頭説歡迎各位參與今天早上的產品設計會議 (Welcome to this morning's product design meeting.)，故本題正解為選項 (D)。

96. 新產品的哪個面向需要兩兩一組討論？
(A) 包裝
(B) 食材
(C) 價格
(D) 外觀

解析 説話者在談話中段要聆聽者們分成兩兩一組，想想蛋糕的外觀要怎麼呈現 (I'd like you all to split into pairs and come up with some ideas for how the cake should look.)，故本題正解為選項 (D)。

97. 請參考圖表。新產品的口味會是什麼？
(A) 草莓旋風
(B) 餅乾遇上奶油
(C) 開心果混合曲
(D) 黑巧克力薄荷

解析 談話後半段説新產品會用賣得最好的冰淇淋口味下去做 (the first cake in our range will use our best-selling flavor of ice cream)。對照圖表可知賣得最好的產品是販售量 40% 的 Strawberry Whirl，故本題正解為選項 (A)。

Questions 98–100 refer to the following talk and map.

> Listen up, everyone. As you know, today is a very important day for us here at the convention center, as **98** it's our first time hosting a large pop concert. Tickets for this concert sold out within three days, so we should expect at least 10,000 fans to turn up tonight. **99** When attendees begin arriving this evening, you'll need to tell them where to go. Make sure they walk toward Hall 1, where the event is being held, and not toward Hall 2. Oh, and I almost forgot...Even though we will sell most band merchandise inside the hall, **100** I'd like to put another merchandise stall out on the street next to Car Park A. Who would be willing to operate the stall?

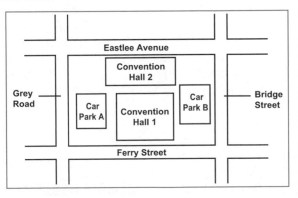

各位聽好了。如同大家所知，今天是會展中心很重

要的日子，這是我們第一次在會議中心舉辦大型流行音樂會。這場音樂會的門票在 3 天內就售完了，所以我們要有預計今晚至少會有一萬名歌迷到場。今天傍晚觀眾進場時，你們必須告訴他們往哪走。要確保他們往舉辦活動的 1 號廳走去，不能讓他們走去 2 號廳。喔，我差點忘了，雖然大部分的樂團周邊商品都會在會場內賣，但我想在停車場 A 旁邊的路上再擺一個周邊商品攤位。誰願意負責那個攤位呢？

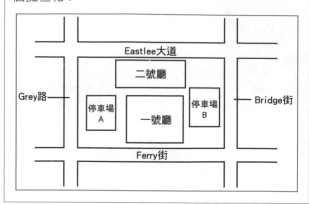

98. 說話者主要在討論什麼？
(A) 一場研討會
(B) 一場演唱會
(C) 一場募款活動
(D) 一場遊行
解析 談話前半段就說到今天是第一次舉辦大型演唱會 (it's our first time hosting a large pop concert)，故本題正解為選項 (B)。

99. 民眾抵達時，聆聽者們要做什麼？
(A) 給他們活動指南
(B) 確認他們的票券
(C) 為他們指引方向
(D) 提供他們小點心
解析 民眾到達後的內容出現在談話中段，聆聽者應該要在他們抵達後幫忙指引方向 (When attendees begin arriving this evening, you'll need to tell them where to go.)，故本題正解為選項 (C)。

100. 請參考圖表。追加的商品攤販會位在何處？
(A) Eastlee 大道
(B) Grey 路
(C) Bridge 街
(D) Ferry 街
解析 說話者在談話的最後說想在停車場 A 旁邊的路上再擺一個商品攤位 (I'd like to put another merchandise stall out on the street next to Car Park A)。對照圖表可知左邊的停車場 A 旁邊的路是 Grey 路，故本題正解為選項 (B)。

Part 5

101.
答案 (A)
譯文 在 Tempo 稅務軟體上確認你最新的信用評分非常容易。
解析 空格內須填入位在 be 動詞 is 後方的補語，且

要能夠說明主詞特性，故本題正解為形容詞補語選項 (A) easy。

102.
答案 (C)
譯文 Kemper 女士的申請表太晚送達，因此無法將她列入那個職位的候選人。
解析 在前方修飾副詞 late，並要是能跟 late 後面的不定詞 to 一同使用的副詞，故本題正解為能構成 "too...to do" 結構的選項 (C) too。

103.
答案 (D)
譯文 所有乘客搭船時都被要求穿救生衣。
解析 此句子是在描述乘客們必須做的事情，因此要以表達「必須做…」的 "be required to do" 結構呈現，故本題正解為選項 (D) required。

104.
答案 (B)
譯文 Andrew Jenkins 市長用一段優美的閉幕詞結束了這個慶典。
解析 空格內須填入能夠在不定冠詞 a 和名詞片語 closing speech 之間修飾名詞的形容詞，故本題正解為選項 (B) beautiful。

105.
答案 (B)
譯文 6 月到 9 月之間，Palm Grove 渡假村接待的客人比 Vincent 海灘的任何一間飯店都還要多。
解析 因為出現兩個時間點，呈現 "A and B" 的結構，因此空格內應填入能夠表達「A 和 B 之間」的介系詞，故本題正解為選項 (B) Between。

106.
答案 (D)
譯文 Michael Zinn 下部動作片的預告造成了很大的宣傳效果。
解析 空格前後有介系詞片語和名詞片語，可知空格內須填入該句子的動詞。空格後方有受詞，因此該動詞應為主動語態。此外，基於主詞及動詞的一致性，單數主詞 The trailer 後方必須接單數動詞。而能夠滿足以上所有條件的為主動語態的現在完成式，故本題正解為選項 (D) has generated。

107.
答案 (D)
譯文 在 Lamp 先生的報告結束後，有興趣的投資人被鼓勵留下做簡短的討論。
解析 作為介系詞 for 的受詞，空格內須填入投資者們在聽完報告後能做的事，故本題正解為有「商討；討論」意思的名詞選項 (D) discussion。

108.
答案 (D)
譯文 O'Hare 迎賓中心提供免費的指引手冊，幫助缺乏經驗的遊客利用轉乘系統。
解析 空格內須填入形容需要轉乘系統相關指引的旅客們特性的形容詞，故本題正解為有

「缺乏經驗的；不熟練的」意思的選項 (D) inexperienced。

109.
答案 (A)
譯文 Brooks 先生的行程與會議日期發生抵觸，因為他已經安排要去渡假了。
解析 空格內須填入位在構成被動語態動詞的 was 和 scheduled 之間的副詞，故本題正解為可擔任這個角色，並有「先前；已經」意思的選項 (A) already。

110.
答案 (A)
譯文 幾間大型娛樂公司都在開發虛擬實境產品，因為顧客的興趣越來越高。
解析 因為空格後方僅有名詞片語，可知空格內應填入介系詞。從文脈可判斷公司是因為顧客越來越感興趣才開發特定產品，故本題正解為有「因為⋯」意思的選項 (A) as a result of。

111.
答案 (D)
譯文 競爭公司們為了招聘一些大有可為的法律系畢業生，越來越多公司都會提供未來有機會成為合夥人的職位。
解析 空格內須填入位在構成現在完成式動詞的 have 和 been offering 之間，負責修飾動詞的副詞，故本題正解為選項 (D) increasingly。

112.
答案 (A)
譯文 多年來，Reilly 塑膠十分活躍在威廉斯堡地區的組織社區服務活動上。
解析 位在 be 動詞後方的空格應為補語，且須為能夠形容主詞 Reilly 塑膠某個特性的形容詞才通順，故本題正解為選項 (A) active。

113.
答案 (C)
譯文 在每週行政會議中，Clifford 女士解釋了整頓辦公室空間的理由。
解析 逗號和空格之間有名詞片語，由此可知空格內應填入介系詞。「在⋯會議中」的語意最為通順，故本題正解為表達「在⋯中；在⋯期間」的選項 (C) During。

114.
答案 (A)
譯文 最近的市場趨勢報告指出大多數的消費者都認為對生態環境無害的清潔產品更有吸引力。
解析 空格後方接了受詞和形容詞 (more desirable) 的受格補語，因此應填入符合此句型結構的動詞，故本題正解為「認為⋯」的選項 (A) find。

115.
答案 (A)
譯文 想停在停車場的最頂層，職員們必須要出示有效的職員證。
解析 空格內須填入能夠描述要在特定空間停車須出

示的職員證特性，故本題正解為有「有效的」之意的形容詞選項 (A) valid。

116.
答案 (A)
譯文 觀眾們應該留意到 Hawkins 主廚在他的食譜中分享很有用的料理建議。
解析 作為 that 子句動詞 shares 的受詞，光是空格前方的 cooking 無法表達完整意思，因此要在空格內填入其他名詞形成複合名詞的結構。故本題正解為與料理相關且能夠分享，有「建議、忠告」意思的選項 (A) advice。

117.
答案 (D)
譯文 Tony Clark 第一部小說的電影版權上週以相當驚人的高價賣給了 Mammoth 影業。
解析 由於受詞是關於費用程度的名詞，空格內須填入能夠有「以⋯價格」意思的介系詞，故本題正解為選項 (D) for。

118.
答案 (B)
譯文 與所有必要文件一起提交的出差支出費用將在審查後立刻報銷。
解析 空格後有一個包含主詞和動詞的子句，故本題正解為能夠連接兩個句子的連接詞選項 (B) as soon as。

119.
答案 (B)
譯文 Sweet Bee 食品行過去 10 年來都一直提供免費的配送到府服務。
解析 由於句子描述的是過去到現在的一段持續時間 for the past decade，由此可知空格內應填入符合該時制的現在完成式，故本題正解為選項 (B) has been offering。

120.
答案 (A)
譯文 我們的新廣告播出後收益節節高升，所以行銷團隊會考慮將廣告活動擴大。
解析 新廣告播出後收益增加，接著考慮要擴大廣告宣傳，根據文脈可推斷空格前後句的關係為「原因＋結果」。由此可知空格內須填入表達結果的連接詞，故本題正解為選項 (A) so。

121.
答案 (B)
譯文 現在新的服務人員都接受了完整的訓練，Huxley 飯店可以開始辦大型的正式活動了。
解析 服務人員完成訓練為能夠舉行正式活動的理由。像這種要表達狀態的變化為某個結果的原因時，會使用意思為「(現在) 因為⋯」的 Now that。故本題正解為選項 (B) Now that。

122.
答案 (C)
譯文 倉庫經理主要的工作就是要讓公司的所有產品維持在有條理的保管狀態。
解析 空格內詞語被形容詞 orderly 修飾，同時又是

作為不定詞 to 使用的動詞 maintain 的受詞，詞性應為名詞。空格內應填入能表達「保管狀態」的詞語，句子才會通順，故本題正解為選項 (C) storage。

123.
答案 (A)
譯文 TechWave 公司新推出的運動生活相機可以潛到 60 公尺深，且功能不會有任何影響。
解析 空格內須填入能夠將表深度或距離的名詞作為受詞使用的動詞，故本題正解為有「到達…，抵達…」意思的選項 (A) reach。

124.
答案 (B)
譯文 雖然監控攝影機比起最新的型號已經有些過時，但還是能夠使用。
解析 空格位在 be 動詞 are 的後方，可知空格內應填入補語。後方的句子用 they 代指監控攝影機，但少了描述監控攝影機特性的形容詞，故本題正解為選項 (B) functional。補充說明，副詞 still 無法作為補語使用。

125.
答案 (C)
譯文 Regal 旅行社很慎重地挑選負責帶海外旅行團的導遊。
解析 能夠和空格前方的 are responsible 一同使用，並表達「承擔…；負責…」的詞語為介系詞 for，故本題正解為選項 (C) for。

126.
答案 (C)
譯文 Tracer 工業能不能賣出它的製造部門就要看它這季的表現了。
解析 從空格後方有兩個動詞 is 和 depends 可知空格內應填入連接詞。由於 its manufacturing division 並非 depends 的主詞，到 division 為止都應該要是能作為 depends 主詞的名詞子句。因 depends 前方沒有缺任何成分，故本題正解應為能夠引導完整子句的名詞子句連接詞選項 (C) Whether。

127.
答案 (D)
譯文 對籌辦娛樂活動有興趣的人必須填人資部門給的提案表格。
解析 空格內須填入能夠和後方介系詞 in 一同使用，並從後方修飾人物的名詞 Individuals，故本題正解為表達「對…有興趣」的選項 (D) interested。

128.
答案 (B)
譯文 帕克斯堡市議會正在尋求大眾對於 Truman 廣場改造工程提案的意見。
解析 空格內須填入能和形容詞 public 搭配使用，並成為動詞 is seeking 受詞的名詞，故本題正解為能夠與 public 一同使用，表達「民眾的意見」的選項 (B) comment。

129.
答案 (B)
譯文 Max 漢堡對自家餐廳的健康與安全規定遠比大部分連鎖速食業者還要多。
解析 空格內須填入能和前方動詞 extend 一同使用的介系詞，故本題正解為有「超過…的水準；越過…」意思的選項 (B) beyond。

130.
答案 (D)
譯文 社區中心的新課程會幫助屋主評估他們替自己的房產評估價值、維護甚至增值的能力。
解析 空格內須填入能將意思為「能力」的 ability 當成受詞的動詞，故本題正解為有「評估…的能力」意思的選項 (D) evaluate。

Part 6
請參考以下網頁回答第 131 至 134 題。

Sherman 商業發展中心坐落於美麗的 Twin Pines 國家公園旁，擁有所有舉辦成功的團隊建立活動需要的設施。 **131** 我們的講師知道要如何讓你的職員發揮他們最大的能力。
我們的計劃要求團隊參與許多 **132** 活動。你的職員必須透過合作一起在森林裡搭避難處，用有限的資源在河上搭橋，並在許多不同的競賽及解決問題的任務中和其他隊伍競爭。 **133** 我們會著重在強化參加者的溝通和團隊合作能力，而這些能力之後也能直接在公司裡運用。想了解計劃的相關細節，或申請團隊建立活動，可以撥打 555-8278。此外，別忘了上我們的新網站 www.sbdc.org/home。你可以在上面找到更多 **134** 關於我們經驗豐富的職員和最新的設施的資訊！

131.
答案 (D)
譯文 (A) 我們的接線員每天 9 點到 5 點都準備好接你的電話。
(B) 你的公司將會從活動上的曝光獲益。
(C) 你可以從多種外燴方案中做選擇。
(D) 我們的講師知道要如何讓你的職員發揮他們最大的能力。
解析 前面的句子在介紹這裡是辦企業團隊建立活動的地方，接著說明該中心有什麼樣的活動。由此可知此處應填入中心的講師們能夠為客戶做些什麼，故本題正解為選項 (D)。

132.
答案 (D)
解析 空格為 participate in 的受詞位置，且須表達在計劃中能體驗到的事情。從後面的內容能夠得知在這個計劃中會做許多不同的事，故本題正解為能夠總結所有體驗的名詞，意思為「活動」的選項 (D) activities。

133.
答案 (B)
解析 從空格後方的內容可得知某人將重點放在強化參加者的溝通和團隊合作能力，而這是該中心該做的事。文章後半段出現用代名詞代指

這個中心的 our brand-new Web site 或 our experienced staff，可知空格內須填入和此處相同的人稱代名詞，並以主詞的形態出現，故本題正解為選項 (B) We。

134.
答案 (C)
解析 空格內須填入適合搭配 find out more 的介系詞，故本題正解為表達「了解更多關於…」時使用的選項 (C) about。

請參考以下電子郵件回答**第 135 至 138 題**。

收件人：inquiries@aceappliances.com
寄件人：mfowler@truemail.net
主旨：Java Press 500
日期：9 月 14 日

尊敬的先生／女士：

我想要 **135** 退掉 Java Press 500 這臺濃縮咖啡機。我新廚房的流理臺不如我當初想的大，我沒有足夠的空間可以放這個產品。我希望我 **136** 能夠從你公司的產品型錄上挑同價格的其他產品。 **137** 我偏好換比較小臺的這個產品。

你可以在 9 月 18 日之前推薦我合適的產品嗎？根據你公司的規定，過了 **138** 那天我就不能退費或更換產品了。

期待收到你的回覆。

Meredith Fowler

135.
答案 (B)
解析 從後面的句子能夠知道因為廚房流理臺沒有能放的空間，想換成其他產品。由此可知寄件人是想要退換貨，故本題正解為有「將…退貨；歸還…」意思的選項 (B) return。

136.
答案 (D)
解析 空格所在的 that 子句是由虛主詞 it 和真主詞 to 不定詞構成的子句，在虛主詞－真主詞句子中，空格內須填入能夠作為補語的形容詞。而根據文意可知該形容詞必須是關於退貨可能性的詞語，故本題正解為選項 (D)。

137.
答案 (D)
譯文 (A) 我這個月沒有收過這樣的型錄。
(B) 我很感謝你提出疑問，我會盡快回覆。
(C) 我有在你的網站上看過它的廣告。
(D) 我偏好換比較小臺的產品。
解析 從前面的句子可以知道因為廚房流理臺沒有能放這個產品的空間，所以想換成其他產品。由此可知此處應填入與更換過後新產品的特性相關的內容，故本題正解為選項 (D)。

138.
答案 (C)
解析 空格所在的句子表達了某個特定時間點之後就不能退費或更換產品，而前面句子提到的日期就是這個時間點，故本題正解為代指該日期的代名詞選項 (C) that。

請參考以下報導回答**第 139 至 142 題**。

COMFLEX 公開新任行銷總監
艾德蒙頓 (11 月 14 日)——在昨天的記者會中，ComFlex 介紹了他們的新網路行銷總監 Clive Jenkins。Jenkins 先生將會負責管理一個為吸引新顧客而 **139** 創造的社群媒體廣告活動部門。

Dimitri Augustus，這間電信公司的創辦人說：「我們對 Jenkins 先生加入我們感到很興奮。他的技術和經驗 **140** 能夠讓我們更進一步且更有效率地接近潛在顧客。」 **141** Jenkins 先生帶著他在這個業界的豐富經歷來到 ComFlex。在他上一間公司 Nova 電信，他花了 12 年的時間開發並執行效果非常好的線上行銷技巧。

ComFlex 提供所有 **142** 類型的電話、電視還有寬頻網路服務，最近變成加拿大著名的供應商。

139.
答案 (D)
解析 空格所在的 that 子句是要修飾前方的名詞片語 a division，表達那個部門所做的工作。一般發生的事情要用現在式，如果要把空格後方的名詞片語當作受詞，空格內的動詞就要是主動語態，故本題正解為主動語態現在式的選項 (D) creates。

140.
答案 (A)
解析 空格內須填入能夠和後方「受詞＋ to do」一起使用的動詞，故本題正解為能夠表達「讓…能夠」的選項 (A)。

141.
答案 (A)
譯文 **(A) Jenkins 先生帶著他在這個業界的豐富經歷來到 ComFlex。**
(B) Jenkins 先生將因為他在艾德蒙頓分公司的業務成就得到表揚。
(C) Jenkins 先生在自己的部門得到升遷的機會。
(D) 如果計劃案成功，Jenkins 先生應該就會留在 ComFlex。
解析 空格後方的句子提到 Jenkins 先生在這個領域有很多年的經歷了，故本題正解為描述相關內容的選項 (A)。

142.
答案 (D)
解析 空格後方羅列的名詞都是 ComFlex 提供的服務類型。故本題正解為能和位在前後的 a full 與介系詞 of 一起使用，表達「所有類型；所有範圍」的選項 (D) range。

請參考以下公告回答**第 143 至 146 題**。

Laney 超市的顧客們請注意：

當你在櫃臺結帳的時候，請留意你每個裝商品的袋子都會被收取 50 分美元。你會看到發票上這筆費用寫著「塑膠袋費用」。 **143** 除非你事先告知店員你不需要塑膠袋，否則店員就會在需要塑膠袋時直接提供並收取費用。

塑膠垃圾會對我們的生態環境造成很大的威脅，所以塑膠袋能以環境友善的方式處理掉非常重要。我們店的主要入口有個桶子，你可以把舊塑膠袋丟進去。我們會確保它們都有好好地被 **144** 回收再利用。讓產品有其他的用途，而不是被當垃圾丟掉。

使用塑膠袋是 **145** 可選擇的，我們鼓勵各位購買一個 3 美元，耐用又可以重複使用的帆布購物袋。 **146** 結帳的時候跟店員買一個就可以了。

143.
答案 (C)
解析 從空格後方的兩個子句看來是要表達「沒有事先說不要塑膠袋的話，就會主動提供並收費」的意思。由此可知空格所在的子句要是帶有「要是沒做…；除非」否定意思的連接詞，故本題正解為選項 (C) Unless。

144.
答案 (C)
解析 空格內的詞語必須要能跟前方 be 動詞 are 一同使用，所以要從非動詞型態的過去分詞 (C) 和現在分詞 (D) 兩者中選一個。that 子句的主詞 they 指的是前面句子提到的 old plastic bags，回收再利用是人為的行為，故本題正解為表被動語態的過去分詞選項 (C) recycled。

145.
答案 (B)
解析 空格內須填入能表達主詞 Using plastic bags(使用塑膠袋這件事) 特性的形容詞，就如同前面段落所說，是否付費使用塑膠袋是交由顧客自己選擇，故本題正解為「可選擇的」的選項 (B) optional。

146.
答案 (A)
譯文 **(A)** 結帳的時候跟我們其中任一個店員買一個就可以了。
(B) 我們有很多類型的產品提供購買。
(C) 捐錢非常感激，但志願服務會更好。
(D) 這就是為什麼要確認塑膠袋有沒有破洞。
解析 前面的句子在鼓勵讀者使用帆布購物袋，故本題正解為用代名詞 one 代指購物袋，告知購買方法的選項 (A)。

Part 7

請參考以下優惠券回答**第 147 至 148 題**。

Lacey 沙龍
開幕禮券

下次預約剪頭髮、修甲或臉部療程時 **147** 帶著這張禮券就能免費按摩頭部或肩膀！這張券在一週中的任何一天都能使用，但只限在我們 Bridge 街上的新分店。

我們可以靠你的協助成長！

148 向你的其中一位朋友、同事或家庭成員介紹我們店和提供的服務項目，你就可以獲得下次療程半價的優惠！ ** 為了享受此優惠，請確認推薦的那個人在預約服務時提供你的姓名。
**(請注意這個優惠僅限一次。)

147. 禮券可以用來兌換什麼免費服務？
(A) 臉部療程
(B) 修甲
(C) 剪髮
(D) 按摩
解析 第一段說明了禮券可以兌換頭部或肩膀的按摩 (exchange it for a complimentary head or shoulder rub)，故本題正解為選項 (D)。

148. 顧客要如何得到半價優惠？
(A) 去 Bridge 街上的分店
(B) 參加開幕活動
(C) 把朋友介紹給店家
(D) 預訂好幾個不同的服務
解析 和問題裡半價有關連的資訊出現在第二段。向你的其中一位朋友、同事或家庭成員介紹該美容院店和提供的服務項目就可以獲得半價優惠 (Tell one of your friends, colleagues, or family members...your next treatment for half price!)，意思為將朋友介紹給店家，故本題正解為選項 (C)。

請參考以下電子郵件回答**第 149 至 150 題**。

收件人：Felicia Munoz <fmunoz@mymail.com>
寄件人：Curtis Wode <cwode@diamond.com>
主旨：Sleeford 公寓
日期：11 月 2 日

親愛的 Munoz 女士：

你上個月提到有興趣租我們的其中一間公寓， **149** 但那時候我們沒有空的公寓能夠出租。我很開心能通知你我們其中一位租客剛剛要求提早解約，而我們在找願意在這個月底入住的人。這間公寓位在 5 樓，擁有能看到 Garfield 公園的好景觀。如果你能盡快就這次最早入住的機會回覆我的話，我將不勝感激。 **150** 如果你已經沒有意願搬到 Sleeford 公寓，我會將這間公寓放到我們線上的清單上。但我會暫緩這樣做，直到收到你的消息前。

敬祝 順心

Curtis Wode
Diamond 不動產

---

149. Wode 先生為什麼連絡 Munoz 女士？
(A) 通知她一個工作機會
(B) 提供不動產公司的詳細資訊
(C) 告訴她公寓大樓有空房
(D) 確認不動產租賃契約的修改事項
解析 連絡的目的在電子郵件開頭，之前沒有空的公寓，現在因為有人要退租就空出來了 (we did not have any vacant properties...one of our tenants has just asked to end her lease early)，故本題正解為選項 (C)。

150. Wode 先生暫緩做什麼？
(A) 更新清單
(B) 打掃公寓
(C) 連絡租戶
(D) 安排看屋
解析 Wode 先生在電子郵件的最後說他會晚點做某件事 (I will hold off on doing that)，此處的 doing that 是前面文章提到的將公寓放到線上清單 (add this unit to our online listings)，故本題正解為選項 (A)。

請參考以下簡訊回答**第 151 至 152 題**。

Gail Weiner	[上午 10:21]

Choi 先生你好。**151** 關於線上購物中心的問題，我還在等你部門的消息。你仔細檢查過問題了嗎？

Arthur Choi	[上午 10:23]

151 我們其中一位新的程式設計師在處理了。她正在對新搜尋引擎和圖像進行最後的點綴。

Gail Weiner	[上午 10:24]

很開心聽到這個消息。我們很多顧客都會抱怨搜尋功能。好的時候你可以告訴我一聲嗎？客服部經理和我想要先測試過，看問題是不是都解決了。

Arthur Choi	[上午 10:26]

沒問題。我們一完成後我會傳訊息給你。**152** 隨時都可以連絡我，如果你對新設計有任何問題。

Gail Weiner	[上午 10:28]

儘管放心。非常感謝。

151. Choi 先生應該是在哪個部門工作？
(A) 網頁設計部
(B) 客服部
(C) 行銷部
(D) 人資部
解析 簡訊開頭 Weiner 女士就說她在等 Choi 先生的部門跟她說線上購物中心的問題 (the problems with our online shopping mall) 處理到哪裡了，Choi 先生回答他們其中一位新的程式設計師在處理了 (One of our new programmers is working on it.)。由此可知 Choi 先生在網頁設

計相關部門工作，故本題正解為選項 (A)。

152. Weiner 女士在上午 10 點 28 分說「儘管放心吧」是想表達什麼意思？
(A) 她會排出時間協助 Choi 先生。
(B) 她確保某項工作會在今天下午完成。
(C) 她很確定顧客們會很滿意。
(D) 如果她有問題就會連絡 Choi 先生。
解析 count on 一般來說是表「確信；信賴…」，it 是指前面說的如果有問題隨時都能連絡 (feel free to get in touch if you have any questions)。也就是要對方相信自己會這麼做的意思，故本題正解為選項 (D)。

請參考以下廣告回答**第 153 至 154 題**。

Knightsbridge 國際電影節 (KIFF)
(10 月 3～5 日)

自從 7 年前首次舉辦活動以來，KIFF 的出席人數幾乎每年都在倍增，而今年的活動預計會是有史以來最多人的一次。與知名電影製作人和 KIFF 創辦人 Rod Livingstone，**153** 還有好幾位世界知名的演員，一同參與首映典禮、電影研討會和年度頒獎典禮。今年的電影節會比往年展示更多獨立電影製作人們的作品，**154(C)** 好幾位業餘導演，例如 Lisa Gehrman 已經被提名贏得最佳新導演獎。

今年的 KIFF **154(A)** 將在 Moxley 禮堂舉辦，不同的活動會有不同的門票價格。**154(B)** 所有門票價格資訊都能在 www.kiff.com/tickets 找到。就像往年一樣，**154(D)** KIFF 會員能夠享有各活動八折的優惠。申請成為會員的相關細節也能在我們的網站找到。

---

153. 從廣告中能夠得知 KIFF 的什麼資訊？
(A) 門票變貴了。
(B) 包含電影製作講座。
(C) 會由歡迎演說揭開序幕。
(D) 會有電影明星參加。
解析 第一段中間有提到了參加活動的人。(several world famous actors for movie premieres, film seminars, and the annual awards show)，故本題正解為選項 (D)。

154. 廣告中並未提到什麼資訊？
(A) 電影節地點
(B) 門票價格
(C) 一位獎項入圍者的名字
(D) 提供給會員的折扣數量
解析 第二段一開始就說到會在 Moxley 禮堂舉辦 (will be held in the Moxley Auditorium)，可知描述活動地點的選項 (A) 正確，第一段最後則說到好幾位業餘導演和 Lisa 入圍了電影界的「最佳新導演獎」(Lisa Gehrman have been nominated to win)，可知選項 (C) 正確。第二段中間則說到 KIFF 會員能有八折折扣 (KIFF members will receive a 20 percent discount)，可知選項 (D) 也正確。不過門票價格必須自己到網站上找，故本題正解為選項 (B)。

請參考以下電子郵件回答**第 155 至 157 題**。

收件人：Tomas Verville <tverville＠livemail.net>
寄件人：Carol Koontz <ckoontz＠weymouthmuseum.com>
主旨：一些細節
日期：5 月 1 日
附件：方向指引

親愛的 Verville 先生：

謹代表 Weymouth 科學博物館，我非常開心你接下了我們館內的導覽工作。156 我們位在本市郊外的新建築快要完成了，我們最近正在移動並擺設所有常態展品。

155 你第一天上班時間是 5 月 11 日上午 8 點半，我們的人資經理 Andy Jackson 會幫你介紹新設施。接著，你會和研發部主管 Glenda Boone 見面，她會更深入地介紹我們的展品。157 你最好帶筆記本和筆做點筆記，因為她很有可能會為你提供大量重要訊息，你稍後可能會想參考。

我在郵件中附上了地圖和簡單的指引，讓你能找到博物館。你抵達後，請告訴停車場管理員你的名字，這樣他就不會跟你收取遊客停車費用。之後你會收到一張職員停車證，這可以讓你每天免費停車。

謹啟

Carol Koontz 館長
Weymouth 科學博物館

155. 為什麼 Koontz 女士要連絡 Verville 先生？
(A) 描述一些新展品
(B) 公布博物館導覽的變化
(C) 提供關於某個工作的資訊
(D) 推薦某人到某個職位

解析 第一段感謝對方接受這個職位後，從第二段開始寫了第一天上班的時間 (At 8:30 A.M. on your first day, which will be May 11)，並詳細説明該做的事，故本題正解為提供工作相關資訊的選項 (C)。

156. 從電子郵件中能夠得知 Weymouth 科學博物館的什麼資訊？
(A) 正在搬去新建築。
(B) 最近聘僱了好幾位導覽員。
(C) 提高了遊客的停車費用。
(D) 每個月都會舉辦不同的展覽。

解析 第一段寫到新建築快要完成了，最近正在移動展品 (Our new premises...we are currently in the process of moving)，代表現在正在搬遷，故本題正解為選項 (A)。

157. Verville 先生被建議做什麼？
(A) 寫筆記
(B) 利用特別通道
(C) 事先連絡 Boone 女士
(D) 在停車場和 Koontz 女士見面

解析 建議對方做某事的內容出現在第二段中段，寄件人寫到最好帶筆記本和筆做點筆記 (It would be a good idea to bring a notepad and pen with you and write things down)，故本題正解為選項 (A)。

請參考以下資訊回答**第 158 至 160 題**。

Telford 物流股份有限公司
158 第二屆年度公司工作坊，5 月 8 日到 10 日
大開曼渡假村，開曼群島

合作折扣

Telford 物流股份有限公司非常開心能夠在美麗的開曼群島上的大開曼渡假村舉辦工作坊。我們公司的第一屆工作坊非常受職員們喜愛，而我們想讓這次的活動比上次更好。作為一位工作坊參加者，你會拿到一整本優惠券，週六上午 9 點於渡假村大廳舉辦的歡迎會就能拿到。當你使用這些優惠券時，必須出示公司的職員證。優惠券的有效日只到工作坊的最後一天，且不能兌換成現金。

在渡假村內，使用優惠券可以在很多地方得到折扣。159(D) 你可以在海灘用八折的價格租借潛水設備，在本館大廳後方的 159(C) 運動中心買到半價的飲料。除此之外，你也可以到位於渡假村內部最東邊的 159(B) 水樂園裡以折扣價買到各式各樣的泳衣和泳鏡。

160 那些想要到渡假村外，去附近的城鎮探索的人，請記得優惠券無法換取任何當地的商品或服務。還有，請確保在出發去城鎮前，帶上信用卡或到大廳用 ATM 領錢，那邊要找 ATM 很困難。位在大廳的 ATM 開放時間是早上 8 點到晚上 8 點。

158. 從資訊中能夠得知 Telford 物流股份有限公司的什麼資訊？
(A) 會替職員安排導遊。
(B) 去年辦了第一屆工作坊。
(C) 總部位在開曼群島。
(D) 工作坊期間每天早上都會開會。

解析 標題寫明第二屆年度公司工作坊 (2nd Annual Company Workshop)。既然今年是第二次舉辦每年都有的活動，表示去年辦了第一屆工作坊，故本題正解為選項 (B)。

159. 工作坊參加者們不能在哪使用優惠券？
(A) 渡假村大廳
(B) 水樂園
(C) 運動中心
(D) 海灘

解析 能夠使用優惠券的地點出現在第二段，該段落最後面寫到可以在水樂園裡以折扣價買到各式各樣的泳衣和泳鏡 (a variety of swimwear...at a discount in the water park)，可知選項 (B) 正確。中間寫到能在運動中心用半價享用飲料 (get half-price beverages in the sports center)，可知選項 (C) 正確。最後是段落前半段寫到能以八折的價格租借潛水設備 (a twenty percent discount on...down on the

beach)，可知選項 (D) 也正確。文章內並未提及渡假村大廳能夠使用優惠券，故本題正解為選項 (A)。

160. 關於渡假村外商店的敘述，何者正確？
(A) 他們比較想收信用卡。
(B) 他們提供特惠活動。
(C) 他們不收職員優惠券。
(D) 他們營業到晚上 8 點。

解析 與渡假村外部購物相關的資訊出現在第三段，該段落提到優惠券無法在渡假村外部換取當地的商品或服務 (cannot be redeemed for any local goods or services)，故本題正解為選項 (C)。

請參考以下公告回答**第 161 至 163 題**。

親愛的職員：

161 我們 Cantor 食品將於 10 月 23 日實施新的洗手規定。在行政大樓或流通倉庫工作的職員不受此次變化的影響，162 但生產線和會直接接觸到食品的員工們會受到影響。他們仍然被要求在輪班前在工廠入口清潔雙手。然而，163 取代過去用洗手皂洗手的方式，生產線職員現在必須使用放在該位置的特殊抗菌巾。

如果你對這個改變有任何疑問，請直接告訴廠長 Maurice Chamberlain。感謝各位協助我們改善衛生規定。

Jim Hamilton
營運經理
Cantor 食品

---

161. 這則公告的目的是什麼？
(A) 公布職員會議
(B) 概述新規定
(C) 提醒職員截止期限
(D) 說明安裝程序的細節

解析 第一段的第一句就說要執行新的規定 (On October 23, Cantor Foods will implement new guidelines related to hand washing practices.)，後面也說明了與之相關的細節，故本題正解為選項 (B)。

162. 誰最可能被公告內的改變影響到？
(A) 行政辦公室職員
(B) 業務專員
(C) 生產線職員
(D) 倉庫職員

解析 第一段點出了不會受影響的職員還有生產線職員會受到該變化的影響 (workers who operate the production line and come into direct contact with food products)，故本題正解為選項 (C)。

163. Hamilton 先生暗示了關於 Cantor 食品的什麼資訊？
(A) 打算要關掉其中一個製造廠。
(B) 每個月都會檢核健康與安全程序。
(C) 收到好幾個客訴。

(D) 之後工廠不會再提供洗手皂。

解析 第一段的最後說到要取代過去用洗手皂洗手的方式，生產線職員現在必須使用放在該位置的特殊抗菌巾清潔手部 (instead of using hand soap as before, ...that will be provided in its place)。由此可知工廠現在不會提供洗手皂了，故本題正解為選項 (D)。

請參考以下報導回答**第 164 至 167 題**。

馬迪納，亞利桑那州，4 月 23 日——WeMOVE 企業今天早上宣布明年要重整當地產業。164 看起來公司已經決定要遷移提供許多馬迪納居民工作機會的主要工廠到新的地點。

Derek Ayala，WeMOVE 的發言人，今天早上宣布公司想對 165 從 40 年前工廠開始運作後和他們共事的所有人表達謝意。Ayala 先生解釋當顧客們都來自亞洲時，公司已經無法繼續經營馬迪納的工廠。

167 Ayala 說：「WeMOVE 會在 7 月關閉該工廠並遷移到亞洲」。工廠確切的位置會在接下來幾週內公布。166 許多職員們不確定他們的未來會如何，也已經開始一系列阻止公司遷移的行動。

---

164. 這篇報導的目的是什麼？
(A) 報導新的就業機會
(B) 通知消費者某個產品的名稱變了
(C) 宣布當地公司的遷移
(D) 解釋更換供應商的風險

解析 這篇報導的重點出現在第一段，主要是要告知這間公司決定遷移工廠 (the company has decided to move its main factory)，故本題正解為選項 (C)。

165. 馬迪納的工廠什麼時候開始運作的？
(A) 大概 40 年前
(B) 大概 30 年前
(C) 大概 20 年前
(D) 大概 10 年前

解析 第二段的 "since it opened four decades ago" 提到了開工廠的時間點，decade 的意思是 10 年，可算出工廠是 40 年前開的，故本題正解為選項 (A)。

166. 根據報導可以推測出什麼事實？
(A) 公司正在經歷銷售量的下滑。
(B) 該工廠已經關閉了。
(C) 部分的職員能保住他們的工作。
(D) 許多職員會被解僱。

解析 第三段中段寫到許多職員們不知道他們的未來會如何 (Many of the workers are unsure of what the future will hold)，這是要表達很多職員受公司遷移影響，內心感到十分恐懼，故本題正解為選項 (D)。

167. 下面這個句子最適合填入 [1]、[2]、[3]、[4] 之中哪一個位置？
「工廠確切的位置會在接下來幾週內公布。」
(A) [1]

(B) [2]
(C) [3]
(D) [4]
解析 這個句子是在敘述日後公布工廠確切位置的一個大概時間點。由於第三段的第一句講到了工廠遷移的時間點 (will be closing down the factory in July and moving it to Asia)，本句應擺在這個句子後方的 [4]，一同描述時間點和地點的相關資訊，語意才會通順，故本題正解為選項 (D)。

請參考以下線上聊天討論回答**第 168 至 171 題**。

Dana Elgort	Rian、Vic，168 170 171 我正好要上車去 Korby 股份有限公司提交我們對設計圖做的修改，但我似乎忘了帶他們總部的新藍圖。我是不是把它放在我的桌子上了？[1:28 P.M.]
Rian Dennehy	對，我看到它了。但你沒辦法直接用說的描述我們做了哪些修改嗎？[1:30 P.M.]
Dana Elgort	用說的效果不夠好。169 修改的地方太過精細，所以對方應該會比較好理解如果他們能親眼看到圖。[1:32 P.M.]
Rian Dennehy	這樣的話，你可能要回到樓上的辦公室取走。[1:34 P.M.]
Vic Jacoby	等等，Dana…你不用等電梯搭上來了。170 171 我可以去地下停車場。[1:36 P.M.]
Dana Elgort	太好了！你可以在電梯外跟我碰頭嗎？我現在就朝那走過去。[1:37 P.M.]
Vic Jacoby	沒問題。你在地下 1 樓還是 2 樓？[1:38 P.M.]
Rian Dennehy	Vic，你怎麼不派一個實習生去就好？[1:39 P.M.]
Vic Jacoby	喔，反正我要去車上拿我的手機充電器。我今天早上因為趕時間忘記拿了。[1:40 P.M.]
Dana Elgort	再次跟你說聲謝謝，Vic。我在地下 2 樓，你快到了嗎？[1:41 P.M.]
Vic Jacoby	我幾分鐘後到，Dana。[1:42 P.M.]

168. Elgort 女士應該是誰？
(A) Korby 股份有限公司的職員
(B) Dennehy 先生的客戶
(C) 一位人資經理
(D) 一位建築師
解析 Elgort 女士在第一則訊息說他們修改了設計，而這個設計圖是關於新建築 (to present the design changes we made, but I seem to have forgotten the new blueprint)。從內容

可判斷這是建築師的工作，故本題正解為選項 (D)。

169. Elgort 女士在下午 1 點 32 分傳的訊息中說到「用說的效果不夠好」，她這句話是想表達什麼？
(A) 她比較想要讓客戶看設計圖。
(B) 她沒有什麼自信發表。
(C) 她覺得某場商業會議結果很糟。
(D) 她相信客戶會接受些微的修改。
解析 這句話的意思是「用說的效果不夠好」。後面的句子又補充修改的地方太過精細，對方還是看設計圖會比較好 (so they'd have a better chance of understanding if they could see them for themselves)。由此可知她是想透過這句話強調自己比較想讓客戶看設計圖，故本題正解為選項 (A)。

170. Elgort 女士人在哪裡？
(A) 她的辦公室
(B) 停車場
(C) 她的車子裡
(D) 在電梯裡
解析 Elgort 女士在第一則訊息中說她正好要上車，接著 Jacoby 先生在 1 點 36 分的訊息說要幫她，並表示自己可以到 Elgort 女士所在的地下停車場 (I can head down to the basement parking garage.)。由此可知 Elgort 女士現在人在停車場，故本題正解為選項 (B)。

171. Jacoby 先生說要幫忙做什麼？
(A) 請一位實習生去協助 Elgort 女士
(B) 讓 Elgort 女士借某個設備
(C) 拿文件給 Elgort 女士
(D) 陪 Elgort 女士去和客戶開會
解析 Jacoby 先生在 1 點 36 分的訊息中說他可以去地下停車場 (I can head down to the basement parking garage.)。這表示他要將對話剛開始時 Elgort 女士說自己忘記拿的設計圖 (I seem to have forgotten the new blueprint) 拿去給她，故本題正解為選項 (C)。

請參考以下報導回答**第 172 至 175 題**。

Hakuna 正在籌備新的製造廠
普勒托利亞 (11 月 16 日)──Hakuna 汽車，南非的一間汽車製造廠最近將總部移到我們的城市，也進一步表示他們已經在 173 喀麥隆的杜亞拉蓋了新製造廠。這間工廠會交由公司在當地的管理分部 Hakuna CAF 管理，173 且在 11 月 25 日開業。
172 這間新工廠展現了公司想要在中非提高市占率的意圖。根據 Hakuna 的執行長 Nelson Aganda 所說：175「在杜亞拉製造汽車將能夠讓我們避掉在該地區過多的交通和配送成本，從一般運送的支出來看，估計最少能減少 50%。因此，我們應該要能夠與總是獨佔該地區銷售量的北非競爭對手競爭。」173 Aganda 先生打算親自在工廠開業儀式上剪綵。
3 年前，Hakuna 第一次嘗試攻進中非汽車市

場。這家汽車製造商在整個地區廣泛宣傳他們的 Hakuna Solaro 車款，強調其合理的價格和驚人的燃油效率。很不幸的，銷售緩慢，不可靠的航線意味著顧客必須要等上好幾週才能買到車。

Hakuna 目前在肯亞的奈洛比和安哥拉的盧安達都有製造廠在運作。 **174** Aganda 先生提到公司為了取得在亞歷山卓蓋製造廠的許可，最近在和埃及政府相關人員接洽。他希望能夠在今年的年底得到許可。

172. 從報導中能夠得知 Hakuna 汽車的什麼資訊？
(A) 在準備推出新款汽車。
(B) 3 年前剛創立。
(C) 想要提高自家公司在中非市場的地位。
(D) 會在某個計劃案上跟北非的汽車製造商合作。

解析 蓋新工廠的目的出現在第二段的第一句，這間新工廠展現了公司想要在中非提高市占率的意圖 (the company's intention to increase its market share in Central Africa)。由此可知該公司是想增強自己現在的地位，故本題正解為選項 (C)。

173. 從報導中能夠得知 Aganda 先生的什麼資訊？
(A) 他會負責管理位在杜亞拉的工廠。
(B) 他相信 Hakuna Solaro 會成功。
(C) 他花了很多時間在中非工作。
(D) 他 11 月要去喀麥隆。

解析 出現 Aganda 先生名字的第二段最後一句話寫到他會為工廠開業儀式剪綵 (Mr. Aganda plans to cut the ribbon at the factory's grand opening event.)，而第一段說到新工廠在喀麥隆 (the new production plant...in Douala, Cameroon)，而開業儀式的時間點是 11 月 (will open on November 25)，故本題正解為選項 (D)。

174. Hakuna 汽車接下來應該會在哪裡蓋下一間製造廠？
(A) 南非
(B) 埃及
(C) 安哥拉
(D) 肯亞

解析 關於其他工廠的訊息出現在第四段後半段，內容中提及該公司最近為了取得蓋製造廠的許可，最近在和埃及政府相關人員接洽 (the firm has recently contacted members of the Egyptian government to request construction permission)，故本題正解為選項 (B)。

175. 下面這個句子最適合填入 [1]、[2]、[3]、[4] 之中哪一個位置？
「從一般運送的支出來看，估計最少能減少 50%。」
(A) [1]
(B) [2]
(C) [3]
(D) [4]

解析 這個句子提出運送支出能夠減少 50%，因此應該填在第二段說到減少運送費用的句子後方，

也就是 [1] 所在的位置，該句成為前句事實的根據，語意才會通順，故本題正解為選項 (A)。

請參考以下電子郵件及預訂確認單回答**第 176 至 180 題**。

收件人：Tina Braymer <tbraymer@worldmail. net>
寄件人：Yvonne Gagne <ygagne@evehotels. com>
主旨：你的住房預訂 (#438119)
日期：8 月 10 日

親愛的 Braymer 女士：

這個月底，我們將接待大量參與本年度 Skyline 軟體與科技大會的講者和活動主辦方。你目前預訂了一間位在 2 樓的房間，但該會議的主辦方要把那層樓全部訂下來，供他們的工作人員和貴賓入住。 **176** 因此，我們想詢問你是否介意換到別的房間，我們會提供一張 50 美元的餐券。該優惠券可以在我們飯店所有分館的餐廳抵用， **177** 使用期限到今年年底。

請看以下 3 間可供選擇的房間，我們希望你會考慮。第 1、2 個選擇和你原本預訂的房型相同，同地點，但不同樓層。

406 號房	Eve 飯店 (Porter 路)	標準房	入住時間：8 月 28 日下午 1 點	退房時間：8 月 30 日上午 11 點
519 號房	Eve 飯店 (Porter 路)	標準房	入住時間：8 月 28 日下午 1 點	退房時間：8 月 30 日上午 11 點

第 3 個選擇是一間豪華房，但這間房間在我們另一間分館，從 Porter 路往北走幾個街區就能抵達。你被收取的費用會和標準房相同。

427 號房	Eve 飯店 (Clement 街)	**178** **180** 豪華房	入住時間：8 月 28 日下午 2 點	**180** 退房時間：8 月 30 日中午 12 點

178 如果你願意換到我們提到的這幾間房間，請撥 555-0177 連絡我們的訂房經理 Harry Henley。如果你想保留原本預訂的房間，我們也能夠理解。但若你能協助我們解決此問題，我們會非常感激。

謹啟

Yvonne Gagne
Eve 飯店集團
客服部

飯店預訂確認單
(預訂號碼 #438119) * 已變更
EVE 飯店，Clement 街 387 號，舊金山，加州 94105
住客姓名：Tina Braymer
178 **180** 預約資訊：豪華房，入住日期：8 月 28 日／退房日期：8 月 30 日
179 附免費早餐

已收款項：550 美元 (信用卡號碼：1867-****-****-2878)
入住時須支付的押金：100 美元

176. 這封電子郵件的目的是什麼？
(A) 鼓勵一位客人換房間
(B) 提供客人如何到飯店的方法
(C) 推薦客人去參加大型會議
(D) 宣傳連鎖飯店的新分館
解析 電子郵件的第一段說連絡收件人是為了詢問她願不願意換到其他房間 (we are contacting you to ask whether you would mind switching to a different room)，故本題正解為選項 (A)。

177. 從電子郵件中能夠得知餐券的什麼資訊？
(A) 只能在 Porter 路飯店使用。
(B) 必須在 12 月 31 日前用掉。
(C) 可以換成現金。
(D) 會寄給 Braymer 女士。
解析 關於餐券的資訊出現在電子郵件第一段的最後，有一句說使用期限到今年年底 (is valid until the end of this year)，也就是 12 月 31 日，故本題正解為選項 (B)。

178. Braymer 女士在收到電子郵件後應該了什麼事？
(A) 連絡活動主辦方
(B) 付款
(C) 回覆電子郵件
(D) 打電話給 Henley 先生
解析 電子郵件最後一段寫到如果有意願換房間，就打電話連絡 Harry Henley (please contact our reservations manager, Harry Henley, at 555-0177)。接著從預定確認單上可以看到飯店先前詢問收件人要換什麼房間時，提及的其中一間豪華房 (Deluxe Room)。由此可知 Braymer 女士打了電話給 Henley 先生，故本題正解為選項 (D)。

179. 從預訂確認單上能知道 Braymer 女士新住宿預訂的何種資訊？
(A) 她用現金付住宿費。
(B) 她必須在抵達時支付 550 美元。
(C) 她會得到一頓免費餐點。
(D) 她會在那間飯店住 3 晚。
解析 預定確認單中段寫了 "Complimentary Breakfast Included"，可知提供了免費早餐，故本題正解為選項 (C)。

180. Braymer 女士什麼時候必須退房？
(A) 上午 11 點
(B) 中午 12 點
(C) 下午 1 點
(D) 下午 2 點
解析 從預定確認單中段可得知 Braymer 女士入住的房型是豪華房 (Deluxe Room)，對照電子郵件中的圖表後，可知豪華房退房時間為中午 12 點 (Check-out by: 12 P.M., August 30)，故本題正解為選項 (B)。

請參考以下廣告及表格回答**第 181 至 185 題**。

Real Talk 的暢銷書朗讀活動即將開始

你是個喜歡看書，想要聽名人閱讀暢銷書摘錄的人嗎？如果是的話，181 請轉到 FM93.1 的 *Real Talk*，收聽我們新推出的名人說書系列。183 我們會邀請一些無論是在舞臺還是在螢幕裡很活躍的知名明星來上節目，朗讀一些最近能在書局買得到的暢銷小說上的摘錄。這個朗讀活動會在 3 月連續 3 週的週三下午 2 點進行現場直播。

這個系列總共要朗讀 3 本書：
● *Future Proof*
——一本由 Angus Fring 寫的科幻小說，朗讀者為 Kenneth Forster
● *Dark Nights in Cairo*
—— 184 一本由 Jade Levy 寫的恐怖／懸疑小說，朗讀者為 Alex Knight
● *The Winding River*
——一本由 Angela Masters 寫的羅曼史小說，朗讀者為 Margaret Kaye

182 有問題想問作者們嗎？請在朗讀時間結束後撥 555-0133 給 *Real Talk* 的主持人 Anna Hargreaves。

如果你打算聽我們任何一個朗讀活動，請透過網站 www.realtalkradio.com 告訴我們你的想法。如果這個活動的反饋很正面，我們會試著讓它成為節目中的固定環節。

---

www.realtalkradio.com/bookreadings/feedback
我們真心希望你享受聆聽我們近期書籍朗讀的環節。正如我們節目的所有面向一樣，我們很重視聽眾們給的反饋。請花一點時間完成下面的問卷調查。

姓名： 184 Frank Mirabito

你最喜歡朗讀書籍活動的哪一點？

184 我認為 Knight 先生的朗讀時間是最令人愉快的。他聲音非常有表現力且非常適合朗讀小說。此外，他朗讀的那本書是我過去 10 年多來最愛的小說之一。184 這是我最喜歡的類型。

我們未來還能如何改進朗讀書籍活動呢？

在朗讀的時候，尤其是 3 月 27 日那一天，185 我覺得朗讀的人的聲音有時候會聽不太清楚。感覺應該是麥克風或擴音設備故障，音量才會不穩定。我覺得下次可以考慮升級一下設備。

181. 從廣告中能夠得知書籍朗讀的什麼資訊？
(A) 會在書局舉辦。
(B) 會在廣播上播出。
(C) 受眾是想成為作家的人們。
(D) 會在同一天舉辦。
解析 廣告的第一段就寫到如果想聽書籍朗讀，就要把收音頻道轉到 FM93.1(tune in to *Real Talk* on 93.1 FM)，故本題正解為選項 (B)。

182. 根據廣告內容，為什麼要連絡 Hargreaves 女士？
(A) 為了加入某個比賽
(B) 為了提問
(C) 為了推薦一位作家
(D) 為了提供一本書的閱讀心得

解析 廣告第三段寫到如果有問題的話，可以打給 Hargreaves 女士 (Have something you'd like to ask the authors? Call *Real Talk*'s host, Anna Hargreaves)，故本題正解為選項 (B)。

183. 關於書籍朗讀者的暗示為何？
(A) 他們都有出版小説。
(B) 他們全職為 *Real Talk* 工作。
(C) 他們都是知名演員。
(D) 他們會被 Hargreaves 面試。

解析 廣告的第一段提到邀請了在舞臺或螢幕裡很活躍的明星上節目 (We will welcome some popular stars of stage and screen to our studio to read excerpts)，故本題正解為選項 (C)。

184. 從表格中能夠得知 Mirabito 先生的什麼資訊？
(A) 他沒辦法聽其中一場朗讀會。
(B) 他最近買了 *The Winding River*。
(C) 他會參加下一場書籍朗讀活動。
(D) 他很喜歡讀懸疑故事。

解析 Mirabito 先生的意見出現在表格中段，他覺得 Knight 讀的那段最令人愉悦 (Mr. Knight's reading was the most enjoyable one)。第一篇廣告中間有提到 Knight 先生要讀的書是驚悚／懸疑小説 (a thriller/mystery novel...read by Alex Knight)，故本題正解為選項 (D)。

185. Mirabito 先生建議朗讀活動的哪一點要改？
(A) 朗讀計劃
(B) 特別來賓
(C) 音訊設備
(D) 書籍類型

解析 Mirabito 先生在表格的最後説聲音偶爾聽不太清楚，還補充可能是麥克風或擴音器壞了 (the readers were occasionally a little hard to hear....the microphone or amplification devices were faulty)。由此可知是音訊設備的問題，故本題正解為選項 (C)。

請參考以下租車規定、車輛檢查表和電子郵件回答**第 186 至 190 題**。

VERNON 租車——租車規定
Torres Megano, B49VGA

規定
這是一個 7 天的租約，從 4 月 11 日至 4 月 17 日，一天的租金是 52 美元，總金額為 364 美元。款項已經在租車的第一天收到。 189 延遲還車會額外收取一天 75 美元的費用。租賃車輛會有加滿的汽油、CD/DVD 播放器和電視螢幕。 186 沒有提供充電線。一天額外支付 15 美元就能增加衛星導航系統。 187 取車必須在我們的 Bayfield Avenue 分店，也要將車還到同樣的地點。

損壞賠償費用
500 美元的損壞賠償費用也會在 4 月 11 日當天收取。這筆費用會依歸還車輛後的車況檢查全數或部分退還給租車者。Vernon 租車在將車子租出去之前會實施全面的檢查，檢查表的複本會提供給租車者。

VERNON 租車——事前車輛評估
日期：4 月 11 日
汽車種類：轎車
汽車型號：Torres Megano
車牌號碼：B49 VGA

評估內容：
電力裝置、煞車、操縱裝置和引擎都已詳細檢查過，確認是在 188 完美的運轉狀態。然而， 190 車輛後座的椅套有一點裂掉的痕跡，且擋風玻璃左下角有個小刮痕。Vernon 租車已知這些損傷，且會全權負責處理。

Vernon Mason   Elsa Buchanan
公司董事長   租車者

收件人：vmason@vernonscarhire.com
寄件人：ebuchanan@ecity.net
主旨：損壞賠償費用
日期：4 月 19 日
附件：B49VGA 評估 .pdf 格式檔案

親愛的 Mason 先生：

我幾天前將一臺Torres Megano歸還至你的公司，但我只拿回部分我所付針對損害賠償費用的押金。我很意外你竟然從我一開始付的錢裡拿了 200 美元。 189 我知道依照貴公司的租車規定，我會被收取 75 美元，但沒道理我會多被扣 125 美元。很明顯地， 190 這是我取車的時候就已經在的裂痕的費用。這點有出現在我附上的評估表中。我取車的時候，你的職員還指那個裂痕給我看。我希望你承認你們犯了錯，並退還我被誤收的 125 美元。

謹啓

Elsa Buchanan

---

186. 租車規定中有提到下列何者？
(A) 還車時油箱必須是滿的。
(B) 車輛租金一天 75 美元。
(C) 公司老闆最近改了規定。
(D) 租車者必須用自己的充電線。

解析 租車規定的第一段中間寫到車上沒有充電線 (Device charging cables are not included.)。也就是説要自己想辦法充電，因此描述其中一個充電方法的選項 (D) 為本題正解。

187. 關於 Vernon 租車的暗示為何？

(A) 擁有不只一間店。
(B) 最近增加了新車款。
(C) 提供獎勵給回訪的顧客。
(D) 專門出租跑車。

解析 租車規定的第一段的最後面強調一定要到特定的分店取車還車 (The vehicle must be picked up at our Bayfield Avenue branch and returned to the same location.)。由此可判斷這家公司有好幾間分店，故本題正解為選項 (A)。

188. 在檢查表中，位在第一段第二行的 "order"，跟哪個詞語意思最相近？
(A) 要求
(B) 狀態
(C) 運送 (貨物)
(D) 命令

解析 該詞語位在 in perfect working order 的結構裡，用來表達機器等物品處在完美的狀態。由此可知意思為「狀態的」另一個名詞選項 (B) 為正解。

189. 為什麼 Buchanan 女士會被罰 75 美元？
(A) 她把車還到錯誤的地點。
(B) 她在開車時出了車禍。
(C) 她把車輛的某些用品弄丟了。
(D) 她晚了一天還車。

解析 電子郵件前半段說到被扣了 75 美元 (I knew that a deduction of $75 would be made...。對照租車規定的前半段，文內提到延遲還車會額外收取一天 75 美元的費用 (Late return of the vehicle...of $75 per day)。由此可知她晚了一天還車，故本題正解為選項 (D)。

190. Buchanan 女士為了什麼事爭辯？
(A) 擋風玻璃上的裂痕是因為意外造成的。
(B) 椅子損壞和她沒有關係。
(C) 車子的性能不令人滿意。
(D) 租車公司給了她錯誤資訊。

解析 根據 Buchanan 女士所寫的電子郵件，Buchanan 女士提出費用有問題，且認為原因是出在車上原本就有的裂痕 (this is for the tear that was already present)，而第二篇文章有寫到後座上有裂痕 (a slight rip...of the vehicle's back seats)。由此可知她是想要告訴對方裂痕原本就存在，不是她的錯，故本題正解為選項 (B)。

請參考以下網頁、申請表和討論區訊息回答**第 191至 195 題**。

英國賞鳥討論區
照片上傳守則

1. 根據我們討論區的規定，**194** 請將你的訊息字數控制在 70 字以內。這樣可以確保訊息簡潔、正確，且沒有不相關的內容。

2. 照片描述必須要遵守「鳥的種類——時間——地點」的格式。**191** 我們的會員都是狂熱的賞鳥迷，所以他們特別感興趣的是能夠不費心的快速瀏覽照片的細節。我們有一個獨立的頁面

來上傳未知的鳥的照片。

請增加一個像是「歐洲斑姬鶲——上午 6 點——斯珀恩角，約克郡」的描述

請避免加上不明確的敘述如「在郊區的小隻咖啡色的鳥」

3. 由於這裡主要是分享照片的討論區，你所發的文必須至少要有一張鳥的照片，且必須要是你自己拍攝的。我們不會批准分享不是你親自拍攝的照片。

英國賞鳥討論區
加入新會員申請表

姓名：Arthur Bedford
電子郵件：abedford@homenet.com
191 賞鳥經驗：10 年
目前任職的公司：Natural World Weekly
愛用的相機：Zenon 650

我有興趣聽到關於為英國賞鳥會成員們舉辦的季度聚會的消息。YES (✓) NO ( )

照片使用相關事項：
請注意上傳到討論區的照片，可能會放到我們網站的照片集錦區。**192** 雖然我們保有使用已上傳照片的權力，我們不會允許其他公司使用。

英國賞鳥討論區

討論區會員：**195** Arthur Bedford
圖片描述：小斑啄木鳥——上午 5 點 45 分——Kirby 森林，坎布里亞
日期：5 月 15 日
訊息：**193** **195** 你們當中部分的人要求一些據說住在我新家附近森林裡的小斑啄木鳥的照片。那麼，我很幸運地在今天早上遛狗時捕捉到其中一隻的照片。雖然我只看到一隻，我的鄰居告訴我這幾週還有在這看到好幾隻。我會睜大眼睛並隨時準備好我的照相機！**194** (72 字)
附件圖片檔：小斑 _ 啄木鳥 _05.15

---

191. 網頁提到關於討論區的什麼資訊？
(A) 被有很多經驗的賞鳥人所使用。
(B) 要求會員們要付年費。
(C) 會員可以建立自己的照片集錦區。
(D) 可接受特定長度的影片。

解析 網頁的第二點寫到會員們是很狂熱的賞鳥迷 (Our members are all avid bird watchers)，而申請表寫到加入的會員已經有觀察鳥 10 年的經驗了 (Years spent bird watching: 10 years)。由此可知使用這個討論區的都是經驗很多的人，故本題正解為選項 (A)。

192. 英國賞鳥討論區向會員們做了什麼保證？
(A) 不會把照片發到他們網站的照片集錦區裡。

(B) 提供拍攝鳥類的小技巧。
(C) 每個月幫會員們辦活動。
(D) 不會跟其他業者分享照片。

解析 關於照片使用的相關事項在申請表的下端，並說明不會讓別間公司使用他們上傳的圖片 (we will not permit other companies to use them)，故本題正解為選項 (D)。

193. 為什麼 Bedford 先生在討論區發了文章？
(A) 請求人推薦賞鳥的地點
(B) 評論某位會員上傳的照片
(C) 回應其他會員們的請求
(D) 請求幫忙辨認一隻鳥

解析 討論區訊息中間有寫到部分會員跟他要照片 (Some of you asked for some pictures)，後續也描述了自己拍照的過程，故本題正解為選項 (C)。

194. Bedford 先生是怎麼違反討論區規定的？
(A) 他圖片的描述不夠詳細。
(B) 他沒有上傳符合數量的照片。
(C) 他發在錯誤的區域。
(D) 他的訊息超過了字數限制。

解析 網頁中的第一項就有說到要控制在 70 個字以內 (Please keep your message under 70 words)，而從討論區訊息可以看到 Bedford 先生總共寫了 72 個字 (72 words)。故本題正解為提到超過字數的選項 (D)。

195. 關於 Bedford 先生，下列何者可能是正確的？
(A) 他最近搬新家。
(B) 他剛開始在雜誌社工作。
(C) 他是討論區的負責人。
(D) 他最近買了相機。

解析 討論區訊息是 Bedford 先生寫的，他提到「會員們中部分人說我新家附近的森林裡有小斑啄木鳥出沒，叫我拍點照片」(Some of you asked for some pictures of the lesser spotted woodpeckers that are rumored to live in the forest near my new house.)。由此可知他最近才剛搬到那個地方，故本題正解為選項 (A)。

請參考以下徵才廣告、資訊和電子郵件回答**第 196 至 200 題**。

職位名稱：游泳池活動籌劃員
地區：洛杉磯西部

Eagle 公寓，位在洛杉磯西部聖塔莫尼卡丘陵地，正在找一位外向的人，為孩子們創造和帶領一個有趣的泳池活動。 197 這位講師必須能在游泳池固定的開放時間早上 9 點半之前帶領一個週末泳池活動。

面試時可與公寓管理員 Torrance 先生協商出一個合理的薪資。 196 活動籌劃員可以自由地創造他或她自己的泳池活動，但都必須經過 Torrance 先生的批准。

如果你有興趣申請這個職位的話，請寄電子郵件到

management@eaglecondos.com，請在主旨處打上「游泳池活動籌劃員」。

在電子郵件中，確保你描述了任何相關的經驗並必須貼上一張近照。

Eagle 公寓
游泳池
游泳池活動日程

游泳池固定的開放時間是上午 9 點半到晚上 7 點半，除了週二和週五，它會在打掃完後，10 點半的時候開放。下面的活動是給孩子們參加的，且會在正常游泳池開放的時間之外舉行。任何小孩都可以參加，只要他或她是一個合格的游泳者。父母們也歡迎在泳池旁邊觀看。

時間	活動	負責人
200 上午 8 點半-上午 9 點半（每週一、三、五）	潛水找東西	Steven Chappelle
下午 7 點半-下午 8 點半（每週一、三、五）	水中有氧	Kate Underwood
197 上午 8 點半-上午 9 點半（每週六、日）	游泳比賽	197 Louis Simpson
下午 7 點半-下午 8 點半（每週六、日）	水球	Natalie Liman

目前所有住在 Eagle 公寓的孩子們可以不用事先預約，直接過來參加活動。 198 住在 Livewell 或 Agostino 兩間鄰近公寓大樓的小朋友，只要爸媽事先到接待櫃臺預約，也可以來參加我們的泳池活動。

收件人：Betty Adams，行政經理
199 寄件人：Neil Torrance，公寓管理員
199 日期：8 月 12 日，週五
主旨：回覆：新泳池活動

Betty 你好：

謝謝你讓我知道目前為了孩子們舉辦的泳池活動進行得如何。孩子們和家長們似乎都對我們安排的新活動感到很開心。 199 200 然而，在昨天的住戶大會上，有人抱怨週間早晨活動造成了噪音。所以，我想請你跟活動籌劃員說一聲，請他想另一個比較沒有噪音的活動。感謝你的幫忙。

敬祝 順心

Neil Torrance
公寓管理員
Eagle 公寓

196. 根據徵才廣告，籌劃員將能決定什麼？
(A) 要提供什麼樣的活動
(B) 幾點活動會開始進行
(C) 幾位小朋友能參與
(D) 活動要在哪裡進行

解析 徵才廣告第二段的最後寫到活動籌劃員可以自由地策畫游泳池的活動 (The activity coordinator is free to create his or her own program)，故本題正解為選項 (A)。

197. 誰應該是最新的泳池活動籌劃員？
(A) Chappelle 先生
(B) Underwood 女士
(C) Simpson 先生
(D) Liman 女士

解析 徵才廣告的第一段說到必須要能在週末游泳池的開放時間9點半之前來帶泳池活動 (available to lead a weekend pool activity before the pool opens for regular use at 9:30 A.M.)。與此有關的還有資訊中的圖表，從週末上午 8 點半到 9 點半可以看到擔任該時間段講師的是 Louis Simpson，故本題正解為選項 (C)。

198. 從活動日程可以知道什麼資訊？
(A) 家長必須一直陪著孩子們。
(B) 住 Eagle 公寓的孩子可以先預約。
(C) 住其他公寓的孩子們也能使用游泳池。
(D) 孩子們被鼓勵帶特定的裝備來。

解析 有活動行程表的資訊的最後一段說住在 Livewell 或 Agostino 兩間鄰近公寓的小朋友，只要爸媽事先到接待櫃臺預約，就可以去參加 (Children living in the adjacent Livewell and Agostino condo buildings may also attend)，故本題正解為選項 (C)。

199. 根據電子郵件內容，Torrance 先生在 8 月 11 日跟誰講過話？
(A) 應徵者
(B) 公寓管理員
(C) 泳池活動籌劃員
(D) 公寓居民

解析 8 月 12 日的電子郵件中 (上端日期為 8 月 12 日，週五) 寫到昨天有住戶在居民大會上抱怨噪音 (However, at the residents meeting yesterday, somebody complained)，因為是昨天，所以可判斷居民提出不滿的日期為 8 月 11 日。此外，電子郵件上段寫了 Torrance 先生是公寓管理員 (Neil Torrance, Condominiums Manager。由此可知他那天跟居民講過話，故本題正解為選項 (D)。

200. 哪一個泳池活動最有可能被換掉？
(A) 潛水找東西
(B) 水中有氧
(C) 水中賽跑
(D) 水球

解析 電子郵件中說有人抱怨週間早晨的活動會造成噪音 (complained about the noise during our midweek morning activity)，所以要尋求解決辦法。從資訊中的圖表可知週間早上的課程只有週一／週三／週五，上午 8 點半到 9 點半的

活動潛水找東西 (Diving For Objects)，故本題正解為選項 (A)。

Note

揮別厚重，迎向高分！
最接近真實多益測驗的模擬題本

特色 1 單回成冊

揮別市面多數多益題本的厚重感，單回裝訂仿照真實測驗，提前適應答題手感。

特色 2 錯題解析

解析本提供深度講解，針對正確答案與誘答選項進行解題，全面掌握答題關鍵。

特色 3 誤答筆記

提供筆記模板，協助深入了解誤答原因，歸納出專屬於自己的學習筆記。